HEIR APPARENT

By

Prue Phillipson

KNOX ROBINSON
PUBLISHING
London • New York

KNOX ROBINSON
PUBLISHING
3rd Floor, 36 Langham Street
Westminster, London W1W 7AP
&
244 5th Avenue, Suite 1861
New York, New York 10001

Knox Robinson Publishing is a specialist, international publisher of historical fiction, historical romance and medieval fantasy.

Printed in the United States of America
and the United Kingdom.

First published by KRP in Great Britain in 2012.
First published by KRP in the United States in 2013.

Download the KRP App in iTunes and Google Play to receive free historical fiction, historical romance and fantasy eBooks delivered directly to your mobile or tablet.

Watch our historical documentaries and book trailers on our channel on YouTube and download our podcasts in iTunes.

www.knoxrobinsonpublishing.com

Other Books by
Prue Phillipson

The Hordens of Horden Hall (Series)
Vengeance Thwarted
Hearts Restored

Prologue
1740

It is three in the morning and in cottage and castle the two women's labour to bring forth has been hard and long. One father sleeps deeply as he always sleeps after a hard day's toil, the blanket over his head, the other sits hunched over his study fire with his hands over his ears.

Outside the temperature has fallen to freezing point and dark clouds from the hills have swallowed up the moon. The midwife, crouched by the struggling woman on the couch, hears the rattling of the first hailstone down the chimney. The meagre fire hisses.

'Oh come, push, push,' she yells. 'The head is here.' There is a last convulsion of muscles and the body slithers out, a big, fine boy, bursting almost at once into a vigorous cry. The noise is drowned by the clattering of a whole battery of hailstones in the chimney and the fire, exhaling a mist of steam, gives up the ghost.

She has bound and cut the cord and is now intent on the need to wrap the child with everything warm she can find. She fails to notice till too late the ghastly flow of blood that has soaked the couch and left the mother limp and white, her face turned to the ceiling, the mouth open, the eyes gaping in astonishment.

The still waiting father in his study removes his hands from his ears and hears silence. He can't detect the feet of a woman running on the thickening white mat in the rear courtyard, the shawl over her head enveloping too the bundle in her arms.

But there is another cry from above and he covers his ears again, bending his head over his desk, blotting out sight and sound. When will this interminable night end?

She has slipped in quietly, seeking the best fire in the castle, when he lifts his head and the candlelight shows him what he has awaited so long. He leaps to his feet, seeing only a small face peeping from many coverings. He is oblivious of the woman and the glistening moisture on her garments. She is smiling, showing him the child.

'A fine boy, sir.'

'A boy,' he repeats, his arms reaching for him. The child squirms and his eyes open wide as the man takes him and unwraps the swaddling garments to look at the body. It is perfect to the tiny curling toes.

The woman reaches a hand to pull the covers over. 'Keep him warm, sir' and she begins to tell the tale of the hailstorm.

'My son, my son,' the man is murmuring, 'my first born son.'

She starts to shake her head but he is still deep in his ecstasy of joy. She hesitates, then, leaving him with the baby, she curtseys low and, hearing noises above, she scuttles out of the room and up the stairs to attend to his wife.

Chapter 1
1761

livia Beattie had lived for eighteen years acting on impulse, usually with success. This time she knew she had made a dreadful mistake. The great white beast beneath her was not a horse she could ride. But how could she admit that to the reluctant groom still holding onto him?

'I don't rightly know just who you are, my lady,' he had said when she had strolled into the stables and requested a mount so she could explore the castle grounds.

She gave him her sweetest smile. 'I am a guest of the castle. My father is the architect from London who will design your missing west wing.'

The groom was no more than a spotty stable hand and hardly deserved so much explanation. This early in the morning no one else was about.

She passed along the stalls dismissing the horses who were too busy munching to meet her gaze and then the great white head had reared up and the challenging brown eye had seduced her.

'Emperor, Miss?' She was no longer M'lady. 'Only Mr Gerard rides Emperor.'

Not knowing who Mr Gerard was she replied, 'Of course I can ride him. I am an experienced horsewoman.' Yes, on the sedate mare her father always hired for her to ride in the London parks.

'Sir Langton gave permission?' the lad persisted and she had been driven into a nod which was as good, or rather as bad, as a spoken lie.

She had not even met Sir Langton yet. She and her father had arrived so late the night before that the housekeeper, with a sour look, had declared, 'The Master and M'lady have gone to their beds thinking you must not be coming till the morning. We don't keep London hours in Yorkshire. I'll show you your rooms and have a tray of refreshments sent up.'

They had been weary enough with travelling to slip quickly into bed but Olivia had woken early with the bird song outside her window and, rousing her maid, Jenny, who slept in the dressing room she had put on her riding skirt and jacket, determined to go out before breakfast and taste the freshness of the April morning.

Last night there had been a full moon and the staging inn at Tadby had consented to send them the final two miles of their journey in an open carriage. The gatekeeper had to be roused from his lodge to let them in and when Olivia saw the straight drive ahead with a milk-white lake and three stepped lawns rising to the castle she was enchanted.

'Papa, it's beautiful!'

'It will be when I've completed it. See how it lacks symmetry.'

'It's still beautiful,' she said.

When Jenny drew the curtains in the morning she had been disappointed to find that she was in a room of the L-shaped east wing that looked onto the courtyard and stables. But that had given her the longing to ride and Jenny had pointed out the back stair which she had been shown by the housekeeper last night. It was too easy. Slipping out by a back door near the kitchen she had heard but not seen any of the busy household of servants. And she had – oh so madly – headed for the stables.

And now the lad was still hanging onto the beast and

pleading, 'Just trot him round the paths, Miss! He's not to go on the lawns.'

Emperor let forth a sound between a snort and a snigger and the lad left go of him or he would have been dragged off his feet. Olivia clung to the pommel of the side-saddle with desperate fingers as Emperor bounded away from the stables, rounded the corner of the truncated west wing, crossed the drive in two strides and made ready to leap the low stone balustrade onto the smooth green sward of the top lawn. There was nothing she could do to stop him.

She shut her eyes and prayed, not daring to turn her head to glimpse the castle glowing golden at the corner of her left eye. Emperor rose into the air and landed and she was still on his back, but when she looked down she could see the dark imprints his hooves were making in the immaculate green.

She clung on. If he was set on plunging into the lake she must slide off onto the bank and pray that it would cushion her fall.

He had leapt the ha-ha onto the second lawn when, looking between his ears, she saw with horror that below the lowest lawn on the path by the lake a man was pushing someone in a sort of bath-chair.

It all happened in seconds as Emperor triumphantly pounded down to the last lawn, sinking more deeply as the ground here was softer and spongier close to the water. He was obviously intending to brush aside any obstacles in his way. Olivia was already half sliding off when she saw the man's appalled face, saw him thrust the wheel-chair forward and jump back himself with a hand up to grab the bridle. She left go at the same moment and almost knocked him off his feet as she landed in a humiliated heap on the path.

Emperor, astonished at the sudden spread of her riding skirt at his feet, skidded to a stop with one hoof pinning down the hem. Olivia looked up at the man who was white-faced and gasping.

'Oh I am so sorry,' she cried out, unable to rise. 'I didn't mean – I didn't know what he was like.'

The man was not looking at her. He had seen something more alarming along the path. Olivia looked too, under the belly of the horse.

The boy who had been in the wheel-chair – he seemed no more than a boy –was hanging onto a low branch of a tree over the bank his crippled legs dangling. The chair was on its side in the water.

'Luke!' yelled the man and, pushing Emperor's bridle at Olivia, he rushed to help him.

Emperor seemed to be grinning down at her with his wicked eye as he lifted his foot and fastidiously planted it one step forward. She rose carefully so as not to startle him and holding tight to the rein she began to whisper soothing words as near to his ear as she could reach. In fact he seemed now more interested in the sight of a human being suspended from a tree and Olivia watched too as the man clasped his arms round the helpless boy and lowered him to the ground, placing his back against the tree. Then he splashed into the lake to retrieve the chair and, finding a rag in his breeches pocket, dried the seat and lifted the invalid onto it.

Seeing how calm Emperor seemed to be now Olivia passed the reins over a post in the bank to which a small rowing boat was moored and hurried up to the chair.

'Oh I am so sorry,' she said again. 'Is the poor cripple all right?'

She was looking up into the face of the man. He was tall and broad but much younger than she had realised, perhaps her own age, with an outdoor face and curly chestnut hair. She would have liked the look of him if he hadn't been staring at her so savagely. Of course by his rough coat and breeches and old boots she knew he was a servant and the whole incident was painfully embarrassing.

And then the lad in the chair spoke.

'I have taken no hurt at all, thank you.' His voice was deep.

Olivia looked at him with a frown and parted lips. The shame of it all had bereft her of speech for a moment. He was certainly young too but he was not a child. His face was long and rather narrow, his hair straight and fair, a little unruly from his acrobatics. Maybe he was aware of this because he seemed suddenly very shy, lowering his eyes and running one hand over his head.

She couldn't assess his status. His voice had sounded cultured and his clothes were neat though he wore only one shoe on his right leg, the other apparently withered and ending below his knee in a loose stocking.

I shouldn't have spoken of him in the third person, she realised. One does with deformed people and of course he's self-conscious about his appearance. Suppose he is the son of the house and the gardener is taking him on his morning constitutional! What a terrible beginning I have made here when I hoped to be the confident young lady from London before a rustic provincial family!

At last the serving-man spoke. 'Well, Miss, who are you that you ride Emperor over my lawns like a mad thing?'

Olivia stared back at him. '*Your* lawns?' His voice had the local tang to it but for a servant his words and manner were the height of impudence. Only it was impossible to rebuke him when she had so recklessly put herself in the wrong.

The cripple murmured, 'Oh Tom, no. The young lady couldn't have known how wild Emperor can be.'

'I was very foolish,' Olivia said, 'but I am Miss Beattie and my father is the London architect who has come to complete the west wing of the castle. We will be staying here for some time and I hope to ride occasionally but I will not venture on that beast again.'

The young man now doffed his hat. 'I'm glad to hear it, Miss, and I apologise if I spoke out of turn but I assist my father, Albert Todd, Head Gardener here, and it will be my task to repair the lawns before Sir Langton sees them.' He looked at the cripple. 'And first I'll have to take my brother in. He's not supposed to be on show before visitors.'

His brother! Olivia marvelled. And with what a bitter tone he said that! Who can it be that decrees the poor youth must be kept out of sight?

'It's too late, Tom.' Luke was looking up towards the castle. 'Here's Sir Langton and another gentleman.'

'My father,' Olivia said, feeling her shame and dismay rising in a hot blush up her neck. Her father had always made jokes of any little scrapes into which her impulsiveness sometimes landed her but this one would surely test his wayward temper to its limit.

The young man called Tom added to her embarrassment by saying with a now friendly grin, 'You see, Miss Beattie, Sir Langton has to have perfection in all things.' He might have been answering her thought about his brother or referring to the mess Emperor had made of the beautiful lawns. No doubt his words were true in both cases. And, she decided, he dislikes his master for his brother's sake for which I applaud him, but I must see the gentleman himself now and size up what I have to face.

The two figures of the master of Castle Kirby and her father had been standing where the main section of the west wing should be if the building had ever been finished. How much they had witnessed she couldn't guess but they were now hastening towards them by the gravelled drive to the west of the lawns.

If she hadn't felt so apprehensive Olivia would have smiled at the contrast between her father and the older man. Her father was big and burly, with his own hair bushing out from under his hat in a light cloud, his cravat loosely tied at his throat and his coat hanging open to show a highly-coloured waistcoat, stretched tight across his stomach, light breeches and white stockings. Beside him Sir Langton's slight dapper figure was immaculately clad in dark colours. She could see as they drew nearer that beneath his three-cornered hat and neat little wig his face was pale and tight-lipped and he walked with clipped paces that hinted at barely restrained anger. Things untoward were obviously anathema to Sir Langton Kirby.

It was some small relief to Olivia to see that her father's cheeks were their usual cheerful red and he was strolling with loose confident strides while his wide mouth seemed to be chuckling.

Olivia retreated a step so that Sir Langton encountered Tom and Luke first.

'What has been going on here, Thomas?' he demanded. 'You had no business to bring your brother into the garden, let alone thrust his chair into the lake. And why is Emperor out?'

Gideon Beattie cried, 'Where Olivia is *something* is always happening.' He gave her a look of fond pride. At least he is on my side, she thought, but I wish he hadn't implied that I am habitually at the centre of trouble.

Now Sir Langton took notice of her and bowed with courtly politeness. 'Miss Beattie.'

She came forward and held out her hand which he kissed though she felt he would rather have taken a slipper to it. Then he turned back to Thomas.

'Take your brother in and see to the repair of the lawns immediately. I say again, how is it that Emperor has been let out?'

Olivia found her voice. 'Pray don't blame *him*, sir. *I* asked for a ride and Emperor looked the most exciting mount. And as for the poor cripple that too was my fault.' They all looked at Luke who blushed hotly. But a flurry of hooves and a tearing sound swung their attention the other way.

Emperor had been struggling to escape from his restraint which he had tightened by trampling round the mooring post but as they looked he finally ripped the post from the bank and galloped away by the lake with the post clattering between his hooves. The boat glided a little way from the bank.

Now Sir Langton's fury exploded. 'He could break his legs! Thomas, after him!'

Thomas ran, Olivia felt impelled to run too and her father followed. Emperor, frustrated by the weight of the post came to a halt himself and turned on them with flaming eyes and snorting nostrils. Thomas shrank from him but Gideon Beattie grabbed the bridle and freed the post practically under the horse's belly while Olivia reached to stroke the coarse mane and again whisper soothing words at Emperor's ear.

A little procession led the subdued animal towards Sir Langton who was waiting with his back to Luke's wheel-chair.

'Thomas, you allowed my guests to deal with that. Was that well done?'

'No, sir, but I was kicked by Emperor's father as a boy and I've never liked horses since.'

Gideon Beattie laughed outright, 'An honest admission, don't you think, Sir Langton?' Olivia couldn't help smiling too with relief that the whole incident seemed to be passing safely into history. But now she knew why Tom had looked so white when Emperor's rearing hooves threatened to crush his brother. The weakness made her warm to him more than ever.

Fortunately two stable hands came running now so he would be spared the task of leading the horse back to his stable. Instead she saw him take hold of the chair to wheel his brother out of sight but hesitated to manoeuvre it past Emperor now quiet between the two stable boys.

'I will have a few words later,' Sir Langton told them in an icy voice. 'No one but Mr Gerard takes out Emperor without my express permission.'

The stable boys bowed low and walked one each side of

Emperor up the path to disappear round the back of the castle.

As Tom passed her to follow with the wheel-chair Olivia murmured to him again, 'I am so sorry for your trouble.'

He gave her a twinkling grin. 'Forget it, Miss. Work's meat and drink to me. It's all the same whatever it is.'

She felt forgiven and was emboldened to whisper, 'Pray tell me, who is Mr Gerard?'

'The son and heir,' Tom replied, not trying to suppress a sneer. 'Away fighting somewhere with the grenadiers. If you never meet him you can see portraits of him all over the castle.'

Well, she thought, as he wheeled Luke up the path, the under-gardener dislikes both his old master and the young one. Perhaps he is a revolutionary at heart. I am intrigued.

'Now sir,' Sir Langton began to Gideon Beattie, 'before our usual hour of breakfast we have still time to walk round the lake if you please when the whole scene will break upon you and you will best be able to understand what I have in mind.' He added in a stiff society voice, 'Are you giving us the pleasure of your company, Miss Beattie?'

She gave a small curtsy in agreement as her father jovially answered the baronet. 'It's plain enough that you want the façade completed, Sir Langton, but to achieve perfection you must continue the west wing back to match the east which means removing those poor little cottages I saw. Then and only then will you have the true grandeur that must originally have been planned.'

Sir Langton swung round at that and Olivia saw the strangest look cross his face. Alarm, dismay, terror even. It died out of his eyes the moment he caught her looking and he abruptly turned and began the progress round the lake.

Puzzling on this she let the two gentlemen walk ahead and listened only perfunctorily to the architectural talk between them. There were fascinating mysteries in this place. And she was curious too about the heir, Gerard. Though she had not expected to find a husband away from London she knew how urgently her father was seeking one for her with wealth and a good pedigree. He would certainly have found out all he could about the Kirbys when Lord P had recommended him to Sir Langton Kirby. If her father knew there was an unmarried heir on the scene he would be all the more eager to come to Yorkshire. She had already guessed that the real reason for the Earl's recommendation was to remove the dangerous Olivia Beattie from London because his son, the viscount, was infatuated with her. But it was a delicate subject she didn't discuss with her father. He disliked the viscount as much as she did but would always maintain that his own professional merit had come to a certain earl's ears.

Of course this Gerard was serving in the army but he would get leave and she could take a look at him. Getting married was something she knew she would have to do preferably before she was twenty but she was already tired of the London beaux who flirted with her. They were shallow, uncultured creatures, giving themselves unwarranted airs and patronising her because she was no heiress and consequently not a serious proposition. Her father was growing anxious for her.

Catching the word London in the men's conversation she stepped closer to listen. It seemed Sir Langton had inquired about the latest news from the capital on the progress of the war.

'Ah, there is a siege, I believe, going on at Belle Isle,' her father said, 'though by this it may be all over. If it succeeds it may bring peace nearer which to my mind would be an excellent outcome.'

'Pardon my ignorance, sir, but where is Belle Isle?' Sir Langton asked.

'Oh some island off the French coast.'

'And why are we endeavouring to take it?'

'I cannot see into the mind of Mr Pitt but I wager it is of

strategic importance. They say our navy has it entirely surrounded but the Frenchies are well entrenched within it.'

'This is a naval operation then?'

'No indeed. I have heard there will be many thousands of troops there as the plan is to land and take the place. But to be plain with you, sir, as one eager to pursue my profession I am only interested in men's attention turning from fighting to improving their houses and building new ones.'

'Very natural, sir, but then I presume you know no one serving under the colours as I do. I too wish hostilities to end that my son be put in no more danger but I have great interest in any battles going forward at the moment. You wouldn't know then what regiments might have embarked on this venture? My son Gerard is a Lieutenant in the Grenadier Company in the Nineteenth Regiment of Foot and I have had no news for some weeks.'

'Alas no. There I fear I am quite unable to help you. Do you receive the London papers here?'

'We do but of course their news is somewhat out of date.'

Olivia wondered to herself what it would be like to live permanently away from the hub of London life but if she could become Lady Kirby, wife of General Sir Gerard Kirby she would have her own stables, her own carriage and be the grandest lady in all the neighbouring parishes. She was already in love with this place, the beds of daffodils bordering the lake, the clipped hedges, early flowering trees, the rolling landscape beyond stretching to humpy blue hills in the west and the wide sky above.

'Do you know London, Sir Langton?' she asked, daring to address him directly.

'We visit London once a year, Miss Beattie,' he answered with dignity, 'though I own I prefer the sweet air here to the smells and grime of the capital.'

'Quite right,' her father cried. 'Look at the beautiful golden colour of your stonework. Everything in London is black with soot.'

They had all paused to view the building from across the lake. The central tower with steps up to its great doors was castellated. That's why they can call it a castle, Olivia thought, but the need for improvement was now very obvious. While the west wing extended for only two sets of mullioned windows, the east boasted six and, as she knew already extended back to form one side of a courtyard. She smiled to herself. Some ancestral Kirby ran out of money. Perhaps they were heavily fined during the Commonwealth for supporting the King.

Her father was telling Sir Langton, 'I am not a disciple of Palladio, nor would his severe lines be suitable here. This place has a flamboyant air and I see now that the perfect finishing touch to crown the central block when the two wings are symmetrical would be a dome. Domes are very much the thing since Wren's on St Paul's and they give a great house like this that extra distinction. You will have seen the fine example at Castle Howard since you dwell within the same county?'

Sir Langton merely bowed. Olivia read everything into that stiff noncommittal reply. He has seen Castle Howard and is green with envy but he is not an earl and he has neither the funds nor the effrontery to copy what the Howards have done.

They walked on, her father commenting on every prospect and placing statues here and fountains there and concluding, 'But where is the mausoleum?'

Sir Langton compressed his thin lips. 'My ancestors are buried in the family vault in Tadby village churchyard. I have no wish to remove their remains to a site within my park.' Her father looked at Olivia and grinned.

By now they had come round the lake again and Sir Langton observed the mooring post lying in the grass and the rowing boat floating just out of reach of the bank. Looking up the lawns he saw Thomas wheeling a barrow of soil down the path from the top lawn to fill the holes in the next lawn.

Here is another job for that busy young man, Olivia thought. All my fault again. 'Papa,' she said, 'could you not use the post to push the boat towards that little promontory where I could catch its rope and pull it up.'

'My dear young lady,' Sir Langton cried, 'I wouldn't hear of such a thing –' but her father had already grabbed the post by its cleaner end and thrust it at the boat, propelling it sideways. Olivia ran onto the little promontory and, drawing her skirts up over her ankles, bent down and grabbed the prow, feeling for the trailing wet rope. As she tried to pull it from the water without marking her skirt she found it heavier than she expected and one foot slipped behind her on the dewy grass. She tumbled forward and landed across the boat with a little shriek.

The impetus would have shoved the boat out again but her father, already coming to help her, was just in time to grab her legs and pull her and the boat in again.

Finding herself unhurt and still clutching the rope she scrambled to her feet, put the rope in his hands, pulled down her skirts behind and couldn't help a rueful smile.

Her father burst out laughing at Sir Langton's appalled expression. 'I tell you, sir, where my Olivia is life is never dull.'

Oh dear, Olivia thought, Sir Langton will be telling his lady dreadful tales of this wild young woman from London. What *can* I do to wipe out the impression I've made and why will Papa add to it with remarks like that?

Thomas had now come running. He took the rope from Gideon Beattie, murmuring apologies, and pulled the boat up onto the grass.

'Fetch a sledge hammer, Thomas,' Sir Langton ordered, 'and restore boat and post to their proper places. Then resume your work on the lawns. Mr Beattie, we must escort your daughter at once to her bedchamber so that her maid can help her repair her appearance. I trust your apparel has received no lasting damage, Miss Beattie. Pray call upon the services of our seamstress if it proves necessary.'

This was said with considerable discomfort, Olivia felt, since the mention of a young lady's apparel would normally lie far outside Sir Langton's borders of propriety. She was taken aback then to see Thomas give her a mischievous wink as he lifted the post into the boat so he could tow it round to its original mooring place.

She rather liked his impudence. It put him in a conspiracy with her over Sir Langton's desperate need for everything to be restored to perfection again. But as to the castle itself, she wondered, will Sir Langton's ideas ever conform to my father's ambitious notions? It's going to be fun to observe them. I think I shall find my time here very rewarding in all ways.

But first, she decided, as they approached the castle and mounted the portico steps, I will change my dress and put some soothing ointment on my breast where I find the edge of the boat has given it a bang after all. It would never do for my gown to reveal a discoloured bruise for I have every intention now of being so demure that Sir Langton will not be ashamed to introduce me to his lady. I know how to please her. I will study all those portraits of the young heir and tell her he is the most handsome young man in the kingdom, however plain he truly is.

She had scarcely lifted her eyes to the grand staircase ahead when Sir Langton laid a hand on her arm and pointed to the large portrait on the wall to her left.

'My son Gerard in his uniform.'

She looked up at the life-sized painting. Plain! He was the most classically beautiful young man she had ever seen. He was partly in profile but one lively brown eye was turned to the observer. The short wig curling below his three-cornered hat showed up a cheek of flawless complexion, one hand rested nonchalantly on the hilt of his sword and his whole air was of casual elegance and awareness of his own perfection of face and figure.

'He's quite magnificent!' she exclaimed.

'There are others of him about the place,' Sir Langton said, with the first genuine smile she had seen from him, 'but you mustn't delay yourself now,' and summoning a maid who was hovering for orders he said, 'Escort Miss Beattie to her bedchamber and make sure her own maid is there to attend her.'

Olivia picked up her skirts and mechanically followed the girl, but all she was thinking was, 'Would I not love to have *that* young man at my feet, pleading for my hand? Can I possibly make him believe that Olivia Beattie is so exciting and witty that he will forego an immense dowry?

She was caressing the polished banister as she reached the top of the stair when Jenny greeted her with, 'Eh, Miss Olivia, what a state you're in!' which brought her down to reality with a bump. In half an hour she must face the mistress of the house at breakfast and when she looked at herself in the mirror above her washstand she saw her grass-stained jacket, a mud splash on her face and her cloud of fair hair escaping all over from its pins.

'Oh Jenny, put me right quickly,' was all she could say. But how she was to keep herself right against all her natural impulses was another matter altogether.

Chapter 2

The hoof-shaped holes had all been repaired though it would take a few more days of grass growth to obliterate every trace of the damage. Thomas Todd straightened his back and looked down to the lake. The rowing boat was lying safely attached to its post and every faded daffodil had been dead-headed. He could go inside and check on Luke in his mid-day dinner break.

He walked round the short west wing to the courtyard and first put his head in at the smaller of the two old cottages that filled the space opposite the stables on the east side.

'Anything for me in your cauldron, Grandmother Witch?'

The old woman seated in a basket chair was indeed stirring a big iron pot on her fire and her sharp nose poking from under her mob cap made him intone, 'Double, double toil and trouble' in a cracked voice.

She grinned, showing her two remaining blackened teeth. 'You can stow that, Tom.' She reached a tin mug off its hook and dipped it in the broth. 'There, I've caught the two bits o'beef in it and you can cut yourself a hunk off that loaf. Betsy brought it from the kitchen 'cos it's last week's baking.'

Tom hacked himself a thick slice and took the mug. He was going out when she said, 'Betsy said there's London folks come.'

'Ay, an architect and his daughter. She tried to ride Emperor and came a cropper.'

'I heard all about that but did you know he wants to knock down this place and yours?'

Tom stopped in the doorway. 'Knock down – ! Who told you that? Why?'

'Mr Granger stepped by and said he'd overheard him telling m'lady.'

Mr Granger was the butler and there was no more reliable authority than he.

She cackled on, 'Oh ay, he says we're in the way when they build the west wing to match the east.'

'Sir Langton would never do that to you, Grandmamma. Mr Granger shouldn't have come frightening you with stories like that.'

'Nay, I'm not frightened. I told Granger he's a silly old doom-monger. I have Sir Langton in my pocket, I said.'

Tom thought, that's true enough. She's the only one can give the Master a piece of her mind and he takes it like a lamb. Must be because she was the midwife who brought Gerard safely into the world.

'Well, I'll go and see Luke's all right. You heard about him dangling from trees I suppose?'

'Oh ay, they bring me the news when there is any. If there's nout to say they don't come near.'

Tom patted her shoulder and left the cottage. He could see his father's hat bobbing in the kitchen garden beyond the courtyard. Albert Todd never bothered with castle gossip but Tom walked over to him and said without preliminaries, 'Did you know this new man from London is advising Sir Langton to knock our houses down?'

His father straightened his back in painful stages pressing on his spade handle. He fastened Thomas with a watery eye. The sun had only just reached this corner, shining over the castle roof, and the April air was chill here.

He waved his free hand to the side elevation of the east wing they could see beyond the intervening courtyard and stables. 'What else – if he has the money? Stands to reason the two wings must match all the way back.'

'Where will we go then?'

His father shrugged his shoulders. 'He'll build us new. The old woman won't be pleased but she cannot live much longer.' Albert Todd always referred to his mother-in-law as 'the old woman'. They rarely spoke to each other. 'Have you cleared the dead bracken from the small copse yet?' he asked Thomas. Evidently he'd said his say on the subject of the cottages.

'I had to mend holes in the lawns first. That foolhardy daughter of the architect rode Emperor over them.'

Now his father did raise an eyebrow. 'Emperor! No woman ever rode Emperor before. Does the Master know?'

'Ay, but I wouldn't say she rode him. She clung on, that was all.'

Thomas left his father as abruptly as he had come. He was picturing Miss Olivia Beattie in his mind's eye, desperation in every inch of her body. He would never forget that first sight of her.

He went into the castle then by the door in the east wing where there was a ramp for Luke's wheel-chair. He strode past the steps down to the kitchen from which a babble of chatter arose and along the passage to the outer corner of the L where Luke had his sitting-room and adjoining small bedchamber. He went in without knocking and found Luke painting at his easel under the window that looked over the lake. The small window facing the eastern woods cast extra light over his shoulder. On the table beside him lay a plate of dinner and a mug of ale untouched.

He looked round and smiled sheepishly at Tom. 'Don't look at it. I can't catch it at all. I saw it in my head – the fresh green of the statuesque trees, the still blue lake, the yellow streak of the daffodils at the edge and she in her red riding jacket, vibrant with life. She was to be a spontaneous child of nature, the goddess of the place.'

He laughed at himself and Tom laughed too. 'If you don't like your painting – though to my mind it's well enough – write her a sonnet. You have half the lines already but how she can be both a child and a goddess I know not.' He set his own mug on the table, dipped his bread in it and said with his mouth full, 'Did you hear what her father proposes, the removal of our cottages? Thank God, you're all right here.'

Luke's eyes became troubled. 'Yes, I did hear that and I am worried for you and father and grandmother.' His eyes strayed to the vast prospect outside the window. 'Don't you know, Tom, I may be all right here but I'd rather be living there with you if only –'

He shook his head, his glance turning to his crippled legs.

That gave Tom a guilty shock. Luke never alluded to his condition, nor had he himself ever felt envy that Sir Langton had allowed his brother to be cared for in the castle. He too had gained much from the arrangement, sitting in as page to Luke with Master Gerard's tutor and absorbing more learning than Gerard himself had ever managed to do. Though it had sometimes made his status as under-gardener seem confined and restricted he also had a store of knowledge he would draw upon all his life. He spoke better than his father. He read the books Luke could take from the castle library. Perhaps, he thought now, it has made me behave above my station today to that young lady but I care not. She's a game one and didn't take offence. But I see how meeting her has hit Luke with his physical state and knocked him out of his usual cheerfulness.

He slapped him on the back. 'Well, eat your dinner, man. There's more meat there than I get in a week.'

'Have some, Tom, please.'

'Nay, I'm teasing you. And don't be troubled for us about the cottages. I've just seen Grandmother and she says she has Sir Langton in her pocket. It beats me why she's so confident but she's always had him eating out of her hand. He would have housed her much better long ago but she's lived there ever since her daughter married father and she intends to die there. He'll leave her be till then.'

He looked at the painting. 'Why did you draw Miss Beattie walking away from you?'

'I couldn't attempt her face and I'll probably never see her again. You'll not be allowed to take me out while they're here in case they're walking or riding in the grounds. But if you see her tell me what she's really like. What colour are her eyes? I know her hair is fair and she has a dimple and her mouth is so – I don't know – very shapely, but –'

'Why, man, you noticed more than I did.'

Tom thought, with alarm, he's smitten with her. Good God, does he have the same urges I do? But he rarely sees a woman – just little Betsy who brings his meals and she's as undeveloped as a child. No wonder Miss Olivia Beattie has captivated him. 'I think I liked her best,' he said, to lighten the atmosphere, 'when she had a splash of mud on her face and her hair was stuck out like a bush.'

He tossed off the mug of broth and ran some of the bread round inside to collect the lumps of meat and vegetables.

Luke had laid down his brushes but his food was still untouched. He said, 'Betsy has talked to her maid Jenny and told me Miss Beattie lost her mother at the age of three. Doesn't that give her an affinity with us, Tom? Mine died when I was born and when Father married again your mother only lived till you were not quite two. We have all been motherless most of our lives. But at least,' he mused, 'Mr Beattie seems an affectionate father.'

Tom felt another burst of sympathy. 'I know the old man doesn't come to see you, Luke, but he can't put feelings into words. Never could that I remember. And he hates going indoors. So come on. Don't get low. Eat your dinner and finish your painting. It's good.'

Luke gave him a wistful smile. He *must* be in love, Tom thought. He's usually such a brisk, happy soul, embarrassingly so considering the life he leads. I've never had to feel sorry for him. He has his paints and his books and fills notebook after notebook from his reading. I wonder if Miss Beattie is a reader. Maybe I could get her to visit him if we have a wet day and she can't go out.

On the other hand, he thought as he popped his mug back in his grandmother's cottage without waking her from her early afternoon nap, I don't want to over-excite the poor lad. He lifted the brim of his hat and scratched his head as he made for the small copse to resume work.

It was only a week later that the weather changed. Luke sat in his room watching the rain streaming across the window that faced the lake. The wind must be in the south west, he reckoned, when the stone lintel provides no shield. What, he wondered, is everyone doing? Mr Beattie and Sir Langton may be discussing plans in the estate office. Is Lady Kirby there too? Is she interested? Would she care if the little cottages were demolished? Will Tom be moved further away from me so that he can't slip in of an evening when his work is finished?

He looked at the third painting he had done of a young woman walking by a lake. It was so far from expressing his wonder at Olivia Beattie that first day that he would have knocked it from his easel if he could have reached it, but just now he was sitting in his desk chair and Betsy had moved the easel when she tidied his room that morning. He wanted to write a poem but no words would come. All he could do was watch the veil of water dimming the lake and the woods. There was no colour left in them.

What was *she* doing? That was what really consumed his thoughts. She must be about the place somewhere, reading, embroidering, playing the piano? His little prison was so far from the principal rooms of the castle on the first floor of the central block that he could hear nothing.

Then there came the sound of feet in the passage and sudden voices just outside his room. The door was flung open. He heard Tom say, 'Come into the sanctum. Luke won't mind.'

He twisted round as best he could. She was in the doorway, hesitating a little but with a merry smile on her face.

Tom said, 'I found a bored young lady wandering the castle. She's come to read with us. I've done all I could in the glasshouses and have permission to spend the rest of the morning with my brother.' He was arranging the one comfortable armchair for Olivia Beattie close to the fire and motioning her into it. Then he came over to Luke, humped him to his wheel chair, drew that beside her and finally pulled the desk chair over for himself to complete the semicircle round the blaze.

Luke was speechless with astonishment at her sudden presence in his room and embarrassment at being parcelled about like this in front of her. Of course it was only what Tom did day in day out. What amazed him too was Tom's ease with her, his total lack of awe at her presence, when he himself dare not even lift his eyes in case she was looking at him.

He could hear her dress rustle as she turned in her chair and then he knew to his dismay what she was looking at as she exclaimed, 'Oh, I think that is I by the lake. Is that your work, Luke?'

'Throw it down, Tom,' he muttered, feeling the blood rush up his neck and face. 'It's not fit to be seen.'

'But it is,' she cried. 'Leave it alone, Thomas. I can look at it when I'm tired of hearing your lessons.'

Thomas laughed aloud at this, making Luke more uncomfortable than ever.

'We're a little old for lessons, Miss Beattie. We're reading Shakespeare. We take parts and I hope you will join in.'

'Oh I love Shakespeare of all things and have seen Garrick on the London stage. I'm sorry, I suppose I thought Luke was younger than he is.'

'He's my *older* brother and I'm eighteen. He just looks young with being small and light because of his legs.'

Luke kept his head bent down. Why had Tom brought her here to put him through this?

But a most extraordinary thing happened then. She rose and fell on her knees before him and put her hands on the very arms of his chair. Her skirts spread around his one poor foot. This was agony.

'Luke,' she said, 'please, will you not look at me?'

He was compelled to meet her gaze as she pushed her face forward and peered up into his but he couldn't speak. She wasn't staring at his poor leg. She was trying to talk to him face to face.

'I'm truly sorry,' she was saying. 'I didn't realise you are older than I. I never met anyone before with – with your trouble. But tell me something. Do you have to sit in a chair all the time? Your arms are so strong – I saw you clutch that branch – could you not have crutches to help you move about like the soldiers who have lost limbs in the wars? Your right leg seems whole even though the knee is a little twisted.'

After a struggle Luke mumbled a reply. 'Soldiers can be proud of their deformity – I was born like this. I should keep hidden.'

She put her weight on the arms of his chair and straightened up with a sigh and resumed her seat. 'That's really sad. I'm so sorry. Well, let us read. Which play are you studying?'

Tom handed her a handsome leather-bound Shakespeare open at the place in *Julius Caesar* where they had left off the evening before.

'We'll share this other one,' he said. 'It's old but has all its pages.' He pulled his chair close to Luke. 'We were in Act One, Scene Two at the exit of Caesar, but now only Brutus and Cassius are in the scene.'

Olivia broke in, 'Oh please, can I be Cassius? He's an unpleasant character but I rather admire his sharp brain and uncompromising ambition. Thomas, you take Brutus, and Luke, please take the few lines of Caesar and Antony when they come in.'

Tom objected, 'Luke is much better than I. He could be a great actor – he makes the words come alive so.'

'Oh no, Tom, please do what Miss Beattie says,' Luke pleaded. 'It is such an honour for us to have her here.' He was still struggling to believe she was sitting there within a foot of him and genuinely wanting to draw him out.

'It is we who are providing her entertainment for a wet morning.' Tom chuckled with a boldness that was incomprehensible to Luke.

'Come, I am ready to begin,' she said. Oh she was so lively, so eager and she loved Shakespeare which was another bond between them all.

'Shall I read from 'Will you go see the order of the course?" she asked and, hearing no objection, away she went, reading with great speed and liveliness.

Now Luke did feel able to lift his eyes and look at her as her lips moved and her whole face was suffused with excitement. Her eyes, he saw, were the blue of the lake in sunshine and when Tom spoke his part he saw them momentarily widen in surprise at the fluency of his reading. She hadn't expected that – from a gardener. Luke glowed with pride at his brother. Though Tom's accent wasn't as refined as hers his understanding of the words was plain to hear.

As the scene went on Luke grew less self-conscious. He was caught up in the drama as he always was when he and Tom read together. It took him out of himself. He was there in Rome, a place seething with the turbulent, changeable mob and dark with the plots of conspirators. He wanted to be involved and when his chance came he was there inside Caesar's mind, that secret dread of assassination, and Antony soothingly answering him, pooh-poohing his doubts. Though speaking to himself in their brief dialogue he was both characters, two different voices and, when he heard Olivia interject, 'We'll go on to the end of the scene with Luke as Casca,' he found a rough, brusque, offhand voice which was how he always heard Casca in his head, for in his long lonely hours he had gone through all the plays, acting them silently to himself.

And so they galloped on to the end of the scene and laid the books down with a mutual grunt and a moment of satisfied silence.

Then Tom looked across at Olivia and said, 'Sometimes we pick out a word or phrase from the scene that we want to debate upon. Will Miss Beattie be pleased to suggest something?'

She sat up straight and without a second's hesitation exclaimed, 'No such mirrors! That's the phrase I noted and I claim the right to apply it in my own way,' and she looked full at Luke. "It is very much lamented, Luke, that you have no such mirrors that will turn your hidden worthiness into your eye.' So, Luke, I will be your mirror. You must not hide in a chair all day. You have a gift. You should be in the drawing-room every time Sir Langton has guests, reading whole scenes, taking every part yourself and displaying your versatility in different voices. I am certain that would be much better entertainment than hearing ill-taught young ladies warbling or strumming the piano. I shall have to speak to Sir Langton. Perhaps he is unaware of your talent.'

'Oh pray, Miss Beattie, do no such thing,' Luke cried, startled into vehemence in his own voice. 'Tom, explain to her. I am allowed to live here but –'

'It's this way,' Tom said. 'Sir Langton decided our cottage was not comfortable for Luke from his earliest childhood so he had a ramp made from the courtyard to the passage and gave him this little room with its adjoining bedchamber and got the blacksmith to construct a chair which has been adapted as he has grown bigger, but Luke is no way part of the castle family. A maid cleans his room and brings him food and I take him out when it's fine but not when there is company staying. He's only a gardener's son, like me, after all.'

'And I know everything has to be perfect in Sir Langton's life,' Olivia cried, rising and pacing about the room. 'And you, Luke, are not, through no fault of your own. I see into his narrow little mind.' She is really angry for me, Luke thought in wonder. Then she turned as if a sudden thought had occurred to her. 'But why – if that is so – has he endured for so long living in an unfinished castle?'

Tom had risen too. If she would walk about he couldn't remain seated. Luke felt his own disability keenly. Could he ever master crutches as she had suggested?

'Luke has studied the history,' Tom said, following her to the window to which Luke now turned his chair so that he could see too what she was suddenly looking at. There was a horseman in the distance approaching up the long drive.

He began tentatively to say, 'A central tower was here in Elizabeth's reign but the baronet in Queen Anne's time started to build the wings. Only he lost money through gambling and no one since has been able to complete it till –'

She interrupted. 'Oh of course, I heard something in London. Your Sir Langton has recently come into a fortune from his younger brother who had no family. Was he not a naval captain who won large prize money and was then killed in action?' Now she leant forward with her face to the window-pane peering sideways to see the main portico. 'This is a messenger with letters. Even Sir Langton has come out despite the rain and is addressing the man. What! Lady Kirby is on the steps too and a great bustle is going on. They are taking the messenger in to interrogate him further. Do go and find out what's happened, Thomas.'

Tom stood his ground, feet stolidly planted apart on the threadbare rug. Luke was amazed at his impudence. 'I'll hear in good time from the servants, Miss Beattie. It's not my place to venture into the family's rooms.'

She abruptly left the window. 'I'll go myself. No one seems to mind if *I* wander around. Did you not find me hovering outside *this* door wondering what was behind it?' She broke into laughter. 'I never expected to find Shakespeare lurking within!' She paused at the door. 'Thank you both for that pleasure.'

She was gone. Luke exchanged a rueful look with his brother. 'Should you not have –?'

'No I should not. It's not for her to give orders to me. 'No such mirrors' indeed. She needs some mirrors from those around her to show her she's only an architect's daughter. Did you see how she took it upon herself to organise the reading when she was our guest? I like her well enough but she's too imperious –'

'Oh Tom, she took kindly interest in me, she has a warm heart. She even praised my wretched painting.'

There came a tap on the door and Betsy entered with a tray.

'You here too, Mr Thomas? I've only enough for one.'

'Nay, my grandmother will have something for me if I go now. What is all the commotion about?' Now the door was ajar they could hear feet running and voices chattering.

'Oh my! It's Mister Gerard. Word's come that he's been

wounded in some battle. M'lady's fainted away and Sir Langton's quite wild with anxiety. The messenger can't tell much but he says Mister Gerard took a musket bullet in the chest. That's sure to be fatal, cook says, so everything's in an uproar. But I remembered you, Mister Luke.'

She laid the tray on a small side table. There were slices of beef, some radishes from the glass houses, a crust of loaf and a jug of ale.

'Thank you, Betsy.' Luke smiled at her. She was a slip of a girl no more than thirteen. 'But that's terrible news for the poor master and mistress. Tell us if you learn more.'

She nodded and scuttled out.

Luke looked up at Tom. 'Castle Kirby without an heir? The Master will break his heart.'

Tom lifted his expressive dark brows and shrugged his shoulders. 'Gerard will come through, I wager. He's indestructible. I rescued him from the lake three times when he was a lad though he's older than I. He fell out of a tree twice without hurt. He's not used up his nine lives yet. You see if I'm not right. Eat your dinner, man.'

'Have some,' Luke urged as he usually did without success.

'Nay, you must get strong for your crutches,' Tom laughed and, returning the Shakespeare volumes to their shelf, he went out.

Luke drew a deep breath. So little usually happened to break the quiet pattern of his life that the morning's drama and the sudden news at the end left him with a quickened pulse and a myriad of reactions. Miss Beattie had been like a flash of lightning in a uniformly grey sky. He was shaken and confused by her interest in him. No one had ever suggested he could learn to walk with crutches. Was that possible? She must not be allowed to think him feeble. Had she not praised Cassius's ambition?

And now this news of Gerard – perhaps fatally wounded! He had spent many hours in Gerard's company when they had their lessons together but there had been no real friendship between them. Gerard loved all forms of sport and insisted on ten minute breaks every hour which was why the school room had early been sited on the ground floor. Then his tutor had told Sir Langton that Luke's quiet concentration would be a good example to Gerard and Sir Langton had consented but only if Luke was removed when he himself came to inspect his son's work. Tom was allowed to sit in then to see to Luke's needs and he too absorbed the lessons with the same speed and dedication that he brought to everything he did.

Looking back, Luke realised how inevitable it was that Gerard the boy would resent them. But it had only made him more determined to be the best horseman, the best tennis player and the best cricketer in the whole county. Once he had achieved these goals Gerard the man became much more affable with his old schoolmates and had taken a very friendly leave of them last New Year when he had gone off in his uniform to rejoin his regiment after the Christmas festivities.

Luke could imagine too well the devastation that would descend on the Castle if the beloved son and heir were gone. He wished Miss Beattie would think of coming back and telling him what more she had learnt.

He ate his dinner slowly but she did not come.

Chapter 3

Olivia, hearing the news from her father, fled up to her bedchamber and hurled herself onto the bed. That beautiful body smashed! She pictured the poor wretch writhing in agony as a surgeon dug for the bullet. She pressed her own breast where the bruise from her fall was still painful and so discoloured that she had had to wear her widest lace tucker on her low evening gown to hide it. If that was sore now what must torn flesh be like. It didn't bear thinking of.

It was a disappointing end too to the pleasant hour she had had with Tom and Luke. She had begun to feel a little lonely in the Castle with her father busy on his drawings. At first she had been in awe of Lady Kirby but had found her a meek, sweet-natured lady, very anxious to please and for ever glancing at her husband for his approval, a state of things which Olivia vowed she would never tolerate when she was married herself. But she hardly knew her well enough yet to be quite at ease with her, so to find a love of Shakespeare in the gardeners' sons had been an astonishing delight. She hoped she hadn't been too forward with Luke. He had seemed no more than a shy boy at first but there were depths there and she was afraid she might have trodden too roughly on his sensibilities. As for brusque Tom she must try to keep his familiarity at a safe distance. But she would certainly want to continue their Shakespeare readings and if Sir Langton found out and disapproved she didn't see what he could do to stop it.

But now she had seen Lady Kirby carried insensible to her room and, in passing the small drawing room, she had observed the stiff, buttoned-up Sir Langton raging up and down, quite out of control, sometimes calling on Gerard's name, sometimes cursing the French, then stopping suddenly and crying out, 'Punished, punished.' He had caught sight of her then and she had run, frightened at the distortion of his features and the wild terror in his eyes. Why 'punished', she wondered. For sending him to join the army? It was another mystery.

But this was what war meant. The agony of families as well as maimed and slaughtered young men. War had been going on, she realised now, from when she was only a young girl and she had heard of battles in far flung places like the Americas and the West Indies. It had been exciting and glamorous to see the officers in their uniforms about the streets of London. Even the sight of soldiers with wooden legs had not suggested the pain and suffering that had gone before. She couldn't herself mourn Gerard Kirby, the man, whom she didn't know but she mourned her nascent hopes of him and for the first time in her life she felt a hatred of fighting and a longing for peace.

Her father tapped on her door and looked in.

'The servants have laid a luncheon in the small dining-room though I doubt if Sir Langton and Lady Kirby will join us. But *we* have no need to lose our appetites unless the project for the castle is set aside.'

She rose and tidied her hair and took his arm. 'Don't you think that's most unfeeling of you, papa?' she said, but he only grinned down at her and patted her hand.

To her surprise Sir Langton and Lady Kirby were awaiting them, she still pale and trembling, he with his face closed up again into its usual composure.

'We are so distressed for you, my lady,' Olivia said now, certain that Sir Langton had insisted on his wife's appearance for the sake of their guests. 'You must be consumed with anxiety. Do you know where your son is? Has he been brought home to England?'

'We know nothing,' Sir Langton answered, 'but that he is in the list of wounded from the battle of Belle Isle. The messenger said he had heard a rumour that he had a chest wound and was in the ship that brought back the first of the wounded but of that we await confirmation.'

Gideon Beattie said brightly, 'But Belle Isle appears to be heading for a great victory. This will surely bring the French to their knees and prepare the way for the ending of the war.'

'As to that I care not if it has carried off our son. If I knew that he is in London now I would take horse at once and go to him but I fear I must await word from his commanding officer. Miss Beattie, can we tempt you to a little of this cold beef? You will pardon us if our appetites are not the equal of yours.'

It was an uncomfortable meal. Olivia knew her father was only at ease when he could be full of cheerful talk. Pale, drawn faces at table made him restless and eager to be away so they didn't linger over the bowl of fruit that was brought in at the end. But as they left the room Sir Langton said, 'Mr Beattie, let me see what progress you have made with your drawings. We will go to my study which adjoins this room and perhaps Miss Beattie will be kind enough to keep Lady Kirby company in the small drawing-room.'

Olivia didn't know what she could possibly say to the poor lady once they were sedately seated not on the sofa but on two of the upright Queen Anne chairs with their curious cabriole legs ending in a claw and ball. When she had studied these on the three unoccupied chairs she looked about the room for inspiration and found it in the many portraits on the walls of a young boy.

'Is this Gerard?' she asked pointing to one, where he stood

self-consciously pretty in green satin holding a stick and hoop.

'Oh yes,' cried Lady Kirby, 'he was no more than seven years old and I had to bribe him with sweetmeats to make him stand still for five minutes at a time and he thought that a torment. And there he is at twelve with his first fishing rod though I don't remember him ever sitting long enough to catch anything.' She had now risen and Olivia was soon following her round the room stopping at every picture of Master Gerard and hearing the stories of his childhood till Lady Kirby stopped suddenly and clung to her and sobbed on her shoulder.

'To think he may be lying in some wretched barrack room, suffering and I not there to comfort him. Or he is dead and cold and they are afraid to tell us. Who can recover from a wound in the chest? Are not the heart and lungs there? How can he live?'

The role of comforter was so unfamiliar to her that Olivia could only stand there, patting her back, gazing over her powdered head out of the window, noticing that the rain had stopped and a shaft of sun through thinning cloud had created a patch of light water on the lake.

Then far off where she knew the great gates were she saw some movement. Was it a carriage approaching? She narrowed her eyes.

'Someone is coming, my lady. Perhaps there will be more news. Yes, it's a carriage, a grand one and four horses.'

Lady Kirby gave a brief glance. 'We have some county friends who may have come to commiserate with us.'

The carriageway swept to the west side of the lake and round to the front of the castle in a graceful curve.

Olivia watched the equipage draw up outside. Footmen from the house came running and two servants emerged from within the carriage and held out their arms to someone inside. A young man appeared, a little slowly and carefully but he descended the steps and stood upright on the ground. The house servants were now cheering and clapping their hands.

'Oh Lady Kirby, please look,' cried Olivia, her own heart pounding with excitement. 'Is that not –? Can it be –?'

Lady Kirby looked. 'Gerard!' she shrieked.

He looked up at the window and waved.

The gesture, the smile hit Olivia like a blow in her midriff. The portraits were nothing. This was a live man and she was overwhelmed by her own daring in ever having imagined him for a moment as a future husband.

Lady Kirby had already run from the room calling to Sir Langton. Olivia followed slowly and saw her father in the study doorway.

'So it seems the young man is safe and well after all.' he said. 'I never thought Sir Langton could move as fast as he did when he saw Mister Gerard emerge from the carriage. Shall we go down to the lobby and pay our respects?'

'Oh not yet. Let them have time – I think we should wait – go back to the drawing-room.'

'What! Are you shy of him? My Olivia shy of a young man? I've never seen such a thing. After all the beaux of London you have put in their places!'

'This is different. He has come back from the dead as it were.'

But while she tugged on his sleeve to draw him back along the gallery they heard a slow procession mounting the great staircase and then a young man's voice called out, 'Where is the young lady who rides Emperor? I demand to meet her.'

Olivia clasped her hands over her mouth, her heart galloping so fast she thought she would faint.

His head and shoulders appeared – he was so much taller than his father and mother – oh God, the portrait hadn't lied but this was an animated beauty, not frozen in a supercilious pose. He was in a dark travelling coat which was not as glamorous as his regimentals but he was real, here right in front of her.

'Is this she, hiding in the gallery?' he exclaimed. 'Present me, Mamma, I beg you.'

Sir Langton and Lady Kirby were now there, supporting him on either side and Olivia could tell at once that Sir Langton resented his son's interest in meeting her. But her father as she expected stepped boldly forward.

'Gideon Beattie, at your service, sir, and delighted to congratulate you on your safe return home. We were desolated earlier to hear reports of your being wounded in action. May I present my daughter, Olivia?'

She just managed to curtsey low without her legs collapsing under her. As she rose he seized her hand and bowed to kiss it but a gasp of pain stopped him.

Sir Langton protested, 'No oh no, take care. He *is* hurt,' but Gerard laughed it away.

'A twinge, that's all.'

Lady Kirby cried, 'Oh come, let us get him to bed. He must be exhausted from his journey.'

'Nonsense,' said Gerard. 'We will all go into the drawing-room and have a dish of tea.'

'Oh indeed, I have given orders for that,' his mother said and she took his arm as if he were made of porcelain and leading him into the small drawing-room, sat him on the sofa by the fire and put a rug over his knees.

Sir Langton went in too and drew a chair close to his son. Gideon Beattie was following but Olivia pulled at his coat.

Gerard looked round. 'Come in, come in. I want to talk about the battle and I must have an audience, especially a young and beautiful one.'

They went in and Olivia took a chair at a distance but Gerard objected, 'I can't swivel round with all these deuced bandages. Come sit where I can talk to you.' She complied, growing in boldness, as he spoke frankly of his injury. 'The fact is a musket bullet took out a piece of ripe Kirby flesh just here' – he laid his hand on his left side below his armpit – 'and put a crack in one rib which is why I'm trussed like a chicken to keep it from moving. The army surgeon advised me to rest three weeks so I set off three days later and travelled in easy stages. Where can I rest better than in my own home?'

'If you'd only written!' Lady Kirby moaned. 'We had such a fright when we heard of you among the wounded.'

'I thought I'd be home before news reached you. But I'm no great correspondent as you well know.'

The tea now arrived and as the maid poured it out and carried it round he began to talk about the battle for Belle Isle.

All the time Olivia was wondering how he had known she had ridden Emperor and what he truly thought of that. He kept looking at her as if to check she was sufficiently impressed as he described how they had been landed at Locmaria Point where the French least expected them.

'We caught them napping all right. Commander Hodgson took a tip from Woolf at Quebec which meant we had to climb a nearly vertical cliff – devilish hard with all our accoutrements. My platoon was splendid. They all made it to the top but I was unlucky to be hit in the first flurry of Frenchies that we met. They were running like the blazes to get inside the Fort at Le Palais but one or two turned and took aim as we got within range of them. I wager it'll all be over there long before I can get back to it.'

'Go back!' cried his mother. 'You'll not go back in the army now?'

'Why would I not? The surgeon says I'll scarcely have a scar to show for it in a month or two and I'll be fit long before then.'

'But the risk!' she moaned. 'When I think of you facing musket bullets I am terrified. What say you, Sir Langton?'

Olivia watched the father turn his eyes on his son and saw

how he struggled not to reveal his intense pride in him. 'I believe the army has been the making of you, Gerard, but now that you have survived this great danger I could wish you to take an interest in your inheritance here. I trust you will overlook with me the plans Mr Beattie is preparing for the west wing.'

Gerard switched his attention to the architect now but Olivia felt it was with scant enthusiasm. 'What's the need for plans? Can't the builders just copy the east wing?'

Her father chuckled. 'Builders work from instructions and Sir Langton tells me the original plans were lost years ago in a fire in the estate office. So I am working backwards as it were from the actual building and reversing the measurements, but also outlining for your father's approval some additions and improvements in line with today's fashions so that Castle Kirby will become the greatest house in Yorkshire, second only to Castle Howard perhaps but that too is in need of renovations.'

'That all sounds very jolly,' Gerard said, 'but what says Miss Beattie? Does it compare with the excitement of the battlefield?'

She felt her cheeks flush up but an idea popped into her mind as to how best to answer him. 'Sir, I have been so moved by the beauty of this place that I could imagine nothing more exciting for you than to ride Emperor over its whole extent, only excepting of course its perfect lawns.' She cast down her eyes but permitted one of her mischievous smiles to play over her lips.

He seemed delighted with this answer. 'By Jove, she's right. The first thing I asked the stable lad was how Emperor was and he begged pardon for allowing a young lady to ride him. I can't wait to be on his back again and perhaps you will accompany me on one of our more sedate mares, Miss Beattie. That was the only thing I regret about the army. I didn't obtain a commission in the cavalry.'

'So you will quit fighting?' Lady Kirby begged.

'Nay, I've not promised that, Mamma. Riding Emperor is

splendid but I can't do it all day and I know no other pleasures of the country that would engage me as much as the army.'

Gideon Beattie said, 'Pray do not be afraid, Lady Kirby, for I am convinced that peace is on the horizon and being in the army may prove no more dangerous than walking the streets of London.'

They had now finished their tea and Lady Kirby pulled the new-fangled bell tassel to summon the maid to remove the tray.

'You will retire to rest now, Gerard,' she pleaded. 'Your room has been prepared and the fire should by this have taken away any chill.'

He stood up carefully. 'First I must greet my old childhood friends, Luke and Tom.'

Sir Langton rose too. 'Hardly necessary on your first day back. Tom will be about the gardens somewhere now it is fine. Tomorrow will do very well.'

'No, I will go down to Luke's den this evening at the hour Tom comes to visit him. But first, I will please Mamma by having a quite unnecessary rest. Miss Beattie,' he gave her his hand, 'I am charmed to have the pleasure of your acquaintance.' This time he did succeed in kissing her hand which she lifted so that he only had to bow his head. She was pleased that he was taller than herself. Being unusually tall for a woman she had literally looked down on many of the young men in London whom she despised.

Her father said, 'Perhaps another day, sir, you will honour me by overlooking my drawings.'

Gerard gave him a nod and a smile and he was gone, both his parents accompanying him along the gallery to the best bedrooms.

Olivia exchanged looks with her father who broke into one of his chuckling laughs. 'Well, there you are, my girl. He's no lover of architecture but he's certainly smitten with you.'

'No!' she exclaimed. And then, 'Oh papa, do you really think so?'

She stood quite still with delight and wonder and then gave a little skip about the room.

Chapter 4

Three weeks later Olivia was walking out alone for the first time since Gerard's arrival. She took several deep breaths, opened and shut her parasol a few times and gradually slowed her pace to one proper for a young lady. It was the high words she had just heard between Gerard and his father that had disturbed her. Were they about herself or about him leaving the army or indeed both? The high words were in fact only Gerard's. He didn't make any effort to moderate his voice. All she could hear of Sir Langton's replies was a thin cold sound like ice crackling.

She knew Gerard's new uniform had been delivered and he was trying it on in his dressing-room while she sat with a book on the recessed velvet seat further along the gallery because he had promised to walk with her before tea.

Evidently his father had joined him because she could hear Gerard say, 'What do you think, sir? A good fit is it not?' Maybe Sir Langton complained of the expense   because Gerard protested, 'But it's not only for tomorrow's ball. I will get a captain's commission when I go back. I wish I'd been there at the siege if that newspaper account was right. They said it was a huge bang when one of our shells hit the magazine and opened up a breach in the wall. That would have been a great sight.'

Then came a remark from his father and Gerard barked, 'With my army pay I am in a position to please myself.' It was the next speech of Sir Langton's – quite a long one – that triggered Gerard's fury and her own agitation.

Gerard seemed to be pacing the room as he shouted, 'If there are funds enough for the new wing why should I look only at heiresses? I say it can be announced tomorrow and I'll return to my regiment next week.'

What! Announce their engagement? He hadn't even asked her yet. He hadn't openly declared his love. Was this how things were in high society? She felt her youth and inexperience and longed for the mother she hardly remembered. Her father of course wanted the match and from the moment of Gerard's arrival had urged her to encourage him but lately he had taken her aside and said, 'I believe Sir Langton is fretting at the attention Mr Gerard is showing you. He could be looking a great deal higher than my poor little Olivia for his precious son. We must be careful not to offend him. I don't want him to terminate our agreement.'

'Oh Papa,' she had cried, 'is my marriage destiny always to be bound up with the progress of your work?'

He had laughed uneasily. 'It's the way of the world. But you hated that young viscount. How are your feelings for this future baronet?'

'I scarcely know him. Lady Kirby often walks with us. He is mostly amiable though he grumbles at the doctor forbidding him to ride yet.'

Of course she had pondered her volatile feelings in their walks together but this dialogue between him and his father was like lighting a fuse under a powder keg. The next thing she had heard had made her think Sir Langton could be leaving the room. Gerard said, 'You think you've had the last word, sir, but I shall be twenty-one in November and independent of you.'

That was when she had jumped up and fled along to the grand staircase and run down to find the great doors open and the balmy May sunshine flooding in. Out she had scuttled and down the easterly path towards the lake.

Now she turned a corner into the formal garden and saw Thomas crouched by the edge of the path digging out a dandelion root. He tossed the plant into the wheelbarrow and straightening his spine stretched and looked critically along the edge of the flower bed. The low box hedge was geometrically perfect and the shrubs behind it free of any discoloured leaves or faded flowers.

'Perfect,' she said behind him, suddenly wanting his company. He swung round and touched his hat to her.

'Your escort neglecting you, Miss Beattie?' he asked with a grin.

She'd forgotten the cheek of the lad. She gave a little toss of the head. 'Does your impertinence know no bounds, Thomas Todd?' But she didn't want to quarrel with him so she went on, 'If you mean Mister Gerard, he is being fitted out in his new regimentals for the ball tomorrow. I gather Sir Langton is not usually generous in his hospitality but now he feels obliged to mark his son's recovery by showing him off to your local gentry.'

'Oh so it's not to celebrate his engagement to you?'

Now she *was* angry. 'How dare you presume – !' She stamped her foot. 'Just because he has walked about with me! The poor young man was frustrated because he couldn't ride. He was bored to tears with nothing to do. And mostly his mother has accompanied us.'

'*You* were bored till you came to read Shakespeare with Luke and me.' He said it as a simple statement of fact, standing before her with his straight open look, his hat pushed back, his dark curls clinging to his forehead damp with perspiration

It was true. That time was the most enjoyable since her arrival. Everything else had been fraught with uncertain emotions. That had been pure pleasure.

'It has taken Luke and me these weeks to finish *Julius Caesar*,' he added. 'The weather has been so fine we have had little time for reading, but Luke hopes you will be Cleopatra if we go on to the next Roman play. I told him you had more interesting company now.'

He must have sensed then that she was embarrassed and cross. She knew she was frowning when she would much rather have laughed with him as she had before.

'Excuse me,' he muttered and turned away to his wheelbarrow.

'Well, if you are not going to be agreeable I will spare you my company,' she said and was going to walk past when he seemed to remember something.

'Oh Miss Beattie,' he cried, as naturally as usual, 'I forgot. There is someone who is very anxious to meet you and if you are free now I could take you to her.'

'And who might that be?'

'My grandmother who lives in the little cottage adjoining my father's. You haven't seen her yet because she doesn't get to church with the rest of the household.'

Olivia had gone each Sunday to please the Kirbys who had been quite shocked to discover that her father proclaimed himself a free-thinker. She had been amused at the procession from the castle of all the servants in strict ranking order, but Luke, she noticed, was never among them.

'No, I didn't know who lived in the smaller cottage,' she said. 'Are those the ones in the way of the new wing? I hope your grandmother doesn't think *I* can save them.'

'No, I'm sure she doesn't. But she has seen you from her window and would be honoured if you paid her a visit. She never goes out, so a young and beautiful face would be a delight to her.'

Now at last Olivia gave him her roguish smile.

'I never marked you down as a flatterer, Sir Tom. Well, lead on, I will visit your grandmother.' It would be a diversion from the knot of emotions and anxieties which she felt helpless to untangle.

He wheeled the barrow ahead of her round the truncated west wing to where the two cottages stood.

'I'll show you in and then empty this at the compost heap by the kitchen garden.'

Tapping at the door of the smaller cottage he opened it and called out, 'I've brought Miss Beattie, Grandmother. Can she come in?'

A husky voice answered and he beckoned her to step over the threshold, which she did gingerly, peering about at the tiny cluttered room before focussing her eyes on the shrunken figure in the basket chair by the hearth.

Uncertain what to say, she began tentatively, 'How are you, Mrs Todd?'

'I'm not Mrs Todd,' the gap-toothed mouth snapped. 'I'm Janet Johnson.'

Behind her Tom exclaimed, 'I'm sorry, I should have told you, Miss Beattie. She is Luke's *mother's* mother, not our father's.'

'Isn't Luke's mother *your* mother too?'

'My Grace is dead,' the old lady gabbled on, 'and that Albert Todd took another wife very quick and had Tom there, but he was punished for it 'cos *she* didn't live above two years and left me to bring him up but he's been a grandson to me and he's a good boy and looks after me now. Away back to your gardening, lad, and you sit down, young lady, and let me look at you.'

Tom asked, 'Don't you want me to make Miss Beattie some tea, Grandmother?'

'I can do it,' she croaked, so with a shrug of the shoulders he left them alone together.

Olivia, wondering what was to come, drew up a three-legged

stool which was all she could see apart from a narrow bed in the corner. The cottage apparently had only one room. She perched on the stool lifting her dress away from the ash-strewn hearthrug as best she could. Some afternoon sunlight was getting through a tiny window that looked west over the side garden but the bigger window faced the stables The old lady's face was half hidden under her cap and an ancient knitted shawl swathed her up to her chin despite the warmth of the day.

'Pray don't trouble about tea,' Olivia said as Mrs Johnson stretched out a knobbly hand to the kettle sitting on the trivet. 'It is just very pleasant to meet you. I have already met your grandson Luke. Perhaps you don't see him so often as Thomas since he is in a wheel-chair.'

Mrs Johnson turned her face towards her then and Olivia saw that her eyes had a startled look. 'Ah Luke! So you've met the cripple have you? But it's the other I've seen you walking out with. He takes you to see the horses but he's not fit to ride yet. What does he say to you when you are alone together?'

'You mean Mr Gerard? We are seldom alone but generally he talks about the army and the action he's seen.'

'Does he make love to you?'

Astonished at this directness Olivia could only stammer, 'We've only known each other three weeks.'

'That's long enough for Gerard.'

Was it? Olivia wondered. Did he flirt with all young ladies? But it hadn't felt like flirting and in the quarrel with his father he seemed to be alluding to a serious attachment. Perhaps he was secretly betrothed to someone else? Her own emotions were in chaos. She loved his looks but was uncertain of his character. At the same time she doubted if she would be able to resist him if he declared that he loved no one but herself. To be truly loved for herself alone, was something that had never happened to her, unless she counted the odious viscount, son of Lord P. He had certainly professed undying devotion but never proposed marriage.

'Tell me about yourself, my lady,' Mrs Johnson said now

Olivia gaped at the sudden change of subject. She tried a little light laugh though it felt inappropriate in that cramped dim space. 'You needn't call me 'my lady', Mrs Johnson. I'm just Miss Beattie, Olivia Beattie.'

'Not an earl's daughter?'

'No indeed.'

'A baronet's?'

'Not even that though if my father makes many more great houses for the nobility he may be knighted one day. Sir Gideon Beattie would sound rather well, would it not?' She was still probing for an answering smile but the staring eyes, a liquid hazel brown, now lit by a sunbeam, still gazed up with grim intensity from the skeletal face.

'Are you not looking for a grand marriage then?'

'Grand? Oh no, but I hope I would love my husband and that we would be comfortable.'

Suddenly the woman did cackle. 'More comfortable than this eh? You'd be too good for Thomas then. I wager?'

'Thomas! You were speaking of Mr Gerard, were you not, whose father, I'm sure would think *him* too good for *me*.'

'Is that so? Too good? Well' – she reached out a claw and patted Olivia's hand – 'you're bonny enough to turn any young man's head. Thank you for coming to see me. One day I may tell you a secret, but who knows? You may not be the one to tell. I've had some bad turns but I'm better now the summer's here. But if I were dying – you'd come to me again, wouldn't you? Would you promise me that?' Now the claw gripped Olivia's wrist. 'Because you may be the one. I had a presentiment –

when I saw you together by the stables. I said it out loud at the time, the way he looked at you. She could be the one, I said to myself. Will you promise?'

Olivia would have promised anything to release the bony grip on her wrist.

'I do, I do, I promise, Mrs Johnson.'

The hand was withdrawn and the eyes lowered. In fact the old lady seemed to disengage herself from the scene entirely. After a moment her head drooped onto her chest and her hands lay limp on the apron covering her skinny knees.

Olivia jumped up in a panic. Had she died there and then? But presently there came a deep sigh and another gentler one.

Well, gracious me, she thought, she's fallen asleep just like that. I suppose I can go. She doesn't smell very pleasant, poor old thing and I'll be glad to get out in the air.

When she stepped outside the first person she saw was not Thomas but Gerard Kirby approaching round the corner of the great house in his new uniform.

She swallowed what felt like her heart leaping into her mouth. He was devastating, the portrait walking towards her, one hand on his sword hilt, the other lifting to sweep off his three-cornered hat at sight of her.

As he drew nearer she saw that far from wearing the supercilious look in the portrait he was in fact quite agitated.

'Miss Beattie! I was searching the gardens for you till Tom said you were here.' He gave her his arm as she rose from the demure curtsey she had dropped and he guided her away beyond the stables, not as she expected towards the front of the house. 'We can be seen from everywhere in this deuced place. I never know which windows they are looking from. Let us head for the small copse.'

Albert Todd was working among the vegetables, she could see, but he had never taken any notice of her nor she of him.

'What is it, Mr Kirby? What has happened?' she asked as he hurried her along.

'They want me to leave the army. It seems my trifling little wound gave them a fright.'

Is that all? she thought. Is he only going to talk of himself as usual?

Then he went on in a rush, 'I would do it to spend time with you, Miss Beattie'– Ah, now what was coming? Her pulses began racing – 'but my father thinks he should take me on the grand tour if peace is declared soon. I'm damned if I want to stare at old ruins and museums and galleries and such. He thinks that's safer than the army but all he really wants is to part you and me.'

They had reached the copse and he drew her under the trees so that her parasol snagged in the branches. Impatiently he took it from her and cast it on the ground and grasped both her hands.

'Don't you know what I feel for you?'

'No, no I don't,' she cried, her voice coming out shrill with excitement. 'You've never spoken. How can I know –?'

'I've *looked* words, haven't I? Damn it I've sought you every day. My mother knows, my father knows, *your* father knows. I spoke to him just now.'

'You spoke to my father!'

'The proper thing. Get his permission to address you –'

'Oh what did he say?' Good heavens – spoken to my father! This was indeed the real thing.

'Oh devil take him. He asked what *my* father thought. He doesn't want to fall out with him of course. When I pressed him he said under other circumstances he would be perfectly agreeable, consider it an honour, the usual claptrap. But what say you, Miss Beattie? Nothing else in the world matters to me. If you are willing they can all go hang.'

He hadn't spoken a word of love. Am I a pretty thing he wants because he's been told he can't have it? When Thomas has spoken of him I've always had the impression he thinks Mr Gerard a spoilt brat.

She lifted her eyes to his. No, that was dangerous. He was too handsome. But what could she read in those eyes? Pleading, yes. What more?

'Why don't you speak?' he cried. 'Don't you love me?'

'I may be only an innocent young girl in your eyes, Mr Kirby, and indeed I am only eighteen but, having lost my mother very young, I have been much with my father among London society and I understand it is the custom for the gentleman to declare *his* love *first*.' She felt very proud of this speech, so cool and measured when the emotions inside her were bouncing up and down like a see-saw.

By way of answer he put his arms round her and pressed his lips on hers. She pushed him away so hard he actually gasped with pain.

'That place – you were right on it. What's up with you?'

'I'm sorry but kissing does not come before love.'

'You're a right stickler! Of course I love you. I fell in love before I ever saw you, when I heard you'd demanded to ride Emperor. By Jove, I thought, that sounds like the girl for me and then I saw you in the gallery, so lovely and pretending to be so shy. But you weren't. Not one of these simpering young ladies. I can't stand that. You were bright and friendly and you handled the old folks so neatly. My mother is quite taken with you. She'd be no trouble but the old man's on his high horse. I'll manage him though. Only say you can love me. I'm not a bad catch. All this will be yours and it'll be a deal grander when your father's finished it. What d'you say? I'm not going down on one knee in these breeches but believe me, I love you, Olivia Beattie and I want to marry you.'

She heaved a deep breath. They were the first such words she had ever heard in her life and they were triumphant music. She had thought before she met him that she would like to have him at her feet. Well, he wasn't going to dirty his new regimentals for her but, as a practical soul, she could see the sense in that. He was so handsome, and to be mistress of this magnificent place! But it had all happened in so short a time. She was scarcely ready for the moment, but oh! it would be so romantic to say yes, here in the wood, surrounded by young beeches wearing their most vivid green against a cloudless sky.

'Olivia, darling Olivia,' he breathed at her ear, 'say you'll marry me. Say yes.'

'Yes, Gerard Kirby, oh yes, yes I will.'

Now he took her in his arms again and she experienced her first ever long-drawn kiss of passion. When she could breathe again she gazed at him – her betrothed, her beautiful, beautiful betrothed. 'Oh I love you,' she burst out. 'Gerard, I love you.' It was true. She did. His love had drawn out hers. There he was – her man, smiling the most divine and radiant smile.

She had provoked another kiss and she could feel his hands longing to explore upwards from her slim waist, a new and exciting sensation, but he withdrew and murmured as he led her out of the wood, 'Damn it, I want you so much but now we must be cunning. It can't be announced while the old man is set against it, so I'll do my tedious duty at the ball tomorrow and dance with some of the county ladies first but we'll contrive one or two dances afterwards, without drawing too much attention to ourselves. I come into my majority in November and by then he'll have to be agreeable. We won't worry ourselves about him.'

'Will I still be here in November?' she wondered aloud. 'My father will soon be setting the builders to work and though the building will take a long time he may only come back to supervise it when it is more advanced.'

'Well, you won't disappear into vapour. If you are in London I'll be sure to be there too. The thing is you're mine from now on.

That's not going to change for anything.'

They were passing the cottages again and Olivia was shocked to realise she had completely forgotten the scene with Mrs Johnson. Goodness, she asked me if I was looking for a grand match and half an hour later I have secured it. She'll never believe it wasn't already all set up. And what will Thomas say, and Luke? Only of course I must say nothing. It's our secret. I wonder what *her* secret was. Nothing particular, I'm sure. I'm afraid she's in her dotage.

'You were visiting the old witch before?' Gerard said. 'Most obliging of you. I must confess she gives me the creeps.'

'But Luke and Tom, her grandsons, were your childhood friends. Do you confide in them?'

He laughed. 'It would hardly be appropriate now. I have a word with them from time to time of course. They are decent lads. Now my mother will be looking forward to her afternoon dish of tea. She likes you there for that, female company you know. I may come in but Father and I had a bit of a set-to and I ought to calm him down before dinner or it'll be deuced embarrassing. I suggest you're pretty distant from now on which will help smooth things over.'

They climbed the steps and he parted from her at the foot of the staircase with a little bow and went through the tall oak door into the truncated west wing to seek his father in the ground floor room used as the estate office. Olivia mounted to the small drawing-room hardly able to believe that such a momentous thing had happened to her since she had descended a mere hour before.

Chapter 5

'Is she coming, Tom?' Luke asked.

Only a week had passed since the ball but the sudden departure of the Kirby family for London had filled Luke with joyful expectation.

A thunderstorm overnight had broken the warm spell of weather and left a grey sky and relentless rain falling. He hoped Sir Langton and Lady Kirby and Mister Gerard had yesterday reached their first staging post en route to London before the storm, but now all he could think of was whether Miss Beattie would join them to read *Antony and Cleopatra* now that she had no other companions.

Tom had just come in and his usual cheery face was sombre.

'I don't know about that,' he said, 'but I've just been speaking with her father. Now that the Master's out of the way he's been interrogating all the out-servants and reckons Jack and Meg could accommodate Grandmother, father and me in their cottage in Tadby. Since their boys went to the war they'd be glad to let us a couple of rooms. So now he wants us out of here as quick as we can. He says the first load of stone for the south face of the west wing will arrive in two days and it should be stored right where our cottages stand – to be handy for the work. They can't put it out on the terrace.'

'You'll be a mile or more away at Jack and Meg's.' Luke felt suddenly bereft at the thought of not having his brother near at hand. 'Jack was here with my new crutches only a week ago and said nothing of this. Is this what Sir Langton ordered before he left?'

Tom grunted and went to the window to peer at the rain. It showed no sign of stopping. 'Mr Beattie won't say directly that Sir Langton gave orders for us to move. He only says there's nothing else that can be done and that the Master agreed to that. Well I say Sir Langton should have come to our father before he left and told him face to face. But we know he hates uncomfortable scenes and I'm not sure he isn't a little afraid of his architect.'

'Afraid of him. Sir Langton! Surely not. But what will you do, Tom?'

Tom had left the door slightly ajar and a voice said, 'He'll read Shakespeare of course while the rain lasts.'

She was there in the doorway again, a volume of Shakespeare in her hand.

A great surge of delight flowed through Luke.

'Oh Miss Beattie, pray come in.'

But Tom said, 'I should be helping Grandmother gather her things together. You know, Miss Beattie, that your father's uprooting the poor old soul?'

She came in and shut the door. For a moment she seemed dashed. 'He says he's found her somewhere more comfortable where she'll have a kind woman companion and you and your father will be in the same house to help look after her.'

'If she can climb the stairs to a wee loft room only fit to store apples in.'

'But the man is the estate carpenter isn't he? And he's going to fit out the room with a new bed and she won't have to make meals because his wife will take her all she needs.'

'All she needs is to change nothing in her way of life and to die in her own bed.' Thomas came away from the window and motioned Miss Beattie to sit down. 'But it's not your fault and as it will take barely ten minutes to pack up what she wants I'll wait till the rain stops. Luke has been longing to read with you.'

Miss Beattie let her eyes rest on Luke and he managed not to drop his own gaze but smile expectantly at her. He wondered if she had noticed what was leaning against the wall behind his easel. He couldn't help glancing towards the spot and she cried out, 'What do I see there? Crutches!'

'I got Jack to make some,' Tom said, 'and Luke has been trying them out this last week. I don't reckon he's fallen over more than a hundred times.'

'Oh Tom, not as much as that.'

Miss Beattie had just sat down but up she jumped again. 'Well let me see.'

This was not what Luke wanted at all. He had only hoped to convince her he was not a poor spiritless creature, but she fetched the crutches and held them out to him. Tom came over too with a grin on his face.

'I'll catch you. But he needs help to get up, Miss Beattie. Can you give him an arm that side?'

Luke was overwhelmed with shame that she should touch him but if it would put Tom in a good humour he was prepared to try. As they supported him upright he wedged the padded ends of the crutches under his armpits and tried not to let any weight at all fall on her. He had already learnt to use his right leg as a balancing aid. Some strength was even beginning to develop in the muscles he had thought useless. With much wobbling and their hands preventing him from falling he managed a few paces.

Tom knew how little he could do and lifted him back to his chair before he fell. But Miss Beattie said, 'Oh that's wonderful. I am so happy that you tried.'

He murmured, 'I do thank you, Miss Beattie, for your

encouragement. No one else has ever thought I could walk at all. But now that Tom is to be living over a mile away he won't be able to help me so much.'

'Nonsense,' said Tom. 'I will be in the gardens every day just the same and shall come in regularly for your exercise. Now you can do what you do better than either of us – act Shakespeare.'

'Yes, indeed,' Miss Beattie said. 'I do believe that if Luke had Mr Garrick's presence on the stage and his power of movement he could excite an audience almost as well. So let us begin. You will be Antony, Luke, to my Cleopatra, but there are many more good parts for you, Thomas. The best way will be if I give out the lesser ones as the scenes go on so we avoid talking to ourselves.'

She settled down and opened the book. 'I took this one from Sir Langton's library. It's marvellous what an air of lightness there is about the place with the family absent. The servants seem so easy as they move about and even sing aloud as they work. It's quite delightful.'

This was a great joy to Luke who had expected her to be very low in spirits now that Mr Gerard was away. It seemed so obvious to everyone else that Sir Langton's sudden decision to catch the end of the London season with his family arose from his wish to separate Gerard from Olivia Beattie. But perhaps their walking about together in the grounds had meant nothing after all.

They had been reading an hour when there came a timid knock on the door. It was the little maid Betsy. She curtseyed when she saw Miss Beattie.

'If you please Mr Luke your father is at the kitchen door asking for Mr Thomas.' Luke was touched that as the newest and lowliest of the servants she appended Mr to almost everyone's names.

'Will he not come in?' Miss Beattie asked. 'I've never met him to speak to.'

'I might persuade him with the Master away.' Tom went out after Betsy.

It was the first time Luke had ever been alone with Miss Beattie and he was devastated with shyness. Fortunately she began to talk about the play.

'Cleopatra is not an attractive character, is she, but her love for Antony seems very passionate. She loathes his absences and wants to know what he's doing every moment. I don't suppose you've ever been in love, Luke, because of course you don't meet people but can you imagine feeling that way – not able to bear someone's absence.'

She's young, Luke thought, and she said herself she has never met anyone like me so I mustn't feel hurt. 'I *can* imagine,' he said softly. 'I may not meet people but I read a great deal.'

'Of course you do, so would you think that's a requirement of being in love?'

Ah, he realised, she thought she was in love with Gerard but now she is in doubt. 'I would say,' he began, growing bolder, 'that Cleopatra loved but didn't trust Antony. Absences are always painful but where love is very deep and two people have known each other a long time they can endure partings because there is perfect trust between them – but they are never completely whole except when they are together.'

She clasped her hands under her chin and looked so very young and wistful that his heart ached for her.

'That's very beautiful,' she said. 'I must remember that.'

Then Thomas walked in with their father and Luke yearned to see his father's usual unsmiling face lighten up for Miss Beattie but all he did was pull at the grey curl on his forehead as his hat was in his hand.

'I'm pleased to meet you, Mr Todd,' Olivia said, not offering her hand as he put his grimy ones behind his back. 'I've been reading Shakespeare with your sons.'

'Ay,' his father said in his broad accent. 'It's all right for young ladies but Tom has work to do. Jack t'carpenter has sent his cart for our things. He'll need it tomorrow so we must move now. Come, Tom.' And he turned and walked to the door again.

Luke felt ashamed at his gracelessness but Albert Todd never used more words than he had to and Miss Beattie didn't seem offended.

'Pray let me come and help Mrs Johnson,' she said. 'Is she to travel in the cart in this rain?'

Tom said, 'There's a tarpaulin in the cart. We'll rig it round her. The rain's not heavy now.'

'Then I shall come and help her get ready and comfort her at this sad removal. We'll finish the play another day.'

She followed Tom and their father without a backward glance at Luke.

Finding himself alone was an all too familiar situation but for once he felt unable to extract from among the cushions on his chair one of the books he was currently reading. He was too disturbed by the upheavals that were happening and in which he could play no part.

But maybe I could, was his astonishing next thought, and he did something he had never done in his life. He propelled himself to his bell-pull and rang the bell.

It was only Betsy who appeared again.

'Do you have any idea, Betsy, where Mr Beattie, the architect, is at this moment?' He didn't expect she would so he was delighted at her ready answer.

'Oh yes, Mr Luke. He's in the office surrounded by his plans. I took him a glass of porter ten minutes ago and there was scarce anywhere to set it down.'

'Are you strong enough to wheel me there, Betsy?'

'Oh yes, sir. I carry the water jugs and coal scuttles. I've got such muscles!'

He laughed. 'Please do then and I beg you not to call me Mr Luke or worse still, sir. I'm Luke and you're Betsy or I shall call you madam or my lady.'

Now she did laugh too as she began pushing him along the passage, through the arched doorway from the east wing to the central lobby, past the foot of the great stairs and through the archway to the west wing which at present housed only the library on the south side and the estate office and storage rooms on the north.

He felt keenly what Olivia had said about the air of freedom and lightness about the place in Sir Langton's absence. He would never normally have ventured here in the middle of the day.

All the same he was nervous of meeting the architect. He hadn't seen him close to since the first day and that had only been embarrassing. But the voice that summoned him in was hearty and the florid face under its bushy hair was smiling.

Luke found it odd to see a man of his age without a wig. Sir Langton's was always neatly curled but Gideon Beattie gave off a general air of dishevelment.

When Betsy had crept out Luke said, 'Pray accept my apologies for troubling you, Mr Beattie. I am Luke Todd and –'

'Yes, yes, I saw you swinging from trees – all my silly girl's fault I believe.'

'Oh but sir, she is kindness itself. She has gone now with my brother and father to help my grandmother's removal to the village. What I wondered, sir, begging your pardon, is whether it is really necessary for Grandmother to be removed so suddenly. She's an old frail lady. I thought Sir Langton's original idea was to complete only the front façade of the house and leave the cottages alone.'

The architect grinned at him across the table but shook his large tousled head.

'He soon saw that wouldn't do at all. People walk round the

whole estate and the rear elevation should be as pleasing as the front. In fact that should become the main entrance with the south elevation called the garden front as at Castle Howard. There the new wing has been completed asymmetrically in the Palladian style and looks decidedly odd but Sir Langton is a perfectionist and perfection is what I must give him. The stables will need rebuilding to create two handsome blocks either side of a pillared archway leading to an imposing north entrance so that visitors' carriages can be brought up close and under cover. Various offices and servants' quarters can be incorporated above and I'm sure accommodation will be found there for your family if they prefer to move back to the castle.'

He drew out a sheet and laid it on the top for Luke to see.

'There. Sir Langton was very pleased with that as a replacement for the present stables and shabby cottages. To complete only the terrace façade of the west wing would leave the north elevation unfit to compare with the south.'

'It's very fine indeed, sir,' Luke said. He couldn't help being won over when his mind's eye compared this with the present shambles of the rear courtyard. He had made a study of architecture among his many interests and he knew all about Castle Howard and the wing added only five years before. His eyes began to scan avidly the other drawings and he wondered to himself if the Kirby estate could ever pay for such grandeur. He doubted if it had a twentieth of the acreage of the Howard land to support it. No doubt Sir Langton had admired it but had he authorised it to be carried out in full?

He began asking Mr Beattie questions about the scales used and other technical details about the drawings.

'Why, you know more than I gave you credit for, Luke Todd!' Mr Beattie guffawed. 'I'd make you Clerk of Works but Sir Langton has already recommended a good man in the village.

Perhaps you also know about the layout of the grounds. There seems to be no proper plan of the whole estate and I believe there should be many embellishments and vantage points to raise the place to a higher status among the great houses of England.'

Luke smiled. He found himself liking Olivia's father more and more. 'Well, sir, I have lived here all my life as Sir Langton has been good enough to let his servants look after me from babyhood, my mother dying when I was born. So I have amused myself from time to time in making maps as my brother has wheeled me everywhere my chair would go. I would be happy to show you my poor work if it would be of any interest. I have also made records of the use of the land, cattle pasture, arable and woodland – just for my own interest though I am sure Sir Langton has all such things in his ledgers.'

'Why you are a walking encyclopaedia!'

'Not walking, sir, but for that very reason I have been able to fill my time with acquiring knowledge.'

'I am astonished that Sir Langton hasn't made you his steward.'

'Oh he doesn't bother with me, sir. I don't think he knows me at all, though he has allowed me to take books from his library when no one is about and he permitted my brother and me to sit in the room with Mr Gerard's tutor when we were young.' He smiled bashfully. 'The tutor said our presence helped to create an atmosphere of learning.'

The architect roared with laughter again. It was plain where Olivia had acquired her gift for ready merriment.

'Yes, I haven't been impressed the last few weeks with Mr Gerard's scholastic attainments. All he wanted to do was ride or shoot and the doctor would permit neither. Well, I would like to see your maps, Mr Todd. Will you take me to them?'

'Oh sir, I should fetch them here –'

'No, no. I thought I had seen most of Castle Kirby but your

quarters have escaped me.' And he came round the table and took hold of Luke's chair.

'It's just at the corner of the East wing sir. I have two windows, one on the lake and one to the east woodland, which is very pleasant.'

And so they arrived back at his room just as Miss Beattie came running in from the rear courtyard. Luke was shocked at her bedraggled state. The shawl she had hastily thrown over her head was soaked and her dress dark with wet and smudged with grime.

Seeing her father and ignoring Luke she burst out, 'Papa! How dare you put an old lady through that? The poor soul clung to her door and Mr Todd had to pick her fingers off it one by one. And now she's being shaken to bits in that cart squashed with the goods from the two cottages and bent under a heavy tarpaulin.'

Her father retorted, 'You should think before you speak, my girl. She'll have a warm fire to welcome her and a clean bed for a change and a kindly body to take care of her.'

'But it was *your* doing, turning her out on a soaking wet day. She kept calling out for Sir Langton. Said she didn't believe the Master would have treated her like this. She knew things and she would tell. I don't know what she meant by that.'

Luke, sitting helpless, felt he must intervene on behalf of his new friend.

'Truly, Miss Beattie, the removal was necessary. The cottages have to go. It was unfortunate about the rain but that was when Jack could spare his cart. That was not Mr Beattie's fault.'

She turned on him like a tiger. 'My father's been working his charm on you too, has he? I'm surprised at that. I thought better of your good nature. Your own grandmother and you don't seem to care about her!'

'Oh I do, Miss Beattie, but your father has most kindly let me see the plans for the north elevation with the handsome stables and new carriage way. They are truly splendid and when finished will provide a home too for all my family.'

'If the shock hasn't killed your grandmother. She'll never live to see them built. Oh yes, my father's plans are beautiful things but they rarely turn into real buildings.'

'That's enough, Olivia. Get to your room and change or you'll catch your death which is no more than you deserve.'

Luke was shocked into silence by this unseemly shouting over his head between father and daughter and she a young lady for whom he had already felt such admiration, no, he had to admit, love. Of course he was in love with her and to see her in her dishevelled state yelling like a hoyden distressed him to the core.

'I'll go,' Olivia said, 'but I'm curious what she knows of you, Papa, that she'll tell Sir Langton when he gets back. Oh and Tom says you needn't set any workmen on the cottages. He has a sledge hammer ready for his return and he alone will level them to the ground. That's how he'll work off *his* anger. That's what he said. And very splendid he looked saying it!'

And she turned and marched off to the stairs, shaking a trail of wet onto the polished oak floor.

Then Luke, unable to look at Mr Beattie, heard him snort with laughter.

'Silly girl. She always was impulsive. Forget it all, Luke. She's a creature of the moment. Now to see these maps of yours.' And he wheeled him into his room.

Chapter 6

Olivia's maid Jenny was not in her room. 'I wager she's gossiping somewhere with the other servants,' she said out loud and began to wrench off her wet stockings.

She had started the day cross, cross with herself for not being devastated by Gerard's absence. Here she was, engaged to him and he had gone off to London only a week after their first ball together in which he had given her one perfunctory dance – and she wasn't pining for him. Oh she wanted him back, his splendid visible presence. She wanted him to hold her and say loving words to her and kiss her. Reading Shakespeare with Tom and Luke had cheered her up till she and Luke had talked about Cleopatra. Do I totally trust Gerard? she asked herself. Is that why I am not mooning about his minute to minute existence without me? No indeed. So what does that say about our love?

In the midst of this bewilderment had come the horrid scene of Mrs Johnson wrenched from her home. It had given her something to be angry about and she had let her tongue loose – and on Luke of all people! She stood, shivering and nearly weeping in her soaking dress.

Luckily Jenny came running in at that moment. 'Someone said you'd been out in the rain, Miss.'

'And where were you? Unless you undo me how am I to get out of this?'

'Gracious, Miss, you're wet right through!' Jenny had her

buttons undone and was feeling her petticoat and corset. 'Have you another day dress to put on, Miss? Your father scolds me when he has to buy you new clothes but I can't keep up with the washing and mending.'

Olivia was struck with fresh contrition. Her new dresses depended on her father earning a good living, and just now she had cast aspersions on his professional skill in bringing plans to fruition. She stepped out of the dress and then the petticoat.

'Oh Jenny, do I speak hastily sometimes?'

'To me, Miss? I don't mind it.'

'But to others. Do I do and say things without thinking?'

'Maybe, Miss, but everyone forgives you 'cos you're so young and pretty.'

Olivia remembered 'no such mirrors' with much discomfiture as Jenny abstracted another corset from the chest and felt her chemise to see if it too was wet. Luckily the corset had acted as a solid barrier.

While Jenny was inserting the stays Olivia became aware of a loud noise outside and went to her window. Down in the courtyard Tom was attacking the walls of the cottages with his sledge-hammer.

The rain had stopped but his shirt was wet either from the morning's downpour or his sweat now. It clung to his body so that she could see the movements of his shoulder blades as he heaved up the hammer and swung it against the walls. What a torso he had! Jenny coming behind her to encase her in her spare corset looked over her shoulder.

'I'n't he strong, Miss! But eh, it's a shame them pretty little cottages knocked all to bits. Oooh!' She squealed as Tom had to jump back as slates came rattling off the roof. He was obviously risking life and limb by weakening the walls first but he continued to bash at them all the way round while Olivia struggled into her clothes and Jenny laced her up.

'Miss, he could look up and see you,' Jenny exclaimed as Olivia stood pressed against the glass while Jenny eased the close-fitting bodice up over her breasts.

'He's far too busy and I wouldn't miss a second of this. Why, you've put my *evening* gown on!'

'It'll have to do while I sponge this down and dry it. There's only your father to see you and he won't notice. It'll save time changing later and you can put your other shawl round you.'

'I shall have to write to Mrs Ledbury to send more dresses. Why did you pack so little?'

'I packed what you said, Miss. How long are we going to be here?'

'You're pining for William, I suppose.' Mrs Ledbury, the housekeeper and William, the general serving man, were all that were left at home in London. Now that Olivia had seen the numbers of servants in Castle Kirby she realised how small her father's household was. When he needed transport he hired it. Here he had had a horse from the stables whenever he wanted to ride out. For the first time she began to realise how far apart were a landed baronet and a not very well-known London architect. Yet she was – secretly – engaged to Gerard Kirby. How had it all happened?

'Nay, Miss,' Jenny was saying, 'William's nothing to me. But that Thomas there – he'd be worth having – if he wasn't a Yorkshireman of course.' She giggled and now that Olivia had her shawl round her they both continued to gaze at the speedy destruction going on outside.

My Gerard is the same build, Olivia thought, and just as strong, I'm sure. I *do* wonder what he's doing now. He promised Sir Langton to look at 'galleries and such tedious things' in the hope that the Grand Tour idea will be dropped. 'I'll go quietly this time,' he had said, 'so the old man will forget his suspicions about us.'

There came a final crash below as the roofs of the two cottages collapsed together and Thomas stood before the ruins, his shoulders heaving and the head of the sledge hammer resting on the ground.

Next morning was fine and the first thing Olivia did after a friendly breakfast with her forgiving father was to go to the stables and request the mare which both Gerard and Sir Langton had said she could ride. She would go and see how Mrs Johnson was. She had not ridden while Gerard was here because he had insisted that if he couldn't ride she must walk to keep him company. She didn't see Tom but she found some of the workmen who were awaiting the delivery of stone clearing away the cottage debris and piling the whole slates and any other usable materials in a corner of the courtyard.

One of the grooms said Emperor must be exercised and he would accompany her so they set off for the village, he restraining Emperor with difficulty when they reached the public highway.

'If you're visiting Jack the Carpenter's house, Miss, I'll take Emperor a gallop round the fields for half an hour.' He pointed out the house when they reached the village and dismounting secured her mare to a tethering post and helped her down. 'She'll stay as quiet as a lamb there, Miss, don't you fret.' And he knocked on the door for her.

When a diminutive woman answered he remounted Emperor who was snorting with impatience and left Olivia to introduce herself.

Meg Summers seemed delighted to see her. 'Poor Mrs Johnson's rambling. She wanted to be up at two in the morning and it took me and Jack and Tom to get her back to bed. Albert Todd sleeps through everything and my Jack said it wasn't man's work but she was so strong, fighting to go home, she was.

'Where am I? Sir Langton must know of this. Where is he? Why doesn't he come?' Over and over for near an hour on the clock till she fell asleep with sheer exhaustion. If you go up, Miss Beattie, maybes you can talk sense into her. I took her porridge but she pushed it away.'

Olivia began mounting the steep narrow stair. 'It's the wee door straight in front,' Mrs Summers called and Olivia tapped on it and bent down to pop her head round. Apart from a bed built under the tiny window and the small table and stool with a Bible on top from the old cottage, there were only three baskets stacked against the opposite wall containing a brass jug, a few pots, her kettle and broth pan and a sack with her clothes pushed inside. Floor and walls had all been scrubbed clean.

Olivia could now make out her form under the blankets. Her nightgown must be as clean as her very white cap as there was no smell, except perhaps a lingering scent of fresh cut timber. Presumably Jack Summers had stored smaller cuts here. It was good of them, Olivia appreciated now, to have made room for the little family at such short notice.

Not wanting to wake Mrs Johnson she took the ancient Bible off the stool and sat down with it on her lap. It was the only book in the place and she wondered if Mrs Johnson could actually read.

She had opened it and was beginning to turn the pages when she saw an eye watching her from the bedclothes. The claw whose grip she remembered so well shot out and closed the book.

'Page a hundred,' croaked the voice.

'Oh! You'd like me to find that?'

'Not now, not now, but remember it.' Mrs Johnson began to sit up in the bed with her eyes fixed on Olivia's face. 'You are the one, aren't you? The one that'll marry Gerard? Where is he and where is Sir Langton? They've taken me away. I was to die there but not till – Only *you've* found me. How did you find me? Where am I?'

'Only in the village with Mr and Mrs Summers. Tom and Albert Todd are living here too but they've gone to work because it's morning, a new day. Mrs Summers is downstairs and she has tea and porridge for you as soon as you're ready to eat it.'

'No, I want to go home. I mustn't be away from Sir Langton. He wouldn't have let them take me away. How did you get here?'

'On horseback.'

'Then sit me up in front of you and take me back.'

'Oh, Mrs Johnson, there's no home for you there till they build you a new one. But they will, I promise you. And you wouldn't see Sir Langton anyway because he's in London and so are Lady Kirby and Mr Gerard and please told tell anyone I'm to marry Gerard because we none of us know the future.'

'No, that we don't and there's many don't know the past either.' She was now sitting bolt upright in the bed, still looking fixedly at Olivia. 'Did you promise to come to me if I was dying or did I dream that? I've had some terrible dreams lately.'

'Yes, I did promise but you are looking very well today, Mrs Johnson. Shall I call Mrs Summers to bring your breakfast now?'

'Mrs Summers?'

'You know them as Meg and Jack I expect. He's the carpenter on the estate. He built you that nice new bed.'

'I want my own bed. I know its ups and downs. Why should I be here?'

'So you can be well looked after and comfortable.'

Olivia went to the door and called, 'Mrs Summers, I think Mrs Johnson could manage her breakfast now. She seems refreshed from her sleep.'

The little woman came trotting up a few minutes later with a wooden tray balancing an earthenware crock of warmed up porridge and a mug of tea.

'You've done her a power o' good, Miss, thank you.'

Olivia whispered, 'She still wants to go home. I've told her they'll build her a new one. She'll understand better when Tom and his father get home from work.'

'They'll not be building a new one soon, will they?' Mrs Summers sounded anxious. She wants their bit of rent, Olivia realised.

She gave her a reassuring smile. 'Not for months or years but we won't tell her that. I'll slip away now but I'll come again if she asks for me.'

She went downstairs where there was a small front parlour on one side of the stair and another room the other side which must be where Jack and Meg slept. The kitchen at the back was the largest room and she presumed the two rooms upstairs had been added later in the roof space when the two boys were born. Where they would sleep when they came on leave she couldn't imagine. Tom and his father obviously had to share their bed. She wondered if her father realised what cramped conditions he had sent them to.

As it was sunny she sat on the bench outside till the groom returned. She felt she had handled the old lady well but she was no nearer making sense of her more mysterious sayings. She would look up page a hundred in her own Bible but when she got back to the castle she found page a hundred was in Leviticus and dealt with burnt offerings and priest's duties. It must be a different edition, she decided, but I'll get to the bottom of it one day.

For the next week the weather stayed fine and work began on the west wing to carry the truncated end forward to the same length as the east. Next time she rode over to the village she found Mrs Johnson dressed and sitting in the kitchen, but rather morose and quiet. There was no chance of a private word in front of Mrs Summers but the little woman said as she showed her out, 'She still wants to see the Master but it does her good knowing you are not far away, Miss Beattie.'

Olivia was left feeling frustrated and restless. The pleasantest times were when Betsy came to whisper to her that Mr Luke and Mr Thomas were at her service which was their sign that Tom had time from his work for a Shakespeare session.

She wondered what Gerard would think if he knew of this. She wanted to write to him but not to mention these secret hours. He had said he would send the address when they had rented a house but no word had come.

One morning however she did receive a letter with the Kirby seal but the hand was definitely female and when she opened it up she found as she feared it was only from Lady Kirby, but at least she had put an address in Grosvenor Square at the top.

Olivia took it out to a seat in the garden to read.

The preliminaries were inquiries after her and her father and the progress of the work and then a paragraph on them settling into their rented house for the rest of the Season and how hot and dusty it was. Then came the real reason for the letter.

'Now I have to confess, dear Miss Beattie, that I am uneasy on several accounts. The rift between Sir Langton and my poor Gerard is no better. They both read the papers for the war news but Gerard is only wishing he could be with his regiment. It seems there was a great ceremony of allowing the beaten French to march out of their citadel on Belle Isle with colours flying, which was very magnanimous of our forces and Gerard is cross at missing it all, but Sir Langton says he is not to go back. The war is not over and indeed Mr Pitt fears Spain will come in. I only follow these things as they affect my boy. He has escaped one bullet which was only inches from his heart and we both worry about him, being our ewe lamb, you know.

'Of course he doesn't want to be told by his father what to do but then young men are like that I believe. We consulted

an eminent physician who says it would be unwise for him to ride yet and that has made him more cross. He disappeared for a whole evening and night and we didn't find out till afterwards that he'd been at the gaming tables at White's. You can't imagine how angry Sir Langton was.

'There is also no question of the Grand Tour until hostilities are over. So if he is not to stay in the army Gerard wants to be back in Yorkshire and I know well what the attraction is there. I only want him to be happy and if your sweet, lively nature can achieve that I would never stand in his way. Of course Sir Langton hopes to secure him a wealthy bride of aristocratic family while we are in London. Pray take no offence at that, my dear Miss Beattie. I myself come from no very grand family but all this brings me to the most painful matter I feel obliged to mention.

'I had not understood that one of Sir Langton's motives in coming away so quickly was to make inquiries about your father's professional standing. As you may know it was Lord P who recommended him to Sir Langton but Lord P is away and his friends will only say that he admired some drawings your father made for one of them but it was impossible to carry them out within the agreed budget and nothing was ever built. I only mention this so that you can have a discreet word with your father. Of course Sir Langton will continue to engage him but I do worry that Mr Beattie has very magnificent ideas and we are not nearly as wealthy as Lord P's friend.

'Please forgive me, dear Miss Beattie, for mentioning these awkward subjects and I'm sure I don't want to distress you over dear Gerard, for if anyone can keep him right I do believe it is your good self, only don't ever let Sir Langton know I said that. Please enjoy all that Castle Kirby can offer and let me know all the news there.

'A letter from you will give great joy to your affectionate friend,
   Sophia Kirby.'

Olivia jumped up when she had read this and walked about very fast while her thoughts chased each other round the uncomfortable matters raised. Gerard didn't come out of it very well though she could sympathise with his longing for freedom from his father's tight control. More uncomfortable was the position of her father, but to have a discreet word with him was impossible in their robust relationship. She would either say nothing at all or tell him outright or even show him the letter.

No, she thought, rounding a corner into the rose garden, I don't want him to know that Gerard has been throwing money away at the gaming tables.

And there in front of her was Thomas Todd dead heading a tall standard rose.

'Morning Miss Beattie.'

She looked him in the eye. 'Tell me, Tom, what do you think of gambling?'

He chuckled at her abruptness, took off his hat and scratched his head.

'Stupid, I'd say, though I've seen my father put twopence on quoits on market day and win sixpence. Next throw he'd lose it trying to make a shilling, so, ay, stupid. Is it your father who gambles?'

'Oh no, well yes, of course when we went to Epsom he backed a horse and was cross afterwards so I suppose he lost but I thought nothing of it at the time. But it *is* stupid. You're right, as usual. Tell me how is Luke progressing with his crutches?'

Tom looked at the sundial. 'It's nearly noon. I promised to go in and help him. Will you come with me?'

She followed him in at once, Lady Kirby's letter momentarily forgotten.

They had finished *Antony and Cleopatra* and Luke was eager to go on to *Coriolanus* which Olivia had never read. So she had been reading it in bed and had pondered deeply on the downfall of the arrogant Roman General. She wondered to herself, have I been too imperious? Did I come to this place, full of pride that I would make a great impression here? Do I still burst out as I did to Luke and Papa over the old lady? But I do believe in standing up for the oppressed. Coriolanus despised the poor and lowly. But I must think first. Coriolanus eventually yielded to the pleading of the women but too late. There is much wisdom to be learnt from Shakespeare. And then it struck her that she had never discussed Shakespeare with Gerard.

They found Luke standing at his window supported by his crutches. Olivia was delighted to see him upright and looking at her with his head up. Though his face was narrow his features were pleasing and his smile was wide and joyful.

'How did you get out of your chair?' Tom asked.

'Betsy came in and her help was enough.'

Luke was obviously pleased to greet Olivia standing up. He took some steps towards her, swinging his body to help the motion and putting some weight on his twisted right leg. She could see that was painful but he was determined to do it.

She clapped her hands with glee. This was all her doing. She had created a new being. 'You'll be able to walk outside soon and enjoy this late June sun. The west wing is growing yard by yard.'

'I do take him to see the progress of the work,' Tom said. 'He has studied your father's plans. I think he would like to be an architect, wouldn't you, Luke?'

'I'd like to be many things – an eighteenth century Leonardo de Vinci would suit me very well.' He was laughing at himself. Was there ever such a quick change in anyone? Olivia thought.

He couldn't even look at me that first time.

'And what do you think of your grandmother?' she asked them both. 'Do you feel she is reconciled to her new place?'

'I'm going to wheel Luke there this evening,' Tom said. 'She needs to be aware the castle is not far away. So it's good of you to call on her, Miss Beattie. She talks of you often, the one that's going to marry Gerard she says.'

'Oh!' Olivia didn't often blush but she felt the blood rush up her cheeks now. 'You mustn't repeat such things. I told her no one can see the future but now it will be all round the village if Mrs Summers has heard her.'

'I daresay it was already,' Tom said coolly. 'The house servants saw you walking the grounds together.'

Luke, back in his chair now, looked up in distress. 'But we must do our best to kill off such rumours, Tom. They are very upsetting to Miss Beattie.'

Tom shrugged his shoulders and grinned at her. 'If they are untrue after all.'

Olivia stamped her foot, 'You, Thomas Todd, have the impudence of the devil. If I ever become mistress here I'll dismiss you at once.' She had hardly finished the words before she began to laugh and in a moment they were all laughing together. She wondered if she was laughing to stop herself crying. Why had he never written, her betrothed lover, if his mother was right that he longed to come back to Yorkshire?

Tom had to go back to his work so Olivia reluctantly headed for the estate office in the west wing to see her father. As she came into the central lobby he burst out of the opposite door exclaiming, 'I can't work with all this noise.'

Seeing her he pranced towards her and whirled her about.

'Ah, what has my little girl been up to?' His moods could change as quickly as her own and she was delighted to be the cause. But she didn't want him to be cross again so now was not the time to tell him of Sir Langton's inquiries.

'I've been to see Luke,' she said.

'A remarkable young man with more sense than his brother. Luke soon saw why the cottages had to come down but maybe Tom has forgiven me since he worked out his feelings with the sledge-hammer in his hand. Since the young master went away you seem to spend your time with those two.'

'Nonsense, papa,' she giggled, hanging onto his arm. 'The occasional word. You are busy and who else is there to talk to?'

'What about Mrs Chorley, the housekeeper?'

'Oh she's a grumpy pudding of a woman and I'm sure she resents me being here.'

'Well, has Gerard written to you yet? You had a letter this morning.'

'No, no it was only from Lady Kirby.'

'May I see it?'

They had walked out into the sunshine down the grand steps and despite the noise of the masons he was leading the way towards the work.

'Don't you want some quiet, papa?' she countered.

'I like to keep an eye on them. I had my window open and it seemed worse indoors. We'll see how much they have done this morning.'

And so, in chatting to the bronzed, half naked men, assessing their progress, examining the length of the trench they had dug for the completion of the garden front wall, he forgot her letter and she didn't trouble to remind him.

It was a week before she exerted herself to reply and then it was a scant letter in comparison with her ladyship's.

'Dear Lady Kirby,
'It was so kind of you to write and consider my feelings
so thoughtfully. I am sure all will be well when we see you

back here and dear Sir Langton will have no further cause to be angry with your son. Mister Gerard will be able to ride Emperor by then and that will cheer his spirits. As for me I do not presume to look as high as a baronet's son. I am gratefully enjoying your charming home and gardens.

'You will be pleased to know that the Todd family have settled in with Mr and Mrs Summers in the village since the removal of the cottages. Mrs Johnson fretted a little and is looking forward to Sir Langton's return and of course yours and Mr Gerard's. She seems uneasy when the family is away from the castle but the old are not fond of changes, are they? I have visited her a few times and she is looking well.

'The work on the west wing is progressing quickly and my father will bear in mind your kind advice and add no embellishments that have not been authorised by Sir Langton. The weather continues fine which is fortunate.

'My father sends his humble greetings to you all and I wish you a pleasant time for the remainder of your stay in London.

'I feel very honoured, your ladyship, that you allow me to sign myself your dutiful friend,
  Olivia Beattie.'

She was very satisfied with this and handed it to one of the footman for it to be sent to the village to meet the post boy. It didn't worry her that she had not in fact shown her father Lady Kirby's letter. At all events it was done and if Gerard knew she had written to his mother maybe he would be encouraged to produce something himself.

What she was not prepared for was the catastrophe that her letter did produce only a week later.

Chapter 7

It was late evening and Olivia was watching the lake from her favourite alcove in the long gallery. The first breeze of sunset flickered across the surface and the red gold light on the water shivered into a thousand flakes.

I don't ever want to leave this place, she told herself.

Mrs Chorley, the dour housekeeper, passed behind her. 'Ay,' she said, ''tis a fine sight on a late summer's evening. Goodnight, Miss Beattie.'

It was the closest she had come to friendliness since their arrival. Olivia stayed a while longer, her eyes mesmerised by the changing colours, then she knocked on her father's door.

'Goodnight, papa.'

''Night, darling.'

She went into her room and closed her door.

Three minutes later there was a sharp tap and the housekeeper put her head in.

'My gracious, Miss Beattie, the Master's back. The carriage is coming up the drive this minute. Will you go down? I must give word about the beds first. I've never known him not send word ahead,' and she disappeared.

Olivia called her father and they ran down.

'I was looking out just now,' she said, 'but the carriage must have been swallowed up in the deepening shadows beyond the lake. Do you think they have all come? But why so suddenly?'

Her father just shook his shaggy head and they reached the foot of the stair as the butler flung back the great doors and grooms came running round from the stables.

Olivia's eyes were caught first by the four glistening horses, heads drooping, their rumps reddened by the last band of light in the western sky. Then she saw the carriage door opened by a groom and out jumped Gerard to hand down his mother.

Olivia was thrilled to feel her heart leap at sight of him but next moment just as horrified at the thunderous face of Sir Langton as he followed.

Servants were all about now, bobbing and bowing, but they allowed Olivia to step first to greet Lady Kirby who to her astonishment folded her in her arms and whispered at her ear, 'Don't be alarmed, dear girl, not your fault at all, but your letter – he would come at once and we've never taken it in such stages you've no idea – Gerard too of course – desperate to come but Sir Langton – it's all about Mrs Johnson – I doubt if he can even be civil to your father. Oh dear and he's right here to welcome us. Mr Beattie –' She laid her fingertips on his hand. 'Pray excuse me, rather tired you know.'

With her lady's maid coming up behind her and Olivia taking her arm she managed the steps and they got her into the hall where she sank onto the velvet couch beneath Gerard's portrait.

A maid came running with a glass of wine. Olivia hovered by her, intensely conscious of the life-size Gerard in front and the real man behind her, evidently determined to speak to her.

She turned and their eyes met.

'Haven't you a word for *me*?' he hissed. 'What did you write to my mother? You would never aim as high as a baronet? You have and you were shot down into his arms. My arms, Olivia. You're mine.'

'Your father,' she murmured, seeing Sir Langton pausing with a fixed look at his son's back.

'Damn my father,' Gerard mouthed.

But Sir Langton pushed into the group. 'Take Lady Kirby upstairs,' he ordered the maid. 'Miss Beattie, will you oblige me with a word in the office.'

It was the nearest room and he took a candle from the first servant who had come running with a tray of lights and carried it through the tall west door.

Olivia, quaking a little but determined not to be intimidated, followed as he lighted her into the office. Some daylight still came through the courtyard window and Sir Langton stepped up to it and looked out. He drew a short sharp breath. He could see stacked stones and sacks of sand and lime mortar but no cottages.

He turned back to her and carefully cleared a small space among the untidily spread plans to set down the candle.

'You have some acquaintance with Mrs Johnson, I believe, Miss Beattie?'

Olivia stood head up and very straight-backed. He had not asked her to sit down and indeed the two chairs also bore piled sketches and written notes. Where could this interview be leading? What was the seemingly intense bond between Sir Langton and Mrs Johnson?

'I have only done what was kind.' Her voice came out too shrilly. 'I visited a lonely old lady in distress.'

He started at the last word but struggled to regain his usual polite composure. 'I am not *censuring* you, Miss Beattie. Indeed I am most grateful for the concern you have shown to an old and valued servant. What did she speak of? What did she say to you?'

The abruptness was back. It was as if the questions had been seething in his mind the whole way from London and courtesy could not restrain them any longer.

Olivia began to feel easier. Whatever strange revelations

Sir Langton feared she had no intention of even hinting that anything untoward had been said. And if Sir Langton was angry with her father for too rapidly ejecting the Todds and Mrs Johnson she could play her part in reassuring him.

'Let me see.' She clasped her chin as if she was trying to recall scraps of a rather uninteresting conversation. 'When I saw her first in her cottage she told me Luke and Tom were half-brothers, which I hadn't realised before. And when she was packing up to move I helped her put her goods into baskets and she was most particular to take her Bible. Then the first time I called on her in the village she asked me how I had come. When I said on horseback – only it wasn't Emperor you can be sure, sir' – with a light laugh – 'she asked me to ride back with her in front.'

'She was desperate to return?'

'Oh but she soon settled. I convinced her that she would have a home at the castle again and that consoled her. My father knows how he will fit very suitable accommodation for her in the new stable block and servants' quarters.'

'Which he will not see built,' Sir Langton suddenly snapped back.

'I beg your pardon?'

'I am sorry to say that I would like you and your father to pack and leave as soon as possible. Perhaps he will see whether *he* relishes the experience of a sudden move.'

Olivia stared round the room completely covered with her father's work.

'Sir, you can't expect –'

'Him to leave all this? But I do. Out of it I will choose what I build. He will be paid of course but I prefer not to have him in my house any longer.'

This was out of all proportion. She looked into his eyes but the candle shone onto implacable depths.

'What has he done? You can see where the workmen have

stored their materials. Surely you expected the cottages to go, Sir Langton?'

'Indeed I did not. It is what I have learnt about your father from my inquiries in London. He acts on his own. He is obsessed with his own ideas. He knew I wanted the garden front completed to harmonise with the east wing but I had not yet decided to extend the west wing rearwards. I cannot work with a man who will not take orders but this I must tell him to his face. I only addressed you first, Miss Beattie, because I know young ladies need more time to pack and if it can be arranged I would prefer you to leave for London tomorrow. I will of course send our own carriage for you to meet the stage coach.'

'Tomorrow!' What in heaven's name would Gerard say? He had rushed from London to see her! This would only make the rift with his father irreparable. How could she leave here with her future prospects in ruins?

Sir Langton had picked up the candle and was motioning her to the door.

'Perhaps you would be kind enough to send your father to me, Miss Beattie.'

She stalked out without replying and picking up her skirts ran up the stairs and almost collided with Gerard who must have been waiting for her.

He grabbed her round the waist. 'You pretty little thing, how fast you move!'

'Not too fast for your father. Did you know he came back to throw us out?'

Jenny was hovering along the gallery outside her bedroom door ready to see her to bed and other servants were scampering about with warming pans and jugs of water and armfuls of clean linen but Olivia didn't care now who saw them together.

Gerard was staring at her, aghast.

'Throw you out? He said nothing of this on the way here.'

'What reason did he give then for the sudden departure?'

'Tired of London, the heat. Wanted to see how the work was going. God knows I was ready to come. London in the season is all very well if a man can ride in the park, hear the news, see the latest fashions, meet friends, play the tables, but living with the parents is so deucedly stuffy. I wanted my girl. Hang it, I'll come back with you.'

'Tomorrow? That's when he wants us gone.'

'Good gad, I couldn't sit in a carriage again as soon as that. These damned roads shake one to bits. But you can be sure I'll come and join you there soon. What the deuce has your father done that's made the old man so furious?'

She began to explain about the cottages but saw over his shoulder her father emerge from his room to see what was going on. She beckoned him and told him to go down to Sir Langton in the estate office.

Gerard grabbed his arm before he could reach the stairs.

'Mr Beattie, you'd better make peace if you can. My father's on his high horse again. You know I want your girl and it doesn't help if you two are at loggerheads.'

Olivia saw her father raise his eyebrows and run his hands through his wild hair as he surveyed the young heir up and down.

'It's you and she that are at the bottom of it, Mr Gerard, if you'll forgive me for saying so. I have no quarrel with your father over the work.'

Olivia shook her head. 'Go down, papa, and speak to him. You'll find out differently I promise you.' She was fighting to hold back tears now as the enormity of leaving Castle Kirby grew upon her. She had been happier here than at any other time in her life, she realised now. The freedom to wander the grounds, to ride when she wanted, the sweet interludes with Tom and Luke, the visits to the village where she was the young lady from the castle, and all the time the hope that this handsome young man who loved her would make her future secure and she would be Lady Kirby, queen of all this one day.

Her father shrugged his big shoulders and descended the stairs.

Gerard drew her into the small drawing-room and shutting the door took her in his arms. She allowed him a long lingering kiss but when her hoop prevented him from pressing his body against her as he was obviously struggling to do his hand went to the fastenings of her bodice.

'No,' she cried. 'I thought you were a gentleman.'

'Gentlemen! Ladies! We're a man and a woman and why we wear such damn silly clothes I know not.'

'I believe hoops are for exactly that purpose – to keep men at arms' length.' She couldn't help her incorrigible laughter from bubbling up as she said it till she remembered this might be their last encounter for a long time, if not for ever.

'Oh Gerard! What are we to do? If you truly love me can we ever be married when your father is so implacable? Will he not disinherit you?'

He dismissed this with a wave of his hand. 'There is no other heir. He would never see the land go out of the family. If your father can get commissions from the nobility he'll change his tune. Anyway he can't keep me chained up. I'll get back to London soon enough. Give me another kiss or I'll go mad.'

Five minutes later they heard her father come up again and call for her. He went to her room and knocked on the door.

Smoothing down her dress and repinning her hair as best she could she hurried out with one backward glance at Gerard, standing grimly, feet apart on the Persian rug.

'There you are,' her father said. 'Jenny didn't know where you were. What have you been up to?' He saw Gerard emerge from the room. 'You'd better leave her alone now, sir. She's not for you. It's all over between us and Castle Kirby. Sir Langton's given orders for the carriage at noon. He'll send for fresh horses from the village. So get your bags packed, my girl. It's London for us again. Nay, don't you give way to tears. That's not my Olivia. It's a fresh chapter, that's all,' and as she came close, wanting to sob on his shoulder, he muttered, 'He's paid me handsomely, so there'll be a new dress or two and better society than you've had in this place.'

Olivia bit her lips and turned into her room to confide her sorrow and anger to Jenny as she prepared her for bed.

Next morning there were many tears from Lady Kirby. 'Why doesn't he wait?' she wailed. 'He's going to ride over to the village to see Mrs Johnson and if he finds her quite happy there is no need for him to be angry any more and you could stay. I was so looking forward to seeing you again, dear Olivia. Mrs Chorley is no sort of a companion. You were always so bright and lively. And oh, my dear, Gerard won't even speak to his father.'

Olivia was too absorbed in her own misery to waste sympathy on Lady Kirby but when she went down to see that all her bags were ready at the door with Jenny sitting guard over her hat box to make sure it wasn't crushed, she knew she must run along the east passage to the little room on the corner and say goodbye to Luke.

She found Tom there, just come in from the garden and he helped Luke rise to his feet and balance on his crutches.

The sight filled Olivia's eyes with tears again. This was the young man she had created from a poor shy neglected creature, just an object to be wheeled about.

Tom, ever practical and unbowed said, 'Well, Miss Beattie, I suppose your father will have work aplenty in London but I doubt if old Harper is clever enough to follow his plans here without his help.'

Olivia had heard her father say of Sir Langton's clerk of works, 'Harper's got the measure of the workmen all right but he's as likely to hold a drawing up the wrong way as the right.'

'I shan't mind what happens if I'm not here to see it,' Olivia said, 'but I shall miss our Shakespeare readings.'

Luke murmured, 'Indeed we will too, Miss Beattie.' He seemed too overcome to say more.

Awkwardly she backed to the door. 'Goodbye Thomas, goodbye Luke.' And then she turned and fled, her handkerchief to her eyes.

When she and her father were seated in the carriage, sweeping round the lake and down the straight drive to the gates, he looked at her sideways.

'What, wet eyes still? I'm not wasting any tears on Castle Kirby. I enjoyed making the designs and if he followed them he'd have had as grand a house as any in the kingdom but I couldn't have worked with him, such a wayward, unpredictable character, and yet he seemed at first to be a precise, orderly sort of fellow. He changed when I first mentioned the cottages would have to go. He became anxious and flustered but I'll swear to God he never forbade it and I was sure he'd see reason once it had happened.'

'Did he say how he found Mrs Johnson this morning?' Olivia asked, peering out at the last glimpse of the castle as the carriage turned out of the gates. 'I hadn't time to go and see the strange old soul.'

'You may be sure he said nothing to me but Lady Kirby shook hands and said it was all very unfortunate and she didn't know why it had happened because Mrs Johnson needed a woman to look after her and Mrs Summers has a heart of gold. Those were her words.' He grinned at her and patted her arm. 'She also said she didn't think Sir Langton would keep Mr Gerard from following us in a little while, so put away that handkerchief and be my merry girl again.'

Chapter 8

Olivia and her father had been back in their small house in Bond Street for three weeks and Gideon Beattie had bought himself a new coat in felted wool with silver gilt buttons. Olivia wasn't sure that the dark maroon colour was suitable with his cloud of fair bushy hair but he came back the next day with his hair cut to nothing and wearing a wig. At first she laughed at his broad face so neatly enclosed. It was a tye wig with short curls at the sides and a queue down the back fastened with a black ribbon. She stood back and considered him carefully, having observed that he was not too pleased at her laughter. He was certainly not the carelessly and flamboyantly dressed father she had always known. In fact in his new coat with matching plain waistcoat and breeches, white stockings and black three-cornered hat he was utterly transformed into a smart man about town and she told him so.

The next day he took her shopping and bought her a beautiful rose-red woven silk at six shillings a yard to have made into an open-fronted gown. The dressmaker suggested an ivory silk petticoat embroidered in rose-red flowers to wear underneath, the bodice having an intricate lace tucker which matched the layered lace sleeves. When Jenny helped her to dress for the first ball since their return which was also very nearly the last of the season she was ecstatic in her praise and bound up her hair into great coils twined with matching ribbons and flowers.

'Eh Miss Olivia, you've never looked so lovely.'

And Gerard not there to see me, Olivia thought. She had had one letter from Lady Kirby which said Sir Langton had invited two of Gerard's fellow lieutenants to stay and Gerard was now riding Emperor and had been out hunting and shooting – but of course was missing his Olivia. The work had been progressing and the ground floor frontage of the extended west wing was taking shape so the appearance of the castle from the lake was not so lopsided.

If Gerard is enjoying himself so much, Olivia thought bitterly, I shall enjoy myself. The ball was given by the fashionable Mrs Fenchurch, a second cousin of her mother. Now that she had been out of London for most of the season Olivia was grateful that the Fenchurch clan had taken note of their return. She understood – as she never had as a child – that her mother had come of a wealthy family and brought a large dowry to her struggling young architect husband. His transformation now was born out of the need to make a fresh impression of success and prosperity. He told everyone he met that he had just completed the improvements to the castle of a baronet and with his beautiful daughter on his arm he was politely received by the assembled guests.

All night Olivia never lacked partners, some of whom had flirted with her before her absence in Yorkshire.

'Where the deuce have you been, Miss Beattie?' one young buck queried, reminding her of Gerard's mode of speech, but he was not nearly as handsome, and even as she danced and chatted with him her heart was aching. Was she really Gerard Kirby's betrothed? 'Mine! You're mine,' he had said and his kisses and fondling had been eager, impatient, passionate in those stolen ten minutes.

But next morning when she was still sleeping Mrs Ledbury, the housekeeper, tapped at her door and came in and drew the curtains onto a scene of London rain.

'Had to wake you, Miss Olivia. There's letters come by different messengers, one for the Master and one for you. I would have let you sleep but it's from Yorkshire in a man's hand and I thought you might –'

Olivia sat up at once. 'Yes please, Mrs Ledbury.' She'd never confided in her about Gerard but Jenny would certainly have told all the goings on in Yorkshire that she knew or had imagined. Mrs Ledbury had only been with them two years, a thin, spare woman, her neck perpetually stretched forward, vulture-like, for gossip. She had been engaged after the death of the comfortable nanny who had been with them since Olivia's mother's death and Olivia was sure she would never grow to like her.

She took the letter from her avid scrutiny and waited till she had gone before breaking the seal. At once she noticed it was not the Kirby seal that came on Lady Kirby's letters. Perhaps Gerard had written it secretly. The handwriting was certainly bold and masculine.

She unfolded it carefully though her fingers were tingling with impatience and then the words sprang out at her 'Dear Miss Beattie –' What was this? The address at the head was 'At J.Summers', Tadby Village, Yorkshire.' Her eyes darted to the foot of the page, 'Your humble servant, Thomas Todd.'

Tom had written! Why? Was the family struck by plague? And 'humble!' When had Master Thomas ever been humble?

She set herself to read it, suddenly fearful that Gerard had been thrown by Emperor and killed.

> *'Dear Miss Beattie,*
> *'Pray forgive me for presuming to write to you. Luke found your address among your father's papers and no one at the castle knows I am taking this liberty. The reason is simply this. My grandmother, Mrs Johnson, was taken last night with a kind of seizure and for a while was bereft of*

speech and movement. This morning she spoke and all she said was, 'Bring the pretty young lady. She's the one I must see.' She repeated it over and over again and was very distressed when we all told her Miss Beattie was in London. She recognised the name then so it is certainly you she meant.

'When Sir Langton heard she was ill he rode over at once but she just looked at him and kept shaking her head. Whether speech has been lost again we can't tell but he sent his own physician in the afternoon who said that she may live on for weeks but if she has another seizure it will certainly be fatal. We are to keep her warm and fed if she will eat but plenty of liquid for which he has prescribed a certain cordial.

'Luke has read over this letter and corrected any errors. He agrees that you should be told but it must be left to you whether you could possibly undertake so arduous a journey again for so uncertain an outcome. He sends his best respects.

'The Kirby Arms in Tadby where the stage changes horses could give you a bed and Mrs Summers swears that she will go herself and inspect it if you write that you are coming. If there is so much as one bug my father and I will sleep there and she will put clean linen on our bed for you.

'I need not say that we will welcome you heartily but we will not feel in the least aggrieved if you ignore this letter completely. We will remain your devoted admirers for the kindness you showed Mrs Johnson and I am honoured to sign myself,

'Your humble servant,
Thomas Todd'

Olivia flung the letter down on the bed. No mention of Gerard! Not a hint. No one at the castle was to know of this. Not even her betrothed lover! Was he there? Had he gone visiting friends? She knew it was the time for country house visits as the London fashion world started to slip back to the country. She got up and stood at the window. Their courtyard at the back of Bond Street looked at other people's mews and the tall, grimy backs of houses. Oh to be at Castle Kirby again! She took up the letter and reread it carefully. Did they believe her too engrossed in London life to even contemplate the trouble of returning to Yorkshire to see a sick old lady? The idea was indeed preposterous so of course she would go. Had she not promised when Mrs Johnson gripped her wrist? The promise had been lightly made but it had not been lightly demanded. She would go and she would seek out Gerard whether his father found out or not. She would demand to know why he had not followed her as he said or at least written to explain himself.

While Jenny helped her to dress she puzzled over the mystery surrounding Mrs Johnson. If she just wants to warn me against Gerard Kirby as a husband I don't want to hear it. He may be a lazy correspondent but until he tells me to my face that he doesn't love me any more he is my man. But why did Mrs Johnson ask for Sir Langton when he was in London and now his presence doesn't satisfy her and she only wants me? Is she just deranged in her mind? And what is the mystery of the hundredth page in her Bible? She was very precise and clear about that.

To Jenny she said suddenly as she laced her up, 'Would you like to go back to Castle Kirby?'

'Oh, Miss, have they asked the Master to go back to the work? He had a letter too this morning.'

'No, but of course he would come with us –' she began when a sharp rap at her door told her he was outside. 'Come in, Papa.'

He walked in, without his wig and still in his morning robe, and said in an oddly portentous voice, 'Jenny, will you leave us.'

Jenny gave a little bob of surprise and scuttled out.

'Papa, Papa, I'm to go back to Castle Kirby.' Olivia held out the letter. 'You will take me?'

He checked in his stride towards her, a look of amazed relief passing over his face. He grinned at the letter he was holding and put it in his pocket.

'They've come round, have they? You're to marry Gerard!' He absolutely leapt at her, clutched her in his arms and whirled her about.

'Papa! Stop it. No, no.'

He put her down. 'No?' His face changed from boyish glee to despair. 'What then? What are you talking about?'

She showed him the letter.

He read it and his frown grew deeper. He slapped his hand on it. 'The impudence of the lad! An under-gardener demanding you make a two hundred mile journey to visit his grandmother!'

'He's not *asking*. He's just telling me about her. He says I can ignore his letter if I want to.'

'And ignore it you will.'

'But I *want* to go.'

'You can't and that's it.'

'Why? I thought you would take me – out of kindness.'

'Kindness won't pay a coach fare.'

'But Papa, you said Sir Langton paid you well. Surely we're rich now? The new clothes –'

'They were money going out to bring money in but it hasn't happened yet.'

He sat down heavily on her bed, dragged his letter out of his pocket and handed it to her.

It was from their landlord. The briefest glance showed her that the rent owing was one hundred and twenty pounds.

'I thought he would wait for it,' her father said. 'I did him some small work on his stables –'

'But Sir Langton's money?'

'We owed tradesmen before we went away. Mrs Ledbury hadn't been paid or William. When I'd settled them we still needed to be well dressed and go about again in society. Work comes on recommendation but Sir Langton had already spread tales and so had his lordship, damn him.'

'But Papa –' She sat down by him. She had never seen him like this with hunched shoulders and drooping head. She looked down on his bare scalp with its sad wisps of fair hair like the few stalks left on a reaped field. 'Are you saying we're *poor*?'

He nodded. 'Worse, we're in debt. We must leave here today and find somewhere cheap. You don't understand. Your mother brought money with her and expected to live as she always had. We've always lived beyond our means. It's easy to get credit from your butcher and wine merchant when you speak of commissions from Lord this and Sir that but it catches up with you in the end. Houses round here have rents of sixty pounds a year. We must live where they are no more than fifteen and we must let Mrs Ledbury go. Will Jenny stay if we ask her to cook and clean?'

Olivia sat staring at the grimy rain running down the windows. It was hard to believe all this. Everything she had wanted had come to her in life and all of a sudden there was to be nothing. Gerard had been in her grasp but he seemed to have slipped away and now even to go to Yorkshire was impossible. She didn't much care about moving house or losing scrawny, inquisitive Mrs Ledbury but Jenny had been hired as a lady's maid. She couldn't be turned into a skivvy. And if she was not to have a lady's maid any more did that mean she was no longer a lady? Her father had said they were worse than poor. A ghastly thought hit her.

'You won't go to prison, Papa, will you?'

He heaved a huge sigh. 'Olivia, there's only one road left. Will you let me look in your mother's jewellery box?'

She leapt up at once and pulled open the small drawer by her bed. 'Of course! I've hardly ever worn them. They're so old fashioned.'

'But valuable. I've kept from asking for them as long as I

could. I loved her you know, my darling, and when she was dying of the fever she kept saying, 'I won't see Olivia wear them but you will.'" His words ended in a choking sob and before Olivia had abstracted the box and found the little key under her handkerchiefs he was howling and shaking and rolling his body about like one demented.

She looked at him with horror, the man she had depended on all her life, reduced to this. Then she turned the key in the box and opened the lid. Even in the feeble daylight from the window the necklaces, rings and bangles shone and sparkled.

She shook her father by the shoulders. 'Stop this, Papa. Look here at these. Will these fetch a hundred and twenty pounds?'

He looked. 'Oh more, more.'

She put the box behind her back. 'You shall have them and pay every debt and move house and dismiss Mrs Ledbury and hire a skivvy if you let me go to Yorkshire with Jenny, but I must have William too because I've never travelled without a man before and I wouldn't know how to manage at all.'

He looked up at her standing before him. His big features were all red blotches and without the wig he looked ugly and ridiculous. I'm the strong one, now, she thought, and I might still bring him back a wealthy son-in-law to please him but he must pull himself together.

'Yes,' he mumbled, 'you'd better go to Yorkshire though the old woman will probably be dead before you get there. Don't stay long in the inn and see that William sleeps before your door. These places are not safe. While you are gone I'll see to the move. I'll keep Mrs Ledbury long enough to help with that. Rents in Aldgate are only fifteen pounds a year and I might get work in the city – not architectural because those opportunities are few during the war but something clerical perhaps.'

'Oh Papa, have you seen this coming – before you got this letter?'

'Well, my love, when no work came to me after our return I knew something must be done soon.'

'But you're a good architect, Papa, aren't you? Luke said your plans were beautiful.'

He got up and put his arms round her. 'Luke! Poor little crippled lad! What did he know, but yes, they were and if that wretched man had had the courage to act on them in their entirety he would have had a castle that looked splendid from every angle. And I thought my girl might live in it one day. What has happened to that nincompoop of a son of his? He wasn't good enough for you but you'd have made a fine mistress of that place.'

'I don't know what's happened but he's not a nincompoop. He's young but he comes of age in November and then we shall see if he can defy his father. Now *my* father is going to take charge of our affairs as a good father should and never let them become tangled up again. Shall I come with you when you sell the jewels? You mustn't let the first buyer have them. You must fight for the best price.'

He squeezed her tight, 'My wise and lovely girl. You write your letter to Thomas Todd – not that I approve of your corresponding with a young man –' and he gave her one of his comical winks – 'but the circumstances are exceptional. I think I can manage the financial transaction.' And he picked up the box.

As he walked out of the room Olivia marvelled at how quickly the jauntiness had returned to his gait. She called Jenny to her.

'As I asked you a little while ago, Jenny, would you like to visit Yorkshire again? We'll take William for protection.'

'Not the Master?'

'No, I'll explain – some of it – as we go. You can start packing my plainest and most serviceable clothes.'

'Goodness, Miss! Are we going today?'

'No, it'll take a few days to arrange I expect but first I must write and say we're coming. You're pleased?'

'Oh yes, it's quite exciting.' She giggled. 'Will I see that nice young gardener again?'

Olivia sat down at her writing desk. 'I should think that is extremely probable.' And she penned 'To Mr Thomas Todd . . .'.

Chapter 9

As the coach approached Tadby it passed the great gates to Castle Kirby. Olivia shrank back against the cushions and Jenny squeaked, 'Ee, Miss, are we really not to be seen there? But the castle always knew what went on in the village.'

'If they find out it can't be helped.'

Olivia reflected that the village also knew what happened in the castle so they would know what Gerard was up to. 'We are doing no one any harm, Jenny. We are two Englishwomen, free to travel where we will and we can be thankful we have got safe here. There's the tower of Tadby Church in the trees.'

She thought wistfully of the Sunday processions to the church. The services had come to mean much more to her because unusually the Parson was a fervent preacher. If she was here on Sunday she wouldn't dare go and risk facing Sir Langton. Perhaps she could go to Dimthwaite, the next village where she had learnt that Jack took Luke in his cart. Luke was very devout she had been happy to learn but had never been allowed to spoil the neat Castle Kirby procession. Sir Langton, she was increasingly feeling, was worse than eccentric. Perhaps he was mad.

Jenny, all excited fingers and thumbs, had begun gathering up the shawls. Olivia leant forward to see the first glimpse of the inn's hanging sign bearing a likeness of the Elizabethan Baronet Kirby. Would there be anyone to meet them? She was weary and very hot. The late July afternoon was stuffy and sticky and yellowing clouds hung over the inn chimney pots.

There was the usual explosion of activity from the inn as the horses were brought to a clattering, steaming standstill. William came clambering down from his seat up top and their bags were handed down to him but the first face Olivia spied behind the scampering inn servants was Thomas Todd's.

His bronzed cheeks were split with a welcoming grin and when she had been safely handed down and Jenny had followed with the shawls and reticules he stepped forward and took both Olivia's hands in his.

She looked into his deep brown eyes a little surprised at this familiarity but she saw only a genuine warmth and thankfulness that she had come and that for a moment he didn't know how to express it except by pressing her hands in his great fists.

Jenny hid shyly behind Olivia's skirts and then Olivia became aware that someone else was watching them from horseback. She looked up and to her amazement saw that it was Luke.

She slipped her hands from Thomas's and stepped over to him, seeing his pony was tethered and he was unable to get down by himself.

'Why, Luke, this is a new triumph.' She had never looked up to him before and she thought his thin features lit by a radiant smile were almost handsome.

'We are all overjoyed to see you safe here, Miss Beattie.' He patted the pony's neck. 'I call him No Such Mirrors because my life has been transformed by the inspiration you gave me in that phrase. The stable lads think it's a foolish name and call him Nonsuch for short. I'm only sorry I still need help to get on and off and I can't greet you properly.'

She held up her hand and he took it. Olivia had tears in her eyes. She had never dreamt in all the long journey that she could feel so happy at being with her Shakespearean companions again.

William, a large gangling figure, was standing among their bags waiting for orders. The inn servants had made no move to carry them inside.

Thomas took charge. 'Miss Beattie, you and your maid are to sleep at Mrs Summers'. My father and I have a room here and you,' to William 'can share it. There's a truckle bed put up for you.'

'Oh Thomas,' Olivia cried, 'did you find bugs there? We can't put you and your father out of your home.'

'Mrs Summers has settled it and there's an end.' He untethered Luke's pony and grabbed two of the bags. 'Bring the rest,' he told William. 'It's no distance.'

Diminutive Mrs Summers was already at her door looking out for them in a very white apron and cap. Sweet peas had grown up from tubs either side of the door and surrounded her with a shower of pink, blue and purple blooms.

'Eh, Miss Beattie, we can't tell you how grateful we are that you've come all this way.' She took her into the tiny front parlour. 'The kettle's boiling. I'll bring some tea directly.'

'But how is Mrs Johnson?' Olivia realised she hadn't yet asked the most important question but she supposed from all the cheerful faces that she had not come too late.

'She's a great deal better. She knows you're coming. I'll take you to her when you've refreshed yourselves. She didn't get back the use of her legs but your room's right by hers.' She smiled at Jenny. 'And this must be little –?'

'Jenny.' Olivia chuckled inwardly. Jenny, though shorter than her mistress. was a head taller than Mrs Summers. 'Pray let her help you in everything. It's so kind of you to let us stay here but I'm sure Mr Todd cannot be too pleased.' There had been no sign of the gardener but he must still be at work at the castle.

'Nay, he's all right. Never says much does Albert Todd but he'll take a little inconvenience in his stride. He's had a rough life, losing two young wives one after the other you might say. Are you stopping just now, Tom?' she called out as he thumped down the stairs from carrying up the bags, 'and Miss Beattie's man? Would he like a jug of ale?'

'I'll see Luke back to the castle,' Thomas said, 'but I'm sure William here would welcome a drink.'

'Will I see Luke again?' Olivia asked.

'Now that he's riding just let anyone try to stop him,' laughed Thomas and out he went and took Luke's rein.

'Ay,' said Mrs Summers, 'that lad's surprised everyone. No one thought he'd amount to anything when he was born and he was stuck in a chair and left to rot if you ask me – except when Thomas grew a bit and was always kind to him. Now I'll bring your tea, Miss Beattie, for I'm sure you're gasping this close day. I'll wager we'll get a thunderstorm tonight.'

Afterwards in their allotted bedroom, where most of the space under the sloping roof was taken up with the bed, Jenny had just begun unpacking when a voice called from the next room, 'Is that Miss Beattie come?'

Olivia was astonished at the strength of the voice. Was this the frail old woman who had had a seizure? The voice called again and she heard Mrs Summers start to come up the stairs.

'I'll go to her,' Olivia called and ducking through the low door onto the square of landing she tapped at Mrs Johnson's door and went in.

The darkening sky made it hard to make out the figure on the bed except for the white nightcap. Mrs Johnson was propped up with pillows and covered with blankets despite the heavy heat in the room. The small casement above the bed stood open but no relief came from outside.

'I'm here,' Olivia said, drawing the stool close to the little bedside table which was cluttered with a cordial bottle, a mug, a platter with a half eaten hunk of bread and jam, and of course the Bible.

As she sat down the claw-like hand appeared as it had done before and flattened itself over the Bible.

'Page a hundred,' came the voice. No other greeting but that.

'I remember.' Now I'm to find out the mystery, Olivia thought. She leant closer. 'Do you want me to look now?'

'No no.' The hand snatched the Bible into the bed. 'When I'm gone. Not till I'm gone. They thought I couldn't hear but I did. The doctor said if I had another turn it would finish me. No one else knows it's page a hundred. I chose you. You are to be married to Gerard, aren't you? When I first saw you I felt it in my bones.'

And when I first saw his portrait so did I, Olivia moaned inwardly.

'I don't know,' she said aloud. 'Sir Langton will not allow it.'

'What's that? Sir Langton can go to hell. He should too.' She suddenly gave a cackling laugh. 'He let them throw me out.' Her hand reappeared without the Bible and she patted Olivia's arm. 'When I'm gone and you've looked at page a hundred he'll let you marry Gerard.'

'What! Why? Oh tell me.'

A flash of lightning lit the room and they both started.

'What's that?' cried Mrs Johnson. 'What happened?'

Thunder growled in the distance. 'Only a storm coming,' Olivia said.' It's still far away. Please explain what you said.'

But the old woman put her hands round her head as another flash came. 'Is God angry?' She peeped out between her fingers. 'He can't be angry with me.' She broke into a babble of speech as if she would drown the low rumbling that was now almost continuous. 'I'm not afraid to go. The parson came when they thought I was going. I heard him saying the prayer for the dying. I couldn't speak or move a jot when he called for repentance but I was nodding away inside. Then he prayed forgiveness over me so I'm all right to go any time – but I had to see you, Miss Beattie.' She had lowered her hands and clasped Olivia's again. 'It comes to me in dreams all the time. Your life is bound up with Castle Kirby. I know that for certain sure. Don't be afraid of Sir Langton Kirby, that's all I say.' Lightning again and louder thunder close on its heels. 'There you are. God's angry with *him*.'

'Why, Mrs Johnson? I have come a very long way to see you. You have more to tell me, haven't you? Is it about Gerard? What do you know of him? He has asked me to be his wife and I did say yes. But if there are things you know about him should I not know them?' She might see him tomorrow. If word got to him that she was here would he not come at once?

Mrs Johnson was shaking her head. 'He never bothered with me from a boy. He's a young man now. He rides, he shoots, he hunts. He went in the army and they say he was wounded but I saw him walking with you. He looked well enough.'

Olivia waited but no more came. And what more do I know of him, she asked herself, except that he also gambles and quarrels with his father and that he fell for my pretty face and kissed me and would have done more if I'd let him. He told me he loved me but was it any more than wanting me as his possession? 'You're mine, you're mine!'

She sat there with Mrs Johnson's hand still resting on her arm, not clutching but tenderly stroking and when she looked into her eyes she saw kindliness.

'You're very young too, my lovely,' she said. 'You've a life ahead of you, a husband and children. Grace was the only one of mine that lived to womanhood and then she went. And her at the castle had a miss and a still before she had the one that lived.'

She stopped suddenly then and her eyes looked frightened. 'You'd better go now. I've said enough. I'm tired. Talking tires me and I forget what I have to say. Only remember page a hundred when I'm gone and all will be well.'

She turned her face to the wall and Olivia went back to her room, frustrated. Half-formed notions rolled about in her head in tune with the ominous growling of the thunder which was producing no deluge of relieving rain. Is this all I came for, she wondered? And then Mrs Summers called that supper was ready and she and Jenny went down.

A tray for one was laid in the parlour but Olivia begged to be allowed to eat with them in the stone-flagged kitchen. Since Jenny knew they were not welcome at the castle but that she hoped to see Mr Gerard she didn't feel any constraint in questioning Mrs Summers in front of her.

'So how are they all at the castle?' she asked as casually as she could.

The answer came freely enough but not at all what she had hoped for.

'Oh they're all in a tizzy over Mr Gerard's disappearance.'

'Disappearance!'

'Ay, well what I say is young men with money in their pockets won't be held back. Sir Langton wanted him to stay at home so he asked two officers from his regiment to keep him company. But when their leave was up he moped about – so Tom told me – till yesterday when he took Emperor and rode away alone. They've sent messages to the gentry round about to see if he's called anywhere but I couldn't say yet if they've heard owt.'

'Only yesterday he left!' Olivia laid down her spoon though the mutton stew was delicious and she was hungry. She thought with dismay, he could have passed us on the road. Dare she hope he was seeking *her*? If only he had written to her! Then it struck her that her father had by now made the move from Bond Street to the small house in Aldgate which he had arranged to rent before she left. Gerard wouldn't be able to find her.

Mrs Summers was looking at her with concern. 'Eh, Miss Beattie, we all knew he was sweet on you and no wonder, I say, for you're as pretty as a picture. Eat your supper and don't be worried about him. He'll turn up. If French bullets couldn't get him I reckon he'll live to old age now. How did you find her upstairs?'

'Oh she was talking in quite a strong voice. But I'm still no wiser about her anxiety to see me.'

'Ay well she was desperate keen for you to come. I hope you won't think you've had a wasted journey. How long do you think you can stay? She might not last. I mind how she used to say that the sign of dying was a sudden rally before the end. She saw a host of women go in childbirth fever so she spoke from knowledge. She brought my lads into the world that's both gone in the navy.'

'I could stay a little, I suppose.' Olivia knew she must ensure she had money to pay Mrs Summers and the bill at the inn. She had been shocked at the tips expected by the coachmen at the different stages of the journey, as well as the turnpike charges, so she must leave enough in her purse to see them back to London. Her mother's jewels would soon be exhausted if her father didn't find work. For the first time in her life she had to weigh up the cost of things and it was a very uncomfortable feeling.

She didn't know whether another conversation with Mrs Johnson would enlighten her any more but she might at least find out something about her from Mrs Summers.

'So Mrs Johnson was a midwife then?' she asked.

'Ay, there's no one round here but she saw them into the world even up to two or three years ago, but you know what they say about cobbler's children. She couldn't do as well for her own as she did for everyone else. Hers died, all of them, except Grace that married Albert Todd and then Grace died too in childbirth and hers was a poor weakling.'

'That was Luke of course. So Mrs Johnson has had a very sad life. Why does she dislike Sir Langton?'

Mrs Summers sat up in evident surprise. 'Eh no I've always thought she looked on him more like a son. Very familiar with him for one in her position but he didn't seemed to mind it from her. He was upset she had to leave her home. He hadn't intended it but maybe she's been telling you he didn't treat her right after all these years. I know it was your father's doing and Tom was angry at first but I reckon Luke talked him round and said it had to be for the sake of the work.' She ladled some more stew into both their bowls. 'I keep out of men's business but one thing I know her ladyship would be very sad not to see you if she knew you were here. The court sits tomorrow at the town and Sir Langton has to go because he's the magistrate. I daresay he'll take the chance to make more inquiries about Mr Gerard. But what I reckon is Lady Kirby would like fine to see you, Miss Beattie, while he's away.'

'I'm happy to see her but I wouldn't think it right to go to the castle without Sir Langton's permission.'

'Eh well, my Jack will have told Joseph, the groom and he'll tell the kitchen and what the kitchen knows soon gets to my lady's maid. We'll see what happens. Here's Jack now.'

A wiry little man came in and doffed his worn hat to Olivia. She had seen him the day of Mrs Johnson's removal and formed the impression he wasn't as enthusiastic about having the old lady as his wife was. His clothes were sandy with saw-dust which filled the grooves above his pocket flaps and the fringes of his coat cuffs. He hung up his hat and scratched his head sending little clouds of dust about the room.

'Mind what you're doing,' Meg Summers admonished him.

'We don't want it in the broth, man.'

'Ay well,' he said, 'you'll need to tidy round tomorrow anyroad for her ladyship's coming to see Miss Beattie.'

Well, Olivia thought, perhaps my journey won't have been wasted. I still have Lady Kirby on my side and for all she seems so timid she may in the end prevail with Sir Langton.

She and Jenny went to bed early, weary from the jolting of the coach. Daylight had faded with the storm but she could hear Meg Summers sweeping up by rushlight. She lay as far as she could from Jenny as the night was so warm but sleep eluded her. Her brain kept chewing over the strange things Mrs Johnson had said but she was no clearer in her mind when heavy rain finally began and she hoped that fresher air in the room would cool her head. The noise was loud and must have disturbed Mrs Johnson because she began to call out just when Olivia was at last falling asleep.

'Ay, God's angry. Punished, punished. It had to come. Punished, punished.'

Olivia's eyes flew open. That was what Sir Langton had cried out when he thought Gerard was badly wounded. What had he done? Was Mrs Johnson herself implicated in something? She had said she felt shriven after the parson's visit. I must find out tomorrow.

There was another shout from the next room. 'Blood! Too much blood.'

Jenny was fast asleep, her nose touching the wall. Olivia had insisted on sleeping on the open side to reach the chamber pot more easily. Now she swung her legs out of bed and crept barefoot into the next room.

She could see by the white blob of the nightcap that Mrs Johnson must be sitting up in bed.

'Hush.' She tried to ease her back on the pillows. 'Go to sleep. It's late.'

'I dreamt blood, oh so much blood. Gerard? Is it Gerard?'

Olivia shuddered. 'No no, he was wounded but he's well now.' Was he? Oh where was he?

'Punished,' the old woman croaked again. 'I knew he would be punished.'

'Gerard punished?'

Now Mrs Johnson seemed to wake properly. 'Who's there? Who are you?'

'Just Olivia, your friend. Olivia Beattie. You've had a nightmare.'

'What's that rushing noise? Where are we?'

'In Meg Summers' house. The noise is rain. We're just under the roof here and it's loud. Go to sleep. I'm in the next room.'

'Ah I remember.' She was feeling for Olivia, gripping her arms. 'I'm not dying yet. Page a hundred when I'm gone. You're the one. No one else.'

'Yes, yes, I know. Go to sleep.' She was able to lie her down now and cover her up. When she seemed to slip straight into sleep, Olivia crept back to her own bed.

She was shivering though not with cold. Drawing nearer to Jenny for comfort she longed to be at home in the London house with her father close by. This was all too eerie and frightening. She wanted the safe cocoon of childhood. And then the desolating thought came that she would never be in her old London home again. Father had given her a strange address in Aldgate and told her to take a sedan chair from the stage coach and William and Jenny could walk behind. Life was in a limbo state. Nothing was sure any more.

After what seemed an age of roaring darkness the rain slackened and the first glimmers of a grey morning found her deeply asleep.

Chapter 10

The sun was high when Jenny woke her gently with a tray of tea, a toasted bun and two eggs.

'Oh Jenny, have I slept late? What are Meg and Jack doing?'

'He was away to work at seven and she's scrubbed the front step and polished everything in sight. They both slept right through the storm.'

Olivia thought, and what of the cry of 'Blood' in the night? That had a ring of *Macbeth* while Meg and Jack sleeping blissfully through it all recalled Shakespeare's insight into the 'vacant mind' of the peasant, oblivious of the cares of kings, going to bed 'crammed with distressful bread' and sleeping so soundly that 'he never sees horrid night, the child of hell.' She couldn't share that with Jenny but maybe she would see Thomas or Luke today. Oh yes, she hoped she would. She warmed to the thought of them both. To Jenny she just said, 'I was kept awake by the rain and Mrs Johnson shouting out in a nightmare.'

'Well it's past ten, Miss, but Mrs Summers says it's ladies' privilege to rise late and Lady Kirby'll not likely come till afternoon.'

All the same Olivia ate her breakfast quickly and then Jenny helped her into the best day dress she had brought with her, fixing the hooped petticoat in place and then lacing the bodice

119

so tightly that she had to complain that her stomach was full and she was hurting her.

When she came down she found it was a beautiful day and the bench outside had already dried from its last night's soaking and Meg Summers was laying her best parlour cushions on it in case her ladyship preferred not to come inside.

'But I think she'll want to see how Mrs Johnson is,' she told Olivia, 'so I'll just run up and see if she looks tidy.'

Olivia had hardly gone outside to enjoy the sunshine when she heard horses' hooves and looking up was amazed to see Lady Kirby riding down the village street escorted only by Luke on his pony. She jumped up at once but saw that several village lads had already run to the mounting block that served this row of cottages and a forest of clamouring arms was eager to help her ladyship down. Then Luke performed an astonishing manoeuvre. He threw his stunted leg behind him while practically lying on the pony's neck and then brought his stronger leg to the ground, clutching the mane while some of the boys who had missed her ladyship drew his crutches from the straps that held them on either flank and shoved them with not unkindly laughter under his armpits.

Lady Kirby sprinkled some coins among the boys as Olivia came forward with a deep curtsey and Meg Summers appeared at the door bobbing up and down in the hope of being noticed.

Lady Kirby raised Olivia and embraced her. 'Dear girl, how good to see you!'

'But Lady Kirby I am honoured that you should come to *me*.'

As most of the women and young children in the village were now gathering, Lady Kirby made for the cottage door, much to Meg Summers' delight. She just had time to grab the cushions and retreat inside with them murmuring, 'Your ladyship will take some tea?'

Her ladyship would so Meg hastened into the kitchen to

put the kettle back on the fire and Olivia found herself swiftly perched on the worn settle while Lady Kirby sank into the one arm chair among the cushions. Luke sat himself on the bench outside the window. Olivia was disappointed that she had scarcely greeted him or congratulated him on his new-found agility but Lady Kirby was losing no time in coming to the purpose of her visit.

'My dear girl, you may have heard that we are all in anxiety at the castle about our poor Gerard. He took Emperor and rode away the day before yesterday we don't know where. Pray tell me if you have any idea of his plans. Has he written to you all these weeks?'

Sadly Olivia shook her head. 'Not a word, my lady.'

Lady Kirby looked desolated, her shoulders drooped, her hands flopped in her lap. 'I thought your visit might have been to meet him. And I wondered if he had gone hoping to intercept you somewhere on the way.'

'I wouldn't have presumed to do that, Lady Kirby. I came because I heard Mrs Johnson was ill and asking for me.'

'That was so good of you. I must go up and see the poor lady while I'm here.'

Meg brought in the tea then and Lady Kirby inquired if Mrs Johnson was well enough to receive a visit.

'Yes, indeed, m'lady, whenever you wish.'

'Leave us for a while then and I'll see her before I go.' Meg bobbed out again like a little bird and Olivia poured the tea.

'I have no excuses for my Gerard,' Lady Kirby said then. 'I believe he has treated you abominably –' Olivia made murmuring denials but she pressed on, 'You see, Sir Langton set his face against the match and now the foolish boy dare not mention it again because he has contracted so many debts which he expects his father to honour. It may be only to escape his wrath that he has gone off like this. He did tell me he was weary of being scolded like a child. I thought perhaps he had followed his two army friends who were here. They live in the county since this is where the regiment was raised but we have sent messages and he has not been seen there. Of course he told his father all the officers gamble and rely on their fathers to help them out but that only made Sir Langton more angry.'

'Do you think he has gone to London?' Olivia didn't like to say 'to see me,' but Lady Kirby was quick to take up the idea.

'Oh my dear he might indeed. He's very obstinate and wants to do just the opposite of what his father asks him. I haven't told Sir Langton but he's taken his new uniform. When he told me he wasn't going to stay in the army I believed him but now I wonder if he intends to rejoin his regiment and I'm so afraid he'll go into action again.'

'Might he not plan to *sell* his uniform?' Olivia was only too well aware now of the need to sell possessions to pay off debts.

'Indeed he might. He can of course sell his commission and make even more, though it was his father bought it for him. If only I *knew*!' And poor Lady Kirby looked about to burst into tears.

If only *I* knew, thought Olivia. She poured Lady Kirby another cup of tea and ventured to ask about the work at the castle.

'Ah that's been another torment for poor Sir Langton. The cottages have gone and he knows your father's designs should be completed but with Gerard's debts I think he wonders if he can.'

Poor Sir Langton indeed! Olivia mused. Poor *Father*! His work is recognised at last but the damage to his reputation has been done.

Lady Olivia didn't seem to realise the implications of what she had said but went on, 'He might just complete the garden front now. Harper, the clerk of works, has been working from the plans but it was only this morning that I discovered who had been helping Harper to understand them. It was Luke.

We've always underestimated Luke.' She turned her head to the window from which they could see him still sitting patiently outside. 'When I first saw him using crutches I asked him if he thought he could ride a pony and he seemed eager to try so I bought him that little one and he now rides round the estate when he knows Sir Langton is indoors. He has completed books of notes about it. He showed me after Sir Langton left this morning and when he knew I was coming to the village he begged to be allowed to escort me. I'm afraid I never knew what a clever young man he is. He was always kept out of the way because of his deformity.' She sighed. 'I wish Gerard took half the interest in his inheritance. But oh, please don't think badly of my boy. He has a loving generous nature and I'm sure all young men in his position sow their wild oats. You would keep him in order,' and she reached a hand and pressed Olivia's. 'Now I think I must go and see the old lady. It was she who brought Gerard into the world you know so I must never forget that – she and a young companion I had in those days, an educated girl whose family had come down in the world, May Tyler she was called. I remember her sitting and holding my hand when Gerard struggled to be born. Then Janet Johnson came and all was well. But poor May caught the fever only a year later and died. I think that's why I was so glad when you came along. I hadn't realised how much I missed a pleasant young lady in the house.'

While Mrs Summers took her upstairs Olivia went out to speak to Luke. It seemed very easy and comfortable to sit down by him and tell him about a little of her disturbed night and how the passage from *Henry the Fifth* had come into her mind that morning.

Luke was delighted and began to recite the whole speech with great animation, quite unaware that a crowd had begun to gather at the moving words, 'I am a king that find thee.' As he launched into the resounding, "'tis not the balm, the sceptre and the ball' to a crescendo at 'the tide of pomp/ That beats upon the high shore of this world,' Olivia felt her very toes curling. At the conclusion he quietly became himself again and was astonished to hear a general clapping.

'My word,' he laughed, blushing a little. 'Where did all these come from?'

'Did I not tell you,' she chuckled, 'that you could entertain a crowd? Even No Such Mirrors pricked his ears up.' And then she told him what Lady Olivia had said of him. He flushed a little more but laughed it away.

'I have been very blessed to have so much time in my life and she has been so kind in giving me my royal steed.'

Olivia laughed with him. It was lovely to be laughing again. She felt suddenly supremely happy, sitting there in the sunshine as the villagers moved slowly away chattering about the unexpected entertainment. She dismissed Mrs Johnson from her mind as no more than an old witch from *Macbeth*.

The moment fled when Mrs Summers peeped out and hissed, 'Her ladyship's ready to go home, Luke.'

It was sad then to see that much as he wanted to leap up and escort her to her horse and help her mount he had to struggle onto his crutches and wave for help to a lad who was feeding a handful of hay to both animals.

Olivia took Lady Kirby's arm and as she walked to the mounting block Lady Kirby said; 'How long will you stay, my dear? I wish I could accommodate you better myself –'

'No, I understand. I am all right here but really I hardly know whether I need to stay for Mrs Johnson's sake.' If Gerard had returned to London she must go back. Had her father left his address with the new tenants? She had no idea and the thought that Gerard might be desperately searching for her after all was a torment. And yet she didn't want to leave here . . .

'She seems well,' Lady Kirby said, 'considering how ill she was. She said little to me but then she never did. It was always Sir Langton she wanted and he has always treated her kindly. He would have given her accommodation in the castle but she never wanted to leave her cottage. That's why he was upset when your father had them demolished. I do regret the way he behaved to Mr Beattie who meant it all for the best, I'm sure, and pray give him my kind remembrances.' Then she kissed Olivia and begged her to let her know if she heard anything of Gerard. 'You can't go tomorrow,' she added, 'since it's Sunday. Will you be in church? I haven't told Sir Langton and I've made sure no one else – Oh dear, it's so very awkward.'

Olivia smiled at Lady Kirby's embarrassment. 'I will rest and keep hidden.' She wouldn't try to walk to Dimthwaite even though Luke might be there. She would almost certainly meet the castle procession on her way back.

Two more nights in that hot little room with Jenny and the risk of Mrs Johnson having another nightmare were not appealing but she said she would be gone on Monday and Lady Kirby kissed her again and was helped by several willing hands to mount her horse. Luke mounted by lying across the pony's neck and reversing the manoeuvre of his dismount. The crutches were inserted into the straps and he sat upright. Olivia waved to him with regret. It was unlikely she would see him again this visit and that meant, she realised with a stab of real pain, that she might never in her life see him again – unless Mrs Johnson had the gift of second sight and her destiny *was* wrapped up somehow with Castle Kirby. But that the revelation of the hundredth page on Mrs Johnson's death would allow her to marry Gerard was surely all madness.

She turned back with an exasperated sigh into the cottage and sent Jenny to the inn to tell William to be sure to reserve their places on the coach for Monday morning.

The rest of the day dragged. Meg gave her a little tour of the back premises of the cottage which were quite extensive with a stable for Jack's dray horse and roofed space for his cart next to the shed with his long carpenter's bench.

'He has most of his tools up at the Castle just now,' Meg said. 'There's doors and window frames to make for the new wing.' She had brought out a pail of scraps and Olivia saw that in a small fenced area next to the shed a dozen hens were scrabbling in the dirt. Meg threw them the scraps and they fought noisily for them.

'The eggs were delicious this morning, Mrs Summers,' Olivia said and the little woman was delighted.

'Ay, they're good layers all of 'em. I can sell spare eggs to neighbours. It all helps.'

Yes, thought Olivia, and how much must I give her for our keep? In Mrs Summers' eyes I'm a wealthy young lady. I wish Father was here to deal with such things. But then she remembered how badly he had managed his money for many years. There and then she resolved to keep a sharp eye on him when she went back.

Later she looked in on Mrs Johnson but she was either sleeping or lying torpidly indifferent to her presence. Not knowing when Sir Langton would come back she dare not venture out in the street and no news came about Gerard.

On Sunday she heard the church bells and peeped from her window to see the villagers walking up the hill towards the church. When Sir Langton and Lady Kirby passed also walking as was their austere habit and followed by most of the castle servants she felt her breath come quickly and her heart pound. Was Sir Langton really unaware of her presence and did he still hate or fear both her and her father? His slight but very upright figure and neat, precise steps showed nothing of any turmoil he might be feeling about the whereabouts of his son. Lady

Kirby however seemed under her large hat to be dabbing her eyes with a handkerchief and waving aside greetings from the few other gentry who were going to the service. Olivia realised she hadn't seen Thomas. Perhaps he had walked beside Luke to Dimthwaite to help him dismount. She was surprised how sad she felt at not seeing either of them again.

The bells had stopped ringing and the village lay deserted when she turned to Jenny and said, 'I'm not going to be a prisoner this fine day. Put your bonnet on. We'll go for a walk.'

They found a footpath following the stream that flowed into the village duck-pond and before they had gone a hundred yards they saw a young man in a sober dark jacket and breeches standing by a gate. Something about his height, breadth of shoulders and the imperious angle of his head under the cocked hat reminded Olivia of Gerard and she stopped in her tracks. It couldn't be. And then he half turned, one hand still on the gatepost, one bright eye towards her, his dark curls caressing his cheek below the hat. His face lit up and he swept off his hat. It was Tom.

Jenny exclaimed, 'Oh Miss, doesn't he look fine in his Sunday best?'

But Olivia couldn't speak. In that moment she had seen the most extraordinary thing – his striking facial likeness to Gerard Kirby.

She stepped smiling towards him but her mind was stripping off layers of mystery. Sir Langton was cold and cruel to his wife and Lady Kirby had had a brief affair with Albert Todd which had produced Gerard. Mrs Johnson knew and Sir Langton knew but he had accepted the boy as his because he had to have an heir. Lady Kirby was in perpetual fear of her husband and he had to cosset Mrs Johnson so that she would not betray the secret that Gerard was illegitimate. But who was being 'punished, punished?' Most people would say Sir Langton had done the noble thing. Or was he to be punished for his cruelty to his wife that had led her to her deceit? Olivia was still trying to fit all the conversations she had had with the old lady into this picture as she held out her hand to Thomas and said lightly, 'You are not in church then?'

'So it seems.' He grinned his usual cheery grin, including Jenny too whose eyes never left his face. 'I dressed for it and then remembered you wouldn't be there so there would be nothing to relieve the tedium on my only day of leisure. Do you think God will forgive me?'

'If He forgives me too for avoiding the anger of Sir Langton who thinks I have designs on his son.'

'And have you not?'

She had forgotten his impudence. 'You know very well my reason for coming – to visit your grandmother.' Was this truly Gerard's half-brother? Or was he also Lady Kirby's son? Would that account for his lordly manner to his superiors? But Mrs Johnson had said 'her at the castle had only one that lived.'

'And I am humbly grateful,' he said, not at all humbly. 'But is it true you are returning to London tomorrow?'

'I fear so. Your grandmother talks nothing but riddles to me but seems well enough to last for years. Can you not tell me anything that will explain her desire to see me?'

They had begun to walk on up the path which had left the stream and was passing through fields of unripe oats. Jenny lagged reluctantly behind.

Thomas considered her question. 'She believes you are to marry Gerard.'

'So? Why does that seem so important to her?' Olivia had to check herself from mentioning the Bible. She alone had been entrusted with that clue and perhaps sharing that with her had relieved the poor creature's deranged mind.

He shrugged. 'She has strange notions. Maybe I should never

have written you that letter. At the time she was so urgent to have you there. It was hard to do nothing.'

'You did right, but tell me something. Why do you yourself never say Gerard's name but with a note of scorn in your voice?' Ah, is that it? Her mind leapt on. Tom knows the history and is jealous of Gerard. Yet jealousy didn't fit Tom's open straightforward nature. It was a puzzle, but an exciting one. Did she want to marry a wrongful heir? The thought of Gerard still thrilled her but it was also very pleasant walking with this easy young man with whom she felt able to talk so freely.

'Well,' he said slowly now. 'I don't think Gerard deserves you. You have more depth, you are so much cleverer. You may not be his equal in the world's eyes but I care little for rank. Nature is a better guide. Those should marry who are drawn naturally to each other.' He paused and looked full at her. Good heavens, what was he saying? Jenny stopped too a few yards off and began picking flowers in the hedge row.

Olivia gazed back at him. She was thinking, he is paying me compliments but he's a gardener's son. I was brought up a lady. My mother was a Fenchurch. The gulf is huge. Or is it any more? My father is a penniless architect. What does anything matter if two people love each other? But surely *Tom* doesn't love me? He's always treated me with a pleasant familiarity, never with tenderness. And how do I look on him? With friendliness certainly and a suspicion that he may be a much better man than Gerard But it's Gerard who kissed and hugged me. It's Gerard who proposed marriage. I am engaged to Gerard.

She turned quickly and began to walk on. As he stepped up beside her with his long strides he said, 'You think my views are too revolutionary.'

'I'm not sure I understand what you're trying to say.'

'I never *tried* to say anything in my life. If I want to say something I'll say it out.' Was he angry? She looked sideways at him and saw his eyes fixed fiercely on her. They had to stand still again and face each other close together in the path.

'Whatever do you mean?' she murmured.

He glanced back at Jenny and saw she was out of hearing. 'I'll say it straight out then. I've been in love with you, Olivia Beattie, since the moment I first saw you. I fought it because I thought you arrogant and a creature of your whims but I find I was wrong or that events have changed you.'

Olivia stared at him. She had not expected to provoke him to this and it fairly took her breath away. Thomas Todd in love with her! Poor Jenny trailing behind with her flowers had had to stop again, perhaps aware that a portentous dialogue was going on. Why couldn't he be in love with Jenny? She was quite a sweet little thing with a snub nose and round cheeks.

But there he was standing before her, his brown eyes – Gerard's eyes – challenging her to answer him.

'Well,' she said, 'you have astonished me, Thomas Todd. But if we are to speak so plainly I have to say I thought your candour amounted to impudence at first. Then I witnessed your kindliness to Luke and to your grandmother and your surprising appreciation of Shakespeare.' She stopped.

'And –?' he queried, his dark eyebrows raised – Gerard's eyebrows.

'And nothing,' she said. 'If you think *I* am in love with *you* you are quite mistaken. We are friends and I really find it hard to believe you can be truly in love with me.'

'That's because I won't grovel or plead. I knew there was no hope before I spoke. No sense in saying it at all but I'm not one for secrets. It's out and now you can forget it, but it's true enough and maybe always will be. Shall we walk on?'

She hesitated, sad and confused. 'No, I don't think so. I must return before the church service is over. I fear Sir Langton will hear anyway that I have been here and Lady Kirby will be scolded for seeing me.'

He shook his head. 'Even his own man is a little afraid of him. No one tells him gossip. Lady Kirby will see to it that he doesn't know.'

'I'm relieved to hear it.' She tried to pick up their old easy way of talking but couldn't help thinking how her father would react if he knew what had just passed. 'An under-gardener daring to say he loves you!' Yet it had happened so naturally and she was not in the least angry. We're both rebels at heart, I suppose. But if he were in Gerard's place . . .

She began to talk quickly in a matter-of-fact voice. 'I suppose it would be wise for me to stay indoors now but I would like your father to come to Meg's house this evening. I haven't seen him and very much want to thank him for his trouble in sleeping at the inn. I'm sure both you and he have been eaten alive.'

He laughed then. 'We have tough skins, both of us.'

As they walked back she kept giving him sidelong glances. Is he as tough as he thinks? He's made light of his disappointment but is he feeling it deep inside? He has great depths this youth and I do like him. But I want to know, I must find out, if I have guessed right about the great Castle Kirby secret.

She paid another brief visit to Mrs Johnson after supper that evening. It was brief because she could get nothing new out of her. She tried saying directly, 'You're so well, Mrs Johnson, I can't wait for page a hundred to hear about Mr Gerard.'

The old woman just pressed her hand and after a moment's thought said, 'If Sir Langton comes and tells me Gerard has set the wedding date against his wishes I shall have words with him, that's all.' The Bible was not in sight so she must have feared Olivia would come and take it in the night. Then she reiterated, 'But you'll come again if I'm dying won't you? You promised me that.'

'It's a long way and travelling is expensive.'

The claw grip crushed her wrist again. 'Promise. I know you're the one.'

Olivia repeated impatiently, 'I promise,' and the hand disappeared again.

She heard voices below then and withdrew abruptly, tired of the old woman's mysteries and frustrated by uncertainty over her own guesses. She struggled to see Lady Kirby in the roll of adulteress, but stranger things had happened. An earl's young wife had run off with a footman the year before. Sir Langton was not a figure to inspire much devotion. She could well imagine though that a man so set on order and perfection in his household would never admit to his wife's unfaithfulness. He would rather claim the fruit of it as his own. But if he went on objecting to Gerard marrying her would he really bow to a threat from Mrs Johnson to tell the secret? That could have been behind the old lady's words when she was torn from her home. 'I don't believe Sir Langton would treat me like this. I know things and will tell.' Was that it? Olivia sighed at the seeming impossibility of finding out more and cautiously descended the steep stairs.

As she had suspected Albert Todd and Thomas were below in the kitchen. She spoke her gratitude, all the time eying Albert up and down as a possible father to Gerard as well as Thomas and Luke. He was rather bowed now, perhaps from the endless planting and weeding but he had been a big tall man in his youth and though his hair was greying she could tell it had been dark brown like his eyes which were impenetrable. He could have been a handsome figure twenty years ago.

He said only, in his broad accent, 'It's been no hardship, Miss. Worse things can happen than that.'

With great embarrassment she held out a small purse. 'I trust that will cover the expense at the inn.' He peered into it and then counted out the coins slowly on his leathery fist. He handed her one back.

'No,' she cried, trying to laugh it off. 'Pray drink my health with it.'

He nodded, touched his forelock and stumped off back to the inn. Could such a man ever have attracted Lady Kirby? She was shaken.

Thomas grinned and even winked at her in his easy way. It was hard to believe what he had spoken that morning, harder still to know how to say goodbye to him.

'I reckon I'll have gone to work in the morning before you leave,' he said.

She held out her hand. 'I don't know whether I'll ever be back here again. I will miss my Shakespearean companions so much.'

Tears began to fill her eyes and she knew he had seen them. To her astonishment she saw his eyes were moist too and he couldn't speak. He just clasped her hand briefly and turned and ran.

As Olivia and Jenny lay in bed that night Jenny whispered, 'Oh Miss Olivia, you knock them all over – Mr Gerard and Luke and Tom. I guess *I* could have *William* but he has nothing to say for himself.'

Olivia noticed only one part of the sentence. 'Not Luke too, Jenny, you can't mean *Luke*.'

Jenny just murmured, 'Oh yes Miss, Luke too.'

Chapter 11

'Oh Father, I'm so happy to have found you.'

Olivia hadn't dared to risk the expense of a hackney coach or worse a sedan chair, not being sure how far her new home was, though the men were gathered at the coaching inn clamouring for passengers. William and Jenny carried their bags and Olivia herself had the shawls and her reticule.

Asking the way had been a frightening experience. There were not many people walking about who looked trustworthy and she feared footpads lurking up the many dark alleys. The filth underfoot and splashes from coaches and carriages soon made her regret her decision to walk though the way was not far after all. But when they had at last found the right house it was hiding in a narrow back street and Olivia felt ashamed that William and Jenny should see it.

The moment her father opened the door, however, beaming with delight at their safe arrival, her relief was so great that she burst into tears.

He made a great fuss of her then and when she had washed and Jenny had unpacked and helped her change into some clean clothes in the small bedroom he had allocated to her, she felt able to take stock of her surroundings.

The first thing she realised was that the house was so tall, narrow and dark that it must be a slit of a larger one divided into two to produce more rent for the landlord. The tiny back and front attics for Jenny and William were reached up a steep stair which she didn't bother to investigate after Jenny told her with a pout that her room was 'smaller than the old woman's at Tadby.' In front of Olivia's room was her father's which was much bigger as the stair came up beside hers. It contained a desk and table as well as the bed and an armchair.

On the next floor down was a sitting-room the depth and width of the house apart from the narrow stair. Her father rather grandly called this the drawing-room. On the ground floor was a small dining-room to the left of the stairs with the kitchen down a few steps behind. Outside stood a wash house in a dirty yard surrounded by high walls with a coal hatch in one wall above the brick built bunker and a door leading to a communal cesspit which served all the houses round about. At least that was better than the open drains in the street which she had seen in some places. But the whole impression of the house was gloomy and enclosed.

Olivia felt tears rising again as she turned to her father and cried, 'Oh Papa, it's like a prison.'

He gave her a hug. 'We won't be here long, I hope. Now you must have some refreshment. Shall we take it into the dining-room or sit here?'

They were standing in the kitchen next to the range where a good fire was blazing and a kettle singing. Two covered dishes were standing on the table.

Olivia stared at her father. 'But where is Mrs Ledbury? And are you saying we are to eat with William and Jenny?' Her experiences at Tadby should have helped to prepare her for this but it was still a shock that it should happen in their own home.

'I told you I would have to let Mrs Ledbury go.' For the first time he had an edge of irritation in his voice. 'I sent William with two plates to catch the pieman as soon as you arrived. We can eat separately if you like but I thought perhaps after your journey with him and Jenny you wouldn't mind. I know your mother would never have dreamt of such a thing but I am a little more Bohemian.'

Olivia thought with a pang of Thomas and his revolutionary ideas.

'Of course, Papa. But how have you managed since Mrs Ledbury left? You have had no servant at all! You brought in the coals yourself.'

'For two days. You forget you have been away only a little longer than a week.'

'Good heavens, it seems an age,' she cried.

'Well,' he went on, 'I have explored Covent Garden which is nearby,' and he produced from the larder shelf a wooden bowl of lettuce, watercress, sliced cucumber and chopped spinach. 'I prepared it myself to eat with the pies,' he said proudly, 'but as for *cooking* food I have no idea at all how it's done, so I hope Jenny can manage. It's expensive to eat in the chop houses or inns. I'm afraid I have made do in the coffee houses where I hoped to meet people who may need my skills.'

'Oh, Papa, with any success?'

He sighed and shook his head. 'Things are bad with the war dragging on but never mind. Let us eat. The pies came hot and are cooling.' Then he called up the stairs for William and Jenny to leave their unpacking and come down.

They were even more astonished to be told to sit down round the scrubbed wooden table with 'Master and Miss.' Olivia, longing to tell her father some of her experiences, knew she must wait till they were alone, but Jenny, when she had overcome her shyness answered Gideon Beattie's questions freely, chattering about incidents on the journeys and then describing Meg Summers' cottage and the old woman who had nightmares the night of the thunderstorm.

'Oh and sir, you wouldn't believe it but Mr Luke is riding a little pony and his legs are stronger, Mrs Summers said, with gripping its sides and he manages his crutches something wonderful. And Mr Todd and Mr Thomas slept at the inn and let William in the same room, didn't they William?' William nodded. 'And Mr Todd snored, you told me, very loud all night.'

'Ay,' said William with a mouthful of pie. He took a swig from the jug of ale and just remembered not to smack his lips.

After the meal Olivia and her father went up to the sitting-room without telling Jenny to wash the dishes. Olivia just said, 'Bring up some more tea, Jenny, I'm thirsty.' She wanted to see how Jenny would slip into her new role which was virtually a maid-of-all-work, a serious demotion from lady's maid.

'So tell me,' her father said, sinking into one of the three armchairs and putting his feet on a small stool, 'is my girl any nearer becoming mistress of Castle Kirby?'

'Further than ever, Papa,' and she told him of Gerard's disappearance.

'But he must have come to London to see you. Did he not promise?'

'Yes, but after so long? Lady Kirby came to see me and she thought it might be so but they were making inquiries round about. I thought he might have sold his uniform if he was low in funds.'

'I'll wager he's in London but tell me about the old lady you went to see. What did she have to say to you that was so urgent?'

Olivia tried to pass over it lightly. 'She was very much better. Of course she's convinced I'm to marry Gerard and I had to tell her Sir Langton disapproves of me. Maybe she'll try to persuade him, that's all.'

'Huh, what can *she* do? And you travelled all that way at great expense to see her!' He sounded angry but changed his tone abruptly. 'Perhaps we can turn it to our advantage. I warrant Mister Gerard has come to London as young men do, whether to see you or not, we can't guess. But if we can find him and get news to the anxious parents we'll be in their good books again.'

'Did you leave word in Bond Street of our new address?'

'I did not. I am not particularly eager to be found yet.'

'More creditors, Papa! But what has happened to Mamma's jewels?'

'I am keeping some in reserve you may be sure. No, we must be cunning now, my girl. First of all, tell me, did Gerard talk about the places he haunts when in London. What did he speak of when you and he wandered about together?'

'He had missed riding in the park. That was usually the morning activity. Of course they went to Spring Gardens and Ranelagh but everyone does that. Oh and Lady Kirby wrote in that letter of hers that he had been gambling at White's Club – much to the anger of his father.'

'White's. I know it, in St James', the elegant end of town. We'll go there tomorrow and make inquiries.'

Olivia wasn't sure that she wanted to be seen in pursuit of Gerard but at that moment Jenny brought in the tea just like a well-trained parlour maid. She had put on a lace-edged cap and apron, had found the best china which Olivia's mother had brought with her and had laid it on a tray with an embroidered cloth.

'We won't use that porcelain,' Gideon Beattie told her, 'unless we have very special visitors. Pack it away in its box and put it at the back of the larder.'

Jenny looked crestfallen. 'I thought Miss Olivia might still like things done daintily, sir.' There was poignancy in that 'still' which Olivia felt keenly.

'It looks beautiful, Jenny,' she said, 'and of course we will use it now you've gone to that trouble but do what Mr Beattie says afterwards.'

'Yes, Miss Olivia.' She curtseyed and added in a rush, 'and will you please very kindly tell me and William our duties. Is there a daily girl coming?'

Olivia looked at her father.

'Your mistress will talk to you afterwards,' he said and Jenny bobbed again and went out, but Olivia felt there was latent rebellion in the tilt of her head.

'I don't want to lose her, Papa.' She couldn't explain to him that the intimacy they had been thrust into at Tadby had made Jenny much more of a confidant. They had almost been like two girls together except when Jenny had had to trail behind on the little walk and when passengers filled up the coach at different stages and Jenny had to go on top with William. 'You know, Papa, I never had an intimate friend. The girls were very superior at that school for young ladies you sent me too. They all had elegant Mammas to take them round the fashionable shops and they thought I was odd because I was interested in masculine things and liked studying and reading serious books. I think I was quite proud to be different but it never brought me any female friends.'

'You poor girl! But it's a male friend you want now and that's what we must find you. Meanwhile do we really need more than two healthy young people to look after us? Come drink your tea and we'll go and seek young Kirby tomorrow.'

This was all very well, Olivia thought, but a man had no idea of household duties. Her father had briefly struggled by on his own, eating out and sending his linen to a laundress but a house like this with London soot creeping endlessly through the ill-fitting casements needed daily cleaning. For four people there would be plenty of cooking to do, coals to fetch, slops to empty and water to be carried to the bedrooms. How could Jenny – if she consented to share these tasks with William – keep her hands nice for helping her mistress to dress and do her hair?

So she wasn't surprised that later that evening she had an uncomfortable half hour with both Jenny and William. William said he was happy to stay and do whatever was asked of him but he stuck up stoutly for Jenny.

'You see, Miss Olivia. She was hired as a lady's maid and that's what she is, not a skivvy.'

'But, Jenny,' Olivia pleaded, 'you told me you came of a big family so you must have helped your mother cook for you all. And when you went into service you started at the bottom. I know you pleased everyone because you were so neat and quick and that's why you moved up. But there was no vacancy for a lady's maid in your first place. That was why you came to me. You hadn't been a lady's maid before that.'

'I know, Miss, but now I am and I don't fancy going back down again. It seems to me that if a lady has come low enough to walk with a gardener – which would have been more fitting for me to do – then it's not right for her to have a lady's maid. If you'll pardon my saying so.'

Ah, that was what rankled, Olivia realised. Jenny's pert little lips were tightly compressed together as she watched for her mistress's reaction.

Olivia thought again of Thomas. He might well have fancied Jenny if I hadn't been there. But he had the nerve to love *me* – if he really meant it – because he doesn't regard rank. What would he do now if he were in my shoes?

Impetuously she took Jenny's hands. 'Suppose we just try to be friends and I'll share the cooking with you?'

The gesture and the words astonished herself as much as Jenny who was quite speechless for a moment. In fact Jenny's rebellion had won Olivia's reluctant admiration. It was a new thing for her to begin to put herself in someone else's place but she could see that Jenny had no need to share their downfall and she had

141

no right to ask it of her. 'Suppose we work together, Jenny,' she repeated, 'and when our fortunes pick up again we'll hire more servants.'

'Eh, that's handsome, ain't it, Jenny' cried William. 'We always did all right when Mrs Ledbury was here but she never had to do heavy or dirty work. She wasn't above dusting and she was a good cook but I always did the rough work. Suppose you give it a go for a week or two.'

Jenny giggled suddenly. 'I never dreamt you'd say that, Miss Olivia. You and me friends and working side by side! Well, I never! Have you ever peeled a potato, Miss?'

Olivia was already beginning to wonder what she had undertaken and how much Jenny would presume upon it but she answered resolutely, 'No I haven't, Jenny, but I don't suppose it's so very difficult. I can learn,' and she looked down at her soft smooth fingers and wondered whatever it would be like.

Chapter 12

There was little time to test the new experiment next day as Gideon Beattie was anxious to set off westward in search of Gerard Kirby. Olivia contented herself with donning an apron and clearing the breakfast dishes while Jenny, nose in the air, took out the chamber-pots to empty.

William had fetched in coals and made the fire so they had had hot chocolate and buttered toast to start the day. Mrs Ledbury had brought their stores from the other house so there was a full crock of butter and a large jar of Churchman's Chocolate which should last a while longer. Then Olivia with very little idea what she was ordering made a list of shopping for Jenny to fetch and told her if she was frightened in the strange streets she could take William with her.

'We can't say when we'll be back so you may make yourselves a dinner of bread and bacon at one or two o'clock when the rooms have been tidied and the stairs swept down and our dirty clothes from the journey laundered.'

Jenny pulled a face and stood with her hands on her hips.

'It's just for today, Jenny. Mr Beattie has business to see to.'

'It's all right, Miss Olivia,' William said and Olivia caught a wink from him to Jenny. Oh heavens, what temptation was she putting in their way by leaving the two young people together!

She felt even more uncomfortable when her father summoned a hackney coach even though the day was fine. He said they couldn't risk the dirt in the streets by walking all the way to St James'. He was dressed in his new maroon coat and breeches and she had put on a pale blue bodice and deeper blue skirt over her hooped petticoat with a light ivory coloured shawl and matching straw hat. She took her parasol and wore pattens in case there was an opportunity for a walk in the park.

She could hardly look at Jenny who had pointedly taken up a position cleaning the dining-room windows to wave her off, but the excitement of passing St Paul's Cathedral and gradually drawing out of the City and entering again the world of elegant squares and green gardens soon put Jenny out of her thoughts. She couldn't imagine they would learn news of Gerard today but it was pleasant to travel with her father beside her and feel at ease again.

They left the hackney coach at St James' Park and Gideon Beattie tipped the driver generously. Would her father ever accept the idea of economy in little things, she wondered.

Here the streets were much cleaner, the dung from the horses being regularly swept up for use on the gardens. Carriages of all sorts and gentlemen on horseback were already taking the air and Olivia began to look eagerly at every grey for the unmistakeable proud head and big shoulders and haunches of Emperor.

She shook her head at her father. 'The place is so vast and people are coming and going all the time the chances of seeing him are very small.'

What she would do or say if she did see him she had no idea. His own mother had said he had treated her abominably. Should she be very aloof and cold? But her father would be most affable himself and highly displeased if she actually discouraged Gerard. And if he's glad to see me, if he still loves me, she decided, I know I couldn't fail to respond.

They refreshed themselves at one of the tea houses and then Gideon Beattie proposed walking to White's in St James' Street.

The afternoon was still sunny and Olivia strolled about outside the club with her parasol while her father made inquiry of the footman at the door if Mr Gerard Kirby was within. Gerard did not appear but another young man came out to speak to her father and she drew near to hear what was said. They had exchanged cards and her father took her hand and introduced her.

'Olivia, this is Sir Peregrine Grant, a friend of Mr Kirby. My daughter Olivia, sir.'

She curtseyed

'Ah, Miss Beattie, the lost Miss Beattie, the much sought-after Miss Beattie,' the young man said, bowing over her hand. He was rather stout and his tightly stretched waistcoat and breeches creased into strained lines as he did so. Olivia's eyes were fascinated with this while her ears took in with a surge of excitement the implications of his words.

'Poor Kirby has been desolate,' he went on 'at not finding you at the address he expected. He has been drowning his sorrows at the tables where he lost half his inheritance in two nights but last night, wonder of wonders, he won it all back and a great deal more. The whole room was gathered at his table as throw after throw came in lucky. We begged him to stop and at last he did, still at the height of his success, so we all benefitted with abundant champagne from his lavish pocket. They were still drinking when I left so I wager he'll be sleeping it off at his lodgings still. I will escort you there directly. Pray just allow me to fetch my hat and cane.' He disappeared inside again.

Olivia looked at her father. 'Oh Papa, do you think we should go now? Gerard won't be pleased to be wakened and it will look as if we have only come because of his winnings. I couldn't bear him to think that.'

But Gideon Beattie pooh-poohed this. 'You heard, girl, he still wants you. We're in, we're made, don't you see? And won't Sir Langton be happy again to have him safe and out of debt and so will m'lady!' He was practically dancing on the paving stones when Sir Peregrine re-emerged, swinging his cane, and gave her his arm.

'It's but two squares away, Miss Beattie. Are you content to walk?'

'Of course, but we hesitate to disturb him now. We only came because I have been in Yorkshire and have a message from his mother.'

'Messages from mothers be blowed, if you'll pardon me for saying so, Miss Beattie. It's you he desires to see. It seems to me you have been chasing each other about the country. He left Yorkshire to seek you in London. But all's well that ends well as they say. I will be in high favour for finding you, I can tell you. I will send up word that I have brought him a present.'

And when they mounted the steps of a house in a fine newly built stone terrace and he rapped on the door with his cane those were the very words he said to the footman, who obviously recognised him and bowed him in at once.

'Tell Mr Kirby Sir Peregrine Grant and friends are here with a present.'

The man looked about for a parcel but obeyed nevertheless, scurrying up the stairs repeating '– here with a present.'

The hallway was a room in itself, Olivia saw, with velvet chairs and a grandfather clock and a cabinet of silverware. The footman had bowed her to a seat but she remained standing, the blood beginning to pound in her head and her breath coming in excited gasps. If only she could have met Gerard alone! But now Sir Peregrine, all giggles, was coaxing her to a seat where she couldn't be seen from the stairs and urging her father too to keep out of sight.

He himself stood at the foot of the stairs and she could hear him exclaim to someone above, 'Why, man, you'd have to be up to dress for dinner. It's past three in the afternoon.'

Then she heard a yawn and Gerard's voice drawled. 'Can't you bring it up whatever it is?'

'No, you're to come down. I promise you you won't be disappointed.'

'My God, it's not Emperor, is it? You've never found that dealer and got my horse back, have you?'

'Better than that.'

'There can't be better than that.'

Olivia bit her lip but now she could hear his footsteps coming down. With difficulty she kept her place. What would he be like? Not his handsome portrait that was certain.

There she was right. A dishevelled figure in a morning robe, his tye wig hastily put on and slightly awry, appeared round the carved newel post. He looked about rubbing his eyes.

She stood up and saw his bleary glance focus suddenly.

'What! Olivia! Is it really you? Have you dropped from the heavens?'

Then he saw her father too. 'Mr Beattie! Oh forgive me, sir, the state I'm in. You rogue,' to Sir Peregrine, 'why did you not let me dress?'

But he came towards her and she tentatively held out her hand.

This he brushed aside, clasping her arms instead as if to feel that she was really there, substantial.

'I'm not dreaming this, am I? Say something so I know you're alive.'

'Good afternoon, Mr Kirby. How are you?'

At this he burst into laughter and clasping her to his chest he pressed his lips to hers so vigorously that her wide-brimmed hat was pushed off her head and hung down her back by its ribbons. He made no apology for this but murmured, 'Now I've got you I've got everything. I'm rich, Olivia. We're rich.'

'But you haven't got Emperor. Nothing is better than Emperor.'

'What! Mischievous as ever! That's what I love about you. Oh I'll get Emperor back but how could I think that villain there could find me a present like this!'

Then they were escorted up to a handsome drawing-room and given tea while Gerard disappeared to dress and returned looking very elegant in a purple jacket, embroidered waistcoat and cream breeches. Olivia kept thinking of the house in Aldgate they had left behind and her rash promise to share the chores with Jenny. Whatever would this baronet-to-be think if he knew to what his lady had fallen?

'You'll dine here of course,' he said. 'I've given orders.'

Sir Peregrine excused himself on the grounds of a prior engagement and after much banter and grateful back-slapping from Gerard he left.

Gerard drew a chair close to Olivia. 'And now tell me everything – where you have been and why I couldn't find you.'

Olivia looked at her father but he seemed to want to leave her to answer so she countered at first by asking, 'And where were you when you promised to follow us to London after your father summarily threw us out?'

He slapped his hand against his head. 'It was deuced awkward. The old man *would* ask two of my fellow officers who were on leave after Belle Isle to come and stay. Of course I had to entertain them.'

'Yes, it was your mother who wrote and told me that.'

'I knew she'd written so – hang it! I'm no hand at letter writing. But after they'd gone I wanted to come at once. But the old man was keeping me deucedly short of funds. So one day when they thought I was calling on a neighbour I packed a pannier and took Emperor and my uniform and sold it in the town so I had enough for the journey. Of course when I arrived I went to your address but you'd gone, no one knew where. I had to sell the horse so I could have some stake money. The rest I think that rogue Peregrine told you. Now it's your turn.'

Olivia looked at her father again and this time he did speak.

'Well, sir, you've been candid about your difficulties and I'll be candid about ours. Your father, I'm afraid, left us in a pickle. He'd disparaged me among his friends and I have had no commissions since our return. It was necessary then for us to rent something smaller. But as your mother will no doubt tell you in her own time Olivia here paid a visit to Yorkshire. She only returned yesterday.'

'What? I was coming here when you were going there? I might have ridden past your coach without knowing. By Jove, why did Mother not tell me she'd asked you?'

This time Gideon Beattie looked at Olivia and she said warily. 'Your mother didn't ask me. I got word from Mrs Johnson's family that she was very ill and begging to see me. They didn't expect me to go but I did and found her much improved. I saw your mother because she kindly came to the village but I'm sure Sir Langton doesn't know I was ever there. All I learnt of you was that you had disappeared and they were making inquiries among their acquaintances. You could have been attacked by highwaymen and left in a ditch somewhere. You really must let your poor mother know that you are safe and well. In fact if you won't write I will. She's a sweet lady and doesn't deserve to be kept in anxiety.'

Gerard grinned at Gideon Beattie. 'I can see how it's going to be when we're married. She'll be keeping me in order all the time.'

Olivia frowned. She didn't like the male assumption that female advice was always nagging and the phrase 'When we are married' was casually spoken while to her it was so portentous. Would they ever be married? How deep was his love? How deep was hers?

The same footman announced that dinner was served and

they moved through into an elegant dining-room with a table that would seat twenty. There didn't seem to be a butler and only the footman and a maid brought in the dinner and left when Gerard told them he would carve. She wondered how Gerard had chosen this house when the rent and servants' pay would be a big expense.

As they sat down he must have guessed her thought. 'This place belongs to the family of Captain Anston, a fellow officer, but they are at their country seat in Surrey and he told me I could bob in here any time I needed a London address and could make use of the few staff they leave behind. I'm sure he wouldn't mind you staying as well. There are plenty of rooms.'

Olivia thought for a moment her father would agree – this house was a world away from theirs in Aldgate – but she could never feel comfortable trespassing in a stranger's house on so flimsy a basis. She was already beginning to worry about when they would get back to Jenny and William.

'That's very kindly meant but it wouldn't be possible,' she said firmly.

'I shall come and call then tomorrow and take you wherever you would like to go. Spring Gardens, Ranelagh and the opera in the evening or a play. You shall choose. This is all I've wanted, to have you to myself in London.' He put several slices of meat on her plate and begged her to help herself to the dish of vegetables. 'You must forgive such a plain dinner but the kitchen had little notice of my having guests. I understand there is a blancmange made and I see plenty of fruit on the sideboard.'

'Delicious,' Gideon Beattie said, 'but I must say, Mr Kirby, things should be on a firm footing before you and Olivia go about openly as an engaged couple.'

'Oh I'll have it put in the newspapers if you like and I can buy her all the rings and bangles she wants tomorrow.'

'You can hardly have it printed that Sir Langton and Lady

Kirby announce the engagement of their son etc etc when they know nothing of it.'

'Well, what do you want me to do, Mr Beattie? I daresay I'll have to face the music at home eventually but I thought a week or two of jollity here while I'm in funds would be very pleasant. That's why I don't want to be in too much of a hurry to write home or I could bring a hornets' nest about our ears. I might be able to put some work in your way too. These Anstons are talking of extending their place in Surrey. Now if you were known to be in with a rich patron my father might change his tune. It was an odd business that about the cottages but now that it's settled down and no harm done I don't see what he's got against you. By Jove, if I could rake in a bit more at the tables I could even help the old man out so he could finish your plans. That scheme you had for a grand entrance on the north side so the carriages could come right in and discharge under cover was pretty splendid.'

'Oh please, Gerard,' Olivia cried, 'no more gambling.'

'But it was so deuced easy. I had the castle mortgaged to the hilt one night and the next it was all back and the coffers overflowing again. I shouldn't have stopped last night. I was on a winning streak.'

Olivia was appalled to hear this. She knew her father had gambled at races and dreaded him catching the notion of easy money again from this man who was to be her husband. She looked at him now, carving himself another slice from the leg of lamb, while picking up the mint leaves with which it was decorated and casually chewing them.

He laughed at her shocked face. 'Don't worry, my darling. I am to be a good boy from now on. It's such a wonder to have you here when I thought I was never going to see you again. Did I not tell you you were mine? I've got you back and I'm going to keep you.'

He wouldn't allow her to leave the table when they were

finished. 'There are no other ladies to accompany you and your father and I have no secrets to discuss. If you'd like tea while we have a glass of port I shall order it at once.'

She was always happy to defy convention so she said, laughing, 'But I would like a glass of port too.'

This delighted both gentlemen so she sipped it carefully, a new experience, while her father asked Gerard to tell him more about the Anstons.

Gerard reached behind him to a silver tray on the sideboard and handed Gideon a card. 'There, that's this address and the Surrey mansion address. They're not nobility but he's made a fortune in the West Indies and would like to think he is. He's certainly wealthier than we are.'

Her father asked if he could write and use Gerard's name as an introduction.

'Of course, of course.' Gerard airily waved a hand. 'It's of no use my promising to write. I know I'd never do it.'

Her father was so interested in learning all he could of this family that it was with great difficulty that Olivia persuaded him they should leave at nine o'clock.

'It's still daylight,' Gerard cried. 'The best time of a London day is between now and two in the morning.'

'But our new neighbourhood is not so pleasant in the late evening. We hope to see you tomorrow, Mr Kirby, and are most grateful for our excellent dinner.'

Gerard, who had drunk freely at dinner, peered at the piece of pasteboard Gideon had put into his hand. 'This card you've given me only has a coffee house address for correspondence. I see what it is. You still have a few creditors and you don't want the bailiffs at your front door. That's nothing to be ashamed of, man. Half the titled people I know live perpetually on credit.'

'And that frightens me,' Olivia said. 'Come, Papa.'

Gerard reluctantly sent the footman for a hackney coach and

Gideon as reluctantly wrote their address on the back of the card.

'Don't come before noon,' Olivia said as Gerard claimed a parting kiss.

'Are there hours before noon?' he laughed.

As soon as they were home Olivia looked about and saw that everything she had asked had been done and William and Jenny were sitting in the kitchen like a comfortable married couple with one candle and a small fire, Jenny mending a tear in Olivia's travelling dress which she had sponged down as best she could. On a string above their heads all the linen was drying.

Jenny said, 'Eh, Miss, we didn't like to go to our beds before you came home. We thought you might have been set on and murdered.'

'You go now. Take a candle each and Mr Beattie and I will make breakfast in the morning.'

'Eh, Miss, what about seeing you to bed? You'd never manage.'

'Well, you can just undo me at the back. I'll come up now and,' she whispered, 'as we're friends I'll tell you what happened today. Goodnight, Papa.'

'I'll look in on you when you're in bed,' he said and his tone was severe.

'Master don't like this new way of going on,' Jenny murmured as they went up the stairs.

Olivia drew her into her bedroom, took the candle from her and set it on the chest of drawers. Then to Jenny's astonishment she gave her a hug.

'I know he doesn't, Jenny, but I need a friend. You and William have been like solid rocks today. We asked so much of you and you haven't let us down.'

She laid aside her shawl and Jenny, seeming confused and embarrassed, began to undo her buttons and laces.

Olivia told her quickly how they had met Mr Gerard and he

153

still wanted to marry her but preferred to keep it from his family for the present.

'Well, Miss, you'll be happy now, I guess, and one day I can go back to being a lady's maid.'

'Oh, Jenny, I hope you will, whatever happens, but tell me, as a friend, is a girl to go on loving a man because *he* loves *her*? Does it make a sort of obligation?'

Jenny took up the sliver-plated brush and comb and began from habit to comb out her hair. 'Funny you should ask that, Miss. William came on a bit strong today and though I like him well enough I wouldn't fancy him that way, if you know what I mean.'

Olivia smiled round at her. 'You fancy Thomas Todd that way?'

'I daresay I do. I couldn't help it.' Olivia sensed that was a delicate matter and wasn't surprised when Jenny turned the subject. 'So, Miss, are you saying you're not so fond of Mr Gerard after all?'

'I love being loved, Jenny.' She too thought about Thomas Todd and how he looked by the gate that day in his Sunday best. Did he give me a thrill, she asked herself, because he looked like Gerard? What did I feel then when he told me in such a matter-of-fact way that he loved me? Did I feel under an obligation to him? I don't think so but I do know that out there somewhere there is a real love waiting for me and that I have a very, very deep love, a love of total respect to give to someone and that someone is not Gerard Kirby.

She turned round and clasped Jenny and began to sob.

'Nay Miss, don't take on. That don't do no good.'

In the midst of her tears Olivia began to laugh hysterically. 'Oh Jenny, it's so ridiculous. *My* father will be very angry if I *don't* marry Gerard and *his* father will be very angry if I do. But I know I could do a lot of good as mistress of Castle Kirby and I love the *place*. But is that enough?'

'I'd say so, Miss, and after all Mr Gerard is a very fine-looking gentleman. When we was at the castle I couldn't help looking at that portrait at the foot of the stairs. I thought, if that man was after me I'd jump at him. Any girl would.'

'I know,' Olivia sighed. 'That was what I thought and I did jump. But I'm afraid that's what I was like, Jenny. I acted and spoke before I thought. I'll always be inclined that way but I do want to be wiser –'

Her father's knock came at her door. Without realising it she was already in her dressing-gown and ready for bed.

'Go Jenny, I've kept you up,' she said and called him in.

Jenny bobbed to Gideon Beattie at the door. 'I haven't to forget how to be a lady's maid, sir.'

'Quite right. Goodnight Jenny.' He closed the door.

'Now Olivia, I've been writing to these Surrey people to introduce myself. It'll be sent off in the morning and I might have a reply within a week. I have good hopes of this one. A man with more money than he knows what to do with and ambitions to make a splash in his county is just the sort of patron I need. So I hope this nonsense of stepping down to the level of servants will stop.'

'Oh Papa, this from you the Bohemian as you called yourself!'

'Things have changed now we've found Gerard. When you're at Castle Kirby you won't go on like this. You'd upset the balance of life. Everyone knows their place there and the daily routine moves smoothly. So we mustn't descend into wrong habits. Now get your beauty sleep for tomorrow. We must keep the young man happy and the old one will come round in good time.'

He went out and Olivia was thankful that the light of the one candle had not allowed him to notice her tearstained face. What will make Gerard happy? she asked herself. Getting his own way of course. Does he care at all about the deep things in life? I saw how bored he looked in Tadby Church when the parson was fervently urging on us our duty to God and our neighbour. Does Gerard strive for anything but his duty to Gerard?

She slipped into bed but felt unready to lie down. She wondered whether the little household at Tadby were all sound asleep by now and how were things at the castle. Was Luke allowed a candle to read late if he chose and was poor Lady Kirby on her knees praying for her vanished son?

She slid her long legs out of bed and felt for her slippers. She would write to Lady Kirby at once and then she would be able to sleep more easily. She had not blown out her candle so she wrapped her dressing-gown round her and took the candle to the tiny chest under the window where there was just room for her writing materials. She wouldn't tell Lady Kirby Gerard's address but she had to let her know he was alive and well.

Chapter 13

On the morning that Olivia Beattie's letter was delivered to Lady Kirby Luke had just come in from riding to the extreme south west corner of the estate. It was his custom to leave his chair by the stables and one of the grooms would wheel him up the ramp and along the east passage to his room. He couldn't manage his crutches on the slope and, besides, the blocks of stone and stacks of timber in the courtyard created too many hazards.

Passing the kitchens he and the groom heard one of the maids excitedly telling Cook, 'Lady Kirby's had a letter and she's run to the Master all smiles so it must be news of Mr Gerard.'

Ten minutes later Lady Kirby herself came down and tapped at his door. This had become quite a common occurrence but he felt very flattered that she should so soon want to share the news with himself.

She sat in the armchair Olivia used when they read Shakespeare. He always thought of it as Olivia's and wondered if he would ever see her in it again. Now her name was the first on Lady Kirby's lips.

'Think of it, that dear Miss Beattie has gone to the trouble of writing to let me know my boy is in London and perfectly well and happy. Why did he not tell us he was going there in the first place?'

Luke understood that this was a rhetorical question so he just expressed his pleasure at the news and asked, 'Are Miss Beattie and her father well?'

'Oh she doesn't say anything about herself except I see that the address is not the same. It seems to be in the City somewhere near St Paul's – not a fashionable address at all. Of course Sir Langton is now talking of going off again because I was so hasty I showed him the letter and he saw who it came from. He thinks *she* must have begged Gerard to come and that's why he rushed off, but you and I know she was in Tadby the day after he left. I kept her visit a secret from Sir Langton at the time but now I daren't tell him because he'll be so cross with me. He hates being kept in the dark. Anyway it's true that she's in London and has met Gerard. That's what's upsetting him. Oh dear! Whatever can I do to stop him heading for London again?'

Her ready confidence astonished Luke till he remembered she had no one else to talk to about it. Mrs Chorley was an efficient housekeeper but hardly a friend. However, Lady Kirby's question gave him an opportunity he had been seeking for several days.

'It's possible, my lady,' he began cautiously, 'that a distraction would keep Sir Langton here. There's a matter he ought to be told about, quite urgently, but as you know he never comes to my room so perhaps you could approach him with it.'

'By all means, if I can understand it. Is it about the west wing?'

'No, my lady, nothing to do with that. There are things going on where Castle Kirby land meets Mr Braintree's.'

'Oh dear, Sir Langton will never go near that spot because he hates to see the mine workings Mr Braintree's started. All noise and dirt, he says, and tearing up a pleasant hillside. He says he'll set some trees alongside the beck to hide it all.'

'Well, it's at the beck where I first discovered it, my lady. After that heavy thunderstorm we had I rode that way and found the beck had been in spate and had actually changed course. A landslip had blocked its old streambed and left exposed a twenty yard long section of the hillside. And this is the important news, my lady. Castle Kirby also has coal.'

'Gracious heavens, I'd better not tell Sir Langton that.'

'But Mr Braintree's men have seen it and there are signs that they have been coming over the wall there and digging it. Have you not heard, my lady, that every landowner in Yorkshire – and Lancashire too for that matter – is hoping to find coal on his land? Coal is a huge source of wealth. Sir Langton could complete all Mr Beattie's beautiful plans if he exploits this resource. When Mr Braintree found it I suspected we must have it too because that same ridge runs through our land for half a mile or more. So I've been studying the geology of these seams and found that though they lie at a slant and in the lower reaches would involve deep mining which is expensive, the ridge produces outcrops which are easily dug. If Sir Langton would ride up and look he could see it plainly with his own eyes.'

Lady Olivia clasped her hands before her face. 'Oh dear,' she said again, 'he'll be very angry if he thinks Mr Braintree's workmen are trespassing. If I tell him that it certainly might keep him here a while.'

That seemed to be the only point she had grasped but if it roused Sir Langton's interest that would be a start, Luke decided.

He watched as she stood up hesitantly. He wanted to reach for his crutches so he could rise too but she waved her hand at him.

'No no, Luke. Stay where you are. Well, I suppose I'd better tell him. I wish he'd come and talk to you about it.'

She turned slowly to the door. She was still a slim graceful figure but he wondered what her hips and legs were really like underneath that huge hoop that swung gently about with her movements. Olivia hadn't worn one so wide so he supposed London fashions were reducing in size.

When she'd gone, still murmuring 'Oh dear me!' he chewed his lower lip in frustration. He had little faith in her ability to put the matter clearly before Sir Langton but if only the baronet could see the possibility of making his fortune he could have Gideon Beattie back and with Beattie would come Olivia and he, Luke Todd, could look on her again.

What was *she* like, the whole of her lovely body? She had assumed he knew nothing of love but to his sorrow he had all the desires and longings of a man and she was the sole object of them.

In half an hour Lady Kirby was back.

'Oh how right I was that he'd be angry with Mr Braintree. He's sent Thomas to mend the wall if it's damaged and he'll have a thorn hedge planted beside it to keep out intruders. But he still wants to go to London. What is the point, he said, of all his efforts to preserve the estate for Gerard if he throws himself away on that designing hussy? Those were his words you understand. My own feelings are quite different. I believe Miss Beattie would be very good for Gerard.'

She sat down again and looked disconsolately at Luke. 'It's very comforting, Luke, to have you to talk to. I can't think how I failed to discover you till now. Of course you were only a boy and I always knew you were quiet and studious which was a good example to Gerard. But now I see what a wise head you have on young shoulders and as you hardly go anywhere you can't betray confidences. It wouldn't be right for me to discuss Sir Langton with the housekeeper and Mrs Chorley is not a comfortable, sympathetic ear anyway. I do hope you don't mind my coming and piling my worries on you.'

He smiled and shook his head. 'On the contrary I am honoured, my lady, and I would never repeat a word you say to me. But pray tell me one more thing about the matter of the coal seams. Does Sir Langton understand the potential value of this asset? Of course it's impossible to say without investigation how extensive the seams are —'

'Oh he exploded about that too when I just hinted the possibility. 'Never,' he cried. 'What! Scar my beautiful land with hideous machines and foul-mouthed mechanics.' So I don't think we'd better mention that again. He'll plant his thorn hedge and his woodland to screen Mr Braintree's work and try to forget all about it.'

Luke sighed and wondered if she had told him who had given him the information. Sir Langton has something very deep against me, he thought. I've always been a blot on his landscape. He said aloud, 'I had intended to set out a schedule of exploratory work that could be done and would have left it in the estate office for him to look at but if he's so adamant against it –'

'No no, don't trouble yourself about it any more, Luke. I'm afraid he'll want to leave for London in a few days and I believe I'll have to go with him to keep the peace if I can. Miss Beattie hasn't said where Gerard is staying. I hope for her sake it is not at her father's house.'

Luke was quite sure Gerard would have to be near his usual haunts in Westminster and St James' but he said nothing to this. He was too sick at heart at the thought that she and Sir Langton would soon see Olivia and possibly make her very unhappy. If she loved Gerard he had to hope for her sake that Sir Langton would consent. But the very notion increased his bitterness. Such a marriage would erode all those good signs in her that he had already observed since the early days when Tom described her as 'imperious.'.

'You're quiet, Luke,' Lady Kirby said. 'You're disappointed about your great discovery.' She got up and patted his arm. 'Have you all you want at hand?'

He assured her he had and she left him to digest his very uncomfortable thoughts till Tom came in to see him at the end of his day's work.

He was later than usual and very weary. Since he preferred

to walk rather than ride it had taken him longer to reach the boundary of Mr Braintree's land and he had put in a day's work repairing the wall, but he was enthusiastic about the coal seams.

'Of course they should be worked,' he said, not sitting in the armchair since his leather breeches were so dirty, but perching on the edge of Luke's desk. 'The stuff's there to be seen with the naked eye. I've been talking to Mr Braintree's foreman. They're going to cut a canal to the river to get their coal out by barge, more cheaply and in much greater quantities than they can by cart. They've been over looking at ours, not *stealing* it he protested but just taking a small sample to show Mr Braintree. It's good coal and if Sir Langton isn't going to work it he thinks Mr Braintree will put in an offer to buy the land.'

'Which our good master will not even look at.'

'If he doesn't he's a fool,' Tom said bluntly. 'The site can't be seen from the castle because of the curve of the hill and it's too far off for any noise to carry. If he worked it himself he could make a deal with Mr Braintree to send the coal to the sea by his canal. He need never see a speck of it himself and the huge London market would be open to him.'

Luke laughed. 'You're as enthusiastic as I was when I first saw it. I was excited by the thought that he could afford to finish the Castle to Mr Beattie's plans and we would get our dear Shakespearean back.'

Tom frowned and shrugged his shoulders. 'We'll get her back if she marries Gerard and then I don't think she'll be encouraged to read Shakespeare with the gardeners' sons.'

'You're sweet on her, aren't you, Tom?'

Tom slid off his perch. 'Never mind that. I'm hungry and Meg will have supper waiting. Oh and Father said Jack came by when I was at the wall and told him Grandmother had a sort of fit this afternoon. I must see how she does. The doctor said she wouldn't survive another seizure but I don't think it can be as bad as that.'

'Bring me word how she is. Do you think Sir Langton knows? Maybe he won't set out for London is she's ill.'

Tom paused at the door. 'Why should he set out for London now he knows Gerard is well?'

Luke realised he had unwittingly betrayed Lady Kirby's confidence. Tom was evidently unaware who had written the letter. 'I suppose to persuade him to come home.'

Tom shrugged his shoulders again. 'I'm for my bed when I've eaten. If Grandmother is no worse Sir Langton will hear news of her in the morning and so will you, Luke. I can't rub your legs tonight. Can you manage yourself?'

Luke smiled and nodded. He often sat massaging his own muscles but Tom had taken to working on them vigorously whenever he had time. But tonight Luke could see that his brother had for once reached his limits and he let him go.

He sat thinking of Olivia and wondering if she was at the opera with Gerard till at last, impatient with such imaginings he trimmed a quill and began to write an equally hopeless report to Sir Langton about his coal seams.

Having sat up late he was still asleep when Tom in fresh linen and renewed vigour strode through his little sitting-room into his adjoining bedchamber and shook him by the shoulder.

'She's gone – Grandmother. Must have slipped away in her sleep. No one heard a sound.'

Luke sat up and sighed and stretched himself. 'Poor old Grandmamma! Well, God rest her soul. I hope she knew nothing of it. She's in a better place now.'

Tom nodded but then he sat down on the bed and leant close to Luke. 'But listen to this. I encountered Sir Langton just setting out for his early walk and of course told him the news. As you well know he's not a man to show his inmost feelings but I'll swear I could see in his eyes a look of – I can only say – *joy*.'

'Joy!'

'Huge relief, perhaps. It was only for a fleeting moment and then he became all grave and solemn and said he was most sorry to hear it and hoped it was peaceful and all that sort of thing.'

'You must have imagined it.'

'I'll swear I didn't. It's very strange.'

Coming from practical, down to earth Tom this sounded convincing but Luke thought of an explanation.

'You know, Tom, Sir Langton is not a truly kind man but he has a fierce sense of duty to the old and helpless. He has never liked to see me anywhere about the place, nevertheless he gave me a home from babyhood. And he always sent his own physician if Grandmother was ill. He was shocked at the notion of turning her out of her house and furiously angry when it happened while he was away. Now his duty to her has ended and any burden of guilt he may have felt about her treatment in her last days has been lifted off him. It would be just the same with me. If I were to die tomorrow I'm sure he would feel vastly relieved.' He laughed a little uncomfortably at the thought.

Tom stood up. 'You may be right. You have a pretty shrewd insight into folks' characters from all your reading. Well, he told me he and her ladyship will be leaving for London the day after Grandmother's funeral so I am to keep watch for trespassers while they are away and I have his permission to dig up any self-sown hawthorn or blackthorn I find in the woods and plant them near the wall to 'keep the villains out' as he put it."

'It seems I wasted my time then writing him a report last night. I won't send it to him now. Do you think he'll allow me to go to Tadby Church for the funeral? He never lets me go there with the castle household for regular services.'

'I'll wheel you, Luke. That will be easiest and he can't refuse that. The Todd family must all be together to follow the coffin. Now I must get to work.'

Luke sighed. 'I have to admit I don't feel sad. I hardly knew

Grandmother well and it seems to have been a happy release after she became bedridden.'

'There I agree but I wonder how Olivia will take the news. She came all that way and felt she hadn't been needed and yet Grandmother seemed desperate to see her before she died.'

'Grandmother loved her bright, pretty face.' Luke sighed again. 'Who could not?'

But Thomas was already on his way out.

Chapter 14

Olivia stood with her hands on the stone parapet and gazed over London. She was so enraptured that she almost forgot Gerard at her side, and the morning of household chores and wrangling with her father that had preceded Gerard's coming.

She had ignored her father's plea to start behaving like a lady again. Her promise had been given to Jenny and William and she would carry it out. She rose early the morning after the dinner with Gerard and would have tried to make the fire but William heard her and ran down to prevent such a trespass on his province. She swept the front step and the kitchen floor when he had the fire lit, emptied her own chamber pot, washed her stockings and prepared the hot chocolate and toast for her Father when he came down. Jenny followed, looking quite aghast.

'You should have waked me, Miss.'

'No, Jenny, I made a promise and I'll keep to it.'

'And what will Gerard say if he finds you in a cap and apron?' her father demanded.

'I shall be dressed and ready for him before noon,' she declared, and she was.

That Gerard hadn't appeared till nearly one in the afternoon had produced the first altercation she had ever had with him.

'You were drinking again till late,' she accused him.

'Of course. What did you expect me to do – leaving me alone

at such an hour? And the trouble the coachman had finding this place! We must get out of here as quickly as we can. I've kept him waiting at the corner of the street.'

'You can dismiss him then. I want to go to Saint Paul's which we can do on foot in a few minutes.'

'What! Look at a Cathedral? What sort of entertainment is that? Is this your idea, Mr Beattie, to gaze upon Wren's work and hope someone will ask you to build another as splendid?'

Gideon Beattie repudiated the idea. He told him he had written to the Anstons and was now going to the inn to hand the letter to the post-boy. He was happy for the young people to look round St Paul's and he would meet them there later.

'Take my letter too, Father,' Olivia said, and then defiantly to Gerard. 'It's to your mother. I haven't told her where you are staying, just that you are alive and well.'

'The deuce you have! She'll tell my father we've been seeing each other and that'll bring the old man down here when we could be enjoying ourselves.'

'If she doesn't say where the news came from he won't know. Anyway it's to go and it is I, not my father, who wishes to view the Cathedral. I haven't seen it since I was too young to appreciate it but finding ourselves living nearby that is what I would most like to do. You gave me leave to choose, don't you remember? So let us set out.'

Gerard looked at her with raised eyebrows. 'Yes, I see I must also remember that this is the young lady who rode Emperor. When I get him back I will have to put her on him again and see whether it is horse or rider who is tamed.'

He took her arm firmly in his and they set out. Have I overstepped the mark, she wondered, but he loved me *because* I rode Emperor. Are all men really the same? They can't abide a dominant woman. But I swear I will never be a Lady Kirby like the present one.

However, it was delightful to walk with this strikingly handsome young man and see the eyes of everyone turning towards them. The day was warm and the streets dry underfoot. If she was to learn her own feelings towards him she must also be pleasant and give him a chance to show himself at his best.

But when they entered the cathedral she yielded up control of her feelings altogether. Her very soul was moved in awe at the miracle of the vast space and a sense of the grandeur of God. I am very small and insignificant was all she could feel. She slid her arm from Gerard's and wandered through the nave and choir, head up, turning this way and that to absorb the immensity of the dome, oblivious of sightseers and of Gerard tapping his cane against his breeches as he followed.

At the entry to the steps he plucked her arm and suggested it might be quite exciting to go up.

'Oh,' she said, aware of him again. She could see a notice about a Stairs-foot fee which brought her down from her ecstasy with a bump. 'We have to pay.'

An official stood there waiting. Gerard readily plucked open his purse and found the coins and they climbed up.

Now here they were in the sunshine with a mild breeze blowing the smoke haze over the outspread city. Olivia found herself moved in a different way. A whole natural landscape had been transformed over centuries into this teeming maze of roads and buildings small and great and it was still growing outwards into the country in all directions. Gerard pointed out Westminster Abbey and the new Westminster Bridge.

'I hear they plan another at Blackfriars,' he said. 'Three bridges over the river will put the ferries out of business.'

'What is the high ground northwards that we can just see above the pall of smoke? Is it the Heath beyond the village of Hampstead? I believe my father took me there once but Lily, my nursemaid, said it was a haunt of highwaymen and wouldn't come.'

Gerard thought it *was* the notorious Heath and then he turned her to look east towards the sea with the docks and ships and boats of every description crowding the river so that it was 'a wonder,' she said, 'that they are not for ever bumping into one another.'

Gerard laughed. 'They do frequently.'

She realised that a constant clamour of warning shouts was rising both from the river and from the streets below. So much noisy swarming humanity on water and land made her sigh for her memories of Yorkshire.

'You seem amazed at it,' Gerard said, 'and you a Londoner!'

'We didn't go about a great deal when I was young. Lily who cared for me after my mother died was rather fat so we just had what she called perambulations to the park nearby. You,' she said, as the thought struck her, 'should be glad to have a mother still living who loves you so distractedly. I have lost both a mother and a loving nanny.'

Gerard frowned. 'You ladies all hang together, don't you? But a fellow has to spread his wings. You've seen birds caught in a net. They'll flap themselves to death to be free.'

Free to do what, she thought, drink and gamble? But she didn't say it aloud. She wanted to know this man, deeply if there were depths to know.

She smiled at him then. 'I know, I do understand.'

The frown vanished and he slipped his arm round her waist. Despite her doubts she loved the feel of it there, the unstated sign that he wanted her and felt she belonged to him, but when another party of sightseers came up she gently removed it and, spying the tiny figure of her father approaching the cathedral, she suggested they go down now.

'Is he going to chaperone us everywhere?' Gerard grumbled as they descended the steps. 'I must get Emperor back and have you mounted and we can ride in the park.'

'How could you bear to lose Emperor at the gaming table?' she asked.

He tried to laugh it away but she could see it mattered greatly to him. 'I suppose I was mad drunk. This fellow says, 'Put your horse on if you're out of funds' and I did but when I started winning again he'd left the table. I think I know the horse dealer he'll have gone to. He wouldn't keep him himself. He'd find Emperor more than he could handle. I say,' he said suddenly, turning to her as they passed back through the cathedral, 'would you mind? Can I leave you with your father for a few hours while I make inquiries? I'll come back when I've retrieved Emperor and we'll dine and go to the opera tonight.'

Olivia acquiesced. She could see the figure of her father at the entrance outlined against the light and looking about for them. 'I believe if Father receives a favourable answer from the Anstons he'll want to travel down to Surrey at once.'

'You won't feel obliged to go with him I hope.'

'No, but I trust you won't try to take advantage of me if I don't.'

'By Jove, I'd like to, but hang it all, I'm a gentleman you know.'

Yes, she thought, he's a gentleman. And what makes a gentleman these days? One who can buy himself in and out of the army if he chooses, mingle at ease with titled people, win and lose at gambling without shame and still get credit from his suppliers. My father has worked hard to be a professional man but if he is without his profession he runs up huge debts at his peril. Yet I am supposed to be honoured that the heir to a castle – even if he might be illegitimate – has chosen me. She put her hand into her father's and squeezed it. It seemed a lifetime ago that she had been so very desperate to have Gerard at her feet.

When he returned later Gerard tried to make light of his failure to trace the horse. 'I've put inquiries about among my friends. Someone will have news soon. Our business now is to enjoy ourselves.'

Olivia wanted to take pleasure over the next few days with strolls in the parks, a visit to the opera and the playhouse – though Gerard absolutely refused to take her to see Garrick in Shakespeare – if only his mood had not been blackened by the absence of any news of his horse.

Although her father went with them it was Gerard who managed watermen when they had a trip down river and sent the footman for tickets and hired coaches and ordered dinners. He did all these things in such a handsome easy manner that Olivia could hardly believe he was still only twenty years old. But then when they were done and they were sitting in a boat on the water or a box at the theatre he would mutter to himself about Emperor.

'I must get him back. What if he's sold to a foreigner and taken out of the country! I'm damned if I can go another day without tracing him.'

He's obsessed with the beast, she thought as she watched his profile. She often found herself looking at him to see if there *was* any resemblance to Thomas Todd but his face was too often distorted with sulking which Tom's never was and in the box at the theatre he would lounge in bored fashion with his legs out and his shoulders hunched while Tom always sat or stood straight-backed or was athletically at work or, she recalled with a pang, reading Shakespeare with the same vigour he brought to every task.

On the fifth morning Gideon Beattie returned from the coffee shop with the letter he had been waiting for. He was in the highest spirits, waving it at Olivia as soon as he came into the house. She read that Mr and Mrs John Anston requested the pleasure of the company of Mr Gideon Beattie at Anston Manor the very next day to discuss improvements to the house.

Jenny and William were permitted to share his delight and the prospect of regular wages put them too into such good humour that Jenny wouldn't hear of Olivia donning a cap and apron that day.

'But I don't know how I'm to leave my girl,' he said to Gerard when he called that afternoon – his hours had slipped from the middle of the day. 'It's not at all the thing for her to be left with two young servants though I don't expect to be away more than a night or two on a first visit. And it's not right for her reputation if she is seen alone with a young man when both their families are away.'

Olivia said, 'I'm perfectly happy with William and Jenny and if you wish me not to stir out of the house while you're away, Papa, I promise not to do so.' She smiled sweetly at Gerard.

'By Jove you shan't be shut up like that,' Gerard said. 'Look, sir, you met my friend Sir Peregrine. His mother, Lady Grant, has returned to town and we can make up a party with them to go about. Nothing could be more respectable. You may be sure I care as much about the reputation of my future wife as you do, sir.'

Gideon Beattie was only too ready to agree to anything that enabled him to go with an easy mind and next day in his best clothes he took the early coach into Surrey.

Olivia dressed carefully as Gerard was to come that afternoon to take her to meet Lady Grant at the new British Museum. The choice of venue sounded very sober and proper and Gerard said it was full of 'Chinese and Arabian treasures and all that sort of thing.'

Not being sure where they were to dine that evening she was having a small meal with William and Jenny in the kitchen when there came a loud rap at the front door. They all jumped and looked at each other. It was too early for Gerard and Olivia felt a sudden panic that the coach to Surrey might have been attacked by highwaymen and her father killed.

'You see who it is, William,' she squeaked and listened in terror behind the kitchen door as she heard him go.

An unknown male voice asked, 'Is this the house of Mr and Miss Beattie?'

William agreed it was and the next words made Olivia gasp and meet Jenny's eyes in horror.

'Sir Langton and Lady Kirby are waiting in their carriage to speak with them.'

It was what Gerard had feared. She had brought a hornets' nest about their ears. She threw a shawl round her shoulders and went out, her knees trembling, and followed the man to where the carriage had stopped round the corner in the wider thoroughfare.

Sir Langton's face appeared at the window. She thought his expression less stern than she expected and opening the door from within he said in his politest tones, 'Miss Beattie, pray excuse us from coming in. Lady Kirby is feeling unwell from the journey and would be most grateful if you would step up and sit with her for a few moments.' He held out his hand and assisted her inside. 'Is your father not at home?'

Lady Kirby, looking pale and anxious, just clasped her other hand with meaningful pressure and made space for her to sit beside her.

'My father has gone into Surrey this morning on business,' Olivia said. 'He will be most sorry to have missed you.'

Lady Kirby kept hold of her hand and with a fearful glance at her husband murmured, 'Where is our bad boy?'

Sir Langton, on the opposite seat, frowned her down.

'May I say, Miss Beattie, that we are most grateful for the letter you sent her ladyship when you knew the anxiety we were feeling. I was unaware at the time that you had visited Tadby but Lady Kirby has since enlightened me. I regret that she imagined

I would not wish to see you at the castle. I fear I acted hastily to both your father and you on the last occasion but I hope I would always extend the courtesy of my house to any acquaintance coming into our neighbourhood.'

Olivia had not expected this. Poor Lady Kirby must have been thoroughly scolded. Sir Langton, having been very discourteous, had since realised his reputation for perfect manners had been seriously damaged and was now struggling painfully to put it right.

'I assure you, Sir, I was comfortable at Mrs Summers' and very pleased to see that Mrs Johnson was so much better than I expected.'

Here Lady Kirby drew in her breath sharply and looked appealingly at her husband.

'I regret to have to tell you, Miss Beattie,' he said, watching Olivia's face intently, 'that Mrs Johnson had another attack a week ago and died some hours later. We left to come here the day after her funeral.'

'Oh!' Olivia felt as if the door to the secrets of Castle Kirby had been slammed shut in her face. 'Did she speak? Did she ask for me again?'

He still had his eyes fixed on her as if it was she who might have a secret to reveal. 'She never regained consciousness. She passed peacefully in her sleep.'

Olivia could only murmur, 'I'm so sorry for the poor soul. I grew fond of her.'

'May I ask why she wanted to see you on the earlier occasion of her seizure?' The question was said lightly enough but Olivia had been interrogated before by him on the same matter and was on her guard at once.

'I can only suppose she took a fancy to me as a fresh face about the place. She hoped to see me again, not perhaps realising I had returned to London.' The answer was given as casually as his question but Olivia's thoughts had flown to the Bible and page one hundred. She daren't ask what was to happen to Mrs Johnson's things. Would she ever now have a chance to find out what was on that mysterious page? What if the secret did relate to the circumstances of Gerard's birth? If she was ever to marry him she *must* find out. If she could only have time alone with Lady Kirby there was a chance she would break down and reveal all she could tell – if indeed it was her secret and not Sir Langton's alone. But page a hundred would still remain a matter of guesswork. Mrs Johnson had been so emphatic that no one else knew of that.

She realised Sir Langton was scrutinising every change in her expression so she looked him full in the face and challenged him with her own question.

'Did you come all the way to London to tell me this, sir?'

He was taken aback by this reversal of roles and a little flustered, Olivia was glad to see, as he answered, 'No indeed, Miss Beattie, as I thought you would be aware, we came to fetch our son home. Perhaps, since you have evidently been meeting him, you could tell us where we can find him.'

Lady Kirby, who was still clasping Olivia's hand and squeezing it whenever Sir Langton sounded at all sarcastic or severe, murmured at her ear, 'We only want an address and then we can drive on and find him, such a trying journey, the dust you know.'

'Mr Gerard is staying at a friend's house, Sir Langton, but if you liked to take my lady to a respectable inn where she could refresh herself and rest and then proceed to the British Museum at four o'clock you will be able to meet Mr Gerard with Lady Grant and her son Sir Peregrine with whose party I am invited to view the treasures.'

'Lady Grant in town at this time of year!' Lady Kirby exclaimed. 'That is most unusual.'

'Gerard informed me she had recently returned to London.' Olivia couldn't help a mischievous look at Sir Langton. 'Perhaps she too has come to town to prevent her son making an unsuitable alliance.' She turned to Lady Kirby and said, 'Pray forgive me. Our home is too humble for me to invite you in.'

'Oh dear,' cried Lady Kirby. 'I don't in the least mind how humble it is, nor do I think you at all unsuitable for Gerard. Sir Langton knows what I think. How are you to get to the Museum? Is Gerard coming to escort you there?'

'That was the arrangement.'

'Then pray let us go in with you and wait for him. All I need is a little water to wash the dust from my eyes, a dish of tea and a bed to lie on for an hour. If that is not troubling you too much, my dear? Who is with you in your father's absence?'

'I have my maid Jenny and our man, William. Of course you are welcome to come in, Lady Kirby. I will be honoured.' And she got up, ready to descend the steps.

The footman at once opened the door.

Sir Langton no doubt felt he was getting left out of these plans.

'And am I to come in too, Miss Beattie?' She inclined her head with a smile as she turned to step out. 'In that case we will send the carriage to the inn we passed where the horses can be put up,' and he followed her out and handed down Lady Kirby, whose maid descended from the top when she saw her mistress on the move.

If I am to accommodate them overnight, thought Olivia, Sir Langton and Lady Kirby will have to have Father's bed and sleep together – a thing they never do at home – and her lady's maid will have to share Jenny's bed and their footman William's. She couldn't help a giggle rising at the thought. Why she was not more apprehensive at the forthcoming encounter with Gerard she couldn't imagine as she conducted Sir Langton and Lady Kirby round the corner to the front of the tall, narrow house and found Jenny anxiously looking out for her.

Jenny's astonishment and dismay was only too obvious as she curtseyed and backed to the kitchen to warn William.

'Bring a tray of tea to the drawing-room, Jenny,' Olivia said, hoping she would unpack the best porcelain. She knew the water jug and bowl were replenished in her bedroom as she had attended to it herself that morning so she led her guests first to the drawing-room and then, apologising for the extra stairs and the steepness of them, she took Lady Kirby to her own room and left her with her maid in the tiny space to manage as best they could.

When she came down Sir Langton was standing in the middle of the drawing-room floor gazing about him at the faded armchairs and threadbare curtains. A handsome portrait of Olivia's mother hung over the fireplace, one of the few good possessions they had brought with them from their last home. But the room looked very stark and bare and the fire was not lit as they had only coals for the kitchen for cooking and boiling water. But the August day was warm and Olivia bit back the apology she was about to utter.

Sir Langton looked round at her, waving his hand at the room and then towards the window where all that could be seen were the blackened walls of the backs of houses in their little alleyway.

'I trust you are not blaming me, Miss Beattie, for this reduction in your circumstances. I gave your father the price agreed for the limited work on the west wing which is now nearing completion.'

'I am aware of that, Sir Langton.' she said, head up and looking him in the eye, 'but by dismissing him you also belittled his skill among your acquaintances and he has found it hard to receive commissions. I trust that the business he is at present engaged in will lead to useful work. He is an excellent architect but everyone needs patrons and he has not been fortunate in that way.'

'And I have not been fortunate enough, Miss Beattie, to be in a position to pay for the additional work he would have imposed on me. Gerard ran up debts when he was serving in the army. Do you know his plans? Is he hoping to rejoin his regiment?'

'He sold his uniform and commission to settle more debts as he will no doubt tell you, sir, but he has since been fortunate at the gaming tables and is now in funds.'

'Gambling again!' Sir Langton paced angrily about the room. 'Cannot you, Miss Beattie, whose opinion he must value, keep him from this folly?'

She just shook her head as Jenny tapped at the door and brought in not merely tea in the porcelain set but thinly cut bread and butter, a plate of sliced beef which she had decorated with watercress and some sweetmeats from the pastry cooks. She must have sent William out at once, using their own meagre pay which Olivia would have to reimburse from the limited resources her father had left her. Gerard in his lordly way had insisted on paying for every expense incurred that week and she had assumed this would continue. She had never imagined having to entertain his parents.

Lady Kirby now reappeared seeking the tea for which she was thirsting.

'Oh my dear Olivia, you shouldn't have gone to all this trouble.' But both she and Sir Langton cleared the plates leaving little opportunity for conversation, to Olivia's relief.

From three o'clock Olivia listened for Gerard's knock. She suspected he would come early knowing her father was away. She was actually eager to see what would happen. The situation, as her father had said, needed to be set in order. There had been no sign of Sir Langton accepting her as Gerard's betrothed but nor had he forbidden her to see him. What difference might the death of Mrs Johnson have made? It must have relieved him of the fear of betrayal – if there was indeed a secret to betray. But would he then harden his heart against her? If only she could get hold of Mrs Johnson's Bible and look at page a hundred!

She found herself standing at the window watching for Gerard while Sir Langton and Lady Kirby sat in uncomfortable silence. Sir Langton had spoken of fetching Gerard home but he must know it was most unlikely he would agree to go. Gerard lived for the desires and pleasures of the moment without a thought for the future. Was I ever like that, she wondered staring at the empty alleyway. If I was I believe I have grown up very quickly in a few months. Perhaps, she thought, with heightening excitement and not a little dread, my own feelings about Gerard Kirby will be clarified in the next hour or two.

Chapter 15

Tired of watching the road Olivia sat down again and tried to make conversation but they were all too on edge. When four o'clock passed and Gerard still hadn't arrived, Sir Langton got up abruptly and said they must make arrangements for their stay. He would send the footman to secure them rooms.

'Of course if I come alone I stay at my Club. As we normally only make one visit a year to London it's an unnecessary expense to keep a house here.'

As he spoke there was a double knock on the door.

'That will be Gerard.' Olivia rose with every appearance of calm but her nervousness had betrayed her into using his Christian name alone, a familiarity that would surely inflame Sir Langton.

Lady Kirby rose too, all excitement, as his feet could be heard bounding up the stairs. He hadn't waited for William or Jenny to announce him but burst into the room and stopped dead with astonishment. For a second his mouth hung open and then his teeth clenched and he muttered at Olivia, 'That damned letter of yours. What did I tell you?'

Sir Langton leapt to his feet like an exploding firework.

'Graceless boy! Mind your language and greet your mother properly who has travelled all this way to find you.'

Gerard gave her a peck on the cheek. 'Well, you know, Mamma, I can't be kept on leading strings.'

'If you would only tell us what you are doing so we are not imagining you slaughtered by highwaymen.'

'And keep your promises like a gentleman,' his father said, ostentatiously examining his pocket watch. 'I understand from Miss Beattie that you are to meet Lady Grant at the British Museum at four. It is already past that hour now.'

Gerard looked at Olivia in surprise. 'You told them that tale, did you? Didn't you realise I invented Lady Grant to satisfy your father?'

'What!' cried Olivia. 'You lied to me!'

'Oh heavens,' said Lady Kirby. 'I knew Lady Grant would never come to town in August. You wicked boy! What would you have done with poor Miss Beattie? Oh Gerard! Beg her forgiveness!'

'Hang it, I had no evil designs on her,' Gerard laughed. 'She's to be my wife after all. I just wanted her to myself.' He looked at his father with an impudent grin. 'Did you never try and get Mother on her own when you were courting.'

'You've been drinking, sir,' declared Sir Langton. 'And at this hour in the afternoon! I am deeply ashamed of your behaviour. I understand you have quit the army so we intend to return with you to Yorkshire as soon as possible.'

'What the blazes am I to do there? It's not two weeks since I escaped.'

Sir Langton, at a disadvantage because of his short stature, looked up at Gerard. 'You will start to learn your duties as heir to Castle Kirby.'

'But I know you, sir. You would never hand over decisions to me.'

'Certainly not until you are more experienced. You do not reach your majority till November and are entirely under my jurisdiction. I hoped the army would instil a spirit of service and discipline in you but I fear that has not yet happened. I am determined however to mould you into a man who could hold a good name in the world, do his duty by his tenants, serve as a justice of the peace and – I would also hope – in Parliament. If you work towards these ends you will be kept in funds but if you are going to waste yourself in a life of pleasure, in drinking and gambling, you will get not a penny from me, sir, and that is my last word.'

They were still all standing up and the atmosphere in the room crackled with excitement. Olivia, watching Gerard's face with fascinated interest, saw a look of cunning come into his eyes.

'Suppose we all sit down and talk about this calmly,' he said.

'Oh, that's right,' cried Lady Kirby flopping into an armchair.

Sir Langton, looking suspicious, resumed his and Gerard, waving Olivia into the remaining one, pulled up the footstool and sat on it with his long legs stretched out and his arms folded across his waistcoat.

'Now, sir, you have put a picture before my eyes of a well-behaved country gentleman which is not perhaps what I'm quite ready for yet at only twenty years of age –'

'No,' his father interrupted, 'I said you must *learn* to be one and first you must unlearn many bad habits which you have already acquired.'

'Well, granted that, grant the learning and the unlearning, what does a man need to help him on this very sober path? He needs a good woman, doesn't he? So what I say, Father, is this: I will do all you say, come back with you, be a good boy –as long as that includes such respectable sports as hunting and shooting and occasional visits to the races which all the country gentlemen do – and on your part you will consent to welcome that good girl there who is not only beautiful, clever, and well-spoken but very definitely a lady – to be my wife.'

'Oh yes,' cried Lady Kirby. 'Oh Sir Langton, is that not what I have been pleading for? She will keep him right, I know it. And her mother was a Fenchurch – I made inquiries – a very good family. Gerard will turn the corner and never give us any more anxiety. You can't say no when he has promised to keep his side of the bargain so very earnestly. I love that dear girl already like a mother. What do you say, Sir Langton? For heaven's sake, speak.'

But Sir Langton was not to be rushed. His thin features and compressed lips revealed only that he would take his own time. Olivia was pleased. She knew if he had said yes at once she was herself on the point of saying no, she would not have Gerard Kirby as any sort of bargain. The mischief in her nature wanted to see Sir Langton's face when she turned down his son. But caution now held her back as it was holding back Sir Langton. She didn't trust Gerard's ability to keep his promise but on the other hand if he did, for her sake, he might become the man she could love and respect. Weighed with that was the attraction of Castle Kirby and the chance to uncover the mystery. She had pondered the possibility of Gerard's illegitimacy and already decided that if it remained known only within the family she wouldn't reject him on that ground. It was the man himself that mattered. And he was not yet a man either in age or outlook.

Gerard was looking from his father to her but she kept her face neutral and it was Sir Langton who replied first.

'We will remain in London a week, Gerard, and you will understand you are on trial. After that I will consider your request and if I feel able to accede to it I will expect you to return with us and continue to prove yourself in your new role. But,' and now he turned in his chair and looked hard at Olivia, 'I would like to hear what Miss Beattie has to say about that suggestion.'

Olivia gave him a smile which she hoped conveyed a total

understanding of his motives. In a week her father might know if he had a lucrative commission and could move to a better neighbourhood. No baronet could take a wife for his son out of this neighbourhood. And Sir Langton would certainly look for a dowry. She was sure there would be no swift marriage but that would give time for each party to size up the other on all fronts.

'I think you are very wise, Sir Langton,' she said, 'in asking Mr Gerard for such proof of his intentions.' She was now looking gravely at Gerard. 'I also will be pleased to see the outcome of such a trial.'

Lady Olivia began, 'My dear, that's so cold coming from you —'

But Gerard had leapt to his feet, knocking over the stool. 'Hang it, Olivia, you agreed to marry me. You said you loved me. What the blazes are you playing at now, going along with my father?'

She found all their eyes on her. She folded her hands in her lap and said softly, 'I didn't know you very well, sir. I need to know you better.'

'Oh he *will* be good, won't you, Gerard? I know you're upset, Olivia, because of that silly business about Lady Grant.'

Sir Langton held up his hand. 'We were all to be quiet and talk sensibly. I have made my proposition and I respect Miss Beattie for her answer. Now I would wish us to leave and you, Gerard, can accompany us to your lodgings so we can see where you are living and we will take rooms nearby. London is quite empty at present so we should have little difficulty. Tomorrow we can start a plan of cultivated activities beginning with the new British Museum. When Mr Beattie returns we will of course be happy to include him in our excursions if he wishes to join us.' He stood up, a slight figure next to his son but none the less imposing.

Gerard's face showed both dismay and anger but he focussed

on the detail of his father's proposal. 'It's of no use going to the British Museum. I was told they make you apply for tickets weeks before and if you're not absolutely in the peerage you might not even get them. And the treasures are not so marvellous – mostly freak animals and plants and bones and that sort of thing.'

'Then we will go to one of the picture galleries. I had hoped when your uncle died to take you on the Grand Tour but with hostilities persisting that is not feasible. You need cultivating, young man, civilising. And you have already caused me expense with your debts. That has got to cease.'

'I'll only ask the price of getting Emperor back,' Gerard said quickly. 'I can't go back to Yorkshire without him.'

'And how did you lose him?'

'Oh some swine tricked me into a wager. I've an idea now which horse dealer has got him and I think he'll take thirty guineas cash though he's worth a deal more.'

'You have the impudence to demand thirty guineas! I understood that for once you had been lucky in this pernicious gambling habit.'

'I was, but word gets out and all the vultures gather then.'

'So you have incurred more debts already?'

Olivia thought of the freedom with which Gerard had been spending for the past few days. Would some men never learn? She was a little afraid that her father might do the same if he found new commissions.

'If you have lost Emperor let that be a lesson to you,' Sir Langton said. 'You will travel home in our carriage. There are horses enough at Castle Kirby for you to ride.'

Gerard kicked the stool across the room. 'Is that how you persuade me to do your bidding, sir? Is that really your last word?'

'Absolutely and finally.'

Lady Kirby held up her hands. 'Oh Sir Langton, could we not find thirty guineas?'

Olivia looked from one to the other. Gerard, she could see, knew he had made a blunder in pressing this now but his lips were set in an obstinate line.

Sir Langton was just as adamant. 'You get nothing until you mend your ways, boy. Now we have trespassed long enough on Miss Beattie's hospitality. I will send for the carriage and we will take you to your lodgings where I would advise you not to stir out again tonight.'

'The deuce you will,' Gerard shouted at him. 'Olivia, don't you forget you're mine. I'll have you one day.'

And he dodged round his mother and was out of the room and down the stairs in a trice. They heard the door slam and Olivia stepping to the window saw him run in the direction of the hackney-coach stand.

Lady Kirby sank back into her chair and began to sob. 'We've lost him again. We nearly had him eating out of our hands and now he's gone off again – and all for thirty guineas. Oh Sir Langton, could we not have stretched a point –?'

Sir Langton wouldn't sit down again. He was very agitated Olivia could see and paced up and down for a few minutes before stopping in front of his wife.

'I fear that has been our big mistake, Sophia. We have been stretching points for Gerard all his life.'

He would have said much more – it was obvious – but for Olivia's presence. She had never before heard him address Lady Kirby by her Christian name. She begged to excuse herself so that they could be alone. But Lady Kirby said, 'You are our lifeline, dear Olivia. You know where his lodgings are, do you not?'

And so half an hour later they were all three in the carriage with Lady Kirby's maid and the footman sitting on top and the groom driving them towards St James'.

What William and Jenny would make of all the goings on

Olivia had no time to consider but she well knew the lives of masters and mistresses were the chief source of entertainment to their servants.

Sir Langton had sunk into profound gloom and said not a word for most of the way. Lady Kirby on the other hand could not keep silence. She bemoaned Gerard's impetuosity, excused it for his youth, deplored his behaviour to Olivia which must make her feel he cared more for his horse than her, assured her that was not the case, pointing out his last words that he would have her one day and constantly reiterating that he was not as bad as he seemed.

At last Sir Langton burst out, 'Anyone who needs so much advocacy is guilty as charged. Pray say no more. I am bitterly disappointed in him, that's all.'

Olivia had said she could direct them once they reached White's which everyone knew. 'It is two squares on and is the house of Mr and Mrs Anston of Surrey. I believe it is about the fifth along on the left as we drive through the Square.'

'One day they will number the houses,' Sir Langton grumbled. 'It should have been done long since with all this new building, one house looking very much like another. Is Gerard sponging on some friends then?'

Olivia explained and added that she was grateful to Gerard for advising her father of the Anstons' plans for the improvement of their Surrey mansion.

'I am pleased to hear he has been of some use at last, especially to your father.'

Then she quickly outlined the excursions he had taken them on and that he could be most lively and generous. Lady Kirby glowed a little at this but Sir Langton only said, 'Generous with *my* money.'

The footman got down and rang the bell but as Olivia feared the Anstons' man said Mr Kirby had been there but had gone out he didn't know where.

Sir Langton guessed White's but Olivia felt that would be too obvious if Gerard wished to throw them off the scent. Lady Kirby was at the edge of exhaustion so they proceeded to Grosvenor Square and found their former house available to rent again. The housekeeper who lived in the attics was set to preparing the beds and the footman was despatched to White's to make inquiries but Mr Kirby had not been there that evening. He was then despatched again to order a dinner to be sent in while the groom settled the horses in the stables at the rear.

'You will dine here, Olivia, and stay the night,' Lady Kirby insisted. 'Pray stay with us while we are in London though I have no idea how long that will be now. Everything is back in the old uncertainty.'

Olivia had told Jenny not to be surprised if she didn't return till the morning so she accepted Lady Kirby's invitation but would go home next day in case her father came back.

They were alone as Sir Langton had chosen to go out till the dinner should be ready so Olivia was not surprised that Lady Kirby became very confidential.

'Sir Langton needs to walk about you know. Things get pent up inside him and only exercise will relieve him. He has thrown his whole life into making Gerard a fit heir and worthy gentleman and he can see it all wasting away before his eyes. Gerard was such a beautiful baby. Sir Langton kept saying to me, 'Is he not perfect in every feature?' He doted on him and the same when he began to toddle about. He looked so pretty in his little dresses and then when he was first put into breeches didn't Sir Langton look so proudly at his boy! No father ever took so much notice of a child. 'Now he's my little man', he would say. 'Look at how he bowls his top. How he runs! How clever he is!' Yes, he was an athletic boy but not clever at his books. That's why Sir Langton kept him at home under a tutor. He thought he would learn more than in the rough world of school. I think he was frightened too to let him out of his sight. He wanted to protect him from danger.'

'Surely,' Olivia couldn't help commenting, 'it was a great change of heart then for him to encourage him to join the army.'

'Oh it was. But you know Gerard used to stand in front of the portraits of his ancestors, especially those in military uniform, looking so grand on horseback some of them, and he'd say, 'I shall do great deeds like them one day, Papa, and have my portrait up' and Sir Langton wanted to please him and promised to look into it when he was bigger. But when he was seventeen and starting to pester him about his promise Sir Langton was reluctant. Then one day the parson was there and told him Gerard had to be allowed to go and see the world or he would never make a man. That was when Sir Langton began to see how close we'd kept him. It was agony for him to let him go – for me too of course but mothers are expected to worry over their ewe lambs – but I don't think it ever occurred to him that Gerard would get into bad ways in the army. We didn't know there was so much drinking and gambling there. The two officers he invited in the summer come of good Yorkshire families, but they put away a great deal of wine between them and their language was quite coarse over the port after dinner he told me. Dear girl, could it just be a stage he's going through? Will he come out perfect again, like a butterfly from a chrysalis?'

'I would be so happy if it were so.'

Olivia was pleased to learn so much about Gerard's upbringing. Two things stood out. As the pride and joy of his parents' lives he expected nothing to go wrong for him in life. Not having been away to school he had flung himself into the army with a belief that popularity was his absolute right. Evidently he had won it with a swagger and lavish generosity. Wounded under fire only added glory and honour. It was freedom on his own that he didn't know how to handle and, she dared to think, falling in love and not being instantly gratified. She began to feel a little sad and sorry for Gerard Kirby.

The other thing that struck her was how mistaken she must have been about his legitimacy. Lady Kirby could surely not have spoken so guilelessly if she had borne him out of wedlock. Perhaps his resemblance to Tom that Sunday was a fleeting coincidence. What then was the mystery that only Mrs Johnson had known? Why did those words 'punished, punished' echo down the years? Sir Langton had uttered them when he had believed Gerard mortally wounded. Surely they expressed more than regret that he had overindulged his son or that he had listened to the parson's advice and let him join the army.

Lady Olivia was studying her wistfully. 'You are so beautiful too. What a couple you would make and what children you would have to please Sir Langton in his old age! His heritage means so much to him. He wants to pass on the estate and the farms in perfect condition, unencumbered by debts. Although the Kirbys were always for the king he is a bit of a Puritan at heart. He is abstemious in his habits and very nice in his dress. He loves order. Perfection and order.' She sighed deeply. 'It has been hard to live up to and I don't think I have always satisfied him. I suffered greatly when I lost two babies, one miscarried and one stillborn. I felt I had failed him dreadfully. You can imagine my relief when they showed me Gerard after a long hard night with only that dear May Tyler – very sweet like you – and poor Janet Johnson who has also gone to her grave. Oh dear, I shouldn't speak of these things to one so young but you'll forgive me, I know.'

'I am honoured at your confidence, Lady Kirby.' That settled it. Gerard was the rightful heir of Castle Kirby. She loved his mother and had begun to sympathise with his father. She loved the place of which she would be mistress. All she had to do now was the hardest thing of all. She had to be sure in her heart that Gerard was capable of reformation.

Chapter 16

Two days later Gerard crept back home looking as if he had not slept since they had seen him last. Word had been left at the Anstons' house and at White's to let him know where his parents were staying. Olivia had been back to the house in Aldgate and confided some of the news to Jenny, but Lady Kirby insisted on the carriage coming to pick her up in the morning so that she could spend the day with them. On the second day a letter had come from Gideon Beattie to say that Mr and Mrs Anston were delighted with his ideas for their property and he would be returning to London in a day or two to fetch Olivia and collect his things for a prolonged stay with them. They were happy for her lady's maid to accompany her and also his man, whom he was calling his assistant. The house in Aldgate could now be given up and Jenny and William would have very comfortable quarters at Anston Manor.

All this was buzzing in Olivia's head when she arrived at the house in Grosvenor Square but she had not had time to tell Lady Kirby the news when the footman announced that Mr Gerard was below and asking if he could come up.

'Asking if he can come up,' cried Lady Kirby, 'in his own house! Olivia, we will go down to him.'

Sir Langton was out on one of his constitutionals so there was no constraint on Lady Kirby's rapid rustling down the stairs except the size of her hooped petticoat.

193

Olivia followed, looking past her at the sorry figure in the hall.

'Oh my boy!' cried Lady Kirby. 'Where have you been? Are you ill?'

Olivia could see very well that he had been drinking and probably losing heavily at the tables all night. How would Sir Langton take this? And what should she do herself? Finally wash her hands of him? Wipe him out as beyond hope and seize the chance to go with her Father to Surrey? That would mean putting behind her Castle Kirby and its mystery and her dear Shakespearean companions for ever.

His first words made her hesitate.

'Oh Mother, oh Olivia, I am so sorry. I am a wretch. Forgive me.'

They helped him upstairs into the elegant drawing-room with its handsome polished furniture and brocade curtains and view across the square to more elegant drawing-rooms and he sank into a chair and covered his face with his hands and wept.

Both ladies fell on their knees before him murmuring words of comfort. But nothing stopped his choking sobs. When his mother took his hands away to offer her pathetic lace handkerchief Olivia saw how sunken were his eyes and how dark the rings below. And he wore no waistcoat. Good heavens, she thought, he has lost the very clothes off his back. His shirt was soiled and smelt of drink and sweat and its ruffles sagged limply down his chest

She rose and went to the door and called the maid to bring a tray of tea and when it came she took it from her at the door to spare her the sight of the young master. He drank greedily when she had poured it out but was still gasping with sobs in between gulps. She stood at the window and watched for Sir Langton coming.

'Where's Father?' were the first words Gerard managed to choke out when his thirst was quenched.

'He'll be here any minute,' Lady Kirby moaned. 'Oh my boy, what have you done?'

'I've ruined him. I've ruined everything. I can't bear to think of it. Olivia, look at me. Why did you not love me? I thought you loved me but you took his side.'

She turned and looked at his pathetic figure. So that was it. He was going to try and blame her. 'You needed testing,' she said.

'And I failed. That's what you're saying. Of course I failed. I began small to get the thirty guineas for Emperor but the run never came. It was all the wrong way, time after time. It gets hold of you. You can't believe the luck won't change. It changed the last time and I knew it must change if I went on all night. But it didn't. He'll kill me. I'd better kill myself first but I haven't even got a sword to do it with.'

He thrashed about in the chair and Olivia could hardly bear to look at him. She went back to the window and saw Sir Langton coming up the steps to the front door.

'He's here, he's here,' she hissed to Lady Kirby.

Gerard heard and struggled to his feet. 'Where can I hide?'

His mother would have rushed him into the nearest dressing-room but Olivia seized his arm. 'Face him, Gerard. You're not a coward. Face him.'

So they were standing up, one each side of him practically holding him upright, when Sir Langton walked into the room.

He sized up the whole situation at a glance and after a long, slow breath, all he said was, 'Thank God, you've come back.'

Gerard broke from their arms and fell at his feet. 'Forgive me. Oh Father, please forgive me.'

Sir Langton stood, staring at the grovelling figure, and Olivia saw his sharp features begin to crumple. He flung aside his cane and bent down and seized Gerard by his shoulders and lifted him up, taller and broader though he was. But Gerard seemed shrunken and as his father's arms went round him he drooped on his shoulder, shaking with sobs.

Lady Kirby was standing with her hands clasped before her face as if in prayer but with a beatific smile in her eyes as she turned them on Olivia. Tears were still running down her face but they seemed to be of joy.

Olivia, to her own astonishment, felt like a spectator at the scene. Here were these three locked in the deepest emotions and her own eyes were dry.

Only once before on the news of Gerard's wounding had she seen Sir Langton Kirby break down as he did now for his shoulders were shaking too and he had hidden his face against Gerard's cheek. It was painful to witness from so tight-lipped a little man but she seemed strangely detached from it all. She didn't even feel able to put her arms round Lady Kirby. It was all rather embarrassing and she was a little ashamed that this was all she felt.

The scene broke up when Sir Langton, perhaps overcome by the weight of Gerard leaning on him, spoke at last, huskily.

'Come, sit down, and tell me all, however bad it is.'

Olivia then broke in. 'Pray excuse me. It's not right for me to intrude here. I'll go to the room you kindly put at my disposal.' And she was heading for the door when Lady Kirby cried, 'But you are also concerned – deeply – one of the family.'

Sir Langton who had got Gerard into an armchair and was drawing up a gilded upright chair from the writing desk to sit close to him, looked up and said, 'Let her go. She is right. This is between him and me.'

Olivia snatched a glance at Lady Kirby's woebegone face at this exclusion of her too and then gladly made her escape.

She sat in the pretty green bedchamber, gazing out of the widow at the square where she noticed the paving stones were becoming darkened by spots of rain. The few pedestrians put up their umbrellas and hurried forward.

She thought about her father's letter. She told herself, all this could be irrelevant to me from now on. In a few days I may be heading off to Surrey and a new chapter in my life. I may read in the newspapers of the bankruptcy of the Kirbys of Yorkshire, if that is indeed what it will come to and I will never know the fate of those whose livelihood depends on the Castle. This did indeed give her a sharp pang of sorrow. What would happen to the Todds? Perhaps gardeners would find work elsewhere or be kept on by the new owners of the castle but what would be the fate of Luke? She thought of him with tenderness and a strange yearning. She recalled how they had sat on Meg Summers' bench in the sunshine and he had declaimed the speech of Henry the Fifth, 'Upon the King . .' and a crowd of villagers had gathered.

I was so happy then, she thought. Now I'm looking into a blank future. I know nothing of these Anstons – and then she recollected with a hollow laugh that they too had an officer son who had no doubt had his portrait painted in his regimentals. Father will be looking to marry me off to him. So have I utterly abandoned Gerard Kirby? Or could this be the turning point in the moulding of his character? If I throw him over will Lady Kirby think I am deserting their sinking ship? She spoke of me as one of the family.

There came a hesitant tap on her door and she realised she was quite cold and stiff with sitting by the window. The rain had cooled the air and there was no fire in the hearth.

She called, 'Come in' and rose to greet Lady Kirby, who held out both her hands and clasped hers.

'Oh my dear, you are cold. I should have had a fire lit here but of course I didn't know – we couldn't any of us have imagined what would happen. Pray come down to the drawing-room and I'll order some fresh tea.'

'What is –? Who is –?'

'Gerard has gone to bed. I've given him a dose of my sleeping powder.' They began to walk down the stairs when she added to Olivia's relief, 'Sir Langton has gone to the study to work things out. We're not sure yet quite how bad it is but of course we'll have to give up renting this house after the week.' She summoned the maid and ordered more tea. Then she closed the drawing-room door on them, drew Olivia to the sofa nearest to the fire and sat beside her, keeping hold of her hand and stroking it gently on her lap.

'It may all be very bad, I can't tell, but oh, Olivia, it is wonderful to have Gerard so contrite and submissive to his father. This repentance and all the good resolutions he promises will make him the man you can truly love. He says he will work at anything. He would go back in the army but we couldn't purchase another commission at present. Of course Sir Langton says you are released from any engagement you feel you contracted to Gerard –'

'It isn't the wealth or position –' Olivia began and then wondered if that were true. Had she not longed to be mistress of Castle Kirby? Would she want to share a garret with Gerard?

'Ah, I knew you would say that. I told Sir Langton you were not a grasping person, but a romantic, a true lover. Gerard's cry before he fell at last into a deep sleep was 'I have lost Olivia' and I tried to tell him you would stand by him for better or worse, richer or poorer but he was too far gone in his grief and self-reproach.'

'Lady Kirby, I am not *married* to him. If I had indeed taken those vows I would certainly keep them.'

Lady Kirby looked at her with widening eyes, slowly absorbing this.

'Oh but if you throw him over you will break his heart!' Then she dropped Olivia's hand and clasped her own over her mouth. 'No no, I mustn't say that. How can I blame you! Everything has changed.' And she began to weep.

Olivia drew a deep sigh. 'Please, Lady Kirby, let me explain things to you. Everything is changing for me too,' and she told her about the letter from her father and how she was shortly expected to go with him to Surrey.

Lady Kirby seemed to find difficulty in taking it in at first but when she had grasped it she said sadly, 'Ah I see how it is, we are going down and you are going up. I'm glad for you, dear.'

'But I don't want to go to Surrey. I don't know these people.'

'Then stay with me. Come back to Yorkshire with us and we will all see it through together.'

The idea was attractive but Olivia was a practical young woman. She was not familiar with financial ruin on a large scale though she understood only too well the difficulties her father had so recently faced, but this of the Kirbys could involve courts and litigation that she knew nothing about. If they found themselves without a home how could they entertain her?

'Please, Lady Kirby, I am very sad and confused and really only wish for the chance to consult with my father. Do you think I might go back to Aldgate now and await his return?'

Lady Kirby got up at once to ring the bell. How used she is to all the devices in the best houses! Will she ever become accustomed to a different sort of life, Olivia wondered.

Lady Kirby had her hand on the tasselled rope. 'I'll order the carriage for you.' But she was hesitating. 'Oh, my dear, if I let you go now I fear we will never see you again. Of course your father will not allow you to have anything more to do with us.'

Olivia couldn't imagine what his feelings would be. He had desperately wanted the match but now . . . She said cautiously, 'Lady Kirby, he – and I of course – will very much want to know how Mr Gerard is. I would stay to speak with him but he must rest now. I can send our man, William, for news in the morning.'

'Oh don't trouble with that. I shall write you a note tomorrow. And now I do believe you still love our boy, deep down. Did not our Lord's parable of the prodigal son show his compassion for the repentant sinner? And though the story doesn't say so I'm certain the boy never gave *his* father any more trouble. I discern Sir Langton now in this forgiving role. He too seems to be a new man although of course he is desperately weighed down by the size of Gerard's debts.' Now she did pull the bell, the carriage was ordered and Olivia left without seeing Sir Langton.

At home she felt it would be unfair to betray to servants any hint of the disaster that had taken place so she ate a simple supper with William and Jenny and told them that Mr Beattie was sure of work for this family in Surrey and was likely to be home soon to make arrangements to go there for a while.

'Ooh Miss Olivia, will he take you? What will happen to us?'

'Let's await his coming, Jenny.'

They didn't have long to wait because Gideon Beattie arrived the next afternoon, brimming with cheerfulness. Minutes after his arrival the Kirby groom on horseback brought Lady Kirby's note. While her father was in his room washing and changing his coat after his journey Olivia read it. It said simply, 'Gerard slept right through till an hour ago and has now eaten a very late breakfast and put on clean linen and his blue coat and embroidered waistcoat in which he looks his handsome self again. He is asking desperately for his Olivia and blames me for letting you go. He is still abject about his behaviour and longs to tell you so. Please pen a little note that you will come tomorrow and we will send the carriage at eleven. Sir Langton is in the City seeing his banker. S.K.'

The groom said he would wait for an answer so Olivia ran upstairs to her father. It wasn't how she wanted to tell him all that had happened in his absence but she tumbled it out as best she could and showed him the letter.

'So he's been a bad boy at the gambling again, has he?'

'But should I go tomorrow? Do you want me to finish with him?'

'Hang it, a baronet is still a baronet. If the family are agreeable now so much the better. We'll both go tomorrow. Of course I should pay my respects to them. Tell her ladyship so.'

So Olivia, hardly imagining where all this would lead, wrote below Lady Kirby's letter. 'My father has just returned and he asks me to say he would like to come and pay his respects to you and Sir Langton and we are both very honoured and grateful that you will kindly send your carriage at eleven. O.B.' She handed this to the groom and he rode away with it.

When it had gone she was seized with grave doubts. Had her father taken in how great was the calamity that seemed to have befallen the Kirbys?

Jenny had put together a dinner of broth and beef with a salad and Olivia who had been eating her meals with her and William in the kitchen told her she and her father had much to talk about and would eat in the little dining-room in the front, though it was a dark, cramped little room and had no fire.

'You don't need to explain your actions to the servants,' her father said as they sat down. 'And we don't need a fire in August. We'll soon be finished with this place, thank God. You should see Anston Manor, Olivia. Well, you will see it soon. The place is dripping money. He's bought up more land round about and that's why he wants a bigger house, twice as big!'

'But how am I to keep in with the Kirbys as you seem to want me to and yet come to Surrey with you?'

'There's no difficulty with that. If you're still to marry Gerard it wouldn't be for a year or two. By then they'll be back on their feet and I'll be able to afford a reasonable dowry that won't put us to shame in allying ourselves with titled people.'

'But Papa, don't you see. Gerard spoke of having *ruined* his father.'

Gideon Beattie shook his head and laughed. 'These big landowners are never ruined. They have their rents coming in regularly and their harvests and the timber in their woods and everyone is happy to give them credit. There is always something they can sell. I wager Lady Kirby has jewels worth ten times what your mother had. And they tided us over nicely though it hurt me to have to part with them.'

Yes, thought Olivia, you were weeping as Sir Langton and his lady are weeping. How quickly you have forgotten the depths of despair you were in! And she wondered if the baronet would even consent to see her father after the way he parted from him at Castle Kirby. She hoped there was no unworthy motive in her father's wish to pay his respects to him. Was it to rub his nose in their change of fortunes?

She blurted out, 'Papa, I do trust you are not going to *crow* over Sir Langton tomorrow. He's a man in great distress.'

'Crow! I wouldn't dream of such a thing. I hope I'm enough of a gentleman to refrain from *crowing*. I think he will be feeling it all too much himself – after dismissing me the way he did – and that will give me all the satisfaction I need. I think I will be able to forgive him quite magnanimously then.'

'Oh Papa!' It was good to have him back and in good humour. 'Now tell me all about these Anstons,' she said.

Chapter 18

'This is where we will live one day,' Gideon Beattie said as they drove into the new world of handsome squares. 'You see how it is, the aristocracy can always keep up appearances. The Kirbys will never give up their own carriage for example. They wouldn't know how to live without it.'

'But if I marry Gerard what will you do, Papa? You couldn't live all alone in a big house like one of these?'

'I'll be travelling about a great deal – up to Yorkshire to stay with Sir Gerard and my daughter and grandchildren and to see how beautifully they have completed their castle –'

'Oh don't say that, Papa. I can't think it will ever happen. Let us get this meeting over and see what the day brings. I hardly know what I wish for but I do know I was not very comfortable when you were away.'

'That's my girl,' said her father. 'The carriage is stopping. Here we are.'

Olivia was thankful that the presence of her father kept all emotions under cover. It was hard to believe it was the same family of two days before.

They were shown into the drawing-room where Sir Langton, very stiff and formal, greeted them first. Then Lady Kirby appeared and gave Gideon her hand very graciously. Finally Gerard strolled in, his shirt cuffs and ruffles immaculate, his jacket buttons gleaming, his eyes bright, his mouth smiling.

Olivia struggled to recall what he had looked like so recently. He was so handsome again. Her stomach seemed to turn over at the sight of him. He shook Gideon Beattie by the hand and inquired after his visit to Surrey. On learning of his success there he looked at his father and Olivia detected a triumphant grin.

'Well, Mr Beattie, I asked for your daughter's hand some while ago and you were pleased to consent if my father was agreeable. I think I can assure you that he is now.'

Sir Langton, still outwardly calm, said softly, 'Gerard, you are in no position to marry. If you ever are I would not object to Miss Beattie. I have come to admire her good sense.'

'Oh she is the dearest girl,' cried Lady Kirby.

Sir Langton then proposed a stroll in St James' Park before a light repast as the day was very fine and warm. Gideon Beattie got up at once while Gerard hung back to let the older generation go ahead. Then he took Olivia's arm and sauntered out with her as if nothing had changed since their strolls of a few days ago.

'You seem very much recovered, sir,' she said.

'Oh come on, Olivia, sir, to me? I know I was in a pretty pickle the other night and I'm sorry you saw me like that. All I needed was a good night's sleep.'

'I wasn't at all sorry to see you in a repentant mood and full of good resolutions.'

'Hang it, I still am. Turning over new leaves and all that sort of thing. But you've got to see that none of it would have happened if the old man had stumped up the thirty guineas for Emperor I'll not rest till I get that horse back.'

She pulled her arm from his on the excuse of putting up her parasol. 'How can you still speak of spending money,' she hissed, 'when you can never repay your father for the sacrifices he will have to make for your folly?'

'Now you're not going to start scolding again, are you? The old man saw his bankers and they'll give him credit. He might have to sell timber or something of that sort which he doesn't like. Every square inch of that estate is to be kept perfect as he always says. Who for, I ask you? For me, when I don't care if he sells a few acres to get me out of Queer Street. All right, all right, don't purse those lips at me. I've learnt my lesson about gambling. It's a fool's game – though it's deuced cosy when a fellow's winning.'

'What are you going to do now to earn your living?'

'Earn my living? The old man wants to keep me at home – you heard him – be the country squire. Perhaps enter parliament, though he made me sit through one debate when I was younger and it was devilish tedious.'

'So how will you ever pay him back?'

'By being a good boy. How else? Why the interrogation? You'll be pretty snug as my lady when the old girl goes. Till then, well we don't have to live at the castle. We'll keep a house in London when we're married. I daresay it won't be for a year or two –'

'It won't ever be, Gerard. I don't want to marry you.'

It was out, impulsively as ever, as she was already groaning to herself. But it's true, it's true. I can't love such a man for the rest of my life – whatever they are all saying to each other over there.

Her father and the Kirbys had crossed the roadway before the park and looked back to see where the young couple had got to. But I am not to be coupled to him, she reiterated in her heart. Why did I let it get to this point? Why did I not tell my father at once that it was over? Why did I let my pity for Lady Kirby weaken my judgment? I knew he was no true prodigal son. He has proved it now. He is shallow, unworthy of the love I have to give. I can't respect him.

He had stood stock still and faced her. 'You can't mean that. We're engaged. You're mine.' He seized her by her arms. 'Damn it, both families are agreed. What are you saying? I lost Emperor. I'm not going to lose you. Mind, I shall get Emperor back one way or another. You see if I don't. But you –! Look here, Olivia, you pledged yourself to me in the small copse. You said you loved me. You can't go back on that. I won't let you.'

Olivia saw that her father and the Kirbys had turned round at the entrance to the park and were waving to them. The roadway between was busy with open carriages and gentlemen and ladies on horseback so they must wait for a gap.

After what she had said she was in no hurry to cross. She could see the consequences beginning to swell into a great cloud of tears and recriminations and accusations. Gerard would go headlong downhill again and it would be all her fault.

She wanted to turn tail and run but there was nowhere now to run. Castle Kirby would be for ever out of bounds and the thought made her quite sick.

In answer to his outburst she could only shake her head. She made a helpless gesture towards the others waiting by the park.

'They can wait,' he said. 'We're not joining them till I get this straight.'

Then all of a sudden his eyes focused on something along the street behind her. They blazed with excitement. 'My God, it is, it's Emperor! Emperor!' His voice roared. 'Emperor!'

'Where?' She turned and heard the hooves at the same time. It was the sound of galloping. People began shouting. The rider was obviously not in control.

'It's Peregrine!' Gerard yelled. 'The fool! He can't manage him.' He thrust Olivia aside and dashed into the street.

'Gerard!' she shrieked. 'Look out!'

A two-horse carriage was bowling briskly along when the driver suddenly became aware of the bolting horse and the man running to catch its rein. There was a melee of clattering wheels and hooves and screams from the ladies in the carriage. Emperor reared up, Peregrine was thrown and his plump body landed in the carriage on the ladies' laps. More vehicles were brought to a screeching halt as their wheels locked with those of swerving carriages from the other direction.

A pandemonium followed of frightened neighs, shouts and flailing hooves as horses rose on their hind legs. Only one beast quietened as its nose nuzzled something motionless on the ground. Emperor had found his master.

Olivia froze to the spot. She daren't go in among the horses' legs but she saw her father and Sir Langton desperately trying to approach from the other side. Lady Kirby appeared to have fainted away and was being supported among a group of onlookers. Grooms were dismounting now and calming their animals and a Constable appeared and tried to take charge with a barrage of orders.

'Clear a way through there. You, move your carriage forward. You there, pull in to the side. There's a gentleman hurt. Watch what you're doing or you'll draw your wheels over him.'

Soon Olivia could see nothing as a small crowd had gathered around the thing that must be the inert figure of Gerard. She still couldn't move. An explosion seemed to be going on in her head. Did I cause this? Is he dead? What will I do if he lives? His father and mother will blame me whether he lives or dies. I refused him and he killed himself. No, he wanted Emperor. He always wanted Emperor more than me.

'Miss Beattie!'

The tousled figure of Sir Peregrine Grant was at her side. How had he got there? She turned to stare at his white face and horrified eyes.

'If only he hadn't yelled his name,' he choked out. 'I was sitting him well till that minute. Hang it all, I only bought him this morning. I knew how much it mattered to Gerard. I was on my way with him. Oh God, Miss Beattie, if he's dead what will they do to me? What can I say to you? What can I say to his parents?'

Olivia was watching the crowd in the middle. Traffic was

stationary in both directions. The constable was turning some of the carriages into the surrounding squares. Then a shout went up that a surgeon had been fetched.

'Make way for the surgeon.' The constable took up the cry, unnecessarily repeating it at the top of his voice.

She turned to Sir Peregrine again. His plump agonised face, the wobbling of his double chin helped to calm her. He was so terrified she had to reassure him. She found her voice and words came out. 'It wasn't your fault. How could anyone blame you? He was mad. He ran straight out without looking. He can't be dead or they wouldn't have fetched a surgeon.'

The surgeon was waving people back and she saw a glimpse of a red stain on Gerard's fawn breeches. Someone called, 'He's speaking. He's not dead.'

They saw the surgeon stand up and look about. 'He's calling for Olivia.'

Oh God! She swayed for a second and Sir Peregrine grabbed at her. She could see her father straighten up and wave frantically for her. Sir Peregrine propelled her forwards towards the group. Now she could see Gerard's upper body. Sir Langton, looking like a grey old man, was supporting his head and shoulders.

She broke into a run and flung herself down beside the body. 'Oh Gerard. I'm here.' There was a gaping wound in his abdomen from which the blood was flowing over his legs. She swallowed back her own heaving stomach.

His eyes opened wide and he smiled. 'Am I done for, Olivia?' he said quite plainly. She looked at the surgeon and he nodded slightly.

'No, you'll live,' she said.

'I will if you love me.'

'I do, I do.'

'Is Emperor dead?'

'No.' She looked about and saw that two men were holding

him with difficulty by the roadside as he pawed the ground. 'He's very much alive.'

'Good. You never saw me ride him, did you? We never had that ride together.' His breath was coming in short gasps now. 'I'll get better. The Frenchies couldn't do for me. You'll see me ride him yet.'

'Yes, I'll see you ride Emperor, Gerard.'

He grimaced, trying to smile. Then all at once his head dropped sideways and she knew he was gone.

Sir Langton gave a howl and dragged him higher into his arms and rocked him. Then there came a shriek from beside the park and Lady Kirby broke from restraining arms and flew to her son. It almost seemed as if the two of them wrestled for the body, Lady Kirby trying to press kisses over the dead face.

Olivia stood up, numb with disbelief. Sir Peregrine's arm was round her and he guided her to the roadside where the surgeon's assistant had a stretcher now in readiness. She stood beside it wondering why time did not go backwards so that this thing could not have happened. She had been speaking to him moments before. It didn't have to go back very far, less than five minutes.

Someone handed a rug out of a carriage and when kindly arms drew the parents aside the body was covered and lifted onto the stretcher.

The Constable was no longer shouting but rapidly asking questions of everyone he could collar. Some had only just arrived but were quite willing to give their opinion. Here was something she could do. She made no effort to follow the dazed parents who were being helped to walk behind the stretcher as it was carried to the house they had so lately left.

Instead she turned to Sir Peregrine and said, 'I'll speak to the Constable. Come with me.'

He seemed to be hesitating, his eyes frightened, but she drew his arm from her waist and tucked her own firmly into it so that he had to accompany her.

'I can tell you it all,' she said in a clear voice to the Constable and she recounted exactly what had happened from the moment Gerard had spied his horse.

In a slow round hand he wrote in his notebook the gentleman's name and his family address in Grosvenor Square. The surgeon was now also standing at his elbow.

'The coroner will wish to see me,' he said. 'There is my card. I am attending the bereaved to their house. They will need attention. And perhaps this young lady?' He looked at Olivia with raised eyebrows. His eyebrows were the largest feature on his face and Olivia took a dislike to them.

'Thank you. I am perfectly well.'

He shook his head in disbelief and followed the stretcher.

The Constable pocketed the card and resumed his painstaking writing of what Olivia had told him.

'So you was the gentleman riding the horse?' he said to Sir Peregrine. 'I reckon you was in charge of a beast what was out of control on a public highway.'

Olivia said patiently, 'I have explained already that it was all the deceased's fault. He used to own the horse and shouted its name very loudly. That startled it.'

'Very well, Ma'am. I think I've got it all. You'll be hearing from us, sir, Ma'am, if you're wanted at the inquest. Are you taking charge of the horse, sir? 'Cos it can't be left loose on the street.'

Sir Peregrine said he would pay the two men who still held him to take him to the nearest inn stables.

'I can't think Sir Langton will have stabling at his house for more than his carriage horses. *I* don't want the beast, that's certain. I'll have to ask him later what I'm to do with him. Let me escort you there now but I shan't come in myself. I confess

I'm all shaken up. Gerard was a good friend. I must say, Miss Beattie, I admire your fortitude. You were a wonder the way you dealt with that constable and I'm very grateful.'

Olivia said nothing more as they walked the few hundred yards to the house.

She was living on the edge of a collapse that would surely come. All she wanted was to be alone in the little green bedroom.

That seclusion was not to happen. The servant showed her at once into the drawing-room saying that the master and mistress were worried that she had been crushed in the crowd.

Her father was sitting there, looking very uncomfortable, but there was no sign of Sir Langton. Lady Kirby jumped up and ran into her arms.

'Oh my dear, you're safe. I thought we had lost you too. Sir Langton is utterly prostrated. The surgeon wants to find out just how our poor darling died but he won't let him near. He's just sitting by Gerard, talking to him, telling him all his hopes and fears for him and then repeating 'Punished, punished' over and over again. I can't comfort him. I've never seen him like this.'

Olivia sank on to the sofa with her. 'Let him be. Let him work his grief out that way.'

'But should I send for a parson? A man of the cloth would surely tell him that this tragedy has not befallen our poor boy because of petty sins like gambling. God is not so cruel. Oh I know there must be a Day of Judgment. I don't understand it all but I don't like to hear him repeating 'punished' like that all the time.'

No, Olivia thought, it's not Gerard he means, it's himself, but she didn't say it aloud. Is it part of the dark mystery or is it because he made a god of the boy, having already lost two children, and now he knows he created a hollow man, for that's what he was and I am not grieving, horrible as his end was. I am cold and dead inside and I must be a beast without feeling.

She put her arms round Lady Kirby, whose tears had been flowing all this time. I do feel sorrow for her because she is selfless. She is thinking more of her husband's grief than her own.

Lady Kirby responded with a loving hug. 'And you, my child? What of you? You have lost your promised husband. That is a terrible thing and you so young. All your hopes dashed, your love snatched away.'

Now Olivia did weep, not for the lost love but for the absence of love. I lied to him in his dying moments. My love, such as it was, had been struggling for a long time against my better judgment and this morning it died completely. And I told him and then *he* died. She was still haunted by the sense that there was a connection between the two happenings. And to have Lady Kirby commiserating with her made her feel a deep-dyed hypocrite. But she couldn't tell her what she had told him. Maybe it was something she would never tell.

The surgeon tapped at the drawing-room door and came in.

'Forgive the intrusion, Lady Kirby. I have managed to get Sir Langton to take a draught – in a cup of chocolate to disguise the taste. It should calm him and he may sleep. I am now able to make a report to the coroner and I've sent for a very good discreet woman from the undertaker's who will lay out the body. As I understand you are from home at present you will no doubt wish the funeral to be at your own church. Arrangements can be made very quietly and privately for the conveyance – you understand. The suddenness of all this has I am sure left you yourself prostrated, also the young lady who I believe was the affianced of the unfortunate young man.' His eyebrows worked vigorously in Olivia's direction. 'If you will permit me to suggest that you both take some of this preparation and retire to bed.' He handed a bottle to Gideon Beattie. 'Perhaps, sir, you will see that it is not left lying about. Two tablespoonfuls in water or any other drink – not alcohol – is sufficient. An excess would be harmful.'

Olivia saw her father take it warily and the surgeon bowed himself out.

Lady Kirby rose. 'I must go to Sir Langton and if he sleeps I will watch over him so I think I will forbear to take this medicine, but do you, dear child. I really have no notion what time of day it is. Pray ring for tea, Mr Beattie, or any refreshment you wish.'

Now her father did seem galvanised into activity. 'You are too kind, Lady Kirby, but under the dreadful circumstances I feel I should not intrude on your hospitality any longer. Business will call me very soon into Surrey and I have matters to attend to. Olivia, I hope you will feel able to accompany me.'

Lady Kirby who had been hesitating at the door came back anxiously into the room. 'Oh Mr Beattie, pray do not take your daughter away. I couldn't bear to part with her. She is my only consolation. I look on her as a daughter. She is indeed the daughter I was so eager to welcome into our family. Pray spare her to me for a while. We will have to go back to Yorkshire when arrangements can be made and I beg you to let her accompany me.'

Olivia met her father's eyes. The prospect of going to Castle Kirby without the danger of having to marry Gerard was suddenly intensely alluring. She would go as friend and comforter to Lady Kirby and no longer in fear or awe of Sir Langton. Oh yes and she would see her friends, her Shakespearean companions, and excitingly, Meg Summers so that she could uncover the secret hidden in Mrs Johnson's Bible.

'Would you mind, Papa?' she said, simply.

He looked disconcerted and flustered. 'Why no, my dear. You know how much I feel for you in this awful thing that's happened. It's right, with the connection that had developed between you and – of course you must be at his funeral. What will we do about poor little Jenny? William I can take with me to Surrey.'

'Oh but you will bring your maid of course,' Lady Kirby cried. 'She is a sweet little thing. Then it is settled. May God bless you, Mr Beattie.' And she burst into a flood of tears again and rushed from the room.

Father and daughter stood looking at each other for a full minute.

Then he shook his head and held out the medicine bottle. 'You don't look prostrated, but take this if you wish.'

'Not for me, Papa, thank you, but I'll take it for Lady Kirby. She may need it to help her sleep tonight.' She peeped out of the door. 'I think she has gone first to the room where they have laid – I can hear her wailing. I must go to her.'

'Practical matters first, my love. I had better not ask for the carriage but I can call a hackney coach to see me home. Now it would be senseless expense not to send Jenny back with your trunks and her own things so she can be with you here. That will save you the trouble of coming back another day when Lady Kirby feels she can spare you for a few hours. Then I can arrange to give up the house and betake myself and William to Surrey as soon as possible. If you should find the Kirbys are indeed bankrupted when they have paid off that wretched boy's debts and all the arrangements for the funeral you'll have to come to me in Surrey. To be honest with you, Olivia, with their financial troubles you are well out of that marriage and I didn't feel you were as devoted to him as he wanted to think.'

She shook her head wordlessly, her lips beginning to quiver.

'There, my precious. You are only nineteen. There are many better fish in the sea. The Anstons have a fine son in the army. I've seen his picture.'

Now she broke into hysterical laughter. 'Don't, pray, don't even think of such a thing. No, you are right I had lost my love for Gerard. I lied to him as he died. Was that terrible?'

'Of course not. I hoped you would say what you did. He died happy.'

'Oh, Papa, that comforts me. Thank you. And believe me, dearest Papa, I shan't bestow my love again till I find a man of truth and nobility of soul. No title, no looks, no money even. Your little girl is growing up.'

'I see that.' He had tears in his eyes too. Then he smiled. 'I'm not so sure about the 'no money' though. We have had our own shock and just because things are looking up it doesn't mean I can give you much at present. I have a few of your mother's rings left and hoped to keep one for you on your marriage. I'll see what I can get at the pawn shop and send something for you by Jenny. Then maybe I can redeem them when I am in funds. I must have enough to buy more drawing materials and for the coach fare into Surrey. But I will write and send a banker's draft when Mr Anston has advanced me an initial payment. I can't have you dependent on these shaky Kirbys.'

It came home to her then that she was indeed embarking in a leaky boat to an uncertain destination and she might not see her father for a long time. She clung to him desperately then till at last she remembered Lady Kirby and tore herself away.

'You'll send Jenny before nightfall.'

'Why yes,' he smiled. 'It's only two in the afternoon. And despite all that's happened I am feeling very empty. God bless you, my darling one. I shall miss you.' And he hurried away down the stairs.

Olivia saw him let himself out without troubling to get the footman to call a hackney. She knew he was crying.

She wiped her own eyes and went to find Lady Kirby. Time was not going to go back. The ghastly thing had happened and if she was not to sink under the horrible images in her own head there was nothing else for her to do but help others to face it.

Chapter 18

One of Mr Braintree's men looked over the wall at Thomas indefatigably planting thorn bushes.

'They'll all come out, man, and the wall too. If Kirby's fool enough to leave the coal in the ground his son won't. Mark my words, in ten years there'll be a road through here and your coal will travel on it to our canal and the sea. There'll be laden barges every day. We're going deeper already. There's tons of the stuff in the ground. You're wasting your time, man.'

Thomas just grinned and thrust in his spade for the next hole. He knew it was true. He knew Braintree's men had plenty of their own work to do and were not likely to come over again now they had established that Kirby coal was the same quality as theirs. But Sir Langton had said plant so he was planting. He trampled round the spiky plant with his great boots. The ground was drier than he could have wished but his father who had an eye for the weather had looked at the sky at first light and said, 'Ay, rain by noon.'

Already clouds were massing in the west. He worked on, his mind sometimes engaged only on the depths of the next hole and sometimes wandering to London to picture Olivia Beattie and what she could be doing now. There had been no word since Sir Langton and Lady Kirby had left but he wanted the job finished before their return. If Sir Langton was so relieved to find his son that he consented to his marriage to Olivia she might come back with them all. He would be happy to see her at a distance but he would never again betray himself as he had to her that Sunday on the field path. It made him hot and uncomfortable to think of it.

When the rain began at noon he just pulled his hat lower over his face and worked on till all the bushes he had gathered were in. Then he shouldered his spade and strode the mile back to the Castle.

The first thing he noticed was that the flag with the Kirby arms was flying at half mast. Good God, had Sir Langton died? Then his morning had indeed been wasted. Gerard would ring every penny out of the land's resources. That was certain.

Not seeing his father in the kitchen garden or glasshouse he made for the door where Luke's ramp went in and yanked off his boots. Voices and wailing sounds were coming from the kitchen. He ran down the stone steps and put his head round the door. Even his father, who rarely mingled with the other servants, was there. Cook had her apron over her face and was howling. The maids had taken their cue from her and were sniffling. Then he saw Sir Langton's groom who had accompanied them to London, seated at the table, his livery white with road dust and a mug of ale in front of him, looking a little smug at the sensation he had produced.

'Is the master dead?' Thomas demanded. He knew his father had charge of the flag and was a stickler for protocol. The last time he had rushed to put it at half mast was in October the year before at the death of George the Second. He wouldn't fly it like that for anyone.

A chorus of voices yelled at him. 'Mr Gerard!'

Gerard! Olivia's dream snatched from her!

He didn't need to ask how it had happened. Everyone began to tell him at once.

The groom silenced them imperiously. 'I'll tell him. I was there.'

He launched into a tale of Mr Gerard gallantly trying to catch Emperor who was galloping down the middle of the street threatening life and limb, crowds scrambling out of the way, carriages swerving in all directions and how the poor man had been knocked down himself and died in his father's arms with the young lady sobbing out her love for him and his poor mother fainting away on the pavement.

'Does Luke know about all this?' Thomas asked.

Cook pulled down her apron to answer. 'Oh he came to the steps to hear what was going on but he was so upset he's gone back again. He's a tender-hearted lad is Luke. I keep breaking out too. I can't help it. I've watched Master Gerard from babyhood. Such a fine boy and the Frenchies had a go at him and we thought he'd gone then. And now to quit the army and get crushed on a London street!' And up went her apron and off she went again.

'He was so handsome,' sniffed little Betsy.

Another of the maids said, 'And there's even Mrs sour-puss Chorley sobbing in the housekeeper's room.'

Sick of the noise Thomas helped himself to a mug of ale and took it into Luke's room.

He found his brother sitting in his wheelchair, white-faced, arms flopped by his sides. He looked up and shook his head at Thomas.

'Oh Tom, I can't bear to think how she must be suffering.'

'Ay, it's bad indeed. I wonder who the heir is now.'

'I can't think of anything but her sorrow.'

'Sir Langton's brother who was killed in a sea battle had no family.'

'We'll never see her again, will we?'

'No, it's not likely.'

'She made our Shakespeare reading so much livelier.'

'We'll have to have another soon and do the best we can on our own.'

'Tom, you don't seem to mind very much.'

'I don't always say all I feel.'

'I'm sorry, Tom. I know that.'

Then Tom sat down and said gravely, 'I think we'll find the master and mistress in worse fettle. They worshipped the ground Gerard walked on, but she – Olivia – I believe she had more sense.'

'Oh Tom, you didn't like Gerard much.'

'There was nothing much to like or dislike.'

'Don't speak ill of the dead.'

'You and I can be honest with each other. He wasn't worthy of her.'

'There I agree but Robert said how she saw him die in the street and was telling him how she loved him. That's what I keep seeing in my head. What a horrible experience for a young girl! She *must* have loved him.'

'We'll never know. Don't dream about it.' Tom gave him a friendly pat on the shoulder. Even to Luke he couldn't express the myriad thoughts that were jostling in his head.

He had declared his love to Olivia and now she was free. But their paths would diverge far away now. The Kirbys could die out as a family. The castle to which he had been attached all his life and from which he had hardly had a day's absence could fall into other hands. He recalled his grandmother saying 'Sir Langton was desperate for an heir. Lady Sophia was a poor thing and produced only dead babies. Then they got Gerard. There's no other Kirbys if his brother don't marry. So he takes good care of Gerard, don't 'e?' Then she would give her long cackling laugh. And now she and Gerard were both gone.

Betsy tapped at the door and peeped in. 'Please Mr Tom, your father says he needs you in the glasshouse.'

'Very well. I'll look in later, Luke. Don't brood on it too much.'

When he found his father they looked at each other and Thomas said, 'Bad business.'

'Ay. But I did the flag.'

'I saw that.'

Then they worked side by side for three hours and said nothing more.

Next day Mrs Chorley called all the servants into the kitchen, a most unusual procedure underlining the gravity of the news. She rarely condescended to come amongst them in that way. Now she stood on an upturned apple box, her cap adorned with black ribbons which bobbed as she spoke. She was holding in her hand the letter from Lady Kirby which Robert the groom had brought.

'It's quite blotted with her tears,' she said in a rare burst of confidence, tapping the letter, 'so as I could hardly read the words in places. She says Sir Langton is too prostrated to give any orders but they will be bringing the poor young master in a few days to be buried in Tadby in the Kirby tomb. I've called you together because it looks as if we'll have to do what we can without orders. I sent word to the parson but we can't know the time till they're safely here. I reckon poor Lady Kirby don't know what to do or can't be thinking of it yet. But *I* know and many of you will too how things were done when the master's brother died and was brought here to be buried. We can't send out the invitations to the gentry but we can order black broadcloth coats and crepe hatbands for any men here that hasn't still got theirs from Captain Kirby's funeral. And every woman and girl should have a black shawl. So go to Elsie anyone as needs something and she'll make the arrangements.' She pointed to the seamstress.

Then her eyes wondered over the solemn array and picked out

Cook. 'Look to the larder if you please, Cook, and see there's joints enough hung and flour and butter and sugar for cakes and sweetmeats for it'll be a big funeral. Order what more you think you need from town.'

Thomas saw her eyes coming in his direction. His father was standing beside him, arms folded on his chest and his brows locked in an impatient frown. He was only happy when his hands were busy.

'Albert and Thomas,' said Mrs Chorley. 'If there are not vegetables and salads a plenty in the kitchen garden we'll need to order more from the market. And have you a good bed of rosemary because everyone will need a sprig?'

Albert growled. 'Ay, I'll see to it.'

Mrs Chorley went on – and how she's loving this, Thomas thought – 'Now, Susan and Lily and Betsy you can get to work at once because the bedrooms can be got ready straight away and the one order m'lady *did* give was it's the best guest room for Miss Beattie who comes with them.'

Thomas felt a quiver of delight run through him but he moved not a muscle when Luke looked up at him from his wheelchair which had been carried down the steps so he could take part. Luke's eyes had lit with a joy he couldn't conceal but it was tempered with anxious concern.

Thomas pressed his hand briefly on his shoulder as Mrs Chorley wound up her address with an exhortation to have the whole place spic and span with black ribbons on all Mr Gerard's portraits and on the armorial bearings on the iron gates to the drive.

'The workmen in the west wing,' she added, 'will have to be sent home till after the funeral. We can't have knocking and banging going on. So the courtyard dust can be dampened down and then swept clean.' She climbed off the apple box murmuring, 'Eh dear, that things should come to this.'

A way was made for her to pass through and with great dignity she returned to her room.

Thomas was trimming the edges of the lower lawn three days later when he heard the horn blown for the gates and then the wheels on the drive. He laid down his shears and snatched off his hat and stood to attention as the carriage passed. The curtains were drawn so he couldn't see inside but he felt acutely the desolation of the occupants in the darkened interior.

It had been decided that all the servants should be lined up silently in the hall to greet the master and mistress so he ran by the footpath round the west wing to the back and through into the entrance hall, to take his place.

The sight of Sir Langton was a shock. His shoulders were bowed and his head down so that it was nearly impossible to glimpse his haggard face. Uprightness and a precise neat walk had always been his distinguishing characteristic. Now he seemed hardly able to shuffle one foot in front of another.

Lady Kirby on the other hand carried herself with dignity though her face was dreadfully pallid and her eyes sunken. And there was Olivia, starkly beautiful in black from head to foot, trying he felt not to look among the familiar faces but concentrate on supporting Lady Kirby towards the stairs.

At the foot, as Sir Langton, like one in a trance, began to mount slowly, Lady Kirby turned and gazed round at the silent crowd. She waved her hand and spoke out in a shrill tone, 'Thank you all.'

There was bowing and curtseying in response and Cook 'broke out' noisily again and had to retreat to the kitchen.

Thomas wheeled Luke back into his room.

'I didn't feel confident that I could balance for long on my crutches,' Luke murmured. Then he looked up at Tom. 'The Master is a broken man.'

'I knew it. A brittle stick soon snaps. M'lady has found a new strength from his weakness.'

'But Olivia! Black is harsh and unforgiving for one so young. Yet could you not feel her vibrant soul within?'

'Nay, if you are going to wax poetic I shall leave you.'

Luke was right though. Olivia had a speaking countenance however hard she tried to conceal her feelings and Thomas was certain that she was thrilled to be back despite the circumstances. Her colour was high and her eyes very much alive.

'Don't go,' Luke said.

'I left my shears by the path.'

'Fetch them and come back.'

'I'll finish the job first.'

He did return, half an hour later, and had been sitting with Luke barely five minutes when there was a knock at the door, not Betsy's diffident tap, but a single clear confident knock. Thomas met Luke's eyes as a flame of hope leapt in his heart.

Luke called, 'Come in!' with the same eagerness and she was there before them, her face radiant, her eyes sparkling with tears, her hands outstretched.

'Miss Beattie!' they said simultaneously and Luke, pressing on the arms of his chair, struggled to rise.

'Oh please,' she cried, 'Olivia. We are friends. It's so good to see you both.' And she took their hands in turn and pressed them.

They both began to express their sympathy but she cut them short.

'No, pray do not. It has all been very dreadful and the images will never go away. They come into my sleep so that I wake up in horror but to you two – because we have had such inspiring times together – I can be honest. I had refused Gerard finally only minutes before it happened. There,' she sank into the armchair she had always used. 'It is such a relief to say it because

224

I dare not tell Lady Kirby and I can't tell Sir Langton because he is taking nothing in at all. Not that I would. He would blame me I expect for – for – what followed. I have blamed myself but I do not truly believe it would have made any difference.'

Thomas felt a spurt of triumph that he had rightly predicted her feelings for Gerard. He tried to catch Luke's eye but he was saying earnestly, 'We understand Gerard was heroically trying to save people in the street from a runaway Emperor.'

Olivia shook her head. 'There was nothing heroic about it. He had one thought – to get his horse back which he had foolishly gambled away. But if that is the tale let it stand. Lady Kirby may take comfort if everyone believes it was a gallant end.'

Thomas asked then, 'Your father is not with you. I suppose you will be returning to him after the funeral?'

She told them then about his new work and how they had no home at present.

'I am here as Lady Kirby's companion for as long as she needs me.' Then she said, 'Has word reached the Castle about Gerard's debts?'

'No,' Thomas said, 'but surely all these young bucks have debts.'

'Not on this scale. Sir Langton will have to mortgage half his property. It may be even worse than that with the expense of the funeral added and of course the west wing improvements.'

Thomas and Luke looked at each other. 'Is that what has broken him so?' Thomas asked.

'No, he knew of it before – before the accident. He went to see his banker Lady Kirby told me, so he was capable then of rational action. Indeed he was so overjoyed at Gerard's contrition and protestations of a new beginning that he seemed to be bearing the financial shock remarkably well. No, it has been since the death, but it seems more than ordinary grief. He mutters things. He strikes himself on the breast. He can't listen to anything said to him. He waves away requests for decisions. Lady Kirby is having to shoulder all the responsibilities. I think that's why she has not fallen completely under the shock. Mrs Chorley is with her now for orders about the funeral. It's so strange to hear her say, 'We can't trouble Sir Langton.' I don't believe she has ever said such a thing in her life before.'

'I'm sure she hasn't,' Tom said. 'She never did anything without his approval. She was terrified of him.'

'Oh Tom, terrified?' Luke said. 'Surely that is too strong. He's a good man.'

'Not always a sensible one. He wouldn't listen about the coal seams.'

'Coal seams?' Olivia echoed, with a puzzled smile and her head charmingly on one side.

'Ah, yes. Lady Kirby has not told you?' Luke said. 'I think she hardly understood it at the time and this awful thing will have quite put it out of her mind. We have coal at Castle Kirby. It could save the place from the bank's clutches.'

'Save it for whom?' Thomas said as the thought struck him. 'Sir Langton has always been fervent about his heritage and passing it on in a state of perfection. But now – there is no heir. And we believe the title will die with him. This will certainly have compounded his sorrow.'

Olivia nodded and rose. 'Lady Kirby may wonder where I am. I left Jenny unpacking my things. I have been given the best guest room.'

'And you should not be down here talking with the gardener's sons,' Thomas said. He knew her well enough to be sure she had no such thought but he couldn't help saying it. It was certainly what the world would say and his heart felt bitter. *I am her equal as one being to another but it can never be.*

She was looking at him reproachfully. 'Oh Tom!' She used the familiar name. 'I hope we will have many happy Shakespeare readings as the nights draw in when all this sorrow is beginning to fade.'

Luke turned a joyful face to her. And then she seemed to recollect something.

'Your poor Grandmother! I have forgotten to say how sorry I was to learn of her passing. I wish I had been with her. Do you know if she asked for me?'

Tom shook his head. 'Meg said she never regained consciousness after the last seizure. She looked very peaceful when we all stood round her coffin. They'd laid her with her treasured Bible beneath her hands and she looked a saintly old woman.'

He saw Olivia start. 'She was buried so, with the Bible?' He nodded. 'Very beautiful,' she said quickly. 'I must go now. I may not visit like this till after the funeral but you will understand.'

With a swish of those awful black weeds she was gone.

Chapter 19

So I will never know the mystery! Olivia bit her lip in frustration as she ran up the stairs to the vast room she had been given with its four poster bed, damask hangings, embroidered bedspread and wide view down the lawns to the lake.

Jenny was carefully hanging up her dresses in the wardrobe. 'I've pressed out the creases, Miss Olivia. There's everything we could want in the dressing room, smoothing iron, curling tongs and so many bottles of perfume. Oh Miss, it's so good to be out of that horrible house in Aldgate and I'm a lady's maid again.' She gave a little skip of glee and then checked herself. 'I'm a wicked girl with the poor young gentleman lying in that dreadful black draped room for everyone to go and pay their respects. And all the banisters hung with black. It makes me feel quite odd inside.'

'It won't be for ever,' Olivia said, longing with all her heart for the funeral to be over. How they were to see Sir Langton through it she couldn't imagine.

In the event the worst moment was at the tomb side after the service itself when his eyes seemed to bore into the names of the Kirby ancestors carved into the stone. He began to shout out 'No, no, it can't be.' The Parson seized his arm in fear that he was going to leap into the tomb. His valet stepped forward nimbly and guided him out to the carriage and got in with him and held onto him till the committal was over. He didn't appear at all at the funeral feast which was graced by all the local gentry.

Olivia heard many voices murmuring, 'It's unhinged his mind. Of course it's the end of the Kirbys. The line's died out. They say the poor lady could have no more after Gerard. Sad day for an ancient family.'

When the county families and the parson had eaten their fill the household servants were invited up in their sober black to clear the plates which they did with great success. Olivia saw Luke, using one crutch and the banister rail, dragging himself upstairs. Thomas carried his other crutch so that he could move about.

Olivia immediately pointed him to a chair and fetched him a plate.

'I would never have dared come up,' he confided to her, 'but I was told Sir Langton had been taken to lie down. This is the first time I have been above the ground floor.'

'Have you never resented being so confined, Luke,' she asked him.

'No. It was the natural order of things. What has been strange lately is having Lady Kirby coming to visit me and most extraordinarily to consult with me. She even came yesterday to tell me she had mentioned the coal seams to Sir Langton again and he seemed to understand because he shouted at her, 'Why? What for? There is nothing left to me. I thought I would go first. I never thought he would go before me.' He says that all the time, she said. She doesn't know how to deal with the business because he won't sign any papers.'

'I know,' sighed Olivia. 'She has confided in me too. I told her the lawyers would surely refrain from pestering her while her son was still unburied but there are some awful sharks with whom Gerard had dealings who were at the house in London as soon as news of what had happened got out. The newspaper sellers were crying it all over town which was terrible for her to hear. Then Sir Langton was able to tell her to direct any creditors to his bank and a constable shooed them away. He was worse on the journey and much worse since our arrival. It's as if he can't bear to be in the place with no Gerard to leave it to. And what is to happen with the west wing? Lady Kirby is frightened to tell the men when to resume, but the north side must be made good before winter. My father's dream of completing the work is out of the question now there are no funds, but some of it is still open to the elements.'

Then Luke asked her about the work her father was doing now and she found herself telling him all she had learnt in the one letter she had received from her father before their journey north.

'Mr Anston made his money in the West Indies.'

'Not through buying and selling slaves, I hope,' Luke said quickly.

She smiled at his vehemence. His sympathetic heart embraced all the world. 'I think mostly from sugar, but I suppose that is worked by slaves,' she admitted. 'They have a son in the army and four daughters. The eldest was widowed at the taking of Quebec and has a boy of her own and a pleasant house on the estate called Anston Grange. My father says Mr Anston is very fat and jolly except when his gout is troubling him and Mrs Anston has taken to my father because he is happy to play cards with her and the daughters in the evening. His plans are going to make their house very grand indeed and he's much relieved that they have more than enough funds to carry them out. I'm so glad he is there because he loves company and he would have found it dreadfully oppressive to spend a long time with Sir Langton who at his best was so very stiff and proper.' She sighed. 'He wouldn't know him now.'

She wanted to talk to Luke about his grandmother then and

see if any hints of a mystery might emerge in his recollections of her but Lady Kirby's maid appeared at her elbow and said she was asking for her.

She realised the servants were beginning to disappear to their duties and that she had been chatting so comfortably and naturally with Luke that she had hardly noticed what was going on.

'Forgive me, Luke. I must leave you. Is Tom still about? Will he help you down?'

Tom appeared as she spoke. He never went far from Luke if he was likely to need his assistance. How stalwart these two were and how she would have loved to have them as her own brothers, she thought, as she passed along the gallery to Lady Kirby's room.

She found her practically in a state of collapse, shaking all over and tears running down her face.

'It's all been too much for her, Miss Beattie,' her maid whispered. 'She bore up wonderfully through the funeral and receiving the guests but it's knocked her down now. Can you talk her into going to bed do you think? I could send one of the footmen to ride after the doctor. He won't have reached home yet.'

'No doctor,' murmured Lady Kirby, 'now I have Olivia' and she took hold of Olivia's hand and began stroking it as she loved to do.

It was the start of many days for Olivia when she could hardly leave Lady Kirby except at night. Even then she would sometimes get a stealthy visit from her maid who slept in the dressing-room next to her mistress, requesting her to come because she had had a nightmare.

After a week or two Sir Langton began to inquire after his wife and Olivia who was utterly weary and longing to walk or ride out on these golden autumn days decided to take a stern line with him. He came shuffling in to Lady Kirby's room in his morning robe and looked at the wan figure in the bed.

'Yes, Sir Langton, Lady Kirby would like you to sit by her. She's not well this morning and you must try to cheer her up.'

He looked at Olivia with some surprise in his dull eyes, a good sign, she thought. Everyone has been treating him as a poor soul who will never recover his bodily or mental health. But why should he not? Time must soften the blow eventually. She would encourage him. Had she not raised up Luke? She began to look on this as a new challenge which would add some variety to her present confined life.

'What's the matter with her?' he asked Olivia as if she were the nurse.

Olivia got up to give him the bedside chair.

'She's worn herself out because she's had to make all the decisions and entertain everybody and now she needs you to play your part.'

Lady Kirby was looking at Olivia in astonishment. No one had ever dared to speak to Sir Langton like that.

'What decisions?' he exclaimed. 'She doesn't need to make decisions.' He sat down heavily and took his wife's hand. 'Are you eating properly?' he asked. 'My dear, you must order whatever you fancy.'

'I have a poor appetite just now,' she murmured, 'but it does me good to see you up and about.'

'Of course I'm up and about,' he said, straightening his spine and lifting his head. 'Why should I not be?'

'You've not been yourself. Mr Unwin called once and I had to send him away. He had papers for you to sign.'

This Olivia knew was the lawyer who had been in touch with Sir Langton's London bank and was still trying to settle the genuine debts and resolve the ones that were in dispute.

'He must come back,' Sir Langton said. 'I should have been told.'

'You were, dear, but you showed no interest.'

'Perhaps I was half asleep. He should have persisted. I think I have been a little tired lately. My eyes are not as good as they were.' He looked up at Olivia as if trying to fit her into some picture in his memory. Olivia felt that he hadn't succeeded because he looked back at his wife and said, 'Does this young lady write a fair hand?'

'Beautiful,' Lady Kirby said, surprised.

'She can be my amanuensis.'

'Miss Beattie is our guest, Sir Langton.'

He gave a slight start at the name and then the veil drew over again. 'Would you object, my dear young lady?'

'Not at all, sir.' Olivia made a swift appraisal of the power it might give her. 'I should be honoured.'

'I'll send for you to the office later then. Now we must see that Lady Kirby breakfasts well and has a little walk to put some colour in those pale cheeks.' And he called for her maid.

Olivia slipped out. He doesn't realise it's nearly noon, she thought as she ran down to impart this new development to Luke.

She found him looking rosy and wind blown after a ride out on his pony. His welcoming smile always thrilled her but today she saw how sweet and bright his face was, the smile lighting his blue eyes and making happy creases at the corners.

She sat down and told him of the change in Sir Langton.

He leant forward eagerly in his chair. 'This couldn't come at a better time. 'Now I could do it pat' as the Bard so succinctly put it.'

Then he went on to tell her how he had by chance intercepted Mr Unwin, the lawyer, as he was leaving after his last fruitless visit. 'I begged him to come in here so I could show him the paper I had written about the coal seams, and also what I had gathered from reading the latest publications on the geology of our part of Yorkshire and other reports of the costs incurred and profits made from similar workings. He became quite animated and confided that Sir Langton's situation is worse than he had feared and this could make all the difference between bankruptcy and solvency. He seemed to assume I was Sir Langton's steward but I explained that I was doing this quite independently on my own initiative and that my status was indeterminate. 'You might call me a ward of the castle,' I told him, 'since I have lived here all my life and my father and brother are gardeners here.' But he was good enough to be impressed with my work so I showed him other studies I had made of how the yield of the land could be improved. Of course I had to admit that I couldn't interest Sir Langton in all this as he never comes near me. But now if you are to be admitted to his office and Mr Unwin comes back you might – between you – be able to slip these things under his nose.'

'I'll certainly try.' Then she looked at him appraisingly. 'You know, Luke, you speak of Sir Langton's neglect without a trace of bitterness. I feel such anger –'

He laughed. 'No, no, you mustn't. Think what I have gained – food and clothing, access to his library, materials for painting and drawing, any of the latest periodicals on any subject. Nothing has ever been denied me but it goes into the accounts under a special code and I try never to make an extravagant demand.'

'But you receive no money yourself?'

'No, but my little pony was a personal present from her ladyship. If sometime we – you and Thomas and I – can resume our Shakespeare readings my happiness will be complete.'

'Oh we will. Now that Sir Langton is beginning to notice his wife again I may not be needed night and day. But truly, Luke, I think you must be a saint. I never met one before but your humility is such a beautiful thing. I could never attain to it. I hope I'm learning but I am still impulsive and selfish.'

He gave her that glorious smile again. 'Remember 'no such

mirrors'? All who have seen your devotion to her ladyship these last few weeks can reflect back to you just how *un*selfish you have been. Ah now here is Betsy with my dinner.' There came her light tap at the door. 'I eat at servant hours which I prefer as I am usually awake very early.'

Betsy came in with his tray and looked shyly up at Olivia. 'Please Miss Beattie I hear the Master has sent to your room for you to attend him in the office.'

'Thank you, Betsy, I'll go at once.'

She passed down the east wing, through into the entrance hall and under the arched doorway to the west wing. The builders had not yet been told to resume but beyond the office and the library the extended wing lay unfinished, the south façade complete but the north lacking windows. And no work had been done on the interior.

She knocked at the office door and awaited Sir Langton's 'Come in.'

He got up from his desk to greet her most affably. 'The workmen are very quiet today,' he said. 'So you will not mind being in here. I had the fire lit though I believe it is a fine day. I seem to have missed my constitutional this morning.'

'Sir Langton,' she said, taking her courage in her hands. 'The workmen were laid off but they should come back to put the window frames and glass in before winter. We will get storms from the north.'

He frowned as if trying to recall something. 'Why were they laid off? Yes, of course they must come back. I'll see to it. Now, pray be seated.' He seemed to have lost his way with this distracting problem. 'I asked you to come –?'

'Was it to write a letter, sir?'

'Ah, that's it.' He resumed his seat and passed a sheet of paper to her headed with the Kirby crest. The silver stand containing quills and ink he moved over the desk top towards her. He also drew a paper from his desk drawer which she read upside down as a banker's draft for thirty guineas.

Good heavens, she thought, is he going to pay me an annual salary as his secretary. Whatever should I do?

But the dilemma was quickly resolved when he said, 'I recollect that Mr Gerard needed this to pay for his horse, Emperor. So you may commence, after whatever the date is 'Dear Gerard . . .''

Now here was a worse dilemma. She gave a fleeting glance at his face but he looked totally composed and was in fact resting his chin on his hand and gazing from the window at the courtyard in exactly the attitude of one thinking how to commence what he wanted to say.

He has wiped out all that has happened and gone back to the thing that has been niggling in his mind. Gerard needed thirty guineas and he never gave it to him so that is the first thing to be put right now he is more himself. She dared not break this train of thought. Maybe it is a blessing that his memory of that horror has gone. I will write it and insert the banker's draft and I can make sure it is never posted. It must be handed to his lawyer when he comes.

'Yes, Sir Langton?' she said, dipping the quill in the ink.

Chapter 20

Lady Kirby, helped by her lady's maid and Olivia, descended from the carriage.

'Where are you going?' Sir Langton called from inside. 'I thought we were to have a drive. We're no further than Tadby Church.'

'Let me have a few minutes – I was suffering from cramp,' Lady Kirby said over her shoulder.

Olivia could hear him mutter, 'Cramp? It's not five minutes since we left home.'

There had been a frost overnight and the north side of the church roof was white. There were patches of white on the grass where the sun had not reached but there was considerable warmth for November and the sky was a glorious blue above the remaining yellow and bronze leaves.

Lady Kirby was clutching a sprig of rosemary and Olivia a few twigs of jasmine bound with a gold ribbon. Out of sight of the carriage now they approached the Kirby vault with its towering stone monument crowned with cherubs and ornamented with the armorial bearings and all the Kirby ancestors' names. Freshly chiselled was 'Gerard Langton Kirby born November 6th 1740, died August 20th 1761 in a tragic accident. Beloved son of Sir Langton Edward George Kirby and Lady Sophia Margaret Kirby.'

Lady Kirby and Olivia laid their little offerings below the

memorial. Lady Kirby dabbed her eyes with her handkerchief and stood a moment with her hands clasped. Olivia tried to say a prayer but kept thinking of the vitality of the young officer who had kissed her in the wood. It was impossible to think of his body down there in the cold stone among the bones of his ancestors. She couldn't raise a tear on this day he had so looked forward to, his coming of age. It was a strange episode in her life and was over, though not blotted out as it was with his father. It was a series of vivid pictures recalling a switchback of emotions that were now as cold as he was.

It was the present that was warm with the pleasure of the company of Luke and Thomas and their now weekly Shakespeare readings.

She felt Lady Kirby shiver and took her arm and then a shadow fell across them. Sir Langton had come softly across the grass to see what they were doing.

He stood transfixed, reading the stone.

'No,' he shouted. 'No.' He jabbed his cane at the words. 'No. That can't be. Who has written that?' He seemed to sway and Olivia caught hold of him and the footman who had followed at a distance leapt forward and held him up. He thrashed his short legs and seemed to be in a paroxysm of anger, repeating, 'No, no.'

Lady Olivia wrung her hands. 'Why did you let him come, John?'

Somehow they got him to the carriage but he had sunk back into his behaviour after the accident, rocking himself and moaning and Olivia could have wept now at all the good work she and the lawyer had achieved in the last weeks, apparently undone at a stroke.

Thank God, she thought as they drove back as quickly as they could, we managed to get his signature on so many necessary papers, often with cunning and subterfuge as to their contents.

The bank had made him a loan on the basis of Luke's report about the coal seams and a mining expert had been hired who was to start work in the spring. The external work on the present extension of the west wing had been completed. Gerard's creditors were all satisfied and Sir Peregrine had written to say he had found a horse breeder willing to pay fifty guineas for Emperor so he was enclosing twenty as he had no wish to profit from the transaction under the tragic circumstances. Olivia remembered with tender amusement how the plump young man had landed in the laps of a carriage-full of young ladies and somehow, amazingly, none of them had been hurt.

Perhaps, despite this setback for Sir Langton, Castle Kirby could carry on as long as Luke had his finger on the pulse of all its activities and the co-operation of Lady Kirby.

Sir Langton was gabbling incessantly as they drove back and got him upstairs to his bed and sent for the doctor. But he went on repeating his questions. Who had put up that memorial? Why had they not told him? How could Gerard be dead? Had he not written to him? He had sent him thirty guineas. Gerard was not dead. Who was this young woman who had written the letters? 'You sat there and wrote to Gerard,' he yelled at Olivia. Then his face contorted and he cried out, 'How could you do that? I held him in my arms. There was blood everywhere.'

It seemed that his memory of the past few weeks was still there but flashes of the accident were coming back. The doctor bled him to check the onset of a fever and prescribed opium in small quantities. He shook his head over him and told Lady Kirby he feared for his sanity. 'You must not expect a full recovery, m'lady.'

With a shiver of fear Olivia recollected Mrs Johnson's nightmare of the blood. There was something sinister in that old woman. Did she have second sight? Was it after all the *future* she was obsessed with, not the past? Did page a hundred contain a prophecy of Gerard's horrible death? But then why would she say 'When I'm gone and you've looked at page a hundred his father will let you marry Gerard'? Oh it was maddening that they had buried her with her Bible. And yet – what did it matter now that Gerard was dead? Only if it could have cleared poor Sir Langton's troubled mind it might have been a blessing.

Lady Kirby was sobbing, 'Oh why did we ever go to the churchyard? What good did it do? The poor darling boy didn't know we were there.' And she had a relapse into raw grief. Yet hers, Olivia could tell was uncomplicated by any other feelings. It was a terrible loss, pure and simple. Sir Langton's though was all admixed with anger, guilt and bewilderment and nothing anyone could say or do seemed for a while to make any difference.

'What shall we do about your father's visit?' Lady Kirby said one morning as November turned into December. 'He was to come for Christmas but is it fit for him to come into such a house. And you, poor dear, have not seen him for so long.'

Olivia wanted very much to see him but one paragraph from his latest letter had given her quite a shock.

'I have already mentioned Mrs Laura Hatfield,' he wrote, *'the widowed daughter of Mr and Mrs Anston. I would so much like you to meet her and she is equally anxious to make your acquaintance. If I tell you that she has been so obliging as to find your not-so-very-old father an agreeable companion and that I am equally attracted to her charm and liveliness you may perhaps guess where this is heading.*

'Although Sir Langton and Lady Kirby have very kindly invited me to join you for Christmas I know that if we announce an official engagement they would feel obliged to invite Laura too and her merry little son, Ralph. This would hardly be appropriate in a house still in mourning. Can they spare you to come to us here? Christmas is very

jolly in this part of Surrey with processions and carolling and much feasting and would I am sure give you a welcome change from your present gloomy surroundings. I know that outside the turnpike roads winter travelling is almost impossible and if the weather is bad you must not think of venturing from home but the Kirbys have kept a good road to Tadby and from there to the town. Then you are on the main turnpike to London. Between London and ourselves the roads are only impassable after exceptionally heavy rain and the Anstons would gladly let me have the carriage to meet you in London. Think of it, my dear, and delight your affectionate father,

Gideon Beattie.'

P.S. Captain Anston, as yet unattached, will have leave for Christmas.'

Olivia had thought about it already, talked of it to Luke and confided to him that she didn't want to go

'Papa has written so much about these Anstons but I can't feel attracted to them at all. They sound loud, proud and horribly wealthy. They drink and play cards but I have never heard of one of them reading a book. They will be very jolly with Papa because they know him well now and he is to be one of the family soon I suppose. I will be expected to embrace three sisters and one whom I will have to accept as a step-mother. I will also acquire a little brother who will make faces and stick his tongue out at me and, worst of all, I will have to keep at bay the advances of a Captain who will ogle me behind enormous whiskers.'

'How do you know,' asked Luke, laughing, 'that you will not enjoy his advances?'

'I couldn't possibly when my heart is here in Castle Kirby. The Kirbys are my family and all that are under this roof, even Mrs Chorley.' She laughed too, a little hysterically. 'And of course the folk at Tadby, including your handsome brother and taciturn father.'

Luke's laughter checked for a moment. 'Tom *is* handsome, isn't he?'

'And clever. I'm sure Captain Anston will be as stupid as his whiskers are large and curling.'

Luke's laugh at that was not quite as spontaneous as it had been before. Ah, she wondered, has Thomas confided to Luke that he once told me he loved me and my casual remark has set Luke wondering if I am beginning to return his love. But I'm not. I truly admire Tom for the way he has raised himself above his humble work and yet still labours at it so conscientiously. But I can't explain that to Luke. I wish Tom could have looked at Jenny but I see now how unlikely that was. But Jenny will see William again if we go to Surrey. He's much more suitable for her. *If* I ever go to Surrey . . .

Lady Kirby's next suggestion came as a relief. 'Winter travel is so dreadful. I'm sure your father would rather wait for spring. Who knows, maybe we will be in a better state to entertain company by then and if we are not you could travel to Surrey to see him.'

So Olivia wrote,

> *'Dearest Papa,*
>
> *'I am truly glad for you if you have found a lady who will make you happy and be a companion for you throughout your life. I haven't told Lady Kirby as it sounds as if the engagement is not quite official yet, but I have to say that we are not fit here to have guests at present. Sir Langton has had a relapse into his former sad state after the accident, crying out and tormenting himself. I am trying to console Lady Kirby who has her own grief to overcome and for whom her husband's condition is an added and heavy*

burden. She would prefer me not to travel in winter but pray thank Mr and Mrs Anston for kindly inviting me to join their Christmas party. Lady Kirby suggests I should ask if I may come in Spring when the roads are better, or she and Sir Langton may be able by then to welcome you here.

'Please do not think I am myself wrapped in gloom. There is much going on here to forward the return of Castle Kirby to some sort of financial security and it interests me very much. You know I am not a sewing and embroidery kind of young lady, brought up as I have been by an educated and cultured father. One day I may find a gentleman who will respect me for that but I don't think it will be Captain Anston!'

She concluded by describing the beautiful autumn at Castle Kirby and how much she was enjoying the view from her window with the changing light on the lake, the rich colour in the woods and the first sparkling frosts.

When the letter had gone she thought wistfully of her father and how she was no longer the first in his affections. Her own future was undetermined. How long could she stay as a guest at Castle Kirby when she was in no way related to the family? Lady Kirby was doing her best with Luke's help to reduce outlay and they had dispensed with the services of the night footman, one of the stable hands and even of Mr Granger, the butler, who was happy to retire to his brother's inn in Dimthwaite.

Olivia was very aware that every extra mouth to feed was a burden on the Castle's expenses. There was no likelihood that Lady Kirby would ever be able to afford a paid companion which was the only status in which Olivia felt she might earn her own living. No doubt her father and his new lady would expect her to come to them when they were married but the prospect riled her independent soul. They would be trying to marry her to Captain Anston and she knew she would rebel. I must be sure when I want to marry and if I am not sure I will never marry. So she resolved and meanwhile her duty was to accompany Lady Kirby about and to try to bring Sir Langton back at least to the state when he viewed her as his amanuensis and was dressed and outwardly showing some rational behaviour.

Once a week Lady Kirby was closeted with Mrs Chorley going over the household accounts. At those times Olivia would read a play with Thomas and Luke and there would be subdued laughter in his room as they bantered among themselves on interpretations and disputed readings.

Lady Kirby had cut down visiting among the neighbouring gentry for reasons of economy. 'I can't return the compliment,' she confided to Olivia, 'with the way Sir Langton is and without guests we can dine so simply.'

Nothing could have shown Olivia more plainly that Lady Kirby did not regard her as a guest which was very touching and indeed they were more like mother and daughter together. This was comforting when her father wrote that he and his Laura had now celebrated their engagement. If Olivia had been coming for Christmas they would have waited but now they hoped to be married at Easter and he planned to come and fetch his daughter to be there for the ceremony and to reside with them thereafter in Anston Grange, the charming house already belonging to his future wife and which he was extending to create a further sitting room and bedroom for Olivia.

Olivia ran down to Luke with this letter. 'He expects me to cut all connection with Castle Kirby and I can't bear the thought. How could I break up our little Shakespearean group? And poor Lady Kirby – I am so fond of her now and she seems to need me. As for Sir Langton, even he is beginning to notice me again. He came into the drawing-room last night and sat with us for an hour and asked me what I was reading. When I told him it was a volume of Milton he begged me to read a little. So I read from *Paradise Lost* and he listened with tears running down his face, making no effort to wipe them away. I got up and gave him my handkerchief. He took it and looked at it as if he didn't know what it was for. So I wiped his face myself and he said, 'Thank you. How kind,' in just his old polite tones. I could have wept myself to see him and of course Lady Kirby did. So how could I desert them?'

'But your father is a generous-hearted understanding man,' Luke said. 'When you explain this he will let you stay as long as you wish. You'll visit him of course from time to time so the new rooms will not be wasted. And of course he will want you there at his wedding and to meet all his new friends.'

'But I feel no desire to go at all. I shall be a fish out of water.'

He laughed again his sweet ready laugh. 'You will come back and enliven us with your descriptions of them all, their mansions, their gardens, the Surrey countryside – of which I have only ever seen illustrations in picture books – and above all Captain Anston's moustachios. I imagine him as something like Don Adriano di Armado in *Love's Labours Lost*.'

'Oh I will, I'll tell you and Thomas everything. I'll keep a satirical diary.'

'That's right. It's the only way I get to see the world through the eyes of others and through my reading. What joy it will be when you are sitting there again in your armchair and telling us all your experiences!'

Put like that Olivia could look forward to it too and his remark about himself made her ashamed. As far as she knew he had never been anywhere beyond Tadby and Dimthwaite.

'Forgive me, Luke, for my selfishness. I have forgotten how little of the world you have seen. Have you never even been in a carriage or coach?'

He shook his head, laughing. 'My only conveyance has been Jack Summers' cart when Thomas lifted me in to go to church in Dimthwaite. But thanks to you I believe I could climb into a carriage now without difficulty, my muscles are so much stronger.'

'And you can ride openly to Tadby on No Such Mirrors now. Sir Langton was so frightened at seeing Gerard's name on the stone that he won't go near the church. I do believe he is being punished for his wickedness all those years when he maintained that your wheel-chair spoilt the symmetry of the Tadby procession. I didn't know about you going to Dimthwaite at first. I wondered if you had been a free-thinker like my father.'

'No indeed,' Luke said, serious again. 'It is there that I find my strength.'

Olivia nodded vigorously. 'I too and I wish Sir Langton could finally seek peace there as well. Lady Kirby feels it so much, sitting in their pew without him. I suppose that's why she loves me to be with her.'

When Christmas came Lady Kirby urged the servants to celebrate in all the traditional ways except that she could allow only a little beyond the usual budget for extra poultry and mincemeat and puddings. So there was carol singing and Olivia was delighted to find that both Thomas, a strong bass and Luke, a sweet tenor, had good voices. She was happy to join them as a servant rather than a family member and when Sir Langton heard faint singing from the kitchen he sent down word that they were all to come up and sing in the drawing-room. He sat listening and again tears ran down his cheeks. Many who had not seen him for weeks were shocked at his sunken appearance.

Looking at him Olivia knew she would never now solve the mystery that was locked in Mrs Johnson's grave. She had felt sure Sir Langton held the key to it but it was impossible now to believe that probing into the recesses of his mind could ever reveal anything. He seemed to live from moment to moment, a body with senses but little capacity for thought.

Chapter 21

In late January Olivia and Sir Langton and Lady Kirby were all three in the small drawing-room when the London papers were brought in. Sir Langton leant forward and picked up the top one and opened it. He could only read large print now but his eyes took in a headline that Spain had declared war.

'Where is the war?' he cried. 'Did we not beat the French? Why would we fight Spain too? This is madness.'

Lady Kirby, startled at his sudden interest in external affairs, just nodded and murmured her agreement that war was madness and tried to hide the paper. She is afraid, Olivia thought, that he will be roused into memories of Gerard at Belle Isle, but when he persisted in asking why Spain was involved Olivia drew her chair close to his and endeavoured to explain. Perhaps there were glimmerings of a mental recovery which ought to be encouraged.

'Do you remember, Sir Langton, that Mr Pitt always warned Spain would come in with France? I read that the Spanish wanted to keep out till their treasure fleet was safely home from the West Indies – for fear of our navy –'

Lady Kirby intervened. 'He's not listening to you, dear.'

Olivia peered at his face and saw that his attention had indeed slipped away. But it was a glimpse perhaps that his mind was not dead but dormant and could be suddenly, if briefly, stirred. She patted his hand as she might a child's and got up and went to the window, thinking of the interminable war.

Gazing at the clean-swept winter landscape she felt utterly remote from it but far away men were pointlessly fighting and dying. Occasionally her father's letters referred to it but it seemed Captain Anston's regiment was not at present involved. 'And you will be delighted to hear,' her father had written in his latest, 'that the Captain has been promised leave to attend his sister's wedding. He is very much looking forward to meeting you.'

She was not particularly delighted but, as the days lengthened, she began to look forward to her father's coming to fetch her. It was important for him to see how close were her ties to Castle Kirby and what a wrench it would be if he tried to tear her away for good. Although Sir Langton had shown no fresh signs of animation since that brief display he continued to request her to read poetry to him and her father must understand how necessary she was to both the Kirbys. He would stay only two nights before he set off with her and Jenny back to Surrey for the wedding but it had to be enough to convince him where her destiny lay.

On the day in early April when she expected her father's arrival she was at her window constantly looking out and when she saw in the far distance some movement at the gates she ran to tell Lady Kirby she believed her father was coming.

'But where shall I take him, Lady Kirby?' she asked. 'Sir Langton is in the small drawing-room and I fear the encounter. He last saw my father in the street by Gerard's body.'

Lady Kirby shuddered. 'You are right as always. Bring him here to my little sitting-room for some tea. I shall be happy to welcome him.'

Olivia thanked her and ran down to the great doors where the footman was already shooting back the bolts as the equipage passed the lake. The very smart figure sitting up on top next to the coachman was William she was delighted to see. He waved his hat to her and as soon as the horses were drawn up he climbed down and opened the door and out jumped her father as sprightly as a young man.

She was in his arms in a moment. How well he looked in a new cocked hat, and dark travelling coat!

'My little girl! More lovely than ever.'

As the grooms came running to see to the horses he drew her attention to the Anstons' post chaise. 'Look what they have sent for our speed and comfort.'

'Very splendid, Papa. You come from unlimited wealth to a penny pinching household.'

He was standing back and admiring the completed façade of the west wing. 'That much is done at least. But oh it does need a dome to achieve the full effect!'

She smiled. 'You will see the courtyard and stables as they were. The poor little cottages need never have gone.'

He shook his head. 'No Kirby will leave it like that when they are next in funds.'

She tucked her arm through his to ascend the steps. 'You forget there are no more Kirbys and I fear Sir Langton will never be fit to authorise any work on the scale you envisaged.'

'A great shame,' he said, 'a very great shame.'

As they reached the upper gallery to turn aside into Lady Kirby's sitting-room the door to the small drawing-room opened and Sir Langton walked out.

Olivia saw her father start at his stooped, shambling figure, but the effect on Sir Langton was catastrophic.

'What!' he cried peering up with difficulty at Gideon Beattie. 'What is this? Where are we? How did he come here?'

Lady Kirby came running from her room and took his arm. 'It's all right, my love. This is just our dear Olivia's father come to us. He won't be here long. He's going to take her for a little holiday. Forgive him, Mr Beattie.' She stretched out her other hand to him and he bowed over it. 'He is not himself.'

Sir Langton turned and glared at her. 'I am quite myself, Sophia. He knocked down the cottages. You think I don't remember things. He knocked them down without my say-so. A man must give orders in his own house. Did I not send you away once?' He addressed Gideon Beattie directly for the first time. 'Have I asked you to come back?'

Olivia saw her father shrug his shoulders helplessly. 'I am so sorry to disturb you in this way, Sir Langton. I can go to the inn at Tadby and call for Olivia the day after tomorrow.' He looked sadly at Lady Kirby. 'He and I were on very good terms in London before – well, before the grievous accident to your poor son,' he added in a low voice.

'Forgive him,' she whispered again. 'His memory is partial. Of course you must not go to the inn. Your room is ready for you, the one you had last time. I will have the tea sent in there and you can be alone with Olivia. I didn't know he was going to start wandering about.'

Sir Langton's head was turning this way, hating to be left out but unable to catch what they were saying.

'He's come for her, has he?' he suddenly demanded. 'Well she can't go. She lives here. This is her home. No one is going to take her away,' and he actually stepped up to Olivia and seized her hands. 'You wouldn't go away. We need you. He can't take her from us, Sophie, can he?' A sob wrenched his throat.

Olivia pressed his hands in hers and touched his cheek with her lips. 'I will come back, dear Sir Langton. It's only for a very little while. I will be back before the daffodils fade in the garden.' She drew him to the gallery window where he could see the yellow blooms breaking out beside the lake. 'Look there, the daffodils. Can you see them?'

Sir Langton obediently screwed up his eyes. Yet he had recognised her father so swiftly! Now he nodded. 'Daffodils. Yes. Very pretty.' Her nearness seemed to have calmed him and Lady Kirby took the chance to whisk her father into the room allotted to him looking over the courtyard.

Olivia began to repeat her promise to be back before the daffodils faded but he interrupted her with, 'I was looking for you – to read to me. Milton's sonnets. Very moving. 'On his blindness' you know. If I lose my sight as I grow old I will find that very comforting.'

She drew him back to the small drawing-room, sat him down in an armchair and read him the sonnet slowly and emphatically. 'Again,' he begged. But before she had finished it the second time his head had drooped back and he had fallen asleep.

She returned to her father. William was in the room helping to unpack his bags.

'William, if you would like to see Jenny she is in my dressing-room sorting my clothes for Surrey,' Olivia said and directed him to the right door.

When they were alone her father sat down on the window seat and sighed a long sigh. 'The man's stark raving mad. I'd never have believed he could go like that.'

'I don't think he's mad, Father. There's something deep inside that is blocking his rational mind – not Gerard's death, although he won't accept that. I'm sure there is something else – from the past. I wish I knew the answer because I believe he could be cured. Well, I think you had best avoid him while you are here. I would go tomorrow but you must rest a day at least.'

'It's all arranged. The horses are bespoke at the various stages and we take up the Anstons' fine bays at the last stage.' He sighed again. 'I shall be happy to get my poor darling out of this place but I don't like you promising to come back so soon. Do you have to come back at all?'

'Oh yes, Papa. You heard what he said. They need me.'

'But how are you to get a husband here? They go nowhere, don't entertain any more, you said. It's not a natural life for a young woman.'

'Papa, I'm only nineteen. Being in a hurry didn't do me any good before.'

'It might have come to something but for the disaster.'

'No, papa. I don't believe Gerard had it in him to change. No, *I* escaped a disaster there and I don't think I'll trust my own judgment for a while. I shall be happy to meet *your* love and then I shall come back. Tell me about her.'

Then her father became animated on the subject of his Laura. 'She's tall and beautiful, glossy dark curls, hazel eyes. She has a deep contralto voice and can play to her own songs. Oh, she's so full of fun and laughter! We get on famously. And then of course she's a loving mother and Ralph and I have hit it off splendidly. All the Anstons are happy souls and you will love the girls. A ready made bevy of sisters. You've lacked a family all these years and I know when you meet them you'll never want to leave them.'

Olivia made no comment on that but she asked, 'Do I have to call Laura Mamma?'

'She *will* be your papa's wife. You hardly remember your own dear mother.'

As the tea was brought in she refrained from describing her picture of a slim form and angelic face tucking her up and singing lullabies in a sweet high voice.

Next day Olivia took her father to see Luke, remembering how impressed he had been with his interest in his plans. Using his crutches Luke took them round the extension to the west wing. It was not yet plastered and the panelling was unfinished but the extent of the long room which would be suitable for balls was very impressive.

'What will happen to you when the Kirby line dies out?' Gideon Beattie asked him in his straightforward way. 'I'm glad to see you getting about without the chair. You could get clerical work in the town I suppose.'

'I'll certainly have to earn my bread, sir, which will be a change for me.'

'It seems to me you're more than earning your bread here. Lady Kirby tells me Sir Langton would be bankrupt without your labours. Have you thought of being apprenticed to an architect? Your mathematical and drawing skills would certainly make you eligible. *I* would be glad to offer you work when I am more established, as I hope to be in the next few years.'

Olivia heard all this with amazement. She had been forgetting Luke's precarious position. Yet again his calm acceptance of life shook her. Now he was thanking her father and telling him he would be honoured if such an opportunity were offered to him in his hour of need. Meanwhile he was happy to be involved in the work at Castle Kirby in co-operation with Mr Unwin, the lawyer, even if they had to resort to a little trickery occasionally to obtain Sir Langton's signature.

'The work on the coal seams is getting underway too, sir, and the mining engineer has great hopes of its profitability.'

'When I come back, Luke,' Olivia said, 'I shall ask for the mare to be saddled and you must ride No Such Mirrors and take me to see all that's going on there.'

'I'll be delighted,' he said and she realised that though she had never had a chance to ride with Gerard over the estate, to do so with Luke would be a much more delightful experience.

'No Such Mirrors!' exclaimed her father. 'A strange name for a horse?'

'I'll explain how it came about on the journey to Surrey,' Olivia promised.

They walked slowly back into the inhabited castle. Tomorrow

I will be away from here, she thought. How strange that will be!

What she couldn't tell her father was how much she was looking forward to her return.

Chapter 22

On a bright April day almost exactly a year after her arrival at Castle Kirby Olivia alighted at Anston Manor, a red brick Tudor building to which later extensions had been haphazardly added, as her father was bursting to explain to her.

'What I plan will involve almost a complete rebuild to produce a solid . . .'

But he got no further as the whole Anston family came out to greet her. She was overwhelmed with kisses and embraces by stout Mrs Anston and a bevy of younger women of whom the most striking was the tall, well-bosomed, statuesque creature with towering headdress and deep warm voice that she realised must be her father's betrothed. The younger sisters were an amorphous group of slender girls whose names she was quite unable to sort out at the first meeting. Mr Anston was almost too fat to bow over her hand and the only young man, apart from the boy Ralph who jumped about trying to draw attention to himself, was tall, thin and both whiskerless and chinless but must be Captain Anston.

The Anstons did everything in a noisy rush so she was soon bustled inside and had hardly taken off her travelling cloak before she found herself seated in a long dining-room that glittered with silver and cut glass under a chandelier of a hundred candles. They all talked at once and young Ralph who seemed to be allowed complete freedom chattered in his high treble above them all. Olivia had Captain Anston on one side and Laura on the other. Both were so eager to show her attention that she found herself constantly turning her head from one to the other as Laura intoned her hopes of their lifelong friendship and Captain Anston threw out staccato questions about her journey and what it was like up there in the north. Were the peasants very rough? Could she understand a word they said?

Olivia told him of two gardener's sons who read Shakespeare and his eyebrows shot up to his wig. He was blest if he could quote a word himself, he said, and that fortunately kept him silent for almost three minutes.

Accustomed as she was to eat what was put before her at Castle Kirby Olivia found herself clearing her plate only to be presented with another course till she felt close to bursting and longed to run away and remove her corset.

She was quite unable to touch the fruit and jellies piled into a decorative mound of simulated flowers on an enormous dish and was thankful when at last the ladies rose and left her father and Mr Anston and the Captain to their port. If that was an ordinary dinner, she thought, whatever would the wedding feast be like?

She had to excuse herself and retire to her bedroom and ask Jenny to unlace her or she thought she would faint. Her room had a Chinese theme with a four poster bed hung with Chinese silk and a wallpaper to match covered with delicate trees and birds. The painted furniture showed intricate scenes of Chinese life and on almost every surface were exquisite ivory figures that she was terrified of knocking over. Everything was pretty in itself but the profusion of patterns and ornaments all together was overwhelming. How will I endure this place for a fortnight, she wondered, and then remembered Luke. She must start her diary soon and copy his outlook by seeking for the best in everything and everybody.

The evening was all talk and excitement. She had to be secretly shown the bridal gown and bridesmaids' dresses and she felt sure her words of praise were not enthusiastic enough by Anston standards. Falling at last into bed she was too weary to write of her impressions and it was not till she woke early the next morning and studied the prospect from her bedroom window that she discovered the best delights that Anston Manor had to offer.

Unlike Castle Kirby, where the wide view stretched for miles towards the level south and in the west to distant blue hills, this was enclosed with trees in all the freshness of spring growth, budding and blossoming weeks ahead of Yorkshire. A stream ran through the garden with ornamental bridges and a little waterfall into a pool with a fountain. Although it was full of fussy detail – stone nymphs and birds and arbours with carved stone seats the effect was pretty and Olivia was sure she would find every day some new feature she hadn't discovered before. Jenny, coming in to dress her, thought it was a paradise and said that she had been made very welcome by the Anstons' servants who were already fond of William.

But for most of her stay Olivia felt her head buzzing and the diary was no more than the briefest jottings. The Anstons were all over her every waking hour. She must walk here, she must see this, there were races to go to, a day at the seaside, card games to play and dinner parties for local gentry. To crown all this activity was the great day of her father's wedding to Laura.

Although she was told over and over again how wonderful it was for her to acquire a mother she couldn't bring herself to see Laura in this light. She was only sixteen years older than herself being ten years younger than her father and though she was profusely affectionate Olivia could feel no bond with her. She read light novels but had no conversation on literature and Olivia found herself growing daily more reserved in her presence.

When the wedding day arrived the weather which had been bright but blustery became perfectly calm.

'A good omen,' her father said. 'But you'll find these Anstons attract good fortune whatever they do. Now you must acknowledge they couldn't have been kinder to you, could they, Olivia?'

'No, indeed, Papa.' Perhaps he feels I haven't been responsive enough, she wondered.

'They are still eager for you to stay, you know. Just because Laura and I will have our little wedding trip to Bath you don't have to run away tomorrow as arranged. They will look after you here and when we come back you can come to the Grange with us.'

'Papa, I couldn't. Of course they have been charming but they don't *need* me, not the way I'm needed at Castle Kirby. Don't look disappointed. This is your special day and I'm so happy for your happiness.'

These few minutes were the only time she had alone with him before the flower-bedecked carriages came to convey the whole party the half mile to church.

During the wedding service when the parson was giving a rather dull address and the Anstons were necessarily silent Olivia found herself reflecting on the year since her father had taken her to Castle Kirby. I am almost a different person and Papa can't understand that. I went there full of myself as a cultivated young lady from London determined to stun these northern country folk with my style and self-confidence. I wasn't expecting to find a husband but that changed when I fell in love with Gerard's portrait. Then I became a silly flustered girl, swept off my feet, as they say. Father's near disgrace and Gerard's death have made me less sure of myself but I hope more thoughtful for others. I have had to endure being foiled of the mystery Mrs Johnson wanted me to know and I have waited ceaselessly on both the Kirbys, so I believe I have begun to learn patience though I will never attain to that of Luke. But now Papa is marrying I am curiously alone and a little adrift.

Tears pricked the back of her eyes as the parson pronounced Gideon and Laura man and wife. She felt a strange presentiment that she would never herself be in that position. Her father had said it was no life for a marriageable young lady at Castle Kirby. I shall grow old as a sort of nursemaid to Sir Langton and confidant to Lady Kirby for where is the man I can truly love and respect and for whom I could promise all that Papa and Laura have just promised? Who do I know that has Luke's qualities for example? No one of course.

A joyful wedding hymn burst on her at this point in her musings. The Anstons sang very heartily though not always in tune and it became impossible to think at all for the rest of the day since the whole neighbourhood appeared to be at the wedding feast and the noise of chatter spilled into all corners of the house and gardens.

She thanked God she was to leave next day shortly before her father and Laura departed for Bath. But that night lying sleepless with her head still ringing she found her thoughts reverting to her own future and the impossibility of ever being satisfied in a husband.

She considered Captain Anston whom they were all thrusting at her. He was not childish and brash like Gerard. He was good-tempered and amiable but his conversation was very limited. She thought of the London beaux who had courted her at her first coming into society when her father was spending above his means to launch her into the world. She thought, briefly, of Gerard himself. What had he got but his looks?

I am spoilt from knowing Luke, she told herself. That's the trouble. No man will ever match him, his pleasing voice, his sweet smile, his courage, his intellect, his insatiable curiosity about the world and people, his wonderful capacity for listening and his brilliance at acting. She longed to be back, telling him all about her stay, just being with him. In fact it was a pain to be away from him but that would soon be put right.

This pleasing thought sent her to sleep at last but was still at work in her dreams and she woke early with the unsatisfied feeling that there was a logical end to her musings and she had so far failed to reach it.

I've been dreaming of Luke, she told herself, and how much I want a husband I could love and admire as I do him. If I ever do marry I will be comparing my poor husband to him all the time and that will do the marriage no good at all. Luke will always be far, far ahead of the field.

She sat bolt upright in bed. But Luke *is* a man, for God's sake! I am a fool. If I want no one but him how could I ever marry someone else? I once told him he could know nothing of love. How could I have been so cruel? I never want to spend my life without him so what else can I do? I will marry Luke.

She hugged herself and began to cry tears of joy.

Soon she was crying and laughing at once. What do his crippled legs matter? They only display his strength of character. His body is shapely and so are the divine features of his face. Dear God, why have you thrown us together if it was not for me to discover that Gerard's looks hid a man of straw and I had the chance to love the best man in all the world if I could only open my eyes and see him under my very nose.

But of course, galloped on her next thought, he would never propose to me. Yet it must happen. Maybe that fleeting conversation between him and my father could be the open door. Papa likes and admires him.

She was so excited she jumped out of bed and went to the window. A soft early light was suffusing the garden. Oh this was the day she was going home. Tomorrow she should be there as the Anstons had promised the post-chaise and four.

Of course I couldn't marry Luke for a long time. We would have nothing at all to live on except the Langton's bounty if the coal workings begin to pay. And what would they say if Luke went away to be apprenticed to my father and took me with him?

Oh dear, that was a hard question. Nevertheless, knowing she could not possibly sleep any more, she wrapped her dressing-gown round her and sat at the curious writing desk to complete her sketchy diary. The pens stood in a silver nest each in the upturned beak of a baby bird while the inkwell had a silver lid topped by the mother bird with a worm in its mouth.

'Nothing in this house is its simple self, Luke,' she wrote, 'but I think I have found my own self amongst all this extravagant pretence. The Anstons have been my mirrors (encased of course in frames adorned with fruit, flowers, butterflies etc) and they reflect back that I am too serious for them, I think too much (which is dangerous as Caesar thought of Cassius) I yearn for a deep, true love, and though I can be full of laughter it is not their baseless shrieks of mirth. Maybe it used to be – a year ago. I think Thomas's mirror showed me I was thoughtless and self-centred which was good for me and I am grateful to him, but Luke, it is in you I have found the one I can love for ever. You are probably not the truest mirror because you only reflect the best in everyone but I love you all the more for that. Let me be your mirror and tell you of your courage, persistence, nobility, kindness, faithfulness, humility, wisdom – oh I could go on and on and never make you proud. I set off soon to come to you and I can hardly wait.'

At this point Jenny arrived to help her dress for the journey. So she scrawled in the front of the diary: 'To be sent to Mr Luke Todd, Castle Kirby in the county of Yorkshire in the event of an accident to me, Olivia Beattie.'

That eventuality covered, she could look forward to the

hazards of the journey without anxiety but she had to keep her happiness hidden during the early breakfast which the whole family attended.

Afterwards the parting from her father was tender. He hoped she would soon think better of it and return to be part of the happy household at Anston Grange. He was sorry to yield her back to the gloom of Castle Kirby. At the last moment he popped a letter to the Kirbys into her reticule, saying only, 'A word of gratitude to them for entertaining you for so long.'

'And a hope they will let me go soon?'

'Not exactly. It's very carefully worded. You know how diplomatic I am.'

'Papa, that is *not* your first attribute.' She tried to laugh it off and he joined in heartily. His own joy, she could see, was irrepressible.

The farewells of the Anstons were boisterous but, Olivia felt, indifferent. She had made the wrong impression in their mirrors. The louder they had talked the quieter she had become. She had seemed aloof from their games and pleasures and now she was so eager to be away that she adjusted her hat too conspicuously after their kisses and they stepped back to allow her to mount up without more ado.

For the journey Jenny sat inside with her and William on top with the Anston coachman. When they were out on the highway Olivia noticed Jenny was very quiet so she asked her if she was sad to be going.

'It's not that, Miss Olivia, but I wonder when I'll see William again after he returns to Surrey.'

'You're not interested in Thomas Todd any more?'

'I was, Miss, but with you about he doesn't hardly know I'm there. And William and me was thrown together in Aldgate when he come on strong, but when we was parted again I got to thinking about him and missed him and it was good to see him when he came to the Castle with Mr Beattie. But now we'll be parted again.'

Olivia realised for the first time how indifferent to the lives and loves of servants masters and mistresses were. While they themselves could come and go hither and thither servants were assumed to attend them no matter what.

She pressed Jenny's hand. 'I think there will be changes one day, Jenny. I may have to let you go to marry William if that is your heart's desire.'

Or, maybe, she thought, William will come to Luke and me. Luke will need a manservant if I take him away from his brother's care. And that's a distressing thought. They are so close and I love Tom too. Oh how lucky the Anstons are to have money to smooth their paths whatever they want to do. But no, that's unworthy of the wife of Luke. I will just be thankful I am in love again and with the best man in the world.

Jenny looked up into her face. 'Are you sad, Miss, to be going away from your father and that very happy home?'

Olivia wiped her eyes. 'No, Jenny. These are tears of happiness. I love Castle Kirby and all who are in it.' She was on the verge of telling Jenny of her love for Luke. Jenny had said that night in Meg Summers' house that she had bowled over Thomas and Luke as well as Mr Gerard and she had never thought of that since. Was it true? If so Jenny was more perceptive than herself. I never thought of Luke in that way till last night. I was as bad as everyone else who thought of him as 'the cripple' but not as a man.

She would tell Jenny when she had found out Luke's own feelings. For now, she squeezed her hand and listened to the horses galloping and the wheels rattling, taking them at each stage nearer and nearer to her love.

Chapter 23

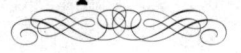

The first thing Lady Kirby said, coming right out to greet her with joy was, 'Oh how Sir Langton has been fretting for you!'

'The daffodils are only just beginning to brown at the edges,' Olivia said, hugging her.

'I know, dear. He didn't forget that remark of yours and has been out to look at them every day. It's been rather dry so when Thomas found out what you'd said he's been watering them daily from the lake in case you were delayed..'

Dear Thomas, Olivia thought. What a delight to have him as a brother!

They went upstairs, Olivia not able to turn aside to Luke's room at the corner of the east wing, as Lady Kirby kept her arm round her waist. There was nothing wild or ostentatious in her affection like the Anstons. It was a quiet deep love.

She was led straight into the small drawing-room where Sir Langton was reclining half asleep in his armchair.

'Look,' cried Lady Kirby, 'look who is here,' and she touched his shoulder.

'What, what!' He sat up and his eyes fixed directly on Olivia.

She gave him a smiling curtsey.

'Ah!' He sighed a long sigh of relief and held out his hand. She ran to him and knelt down and kissed it. But he patted her head and raised her up. 'You won't go away again, will you?'

She shook her head, not daring to put a promise into words since his memory for such things seemed so acute.

Before settling into her room and changing her travelling clothes as it was nearly dinner time she handed Lady Kirby her father's letter. It was addressed to them both so Lady Kirby said she would let Sir Langton open it first and then she would read it to him. 'He has spectacles but he is too vain to wear them,' she confided with a little laugh.

When Olivia entered the small dining-room she saw Sir Langton at the window and joined him there. The early evening sun bathed the lake and the daffodils so that the colours glowed.

He turned to look at her and she thought she had not seen his eyes so bright and aware for a long time. He put his hand on her arm.

'My dear, I fear we have been very selfish in demanding your presence with us here.' Oh, she thought, he has read Papa's letter. 'Your father quite rightly reminds us that you are of an age to be married and he kindly hopes my health has improved sufficiently for us to go about a little more and entertain so that you may meet people.'

'I didn't ask him to say that,' she blurted out. 'I am very contented here.' As she said it her eyes caught a movement at the far end of the lake and her heart bounded with joy. It was Luke on his pony returning to the stables. Her face must have shone because Lady Kirby joined them and looked to see what had excited her.

Olivia couldn't help it. She turned to her and exclaimed, 'Please don't trouble to search for a husband for me. There is the man.'

As soon as she said it she knew her impetuosity had been madness.

Sir Langton couldn't see anything so he cried out, 'Where, what? Who is she speaking of?'

Lady Kirby had caught a glimpse before the stonework of the window had hidden Luke from view.

'You don't mean – the gardener's son!'

Sir Langton glared round. 'What – young Todd. If he has dared to speak to you I will have words with Albert.'

Olivia frantically tried to undo what she had started. 'No one has spoken to me, sir. No one at all. I was just saying I could see a man I could admire.' She noticed the footman had come in with the soup. 'Pray, let us sit down. I shouldn't have spoken. But I do not want anything my father has said to trouble you at all.'

Sir Langton, still peering about the grounds for a sight of Thomas, came reluctantly away from the window.

Lady Kirby hissed softly at Olivia's ear, 'But you sounded as if you meant it. And it was Luke! No one could marry *Luke*. He's not a whole man. Surely you couldn't have meant it?'

But Sir Langton was suspicious of anything spoken under the breath.

'What are you saying?' he demanded of Lady Kirby as he took his place at the head of the table. 'It's not for you to pooh-pooh her father's letter. He was quite right and if the poor girl has met so few men that she starts admiring the gardener's son we must do something about it.' He said grace in a solemn tone and then attacked his soup. 'I daresay Thomas Todd is a fine figure of a young man but he would no more lift his eyes to a young lady like you than hope to fly to the moon. If he has he will find himself out on his ear, that's certain.'

Now Olivia was truly in a dilemma. Once Sir Langton had an idea in his head in his present mental state he could cling desperately to it – as he had to the promise about the daffodils – and if he walked in the garden and found Thomas he was more than likely to interrogate him on the subject. Thomas was far too honest to deny he had declared his love but he would be deeply shocked and hurt that she had betrayed him. She was furious with herself and also with Lady Kirby for what she had just whispered. Luke not a whole man! He was the most complete human being she had ever met.

Lady Kirby now tried to diffuse the tension by asking about Olivia's visit and she had to do her best to describe her father's wedding and his new bride and the family. She was sure, watching Sir Langton's face, that he was still brooding on what had passed and not listening to her at all.

She struggled to eat although she had been hungry before the meal. I must save Thomas, she kept thinking, and to do so I must make clear it was Luke I meant. As I intend to marry Luke sometime have I anything to lose by proclaiming it now? Lady Kirby would never let Sir Langton dismiss him. She knows how valuable he is, whole or not. She is watching me now as if she can read my mind. My cursed face reveals too much. I shall have to be open with her. After all how can Luke be blamed when he knows nothing of my intention? A line from Shakespeare came into her head. 'Send for the man and ask him.' Oh how she longed to see him but perhaps she would not get a chance today.

Betsy, who had been promoted to serving, shyly offered her some more venison. She shook her head.

'Oh pray eat, my dear,' Lady Kirby said, but she couldn't take any more.

There was an apple pie and sauce to follow which she only nibbled at and at last she and Lady Kirby were able to leave the table and abandon Sir Langton to a lonely port. As he was always very abstemious Olivia didn't feel he would stay very long. Over tea in the small drawing-room she must explain it all to Lady Kirby.

'Dear Lady Kirby,' she began at once, 'you know me so well now. I believe you guessed how my feelings about Gerard changed. You know I would never deceive you. It was while I was in Surrey that I awoke to my true feelings about Luke. He has no idea whatever and wouldn't dream of such a thing but I do love him.'

Lady Kirby had sent Betsy away when she had brought in the tea tray, saying she herself would pour out. Now she paused with the teapot in her hand.

'Admire him perhaps for striving to overcome his condition – but love as woman to man? Surely not.'

'Yes, a hundred times yes. And he is far from being just a gardener's son. Brought up here he has learnt cultured ways and has educated himself far beyond most young men.'

'Oh I am fond of him myself. I seek his advice. He is wise beyond his years but he can't escape from his parentage and because of that your father would never consent.' She finally succeeded in pouring two cups of tea.

Olivia jumped up to fetch hers but felt compelled to kneel beside Lady Kirby's chair and plead her cause more intimately.

'Do you not remember coming to that house in Aldgate? We are not aristocracy, hardly even gentry –'

Lady Kirby waved this aside. 'Your father had a little temporary difficulty. He is well placed now, related to the Anstons. These days wealth through trade raises many unlikely people into society – I don't mean your father. He is certainly a gentleman. Architecture is a very gentlemanly profession. Look at Wren and Vanburgh. And your mother was a Fenchurch. You say Luke would never aspire to your hand –'

'I know he wouldn't but if I tell him my love I don't believe –'

'Oh no! That would be so unladylike. *You* propose to *him*! Olivia, what *can* you be thinking of?'

Sir Langton walked in. Olivia scrambled to her feet and returned to her chair.

'What is going on between you ladies?' he demanded in his old imperious voice. 'I am being kept in the dark as usual.'

Lady Kirby burst out, 'No indeed. It is your advice we need.

Olivia has no interest in Thomas. It's his brother and she would like to propose to him herself. Now that is not proper at all, is it?'

Shocked at the suddenness of this revelation Olivia clasped her hands before her face, biting her thumbs and peeping at Sir Langton over her knuckles.

He stood rigid, his mouth slightly agape and his eyes staring. 'What! Brother? Whose? What are you talking about, Sophia?' Then he seemed to take a grip on himself and answered her question. 'No, of course. It's impossible. I mean it's not proper at all.' He turned his eyes on Olivia. 'You're not yourself. Tired, been travelling. You'd better go to bed.'

But now that it was out and she believed she was talking to the Sir Langton who had always refused to acknowledge Luke's existence she felt angry. It was time to challenge him on this and if Lady Kirby could be bold and blunt with him so could she.

'We are talking about Luke Todd, Sir Langton, who is a cripple and has lived here under your nose all his life. I love him and I would like to marry him but he knows nothing of this at all.'

At the word 'cripple' Sir Langton who was still standing up began to flap his arms before his face as if he was swotting flies. 'No no no. Forget it. No. Marry? He can't marry. No. He's nothing. Go away.' His hand movements were directed at her now to wipe her out of his line of vision.

Lady Kirby cried, 'You're upsetting him, Olivia. Leave it for now.'

'But he is not *nothing*.' Olivia stamped her foot. 'He is good, hard-working, kind, humble –'

Sir Langton's face went a fiery red and he shouted, 'He does not exist. Stop this. Go away. I told you to go to bed, didn't I?'

Lady Kirby had now risen in terror. She practically pushed Olivia from the room. 'Oh do, go, he'll have a fit.'

'I'm sorry,' Olivia pleaded at the door, 'but he must learn sometime all that Luke has done for him.'

'I know, I know, but not now. Just go.'

So Olivia fled and the door was firmly shut on her. She stood in the gallery for a moment half bewailing her own rashness and half glad that she had broken through the fog that was Sir Langton's mind.

Then she turned and ran, not to her own room, but to the one place where she was longing to be.

Chapter 24

In a few seconds she was down the stairs and along the east passage, tapping at Luke's door and walking in without waiting for a word. He was not in his little sitting-room but the door to his bedchamber was half open.

'Luke!' she called. There was a scrambling noise and a bang which sounded like one of his crutches falling to the ground. 'Oh Luke, are you all right?'

'Yes,' came his voice. 'I'm so sorry, Miss Beattie. I didn't expect you. I'm just – I'm just covering myself up. I often go early to bed so I can read a while.'

'Oh Luke, forgive me.' She stood embarrassed. She hadn't thought of that possibility. 'I just had to see you. I'll go away.'

'No, please don't. I'm all right but if you don't mind it would be easier if you came to me.' He gave a shy laugh. 'I'm – er – it's all right. If you don't mind.'

She stood in the doorway with great trepidation. Oh he was wonderful! He was sitting up in the bed with a bed gown pulled round his shoulders and the covers drawn up to his waist. His fair hair was tousled as if he'd just snatched off his nightcap but his whole face was suffused with delight at seeing her and with only a touch of natural embarrassment at his predicament.

She didn't dare move or she would have leapt onto the bed and taken him in her arms. This is how she was going to see him when he was her husband. Here was a picture of their future intimacy. She swallowed hard but couldn't help tears of love and joy welling out.

'What is it?' he asked, suddenly alarmed.

'Oh Luke, Luke, I love you. Please, you have to love me too because I'm going to marry you. No one can stop me.'

He fell back on his pillow and began shaking his head. Then he started forward again, his hands in a praying attitude. His eyes looked utterly bewildered.

'Is this a play – you're acting something?'

In turn, shaking her head and sobbing and laughing, she choked out, 'No play. I can't act this well. It's all true. I found out when I was in Surrey.'

'Found out what?'

'How much I love you. I've told them upstairs just now, Sir and Lady. I've told them I am going to marry you. That's why I've rushed down. It's only fair you should know. They said I wasn't allowed to propose because I'm a woman but I don't care. Just tell me you'll have me and then I might be able to come nearer. I might even be allowed to kiss you if we're engaged. Don't look so astonished.'

He shook his head again and his smile was disbelieving. 'I know we're in a dream and I'll wake up in a moment – but I don't want to. I've had them before and they're always dreams. Only this one seemed so real. I remember dropping my crutch.'

'Luke –' She took a step towards him. 'This is *not* a dream.' She reached a hand to the bed and felt for his one foot and pinched it. He started, so she rushed on, 'You said you have dreams – about *me*? Is that what you meant? Does that mean you love me? I won't come nearer till you say the words.'

'Miss Beattie –'

She stamped her foot. 'Olivia – and we are not acting *Twelfth Night* – this is truly me having returned today from my visit to Surrey where Captain Anston does not have one vestige of a whisker, nor even a chin to wear one on, and I have come to my senses and found out who is the man I want for the rest of my life and it is you. Now do you believe me?'

'I believe you are talking to me. I *think* I am awake.'

'Well, then tell me. Could you possibly ever return my love – as the gentleman generally says to the lady?'

Now his lips trembled and his eyes shone with tears. 'I have loved you since the day I first saw you, riding Emperor. But you – how could you possibly love *me*?'

'Ha, that's what Lady Numskull said at first. He's not a whole man, she said. Whole? I said, he's the wholest man I could ever hope to meet.'

Tears ran down his face. 'You mean you've really told them this. I can't – I can't begin to take this in. What did Sir Langton say?'

'He went bright red and is probably having a fit this minute. That's why I had to escape. So, Luke Todd, I haven't had a proper answer yet. Will you marry me?'

'I'm still struggling to believe this is really happening. Marry you! Marry *you*! I never thought marriage would happen to me at all. Ever. But you! Nothing in heaven or earth could give me greater joy. But how could we possibly –'

'Enough. You've said it.' She closed the gap between them and sitting down on the edge of the bed flung her arms round him, her own man, her love for ever. She kissed him full on the lips.

He held her tight for a moment, his breath coming fast, and then his hands gently but firmly tried to push her away.

'You know it is impossible. I have nothing. Not a penny to my name, no home, no status –'

'My father would offer you an apprenticeship. We're not talking about *tomorrow* or even next year. At least we can know in our hearts that we are pledged to each other.'

His eyes still shone with joy but he gave a great sigh and moved his hands in a gesture of hopelessness. 'You say you've told them upstairs. Tomorrow is almost certainly when Sir Langton will throw me out. I suppose I could crawl up the stairs at Meg Summers' to the room my grandmother had and Tom would have to sleep with Father again – but how could Meg feed another mouth for no payment?'

'Oh Luke, you are so practical and I thought I was but I rush madly into things. I should have said nothing to anyone before I spoke to you. But you are far too important here for them ever to want to get rid of you. Lady K knows that and I fear I've so upset Sir that he will relapse into madness again. You are steward here in all but name.'

'There is much in that 'all but' as the bard might have said. But, oh Olivia, will you tell Tom what you have just told me? Tom loves you – I know it.'

She stood up and walked a few paces round the small space between his bed and a narrow wardrobe. The room was very bare, she realised. 'Tom is too generous-hearted to grudge you anything,' she said, facing him again. 'I love Tom in a very different way. He has the same assertive rebel streak that I have and we will make brother and sister very happily, never man and wife. But you, Luke, you are perfect.'

He covered his face then with his hands and sobbed. She was there with her arms again hugging him. 'I know, I know, you have lived all your life under the shadow of being *im*perfect. I can never forgive Sir Langton for that.'

They heard footsteps in the passage. She started back.

'No one must find you here,' Luke whispered. The footsteps passed. 'Go quickly. It's late. Your reputation!'

'Hang my reputation, but I will go for your sake.' She withdrew as far as the open door to his sitting-room. Then she wagged a finger at him as he looked up with a smile of such love through his tears. 'When you wake in the morning don't tell yourself it was a dream. Here' – she took a handkerchief from her bosom – 'there's the proof of its reality.' He took it and kissed it and wiped his eyes.

She slipped out of the room and found Jenny in the passage.

'Oh Miss Olivia, I've been to the kitchen. I didn't know where you were. Lady Kirby came to your room for you. Sir Langton has locked himself in his dressing-room and is moaning and shouting something terrible.'

'All right, I'll come.'

She ran back up again, aware now of sounds of banging and groaning. She knew Lady Kirby would still be angry with her but at least she was desperate enough to need her help. I can sort the world out now, she was thinking, now I am sure of Luke.

'What can I do?' Lady Kirby wailed as soon as she saw her. 'He'll injure himself. He must be striking his head against the wall.'

'You could send for a footman to break down the door,' Olivia suggested.

This was done and after one blow of the man's shoulder the dressing-room door was opened from within.

'Of course! He can't bear damage to his property,' Lady Kirby muttered to her. 'You *are* clever, Olivia, but oh, you had no right to upset him like this.'

He looked out and barked, 'Is there a fire? Can a gentleman not have a moment's peace alone in his own home?'

Olivia had shrunk round the corner of the passage so he saw only Lady Kirby.

'We all wanted peace to go to bed,' she was saying. 'You were making such a noise. Come to bed now, dear, and everything will look much better in the morning.'

Olivia, hearing no objection from Sir Langton slipped into her own room where Jenny awaited her, full of curiosity.

'What made him mad, Miss? He was so pleased to see you at first.'

Olivia sighed. She would tell Jenny but not now. Her inward happiness was intense but the weariness of the journey and the emotions of the last few hours had sapped her vitality. 'We can't account for his goings-on, Jenny. I don't believe he will ever be his old self again. Just unpin me and then you must go to bed.'

'Eh, poor old gentleman,' Jenny said.

When Olivia fell into bed herself quarter of an hour later she thought she would sleep at once but her mind was too full. Why did Sir Langton want to blot Luke out of existence? Luke was the most wonderful character. It was a privilege for anyone to know him and she, fortunate she, had secured him for life. But if ever a man appeared to have something on his conscience it was Sir Langton Kirby.

Or, she mused, am I suffering from an over-vivid imagination? Sir Langton is just a stiff awkward character with a mind bent on perfection and passing on his inheritance inviolate. No wonder his poor brain has been unhinged by the death of his heir and the perilous state of his property. But she didn't really believe that was the case. So many signs pointed to there being something more. Thinking of it was not going to resolve it, however, so she let her thoughts flit to Tom. He at least was an open book but telling him of her proposal to Luke was not going to be easy. She had leapt impulsively into a sea of happiness and was not drowning. In fact she was sure that it was the best impulse she had ever had in her life but she could see that the ripples would keep going far and wide. While she was mentally rehearsing the words in which she would tell Tom what she had done she at last fell asleep.

Chapter 25

The night was mild and she had left her window open. So the singing of birds roused her early and she went to the window in her nightdress and gazed out listening to the chorus of tweets and twitterings and absorbing the breathless beauty of the scene. As she looked the sun cleared the eastern horizon and fingers of light shot through the far wood and spread across the lake. I am in love with this place but when Luke and I marry our future is likely to be far away from here. If only Sir Langton would die Lady Kirby might make Luke her official steward and then we could stay.

Long before the breakfast hour she peeped out of her room and saw Betsy dusting down the curved banisters. 'Come in and help fasten my corset,' she whispered. 'I want to walk in the grounds.'

'Oh Miss, I'm not fit to –'

'Come. It won't take a moment. I don't want to wake Jenny yet.'

When she was done and Betsy had scurried back to her task Olivia went down and let herself out of the great doors, taking deep breaths of the sharp air. The sky was an arch of duck-egg blue, shading to gold at the rim. Below her feet and all about her the world was sparkling, every dewdrop a star of light. She wandered up and down the paths and then out of curiosity headed out to where she knew the border with Mr Braintree's land lay. There was quite a worn path now with the hoofmarks of Luke's pony and Tom's huge boot-prints clearly visible. After a while she saw a figure ahead among a plantation of young trees. It was Tom himself.

She strode forward gladly, eager to have her hard task over and done with. She waved and called to attract his attention.

He looked up and raised his hat and walked towards her. He seemed so pleased to see her that quivers of apprehension shot through her. She must break the news now but she had not yet resolved how to do it.

'You're out early,' she called. 'What are you busy with?'

'It's the new wood to hide the coal workings. Now the buds are here I can see any saplings that have not taken root or have died over winter.' He looked her up and down. 'You look well, Miss Beattie. You enjoyed your stay in Surrey?'

She held out her hand to him.

'Nay,' he laughed. 'Mine are not clean.' He showed her his right hand.

'It's healthy dirt.' And she took it before he could withdraw it. Still clasping it she said quickly, 'and I am not Miss Beattie. Olivia, please, for we will be brother and sister when I am married to Luke.' There, it was said.

His mouth fell open. 'Married – to *Luke*!' His hands flopped to his sides. Olivia cursed her hasty tongue but how could she have broken it gently? And she didn't like the way he emphasised Luke's name which had echoes of Lady Kirby's shocked reaction.

So she said with some asperity, 'Now surely *you* don't think he is never to be married. He is a young man after all.'

He swallowed and said with difficulty, 'I hadn't supposed he would – but – I thought you were going to say – Captain Anston.'

She laughed at that. 'Him! Never. He is a worm and no man. Oh Tom, please, I want you to be glad for us. You were Luke's

282

first thought. Please, try not to *mind* my marrying him.'

He hesitated. 'No-no, but *how*?'

'The parson will do it in Tadby Church.'

'I didn't mean –' He shook his head.

'Speak out,' she said. 'You have always had the courage to speak your mind.'

'Well,' he said, '*I* have little enough prospect of marriage with my meagre savings but *Luke*! Are you suddenly so wealthy you can pick whom you please?'

She thought, he *is* hurt and angry. Of course he is. He told his love as something hopeless because of the distance between us and now I have chosen his unlikely brother. 'No, Tom,' she said deliberately using the diminutive, 'but I love him. I asked him and I find he loves me. We will find a way somehow. Tom, I love you but not like that. We would be Beatrice and Benedict.'

'They got married and lived happily ever after.'

'We don't know that and I must say I've always doubted it. They are both too bold and assertive. Luke will act as a wonderful break on all my impulsive follies. Can you be reconciled to the idea?'

'I'll have to, won't I? But I can't imagine what your father will say.' Then he grinned at her and ran his hand through his thick dark curls. 'Well, I have to say, if you can never be mine – which I never supposed – I'd rather Luke had you as anyone else in the world. He's a wonder, is Luke and he deserves some happiness.'

She flung her arms round him then and kissed his bronzed cheek.

'Bless you, brother, for saying that. You are a trump, Thomas Todd.'

He pursed his lips in a comical smile and put his fingers to the place.

'Well, thanks for that, Sister Olivia.'

She did a little skip round the nearest tree.

'I'm so happy I could sing with the birds, but now I must remember the sad side of the coin. I told Sir and her ladyship last night and he has relapsed into his worst state since Gerard's death. So she is very cross with me and I have to think how I can calm him down. If only I could fathom the mystery that I believe still lurks in the past – which I'm sure your grandmother knew – I might find an answer. Last night he said that Luke did not exist. I'm sure he's not mad. His mind is troubled.'

Thomas shrugged his shoulders. 'I've lived with his strange attitude to Luke since babyhood. There are people who find any sort of freak terrifying.'

'Freak!' she cried. 'Luke is not a freak.'

'Of course he isn't to me, but Sir Langton is an odd man.'

He turned aside to pluck up a small dead sapling. 'I've known him look with revulsion on something like that and all withered flowers must be dead-headed at once. That's why he will never look at the coal workings. His estate is marred. Men are gouging holes in it.' He gave a rueful laugh. 'And that's why gardening for him never stops for a moment.'

'And I'm interrupting you. But I must *do* something. Perhaps if I call on Meg Summers today . . .? She might remember things your grandmother said. Would she be up and about now?'

'Certainly. But you can't have had your own breakfast yet.'

'I think I'll miss it. I'm not so anxious to go back in just now. I know it's cowardly but I don't want to face them yet and I love the walk to the village.'

He shrugged his shoulders again and let her go with a grin and a wave.

Olivia walked fast, much relieved that that interview was over. Now she could enjoy the rare solitude and freedom of motion. If she walked out with Lady Kirby it was at her slower pace and if Sir Langton was with them it was usually in the carriage as it had been the disastrous day when he saw Gerard's memorial.

It was still only half past seven when she reached Meg Summers' cottage. There was no answer to her knock so she peeped in and hearing noises in the back yard realised Meg was feeding the chickens. She walked through to the kitchen and was about to step out of the back door when she noticed an open Bible on the kitchen table. Beside it was a slate with chalked letters printed on it large. GOD, ADAM, EVE.

She was looking at this curiously when Meg exclaimed behind her, 'Why, Miss Beattie, I didn't hear you. It's mighty early for visiting.' Then she too noticed the Bible. 'Oh!' She closed it and popped it behind the bread crock. 'It's just Tom teaching me to read. I felt ashamed I couldn't when he can read great words like Nebuchadnezzar as easy as the parson. You've been away in the south I hear. Fancy coming to see me so soon. I'm sure I'm honoured.'

But Olivia was tense with excitement. She was sure she had recognised that Bible when she briefly saw the outer cover. The black spine was worn in places to a reddish brown exactly as Mrs Johnson's had been.

'And I'm very happy to see you,' she replied to Meg as naturally as possible. 'I think it's splendid of you to be learning to read.' As Meg was putting the kettle on the fire she casually drew the Bible from behind the bread crock and opened the cover. Inside was written in a round hand 'Janet Johnson her book.'

Meg looked up and saw her. 'What you doing, Miss?' She sounded frightened.

Olivia managed to answer easily, 'I just wondered how far you had got and whether you would read to me.'

'Nay, we just started two days ago. I learnt them words,' pointing to the slate. She reached for the Bible.

'Mrs Summers,' Olivia said, looking fixedly at her and keeping hold of the book. 'I thought Mrs Johnson's Bible was buried with her.'

'Oh Miss.' Meg was devastated. 'Oh Miss. You won't tell. I thought it such a shame and I hadn't one in the house if hers went. I was the last in before they come to nail her down and they didn't see. Tom doesn't know but it's my own. He said when you have a minute see if you can find them words in the first few pages and tell me tonight. I've always felt bad about it ever since in case it was stealing from the dead.'

Olivia, trying to still the rapid beating of her heart, said with all the vehemence she could muster, 'It wasn't, Mrs Summers, it wasn't stealing. Mrs Johnson would have wanted you to have it and as it happens she asked me to look for something in it after she was dead so she certainly didn't intend it to be buried with her.'

'Eh, Miss did she really say that? You make me feel so much better. But there ain't nothing in it, unless someone had a look before they put it in her coffin.' She took the Bible, turning it up carefully and giving it a little shake. 'I never found anything either, honest, Miss Beattie. I've had it hidden in fact, because of feeling bad but when Tom said to look for the words I did get it out.'

Olivia could scarcely contain her impatience. 'If you make us both a nice cup of tea, Mrs Summers, I'll just have a look. Mrs Johnson seemed to suggest there was a message on one of the pages. I don't why but she said she'd only told *me*.'

'Oh she took a fancy to you, Miss Beattie. And she knew I couldn't read, see. She wasn't much of a reader herself but it'll make sense to anyone clever like you.'

She was setting out her best cups while Olivia, wishing she could be alone, was feverishly turning the pages and finding the nineties. Ninety-nine. She turned over – one hundred and two! What! Where was a hundred? She turned back. Ah, the page was too thick. It was two somehow pasted together, pages 100 and 101, and there was something between. She could feel an outline.

Meg was watching her.

'I think there's something but it's glued down,' Olivia said lightly. 'Have you some scissors, Meg?'

Meg clasped her hands across her chest. 'Cut a Bible! That's bad luck.'

Olivia was trying very gently to prise the pages apart but she felt a tear begin. With Meg's frightened eyes fixed on her as if she was handling an explosive she tried the bottom edge. No, that was very secure. The top edge. Ah, here was a little gap. Was it possible to get two fingers in and draw the paper out? She could feel the top of it. It was thin paper. She pulled gently. No, it was too wide for the gap. She looked about. On the dresser was an earthenware pot with knives in it.

'Which is your sharpest?' she asked. 'I promise not to cut the paper but if I can ease the two pages apart just an inch I think I can abstract this. It *is* a message for me because Mrs Johnson said it was page a hundred and I went straight for that. If she meant me to have it I would be wronging her memory not to read it.'

'Eh well. Miss, put like that you've got to try.' Meg drew out a lethal looking object. 'There's nothing sharper than that meat knife but be careful. Only my Jack carves with it. He won't let me.'

Olivia took it and handed Meg the Bible. 'If you hold it like that, so – I can delicately slip the knife – There!' She set the knife back in the pot and inserted her fingers into the enlarged slit and drew out the thin folded sheet. 'There now you need never worry about the Bible again. When you get to pages a hundred and a hundred and one get Jack to lever them properly apart so you can read them.'

Meg roared with laughter. 'I'll be dead long afore I get as far as that. But what do it say, Miss? Happen it says you're to have her Bible.'

'If it does I'll give it to you. I have my own. Well I think I'll just take it to read at the Castle.' She gave it a fleeting glance.

'I'm afraid the ink has faded and I'll also need my magnifying glass.' She held it so Meg could see.

'By, Miss, it *is* writ small. I can't see Janet writing that.'

'No well, I think I know what it'll be about.' She took a drink from the cup Meg pushed towards her. 'Mrs Johnson always seemed sure I was to marry poor Mr Gerard. She kept saying, 'You're the one.' So I think it'll be some tale of his childhood or perhaps something he always said he wanted to give his wife, something at the castle which he confided to her.'

'Ay, maybe a love poem he wrote when he was still a lad and was too shy to give it to any but his grandmother. Will you tell me when you find out?'

'If it's not *very* private.' Olivia beamed at her, drank off her tea and rose to go.

'Eh but you've not had a bite to eat. You cannot have had breakfast. They'll only be starting now up at t'Castle.'

'Then I'll just be in time if I hurry. I was up with the birds you see and it was such a fine morning I thought I'll go and see dear Mrs Summers. She won't mind.'

'Mind! Nay I'm that pleased the way it turned out.' Meg came to the door and waved her off.

When she had left the village behind Olivia broke into a run. As soon as she was inside the small side gate to the Castle grounds which provided walkers the short-cut to the village she made sure no on was in sight and opened the paper again. Even in the sunlight it was hard to read but she could make out a name at the top – Janet Johnson – and at the bottom – May Tyler. That was the young woman who had been with Lady Kirby when Gerard was born, assisting Mrs Johnson, the midwife. She folded the paper and began to run again. There truly *was* a mystery surrounding Gerard's birth and she was within minutes of finding it out.

Chapter 26

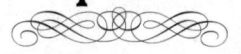

Olivia had told half a lie to Mrs Summers. It wasn't she who had a magnifying glass. It was Luke. She had seen it on top of a map he had been studying once. So she slipped in the back way, passed the kitchen where she could hear clattering and knocked on his door. This time she waited for his 'Come in' and then she was inside and in his arms.

'You've been hunted for,' he said, when he could speak.

'I know, I know. But we must be quick now before anyone interrupts us.'

He was alert at once and she swiftly sketched the background to her quest and how she had found the paper. 'We'll need your magnifying glass.'

He pulled his chair towards his table which had a small drawer below. He put his hand in and laid it instantly on the required tool.

'How orderly you are! You'll regulate our home so beautifully. Now, can you make this out? The ink has faded.'

He held it to the sunlight and picked up the glass. 'Should *you* not read it? It must be private to you.'

'Nothing is private from you. You read it.'

'Very well. It starts, 'The testimony of Janet Johnson.' I wonder if she meant testament. It could be a will.'

'Just read it, read it.' She was hopping with impatience.

'Very well. She goes on, 'I was midwife on the night of

November 6th 1740 to Lady Sophia Kirby and my daughter, Mrs Grace Todd.'

'What!' broke in Olivia, 'you and Gerard were born on the same day?'

'I was told the next day.'

'No one celebrated your coming of age last November?'

'No. Why should they?'

'Well, go on, go on.'

"My daughter died in giving birth to a son. The night was bitter cold and a hailstorm put out the fire. I carried the child to the castle to keep him warm. The nearest fire was in Sir Langton Kirby's study where he awaited the birth of his child.'

'You must have been told wrong. This says you were born first.'

Luke's eyes were skimming down the page. 'I can't – I can't believe this.' The blood was draining from his cheeks. 'Here, you look. Can it be true?'

Trembling, she took the paper and the glass. His eyes must be excellent because she found the thin small letters difficult. "I showed him my grandson and he looked him all over and said, 'My firstborn son'. I tried to tell him his mistake but I heard cries from Lady Kirby and her attendant May Tyler so I went up and an hour later a boy was born. Lady Kirby was not –' What is that word –'

'Conscious,' murmured Luke.

'Not conscious, so I took the boy to show Sir Langton. He was cradling my grandson. 'Is he not perfect, my boy' he kept saying. I showed him his true son but the child was' – no, no, 'deformed in its legs."

She stopped and they stared into each other's eyes.

'You are a Kirby,' she said. 'Luke, you are the heir.'

He kept shaking his head. 'It can't be right. No man could do that.'

'But he did, he did. This is what has been eating him away.

Oh you see how it was – when Gerard died – he couldn't acknowledge *you*! He had always blotted you out. It would have meant confessing to his crime.' She slapped her hand to her head. 'Gerard *was* Tom's brother! I saw the likeness. But how could I have imagined – and she doesn't know! Lady Kirby does not know that she gave birth to you. Luke, she's your mother!'

'You'd better read on. I didn't see further than that.' He could scarcely speak.

She turned her eyes to the paper. 'It goes on, 'I told him plain, 'This is your son, sir,' but he denied it with oaths, clinging all the time to my grandson. Then he got up and carried him upstairs and laid him by his wife. I followed behind with his true son but May saw and heard it all. Lady Kirby opened her eyes. She was very weak. He said, 'Look at our lovely boy. You've done it at last, Sophia. Our perfect boy, our heir.' She wept tears of joy for she had lost two other babies' – Oh Luke, Lady Kirby told me that herself and about this young woman, May Tyler. It all rings true – but I'll go on – 'had lost two other babies and had no belief she could ever please her husband. I saw those tears. May God forgive me, I never enlightened her. I called May out of the room and we were in torment over what to do. I swear it was not that I wished to see my grandson promoted above his station but we both loved Lady Kirby and my poor Grace was dead. I took the crippled boy and showed him to Albert Todd who had slept the night through. He was too grieved for Grace to care much about the child so we found a wet–nurse in the village and Sir Langton said he could be cared for at the castle. This is God's truth that the boy they call Gerard is Albert and Grace Todd's son and the boy they call Luke is Sir Langton and Lady Kirby's son. Spoken by me this first day of December 1740 and written down by May Tyler."

Olivia laid down the paper and stared at him over her clasped hands. 'Oh Luke, he should be hung drawn and quartered. He should be burnt at the stake.'

'No, hush, hush. Has he not been punished already?'

'Punished, punished.' How well she remembered those words and the cries of anguish that accompanied them!

'Luke, what are we going to do now?'

'We could destroy the paper.'

'No, no! Never! You are the heir! You will be Sir Luke Kirby. This which you have worked so hard to preserve is yours.'

'I don't see how I can accept it if it means suffering for Sir Langton and Lady Kirby. Let things stay as they are.'

'Now, Luke, for once you are not thinking clearly.' She stopped. There was a knock at the door. She opened it a crack. It was only Jenny.

'Oh Miss Olivia. They are worried about you. Please come upstairs.'

'I will – at once.' She turned back to pick up the paper.

'No!' cried Luke. 'Not now. He might tear it up. Let me make a copy. Do nothing now. It's too soon. It's so sudden –'

There was sense in having a copy so she left it, but the revelation was like a flame inside her, too hot to hold back. She ran up behind Jenny and found Sir Langton and Lady Kirby in the small dining-room with the remains of breakfast still on the table.

Sir Langton glowered at her and Lady Kirby exclaimed, 'Olivia, where have you been? You went out so early!'

'It was a lovely morning, that's all. I'm sorry if I upset you but it was good that I did because I have found out all that has been troubling you, Sir Langton.'

He started. 'What? Troubling *me*? *You* have been troubling me – saying outrageous things, behaving oddly. If you live under this roof you must conform to Castle Kirby time-keeping. You have learnt strange habits since you went away.'

'No habits that I have learnt, Sir Langton, are as bad as exchanging babies.'

She was standing over him, staring him down and took great satisfaction in seeing her words filter into his brain and his face begin to contort, his body to tremble.

Lady Kirby jumped up. 'Olivia, are you mad? Exchanging babies.'

Now Sir Langton turned to aggression. He got to his feet and yelled, 'Get her out of here. Get her away.'

'No.' Olivia took a pace back in case he attacked her but then stood her ground. 'Lady Kirby, this is a boil that must be lanced and then he will be better. I do not wish to shock you of all people whom I love as a mother but I have found out what Sir Langton did twenty-one years ago.'

He fell back onto his chair, nearly tipping it over. His face had turned a greenish white.

Lady Kirby ran round the table to him and her eyes blazed with fury at Olivia. 'You will kill him. Be silent. I can forgive him anything he did as a young man.' Then her face too began to crumple. 'Exchanging babies?' she breathed.

'Yes, Lady Kirby,' Olivia said quietly. 'You thought you lost a son last summer but you still have a son. Luke is your son. Gerard was Albert Todd's son.'

Sir Langton uttered a howl of pain as Lady Kirby turned a face of shock and disbelief to his. Then a light seemed to come into her eyes and she looked back at Olivia with the former fierce stare.

'You're saying this because you want to marry Luke. Of course you are. How dare you? You want to be Lady Kirby, do you? *Luke* our son!'

It had not yet struck Olivia that she could become Lady Kirby but now she saw what a chance this gave her to move Sir Langton whose distraught state seemed momentarily lost on Lady Kirby.

She flung herself on her knees before Sir Langton. 'Tell her, oh tell her and you will be free. When I said I'd marry Luke I didn't know this. Thank God I didn't so no one can suspect my motives. To me he was Luke Todd, Tom's brother but you know he is not. Now think, think what it means. You grieved for Gerard because you had lost your heir and the Kirbys would die out of Castle Kirby for ever. But you have *not* lost an heir. If I marry Luke we will produce a family of true Kirbys.'

She realised she had taken hold of his hands. He was staring at her and she had no idea whether he had understood, whether it was possible for her words to eradicate his fearful shock and give him hope.

Lady Kirby now came round and pulled her quite roughly to her feet. 'Olivia, what you are saying? I don't know where you heard such things. It's not possible. Would *I* not know? I gave birth to Gerard. Someone has been saying terrible things.'

'I have a paper,' Olivia said, breathing hard and trying now to speak very gently, 'a paper written by May Tyler for Janet Johnson. It only came to light by chance this morning.'

Sir Langton uttered another cry as Lady Kirby repeated the names.

'Don't, don't, Sophie,' he managed to choke out. 'Stop questioning her. Stop it. You don't know. You know nothing.'

'What do you mean? I gave birth to Gerard. You're mad. She's mad.'

'No, no.' Sir Langton grabbed at her dress, pulling her towards him. He spoke into its folds. 'You had fainted. I laid him beside you. I had to do it. He was perfect. Can't you see? The other was – no good. I wanted to please you. You would have been so hurt – a weakling again. Your heart would have broken. I did it for you. He was so beautiful. I didn't think – that thing – that other thing would live.' He broke down into gasping sobs. 'I did it for you.'

Olivia drew a deep sigh of relief. The words had been spoken. He would be released. But Lady Kirby was staring at him in disbelief.

'What have you said? Gerard was not –' She swung her gaze to Olivia. 'Luke is –?' When Olivia didn't answer immediately she cried, 'Show me this paper.'

'Certainly I will. It's in Luke's room. Shall I fetch it now?' Her quiet tone seemed to help Lady Kirby master herself.

'No, I will come down.' But Sir Langton gripped the skirt of her dress.

'Sophie, look at me.' He seemed to have shrunk, his back was bowed. He peered up at her like a pleading dog. 'I did it for you.'

She pulled her skirt from his grasp and walked to the door. 'Come, Olivia.'

Olivia looked back at him with a yearning pity and then followed Lady Kirby.

He is only fifty, she thought as she ran down the stairs. He won't die from this shock. He's a free man now. He can have happy years ahead of him. Now he is rid of this weight of guilt he will live again.

They tapped at Luke's door and entered. He was at his table, pen in hand. Olivia could see he was on the last line of the copy.

Grasping the table he hauled himself up and grabbed one crutch which was leaning within reach.

Lady Kirby was obviously very moved at the sight of him but she held out her hand for the paper.

'Show her the original,' Olivia said. 'Sir Langton has confessed.' He handed it to her. He too, she could see, was looking at this woman with new wondering eyes.

'I can scarcely read this. But it's true. I see it's true. Give me the copy.'

She stood by the window and read it through. 'Yes, I see how it could have happened. But he didn't do it for me.' She turned to Luke. 'Sit down again.' He did so. Then she knelt by him and clasped her arms round him and burst into a passion of weeping.

'Oh Luke, *I* would never have rejected you. Have I not loved you since I came to know you well?'

His head was bowed over hers as he sobbed too. 'And I you. It's not too late is it for us to be mother and son?'

'Oh no,' she cried. 'It's not too late.'

Olivia watched with tears running unchecked down her face.

They clung together for many minutes and then Olivia said, 'It may not be too late for you to have a father too. I think I should go back and see what he is doing.'

Lady Kirby rose. 'You'll never be able to forgive him, Luke. I cannot.'

'Oh but I will. Should I go to him now? I can get up the stairs with some help. Olivia, you were right to break it though I was afraid. It was all so sudden. I couldn't take it in as quickly as you. My identity was changed at a stroke. A family of grandmother, father, brother was snatched away and a new, a lovely, a beautiful mother has been given me.' He squeezed Lady Kirby's hand. 'But you, Olivia, knew it must be told. You have the most amazing courage.'

'I don't deserve that,' she said. 'I spoke on impulse as I always do.'

'And I was cruel to you upstairs,' Lady Kirby said. Then she looked from one to the other in wonder. 'You will be married, you two. Olivia, dear girl, you will he married to my son. You will be my daughter. Oh you have been a daughter to me all these months. I think I am beginning to be very happy. Yes, we will all go upstairs now.'

They had started along the passage when a footman came running toward them.

'My lady, come to the office quickly. The master has armed himself with a pistol.'

They all broke into a run, even Luke swung forward on his crutches at a faster pace than he had ever attempted before.

Olivia was there first. The office door stood open and Sir Langton was inside fumbling at the lock on a drawer in his desk. The pistol was in his other hand.

It's not loaded, she realised. He's looking for powder and shot.

He turned a wretched face towards her, his cheeks wet with tears. 'I can't find the key. I don't know where the key is.'

He was so helpless that she was able to take the pistol from his limp hands as Lady Kirby came up with Luke close behind.

'What were you doing?' she cried.

'I've done wrong,' he said, not looking up and Olivia saw that Luke was now careful to keep out of sight.

'Would you have added another wrong, Langton? You were going to take your own life?'

'I couldn't find the key,' he mumbled.

The footman was still hovering and Lady Kirby sent him for a glass of brandy. She sat Sir Langton in his office chair and pulled up the other beside it. Olivia looked at Luke just outside the door.

'Shall we leave them?' she murmured to him.

Lady Kirby called out, 'Stay and you come in, Luke. Now Langton' – Olivia had never before heard her use the name without the title – 'there is your son. He and this dear girl are going to marry. Do you not want to see your grandchildren running about the lawns?'

Now he did look up but only as far as Luke's legs. He seemed to be seeing them for the first time since he had rejected the deformed baby. He gazed for a full minute. 'That is the child? He can stand?'

'I can ride too, sir.'

Sir Langton shook his head slowly from side to side. 'That is my son?'

'Yes, sir.' There was a long tense silence while they all watched Sir Langton. Would he address Luke directly?

Very, very slowly he moved his gaze up Luke's body till he met his eyes.

Luke struggled to keep his face still. Olivia knew he was torn as to whether he should speak first.

But it was Sir Langton who spoke.

'Can you have children?' he asked in a quiet wondering voice.

Luke blushed and swallowed hard. Olivia pressed his hand and beamed courage into him.

'Sir,' he said, still bright red, 'I do not procreate with my legs.'

Sir Langton nodded as if he could see the reasonableness of the answer. 'And you are my son?'

'If you will have me, sir.'

The old frown of bewilderment reappeared. 'But where have you been all this time?' Olivia thought, his sanity is coming and going like the sun between clouds.

'Here, sir, and very grateful for my board and lodging and above all my education.'

'You have grown into a man.' He said it as a statement of an astonishing fact.

Lady Kirby tapped him on the arm. 'And who has kept Castle Kirby running for the past year? Who has dealt with the debts, the lawyers, the coal workings which will save the Castle, talked to the tenants, planned the crops, improved the sale of produce? Your son.'

Sir Langton continued to stare at Luke. After a silence he said, 'But that is right. If the father is ill, the son is in charge. I always said he should be interested in the estate but he never was.'

'Oh Langton, that was Gerard.'

Pain shot across his face. 'Gerard? Did he not – there was blood everywhere – but – his name was on the stone. That was not right. I knew it. But what could be done? No no. The world will have to know.'

Now he is seeing consequences, a good sign, a wonderful sign, Olivia felt.

He clutched his hands about his head. 'The parson – the baptismal records, the burial –?'

'Sir, let things stand as they are,' Luke said.

'No, no, that wouldn't be right.' The effort of thought made deep lines on his face. 'There must be order in everything. It must be put right.' He shook his head as if it were too much for him. 'How can it be put right, Sophia?'

'I will tell the parson and Albert Todd. The records can be corrected. Gerard's name on the stone – I don't know.' She looked at Olivia.

Luke said, 'The word 'adopted' could be carved in perhaps.'

The footman came with the brandy. When Sir Langton had drunk some a little colour came back into his face.

'Come now, let us go upstairs,' Lady Kirby said, giving him her arm. 'All these things can be worked out. You need not meet anyone yourself till it is all forgotten.'

Olivia slipped the pistol into the case she saw lying open on the desk. He caught the movement as he got up. 'I should have done it. I know you can't ever forgive me, Sophie. It can't be wiped out. If records are made right my infamy will stand there for all generations. I should have done it.'

'I can, I will forgive you,' she murmured at his ear as they passed through together into the entrance lobby and began to climb the stairs very slowly. She looked back at Luke and Olivia. 'It will take time,' she said, 'it will take time for all of us but we will start using a corner of the long dining-room for dinner. We will eat downstairs as a family. That's what we must do. I'll give the orders.'

Sir Langton checked on the stairs. '*I* will give the orders.'

'Of course, dear,' they heard Lady Kirby say.

As Luke and Olivia returned to his room he said softly, 'I think my mother has come out of this very well. I'm just trying how that sounds and I like it.'

They found Luke's door open and Tom standing at the window reading Janet Johnson's testimony.

He turned round with a very stern face. 'Was it wise to leave this lying about?'

'Oh, Tom,' Luke exclaimed, 'I'm sorry you should find out like this. It has been a bewildering day for us all.'

'I came in to congratulate you, Luke, on securing this young lady. Now I find you have secured a baronetcy as well. Did you know of the existence of this already, Olivia, when you went to Tadby this morning – to procure it?'

'No, I did not. I knew there was something for me in Mrs Johnson's Bible but I believed it buried with her. You told me it was. But it seems Meg Summers removed it – for which we are all truly grateful. Sir Langton is relieved of the burden of a hidden sin and he and Lady Kirby have gained a son.'

'And you are to marry the heir which was what you hoped to achieve with Gerard. Good fortune strikes at your second attempt.'

'Stop this, Tom,' Luke cried. 'Why are you angry? You were the next person we would have told and of course our – your father.'

'Yes, while you have all gained each other I have lost two brothers and my father two sons. We should have mourned Gerard whom we never enjoyed and the one we thought we had is not ours at all. I'd better go and tell my father before some of the servants blurt it out.' He made for the door.

'Oh Tom, nothing has changed between us,' Luke pleaded.

'Really? When I am head gardener and you are Sir Luke it is I that will be doffing my hat to you.' And he stalked out.

Luke looked after him with sorrow in his eyes. 'If this is to be the price I wish it had never happened.'

'He'll be back soon,' Olivia said. 'It's not in his nature to sulk.'

In fact he was back half an hour later when Luke had made another copy of the letter as insurance against loss.

Tom held out his hand to Luke and then embraced him. 'Forgive me. It was the shock. If you'll let me we're always be brothers.'

Olivia hugged him in turn. 'Madam,' he mocked, 'you are not remotely related to me now. Is not this unseemly?'

'I fling convention to the winds,' she said. 'Do you imagine our Shakespeare readings will stop now? We will forever be the trio of the Bard's disciples.'

'Good,' he said with his old frank grin

'Did you see your father?' Luke asked.

'I did.'

'Whatever could he say to such a tale?'

'I always knew Albert Todd was a man of great wisdom. He said, 'My Grace never knew what babe she bore and it's too late for me to be fretting' and he went on watering the lettuce plants. Quarter of an hour later he said, 'If you're seeing the lad wish him well from me. He deserves it."

'God bless him. Of course I will go to him and talk with him about it all.'

Tom shook his head. 'You won't get more out of him than I've told you. He's said his last word on the matter. I think I've come off with the best father.'

Olivia said, 'But I have great hopes for Sir Langton when the knowledge of what he did has faded from other people's minds. I think he will be a humble, gentle old man.'

'Are you sure?' Luke said with a smile. 'You heard him on the stairs just now. '*I* will give the orders."

Chapter 27

'Sir Langton would hardly sit still for a moment,' Lady Kirby confided to Olivia as they walked out together into the sunshine later that morning. 'I thought we could have a little light refreshment and talk of it openly. I wanted him to admit he did it for himself, not for me. I would have listened if he could have relived it quietly and honestly but he would hardly pause to eat. 'I must be talking to my son,' he kept saying. 'I must leave everything shipshape for him and his lady. His wedding must not be lavish but it must be fit for the heir to Castle Kirby.' I think, Olivia, he might have had too much brandy. He's not used to it you know but certainly his energy bubbled up as never before and now he is quite possessed with the idea of his son. He doesn't say the name *Luke*. It is 'my son this' and 'my son that.' Not 'our son," she added ruefully. 'He is closeted in the office with him now.'

'I know,' said Olivia, 'and Luke hopes to persuade him to go out and speak to Albert Todd. But perhaps he's not ready for that yet.'

'Oh he has moved far beyond the past and present into the future. The future is so much more comfortable for his poor brain. It did make me think, my dear, how important it is for you to write to your father. Have you done that yet?'

'I have hardly drawn breath, Lady Kirby, after today's extraordinary happenings.'

303

'Ah yes, I am in a whirl too. I had to take a little brandy to stop Langton holding the bottle beside him and then I got Betsy to run away with it. But I think it should not be till September.'

'What, Lady Kirby?'

'Your wedding of course. By then you see it'll be over a year since – I mean it wouldn't seem proper even though he wasn't – Shall we sit down here?' There was a seat on the terrace facing the lake.

'I must confess,' she went on quickly, 'I never mourned that wretched boy as a mother should. I always felt he was more his father's boy but Sir Langton wouldn't discipline him till he was too old for it and after that I seemed to do nothing but worry about him. But I'll tell you something no one knew except poor May Tyler. When I was nursing Gerard the day he was born I heard another baby cry and I asked May whose it was. She said Grace Todd had died giving birth and a wet-nurse had been sent for but she wasn't come yet. I said to May, 'Bring the wee thing to me' and she did and I gave him the breast. 'He's deformed in his legs,' she said. I wondered why she sounded odd and ran out quickly, but I nursed him to sleep and he looked so thin and frail compared to – you know – Oh I wish I'd been allowed to go on loving him – all his childhood was lost to me –' And she began to sob.

Olivia sat with her arm round her for a long time while she cried for the years of love she had been prevented from giving. All the time her own mind was absorbed with the idea of being married to Luke in less than six months.

I only knew a few days ago that I loved him, she realised with amazement, but it was there, maturing, all the time I was half in love with Gerard. Yes, I'll write and tell Papa, but he may not get it till he and Laura return from Bath. At least he can hardly object. Lapsed radical that he is he certainly fancied being connected to a baronet.

Lady Kirby at last drew a long sigh and looked at Olivia with a smile lighting her reddened eyes. 'Did I not say I thought I was going to be very happy? I must put weeping behind me now.'

They heard the sound of Luke's crutches and then Sir Langton's voice saying, 'He will have a very generous pension of course when we are in funds again.'

'Oh I'm glad,' Olivia said. 'They must have been to see Albert Todd after all.' She rose as they came in sight. Sir Langton looked astonishingly like his old dapper self, while Luke who had been on his crutches for a long time and engaged in wearying explanations of the office papers, looked pale with exhaustion.

The ladies made as much room for them on the seat as their hooped petticoats would allow and Olivia whispered to Luke, 'What pearls of wisdom did Albert let fall?'

Luke tried to suppress a laugh as he whispered back, 'After much wiping of his hand on his breeches he was persuaded to shake Sir's hand and all he said was, 'He was no use to me in the garden, anyroad. T'other mighta been but I got Tom and he's worth two o' the best.' That was it. I shall tell Tom because he scarcely ever gets a word of praise'

Sir Langton was animatedly telling Lady Kirby that his son 'had managed so well that the debt to the bank would be paid off by next quarter day.'

'So we can celebrate the wedding in September?'

'Assuredly.'

'There you are, Olivia. Write to your father and tell him. Of course he must bring his bride and I think you said there were unmarried sisters. That's the bridesmaids settled. Now, can we accommodate the whole family here? If the interior of the west wing were finished – well, you must make me a list of their names and we will bring rooms into use in the east wing that are lying idle. Oh it will be so exciting! Nothing like this has happened at the castle in my time.'

'My son,' said Sir Langton, 'is such an efficient manager that I have every confidence we will have the funds by then to do the thing properly. He overstepped the mark a little over these infernal coal seams. Says I signed a paper about it but I wasn't quite myself for a while and decisions had to be made. I don't like it but he says we'll neither hear nor see it. This is the new modern world and I suppose in due course I will have to take a back seat and let it all happen.'

'I trust, sir,' Luke said, 'you will be hale and hearty enough to keep the reins in your hands for a long time. Perhaps we could ride over together soon and you could see if it is all being done in orderly fashion.'

'Now you see, Sophia, how my son defers to me. That's the proper way. That's how I always planned it would be – my son learning how to take over when the time came.'

'*Our* son,' Lady Kirby said under her breath, squeezing Luke's hand.

I hope, Olivia thought, I can endure this new Sir Langton with the same patience Luke shows. The man has simply thrown away his burden of guilt. None of his county acquaintances will dare to speak of it to him direct. Neither Luke nor Albert Todd will press for legal redress so the story may well go about as an accidental mix up only coming to light through the confessions of a now dead midwife. That's how Meg Summers and the village will hear of it. Poor Janet Johnson! The parson and the lawyer will have to see the paper, I suppose, and maybe in secret Sir Langton will ask to be shriven if that is not too Roman a word for a good Church of England man.'

She got up and said she would go and write to her father. Luke struggled onto his crutches to accompany her and Sir Langton said, 'We must fix you up, son, with a wooden leg. All the wounded soldiers get one. Then you may be able to manage with only a stick.' He slid his hand under his wig and scratched his head. 'What was the name of that battle, Sophia, where he got it?'

Lady Kirby looked at him in alarm. 'Got it, Langton?'

'Belle Isle,' he cried. 'See, I remembered. Belle Isle.'

Olivia looked at Luke, who just smiled back at her.

'You could though, couldn't you?' she said. 'Get used to one. You learnt to manage crutches and ride No Such Mirrors, didn't you?'

'Thanks to you, I did. I shall certainly try. I intend to walk down the aisle with you on my arm.'

Then she couldn't wait to write to her father to share the miracle with him.

When his answer came at last full of joy and excitement she found he had enclosed a letter to Sir Langton and Lady Kirby which he said she might read first.

'Dear Sir Langton and Lady Kirby', he wrote, 'it is with the greatest pleasure that I give my consent to the marriage of my daughter, Olivia, to your son, Luke. He is a young man whom I admire greatly for his many excellent qualities and I feel honoured to be linked with you through this happy alliance.

'My wife and I are also deeply grateful for the way you have taken my daughter under your wing and are happy to wait upon you on the occasion of the nuptials in your lovely surroundings at Castle Kirby.

'I am not in a position yet to settle a large sum upon my daughter, though I am pleased to report that I have recently received several new commissions, but I would be most happy to complete the plans for the castle which I originally suggested, at no further charge to yourself, but only of course if this arrangement is agreeable to you. Your son was pleased to look upon the plans with considerable favour when I *showed them to him.*

'My wife and all her family send you their respectful greetings and look forward to the honour of making your acquaintance.

'I remain your humble servant,

'Gideon Beattie.'

When this had been sealed and handed over Olivia and Luke waited with some trepidation to see how it was received.

Half an hour later Luke was sent for to the office.

'You must tell me word for word what he says,' Olivia begged.

It was not till after a light luncheon now served downstairs at one end of the long dining-room that Luke had a chance to report what happened.

'The first thing Sir Langton did was slap his hand on the letter and exclaim, 'Does this mean the man is offering his services in place of a dowry for his daughter?' 'No sir,' I said, 'he is committing himself to a huge future expense if the splendid new entrance, stable block and servants' quarters linking the east wing and completed west wing are finally finished.' Then Sir Langton – I keep forgetting to call him my father – looked quite cross. 'Thinks I can't afford it eh? I call that patronising from a man in his position. We'll do it, my son, at *our* expense. I don't mind him coming here and giving his services if that's what he wants but the materials we will provide ourselves. Can we do that? What do you say?' I told him that with the demand for coal increasing all the time we should be able to.'

'Are you sure?' cried Olivia.

'It'll take time. But I told him we would have a castle to rival the Howards. So he wanted to look at the plans again and as they were still there in his desk I took them out. 'Ah yes,' he said, 'he wanted a dome, called it the crowning glory. That I think is an extravagance.' And he covered the dome with his hand. 'We will dispense with the dome. A vulgar excrescence. The rest is beautiful, harmonious, perfect.' I had to agree so I hope your father won't be too disappointed.'

'He can put one on Anston Manor,' laughed Olivia and kissed him.

That same evening Luke, mounted on No Such Mirrors, and Olivia on her favourite mare rode out on one of their now regular rides round the estate. They soon spotted Tom digging about among the young trees planted to screen the coal workings. They rode down to him and he doffed his hat and made them a mock courtly bow.

Olivia thought how splendid he looked. 'You're working late, Tom.'

'What better thing to do on an evening like this? The darling buds of May are all out and I'm enjoying them before the rough winds do shake them.'

'You and your father will get your new home at the Castle,' Luke said and told him about Gideon Beattie's proposal.

Tom grinned. 'That'll take years and if the war ends soon Meg's boys will be back and wanting their rooms.'

'We have to beat Spain first,' Luke said. 'The news is that the fleet have gone to take Cuba. Meg's boys are in the navy. They'll be a long while yet.'

'Well, when they do come I shall dwell here in the Forest of Arden, the beck for water and the trees for shade. But truly, do you think our baronet has returned to his senses. Does it never bother you that he has not been punished for what he did?'

'Punished, punished,' echoed in Olivia's head. She looked at Luke.

'No, Tom. His sanity is far from secure. He is afraid to meet people in case he says something illogical or worse still ludicrous. He has resigned from the magistracy and after church on Sundays he just smiles and says 'Good morning' to everyone.

He is physically well but mentally a shadow of his old self and he knows it. I would never want to impose more punishment on him than that.'

Tom nodded. 'Then I suggest *All's Well that Ends Well* for our next play reading and if these mild evening hours persist into June we should entertain the castle family with an outdoor performance. Perhaps *Midsummer Night's Dream* would be most entertaining for the groundlings.'

He grinned and turned back to his wheelbarrow which was brimming with rich brown compost and he continued digging it in round the young saplings.

'We'll do that,' Luke said and Olivia remembered how she had urged him a lifetime ago to perform publicly. That mirror had reflected to some purpose at last.

They rode back via the crest of the hill that gave them their favourite view.

The castle stood over to their right, a mass of golden stone with a fresh mist of green hanging over the woods beyond and the foreshortened lake lying like a pearl in the dip of the valley. Far away in the distance the soft blue hills faded into the western horizon.

'I couldn't be more happy in heaven,' Olivia said and then she giggled her infectious laugh. 'I hope God will forgive me for thinking that!'

'I will be even more happy when we are married. Can we go back now? I want very much to kiss you and I daren't try to do it on horseback in case I fall off.'

They rode home in a gale of laughter.

Tom, who had seen them on the hill silhouetted against the sky, returned to his digging. At least the earth was still here and the grass and the trees still growing. He could be happy too.

Epilogue
1763

In Surrey and Yorkshire the two women's labours progress well. The August day is balmy and hearts are glad because the world is at peace after seven long years. Both births are expected before nightfall. In Surrey a mother and three sisters take turns to sit with the labouring woman while her first born son in the garden below her window plays tennis with his step-father to keep his mind from anxiety about both his wife and daughter. Not aware yet that she too is in labour he knows it is imminent and it is a question whether his child will be born before or after his grandchild.

His father-in-law, leaning on a stick because of his gout, walks painfully down from the Manor to the Grange to see how things are going.

'If she's in pain like mine,' he says, as the tennis players pause to greet him, 'I'm sorry for her. But she went through it for you, you scamp,' he tells his grandson, 'and before you know where you are you'll have a brother or sister. There now, what did I say? Did I not hear a baby cry?'

A window opens above their heads and four female voices shrill, 'A beautiful girl.'

'Good,' says the boy trailing behind the others as they enter by the garden door, 'I'm still the only male.'

His step-father's thoughts fly briefly from his new baby daughter to his grown-up one far away. Not normally a praying man he says in his heart, God grant her a like safe delivery.

In Yorkshire the expectant father, forbidden by social norms from the place he yearns to be – beside his wife, holding her hand, bathing her head – has to endure the fanatical pacing up and down of the impatient little figure of his father before his study window in the newly finished West Wing where the younger couples' quarters lie. He knows his mother will not leave his wife, though a doctor and midwife are both present as befits the arrival of the heir.

His valet brings him tea and tells him that the lady's maid is standing by in the gallery to bring him instant news.

'And here she comes, Sir!'

The girl almost falls down the stairs in her haste. 'Oh, sir, a boy, a beautiful boy. They say you may come.'

'Get me up there, William.' He grabs his stick and the man's arm. 'And Jenny, give me a start before you tell the Master or he'll get there before me.'

It is a close run thing but he has time to get to her bedside and see her cradling the tiny infant. She is radiant.

Behind him pants his father who has one thought only to be the first to hold the child after its mother.

He unwraps the hastily placed covers and sees the little form from its fuzz of fair hair to its tiny curling toes. 'My grandson,' he says, 'my perfect, perfect grandson.'

His wife, his son, his daughter-in-law exchange glances which express a momentary shiver of apprehension swiftly swept away by the love and joy that have followed complete forgiveness.

THE END

The Folly at Falconbridge Hall

By

Maggi Andersen

Chapter One

1894 Clapham, England

Vanessa Ashley planned to arrive at her destination cool and composed, but she felt like a wilting lily. She dabbed her handkerchief at the sweat trickling into her collar as heat gathered beneath her chip-straw bonnet. Clapham High Street Railway Station was a noisy and smelly hub of activity, luckily the residence that was to be her new home lay in the countryside.

A short, bearded man approached her and politely touched his hat. 'For Falconbridge Hall, miss?'

'Yes, I'm Miss Ashley. Thank you . . . Mr.?'

'They just call me Capstick, Miss Ashley. This way.' He led her to a trap. After he'd loaded her trunk and her bicycle on board, they seated themselves. He slapped the reins and told the horse to walk on. 'You're the new governess?'

She smiled. 'Yes.'

'Another one,' he muttered and shook his head.

Startled, Vanessa stared at him. 'How many have there been?'

'A few. They don't stay long.'

'But why?'

Capstick declined to comment. He just grunted and shook his head.

'Well, I intend to.' Vanessa straightened her shoulders. It was true she had never wished to be a governess. Even though she was still quite young, her wish for children of her own now seemed unlikely, and if this was to be her fate, she intended to make the best of it. A person without funds, indifferent looks, and a lack of grace had no other course open to them.

'Good luck to yer, then.' Capstick grinned at her, revealing a large gap in his front teeth.

With reassuring skill, he negotiated around a horse-drawn tram as they passed the bandstand on the common and then drove down tree-lined avenues. Villas were soon replaced by streets of gracious homes set amid beautiful gardens. A sign, reading Clapham Park Estate, appeared, followed by larger country houses on acreages.

They passed the last of the houses and were out in the countryside now. Green fields crisscrossed by hedgerows stretched away to a line of forest in the distance. The trap followed the road beside a high brick wall for about a mile until they came to a pair of impressive wrought iron gates with Falconbridge Hall emblazoned on them in gold lettering. Capstick drove through, and a house appeared above the trees. Many chimneys rose from the massive slate roof.

Ahead of them, a stocky dark-haired man rode a magnificent bay horse across the lawn and vaulted a hedge. Vanessa had a glimpse of dark, gypsy eyes and a white smile beneath a black moustache. Before they drew level, he turned the animal and rode towards the woods.

'Who was that?' she couldn't help asking, watching him disappear into the trees.

'That's the groom, Lovel, exercising the master's horse.' Capstick shook his head. 'The gardeners will not be pleased.'

The gravel drive bordered by lime trees curved around through formal gardens to the front of the house where he left her, disappearing with her trunk and bicycle toward the rear entrance and, she presumed, the coach house and stables.

THE FOLLY AT FALCONBRIDGE HALL

The sprawling red brick house had sandstone trim around the windows and a tower at one end, ivy covered its walls. It was older and far bigger than those they'd passed on their way from the station. The house had settled into its surroundings, and she had the feeling it had been here for a very long time while the urban sprawl of Clapham edged ever closer.

Conscious that she looked rumpled and untidy, Vanessa smoothed the skirt of her olive green linen dress and straightened the limp white collar with travel-stained cotton gloves. She picked up her bag and stepped up to the paneled door flanked by stout white columns.

Before she could knock, a maid wearing a mobcap and a white apron over her grey floral dress opened the door. 'Miss Ashley? Please come in.'

Surprised not to be met by a butler in such an establishment, Vanessa stepped into the wide entrance hall. One of those new inventions, the telephone sat on a table. A fine Persian carpet ran the length of the parquet floor, pale green satin papered the walls, and fringed and tasseled emerald velvet drapes hung from the windows. Potted ferns clustered in corners, and a gracious staircase led upward. Despite fractured light filtering down from a stained-glass window above the stair, the house was so gloomy inside dusk might have fallen.

'The master's in his study, miss. Please wait here while I announce you.'

Vanessa sank gratefully onto the edge of a straight-backed chair. It had been hours since she'd had a drink, and her mouth was horribly parched. Now her knees had developed a worrying tendency to tremble. To distract herself, she studied the remarkable flesh tones on the naked woman's torso of the oil painting hanging on the opposite wall. A François Boucher if she was not mistaken. More flesh than was decent, surely.

Her father had preferred the sea and boats as his subjects. He considered the naked body to be soft pornography and not fine art but altered his opinion after nudes became an important asset to any wealthy man's collection and began to fetch high prices. More than once, Vanessa had come across nude models posing in his studio, barely covered by drapery and, sometimes, wearing nothing at all.

At the thought of her father and their home in Cornwall, a wave of homesickness passed over her; she had never envisaged such a drastic change in fortune. She swallowed and focused her mind on the letter and the offer that had brought her here.

In his fine script, the viscount had been brief and to the point. He was a widower with a young daughter in need of tutoring. An associate of her uncle's had approached him on her behalf. She'd read his words with disquiet. He sounded so business-like and … unsympathetic. He had been informed that her mother and father died from the influenza, but his few words of condolence failed to make her more confident of what lay ahead.

The maid's head appeared over the banister rail. 'The master will see you now.'

Vanessa walked up the wide oak stair to where the maid awaited outside a door. A deep voice answered her knock. Vanessa turned the knob thinking how she would have liked to wash before meeting her new employer; it was difficult to appear cool and in control when so hot.

The room she entered was also gloomy. A gas lamp glowed where a man sat in shirtsleeves and braces, his dark head bent over a desk. She took two uncertain steps and paused in the middle of a crimson Persian rug. Vanessa clasped her hands together and inspected the room. Shelves of leather-bound books lined one wall. Heavy bronze velvet drapes, pulled halfway across the small-paned windows, framed a narrow but magnificent view of parkland where broad graveled walks trailed away through well-grown trees. She suffered a sudden urge to walk across, pull the curtains back and throw open a window.

Lord Falconbridge put down the butterfly under-glass he had been examining and pushed back his leather chair, rising to his feet. As she edged closer, he donned his coat and came to shake her hand. 'Miss Ashley.'

'How do you do, my lord?'

He motioned her to sit then sat himself.

He would be in his mid-thirties, she guessed. His good looks made her feel even more untidy. His dark hair swept off a widow's peak, and he had a deep cleft in his chin. He removed his glasses, and his eyes were a similar bright blue to the butterfly. Dark brows met in an absent-minded frown as if she was an unwelcome distraction. 'Welcome to Falconbridge Hall. I hope you had a good journey?'

'Yes, thank you, my lord.'

'You've come quite a long way. You must be tired.'

'I broke my journey with an aunt in Taunton, my lord.' Her aunt was quite elderly, and Vanessa had slept on the sofa, but she didn't feel at all tired. She expected fatigue would strike once the initial rush of excitement had faded.

'My sympathies for your loss, Miss Ashley.'

'Thank you.'

'You have had no experience as a governess, I believe.'

'No.'

'Do you like children?'

'Very much, my lord.'

'Then you have had some involvement with them.'

'Yes, I was very fond of my neighbors' children. I minded them quite often as their parents were both in business.'

'You had no opportunity to marry in Cornwall?'

'I had one offer, my lord.' The widowed vicar, Harold Ponsonby, had offered, in an attempt to rescue her from the heathenish den of iniquity in which he found her.

He eyed her. 'And you refused him?'

Might he think her imprudent? 'Yes.'

'Do you have a particular skill, Miss Ashley, which you can impart to my daughter?'

'No, my lord.' She drew in a breath. She had not expected such a question. 'Sadly, I did not inherit my father's artistic talent, but I have my mother's enquiring mind and her interest in history and politics.'

'Politics?' He stared at her rather long, and she wished again that she'd had time to tidy herself. 'We shall see how you get on. The rest of the day is your own. We will discuss your duties in the library tomorrow at ten. Mrs. Royce, my housekeeper, will show you to your room.' With an abstracted glance at his desk, he rose and went to pull the bell.

The mahogany desktop was completely covered with pens and papers, a microscope, a probe of some kind, a set of long-handled tweezers, a large magnifying glass and a small hand-held one, tomes stacked one on top of the other in danger of toppling, and the butterfly in its glass prison, its beautiful wings pinned down, never to soar again. Caught by its beauty and premature death, Keats's poem *Ode to a Grecian Urn*, rushed into her head. 'Thou, silent form, dost tease us out of thought…As doth eternity.'

The viscount swiveled, and his eyebrows shot up. 'Pardon?'

Vanessa jumped to her feet as heat flooded her cheeks. She'd said the words aloud. She must have had too much sun. 'Keats, my lord.'

'Are you a devotee of the Romantics?'

'Not especially.' Annoyed with herself and, irrationally, with him for pursuing it, she said, 'Forgive me, it was a random thought.'

He folded his arms and studied her. 'You are given to spouting random philosophical thoughts?'

She tugged at her damp collar. 'Not usually. I'm a little tired, and it's been so hot.' Hastening to change the subject, she stepped over to the wall covered in framed butterflies of all sizes and colors. One particular specimen caught her eye. 'Exquisite.'

She felt his presence disturbingly close behind her. 'Which?'

She pointed. 'This one, with patches of crimson and deep blue on its wings.'

'You have a good eye. That's a *Nymphalidae* from Peru. Do you know much about butterflies?' She looked at him, finding his blue eyes had brightened.

'Very little, I'm afraid,' she said, aware her contribution to this discussion would prove disappointing. 'We get many orange ones with black spots in Cornwall.'

'Dark green Fritillary.' The interested light in his eyes faded.

'That can't be. They're orange,' she said.

'That is their name, dark green Fritillary.'

'Why would they call it dark green when …?' Her voice died away at the impatience in his face.

'That species is common and of little interest.' He studied her. 'Unless you took notice of some interesting aspect of their habitats?'

'No, not precisely, my lord … uh, they seemed to gather in trees and grasses ….' She nipped at her lip with her teeth, as he nodded and turned away. Would a governess be required to know much about butterflies or botany? Beyond Cornwall, her knowledge of flora and fauna was barely worthy of comment.

A woman entered the room, her neat figure garbed in black bombazine, with a lacy cap over her brown hair and a watch pinned to her breast. A large bunch of keys jangled at her waist. Vanessa thought her to be in her early-forties. She had a pointed nose and sharp eyes that looked like they would miss little.

'Ah. Mrs. Royce, this is the new governess, Miss Ashley. Please give her a tour of the day nursery and school room and introduce my daughter to her before you take her to her quarters.'

'Yes, milord.'

'Miss Ashley.' His lordship nodded. 'I shall see you here again at ten o'clock tomorrow. We'll discuss your plans for teaching my daughter. I'm extremely keen that she becomes proficient in mathematics, the French language, and botany.'

'Botany, my lord?' Vanessa's fears were realized. Completely unprepared, she looked around wildly at the books lining his shelves. Might she have time to bone up on it? She read some knowledge of her discomfort in his eyes and lifted her chin. 'Surely English and history are equally as important?'

'That goes without saying.' He turned back to his desk. 'Tomorrow at ten.'

Summarily dismissed, Vanessa followed the housekeeper along the corridor. Did she catch a satisfied gleam in his eye before he turned away? Her mind filled with questions. Was it going to be difficult to work for him? Might it be why governesses did not stay long here?

Mrs. Royce glanced at Vanessa's wrinkled gown and scuffed shoes. 'You'll be suffering from the heat, I expect. We've had the devil of a summer.' Without waiting for a reply, she opened the day nursery door as a young maid jumped up. She dropped her sewing as she bobbed.

'This is the nursery maid. Agnes.'

Vanessa greeted the maid as Mrs. Royce approached the child who hadn't acknowledged their presence. 'Miss Blythe, this is Miss Ashley, your new governess.'

Blythe looked up from where she knelt beside a doll's house with the distant expression of someone woken suddenly. A ragdoll with a china face lay in a tumbled heap beside her. Slender brows frowned at the intrusion, reminding Vanessa of her father. She climbed to her feet.

'Please to meet you, Miss Blythe.' Vanessa smiled and stretched out her hand. 'I've so looked forward to this moment.'

'How do you do?' Blythe said politely. Blythe slipped her little hand into Vanessa's and, after the merest touch, withdrew it. She had inherited the black hair and blue eyes of her father, and his height; at ten, Blythe almost reached Mrs. Royce's shoulder.

'It's almost time for afternoon tea,' Mrs. Royce said. 'I'll take you to your room, Miss Ashley.'

The housekeeper shut the nursery door and led Vanessa down the corridor.

Her new charge seemed quite subdued. Vanessa wondered if the girl spent much time shut up in the day nursery with the maid. She planned to change that immediately. A child should be outside in the fresh air in the cooler part of the day. Vanessa had spied a lovely shady folly through the trees, like some ancient relic from the past. She hurried to catch Mrs. Royce, who was walking briskly along the corridor.

They climbed up a narrow stairway.

'How many on the staff here?' Vanessa asked to break the silence.

'Twenty house staff. Dorcas is the head maid. The butler is away at present.'

'I didn't see a footman.'

Mrs. Royce firmed her lips. 'We have none.' She stopped and threw open a door. 'This is the schoolroom.'

It was a good-sized attic room with comfortable chairs, a table, a child's desk, and a slate blackboard on a stand. 'Excellent,' Vanessa said with satisfaction.

At the end of the corridor was Vanessa's bedroom, its sloping walls covered in a daisy-patterned paper and hung with pressed flowers in frames. The white-painted iron bed had a floral coverlet, and a writing desk stood beside it. An upholstered chair was placed near the fireplace, which had a wide shelf above the mantel where Vanessa could put the few things she'd brought with her. A rug covered the floorboards. The small room looked snug. Surprised at her good fortune, Vanessa said, 'How nice. I shall feel very much at home here.' The curtains were closed, and the room stuffy. She crossed to the window and drew them back, looking down over verdant lawns and trees to the picturesque folly. Its circular roof was supported by decorative round columns, and it overlooked an ornamental lake.

'I do hope so.' Mrs. Royce firmed her lips. 'Blythe needs stability.'

Had she lacked it thus far? Unsure how to reply, Vanessa found she wasn't required to, for Mrs. Royce, who appeared to be a woman of few words, already stood at the door. She gestured. 'We have all modern plumbing here. There's a lavatory and bathroom for your use on this floor. Tea will be brought to your room at four. From tomorrow, you shall take it in the schoolroom with Miss Blythe.'

As soon as the door closed behind the housekeeper, Vanessa rushed to open the window. A sultry breeze wafted in, but she relished the light and the fresh air.

In the bathroom, she found the bathtub had a mahogany surround, and hot and cold water issued forth from a noisy gas geyser. Delighted, Vanessa resisted the urge to bathe and made do by washing her hands. She looked into the mirror and cringed when she spied the dark smudge on her nose. Her eyes went large with alarm. What had the viscount thought of her! She scrubbed her face with a washcloth until it glowed and sponged her hot neck with cool water.

Her trunk had arrived while she was in the bathroom. Having recently discarded her mourning clothes, she changed into a fresh grey skirt and white blouse, cinching it in with a wide belt. After tidying her hair, she dabbed on a little lily of the valley scent, adding some to her handkerchief.

She removed her few precious possessions from the trunk, arranging her pearl-handled brush and comb set on the dresser, beside her mother's miniature, wrought by her father's hand with love in each stroke of his brush. Gazing at it brought tears to her eyes. She dabbed at them with her handkerchief then bent over the trunk to take out her father's books on art and her mother's history books, along with her own. She arranged them on the shelf, adding the pretty shells she'd gathered from the Cornish shore.

Having unpacked her few gowns and underthings, she sank onto the bed. It was still hard to believe her comfortable life by the seaside was gone. That it had come to this, a servant in another man's house. Her parents would not have approved, but what choice did she have? Her mother had been an educated woman with an interest in politics. She had joined with many like-minded people in her fight for women's rights. She had been sought by politicians and reformers alike. Women had crowded into the parlor for meetings. Her father felt less passion for her mother's causes. He would cast them a fond smile before disappearing into his studio to paint.

The tea tray arrived soon after a bell pealed through the house. Feather-light, fluffy scones with plum jam and a wedge of fruitcake accompanied the pot of tea. She savored the last drops of a good, strong cup and poured another. Every crumb consumed, she felt much livelier afterwards.

Vanessa slipped out to explore the enormous house. She passed room upon room with curtains drawn. On the ground floor, she walked through a doorway into a burst of sunlight and blinked, finding herself in a conservatory, a long glass room on the sunny southern side of the house.

A scream chilled her blood.

Heart pounding, Vanessa hurried forward. In amongst large tubs of bright orange cumquats, a table was laden with delectable treats. Blythe sat alone nibbling a piece of iced cake and swinging her legs.

'What was that unearthly scream?' Vanessa asked, gazing around. The answer to her question came from a gilded birdcage. A large brightly plumaged bird sat on a perch and called again.

'That's the macaw Father brought back from South America,' Blythe said.

Vanessa went over to the cage. With a crimson breast, bright blue and green feathers, and a decidedly beady eye, the bird was truly magnificent. It turned its head to study her. 'Might it want something?'

'It would like some nuts I expect.'

As Vanessa had no nuts to offer it, she returned to the table. 'I've been exploring.'

Blythe nodded.

'You have a lovely house.'

'Thank you.' The child turned her attention to her glass of milk.

'It's nice to sit in the sun, isn't it?' Vanessa said, hoping to draw the child into conversation.

'I suppose it is.' Blythe gave her a quick glance. 'I'm taking tea with my father.'

'Is this a special occasion?'

'Yes, we don't do it often.'

Feeling like an intruder, Vanessa turned to go.

The contrast of this room with the rest of the house was stark. The sun touched the glossy leaves of the potted plants, turning them vivid green, and the air smelled of earth and fragrant orchids. Outside, a bluebottle batted in vain against the glass. Vanessa might have entered a tropical forest. She couldn't help searching the cathedral glass ceiling for butterflies and smiled wryly as she turned to go.

'You find something amusing?'

Lord Falconbridge stepped through the door. She hadn't expected to see him until their appointment tomorrow. He had removed his glasses and now wore a marine blue coat with a striped cravat at his throat.

'Do sit down, Miss Ashley.'

'No thank you, my lord. I've had my tea.' She stood with her hands clasped in front of her, hoping he'd dismiss her so she could continue her reconnoiter of the house.

He pulled out a chair for her. 'If you don't sit, I shall have to remain standing, and I wish to have my tea.'

'Thank you.' She sank onto the chair he'd offered her.

He sat next to his daughter and leaned back, crossing one long leg over the other. The bright light revealed lines at the corners of his eyes, probably from his time spent in a hot climate. She dropped her gaze, aware that his lordship's intense blue eyes searched her face with more interest now than they had on their first meeting. It was so concentrated a gaze that her fingers curled, and she resisted straightening her collar. She could only be glad she'd dealt with that smudge.

He could hardly be admiring her profile. When her father had painted her portrait, he always transformed her retroussé nose into one of classical proportions.

'Mother had a similar coloring to Miss Ashley, didn't she, Father?' Blythe said.

'Your mother's hair was auburn,' he said. His voice lacked any sign of grief. Blythe, too, showed little emotion when she mentioned her mother. Perhaps Lady Falconbridge had passed away many years before. 'Miss Ashley's is reddish-gold rather like a *Hypanartia cinderella*,' he said, nodding to her.

'From Peru,' Blythe said.

'Is it?' Vanessa asked, transfixed by his lordship's blue eyes.

'Yes, and you share your first name with the *Vanessa cardui*, a butterfly with a strange pattern of flying, a sort of screw shape. Like this.' He made a circular downward spiral with his finger.

Was he teasing her? She looked at him suspiciously. 'I trust it's only my name that reminds you of it, my lord.'

He smiled. 'Butterflies are quite fascinating in their diversity, Miss Ashley.'

She wished he didn't always sound as though he was giving a lecture. Might he be visualizing her under glass?

Vanessa attempted to change the subject. She didn't care to be compared to his lordship's butterflies. 'Do you like to read, Miss Blythe?'

Blythe's eyes lit up. 'Oh yes. I love books.'

Pleased, Vanessa said, 'We can enjoy them together.'

'Then I shall allow you free reign over my library, Miss Ashley.' His lordship put down his cup. He pulled one of Blythe's locks, stood, nodded to Vanessa, and strode from the conservatory.

Blythe and Vanessa stared after him in silence.

Vanessa felt strangely flat. Had her appearance disappointed him? She hadn't been employed for her looks, surely.

She had decided to return to her room when Blythe spoke. 'My party frock is pink. What color is yours?'

Vanessa widened her eyes. 'I didn't bring one. There will be little reason to wear it.'

'Father has invited guests next week. There will be music.'

'Oh. Well, how nice. But governesses don't go to parties.'

'Miss Lillicrop did.'

'Did she?'

Thick black lashes hid Blythe's blue eyes from view like a shutter over a window. 'I watched her from my window. She danced on the terrace.'

Vanessa would have loved to ask with whom, but Mrs. Royce appeared with the maid to clear away the tea things.

'What books have you read, Blythe?' Vanessa asked.

'*Alice's Adventures in Wonderland* is my favorite.' The girl's face flushed with pleasure.

'There are many wonderful stories, and I promise we'll read a new one every few weeks.' Vanessa ran a list of texts through her mind.

'How nice you seem,' Blythe said in her cool little voice. 'Will you stay longer than Miss Lillicrop?'

'I certainly plan to,' Vanessa said, her curiosity aroused.

Mrs. Royce spoke from the doorway. 'Your music teacher is waiting, Miss Blythe.'

'Goodbye.' Blythe climbed down from the chair and left the room.

'I gather Miss Lillicrop was the former governess?' Vanessa asked the housekeeper.

'That is correct.'

'She didn't stay long?'

'A few months.'

'Did something happen for her to leave so soon?'

'You'd best ask the master about that.' Mrs. Royce's tone made it quite clear she would discuss it no further.

Left to her own devices, Vanessa walked out into the garden.

Julian glanced out the window and saw his new employee cross the terrace with a determined stride. She had been a surprise. He was glad women had dispensed with the bustle; he liked the natural sway of a woman's hips. He had met Miss Ashley's grandfather, the Earl of Gresham, but never her father, the ne'er-do-well younger son who had cut himself adrift from his family and left his daughter penniless. Julian found the former earl to be too haughty for his tastes, couldn't see beyond the end of his long nose, and the elder son now in possession of the title was no better, or so he'd heard. He returned to his ledger, this wouldn't get his work done. He had much to do before departing for the Amazon.

Vanessa took the path that seemed to lead to the lake. The air was still and hot, and all the flowers and plants in the garden beds drooped. She entered a thick copse of trees where the overhead branches blocked out the sky, and moments later, emerged beside the lake. As she approached the folly, a welcome fresh breeze blew the damp curls from her brow. It was a most unusual structure, the Grecian columns intricately carved with leaves and flowers. Steps led up to the arched front overlooking the water. Inside, she found a rather decadent looking crimson velvet chaise longue, several wicker chairs and a table. A nice place to bring Blythe for a picnic she decided.

Vanessa returned to her bedroom. She curled up in a chintz chair, her chin propped in her hand. Her new employer filled her thoughts. She'd never met anyone like him. She was glad to find him so interesting, but was there something cold blooded about killing insects and placing them under glass?

Blythe seemed too subdued for her liking. It might be due to shyness, but she doubted it. She would have to wait and see. Vanessa considered herself to have been a luckier child than Blythe, having been blessed with a loving mother until fully grown. She had enjoyed far more freedom, which mattered more than material things. How carefree she'd been, at least until the last year when things had gone terribly wrong.

At the thought of her parents, she pulled out her handkerchief and allowed herself a moment's reflection on the past.

Vanessa sighed, dried her eyes, and moved to the desk to prepare the lessons. When satisfied with the list, she placed it inside the desk drawer. When she tried to close it again, the drawer stuck. She pulled it out farther and peered inside. At the back was a scrunched up piece of paper. Smoothing it out on the desk, she discovered it was a detailed drawing of a butterfly, its wings colored crimson, just like the one in his lordship's study. It would appear that the previous governess had drawn it. So finely detailed, it gave clue to her expert knowledge of butterflies. She replaced it and closed the drawer. What would cause such a competent person to leave Falconbridge Hall so suddenly?